Jasmine

Louise

Thanks so much, dear friend, for all your encouragement and leadership and prayers!

Love,
April

April McGowan

JASMINE

WhiteFire Publishing
13607 Bedford Rd NE
Cumberland, MD 21502

ISBN: 978-1-939023-09-4 (digital)
          978-1-939023-08-7 (print)

For Ken, Madeline, and Seth

"But we have this treasure in jars of clay to show that this all-surpassing power is from God and not from us. We are hard pressed on every side, but not crushed; perplexed, but not in despair; persecuted, but not abandoned; struck down, but not destroyed."

~2 Corinthians 4:7-9 (NIV)

Even Angels Cry

Oh sister if you wake up in the night
Walls are falling letting in the light
No need to worry baby even angels cry

I whisper you don't have to worry we'll survive
Forced smiles underneath
The brittle frozen light
Proof that you're alive
Cold fingers find the curve
Below your tired eyes
No comfort in familiar places not this time
You hold it deep inside

No flood warnings still the waters rise
Flowers through asphalt
Diamonds in the pockets of your eyes
Turn your face and hide
I saw a woman with ribbons in her hair
Old and lonely
So beautiful I had to stop and stare
The well will not run dry run dry

Oh sister if you wake up in the night
Walls are falling letting in the light
No need to worry baby even angels cry
Sister if you wake up in the night
Walls are falling letting in the light
(It'll) be alright baby even angels cry
Please don't worry not tonight

One

The cold from the linoleum floor cut through Jasmine's jeans as she sat with her back braced against the hospital wall. Her eyes sagged closed as her mind whirred from exhaustion and worry. Sleep beckoned, and strange images flitted through her mind, flashing in odd synchronicity with the flickering fluorescents overhead.

Someone jiggled her shoulder, pressing down, squeezing. Survival instincts kicked in, and she reached back to draw her knife from the waist of her pants. When her fingers came up empty, her other hand came around and snatched the throat of her attacker. Her foggy mind engaged as her assailant choked out her name.

"Jazz?"

Jasmine's eyes widened in recognition, and she released her grip. Officer Banner sank back on the floor, scooting away from her, rubbing his throat, and coughing. She ran her fingers through her hair and avoided eye contact, hoping he wouldn't ask for an explanation. There wasn't one—none worth giving. He should know better than to touch someone who was asleep.

"What's going on?" Jasmine stood on shaky legs, glancing toward the hospital room door. She tucked a loose strand of black hair behind her ear and stretched.

Open mouthed, Officer Banner stared at her. "I was going to tell you she's awake." He continued to rub his throat.

"Good." Avoiding his stare, she hurried toward the room. Before she could enter, his partner came out.

"Officer Gerry." She greeted the female officer with a nod.

"Jazz. Did you see what happened?"

"No, I found Misty outside our complex. I'd just finished a late dinner when I heard her scream, and I ran out. She'd been beaten, and by the time I got out there she was unconscious. I called an ambulance, and we've been here since waiting for treatment. What time is it, anyway?"

Ned Banner glanced at his watch. "Zero-four-hundred."

"Has Misty said anything about the attack?" Jasmine caught the look Gerry shot to Banner. "What?"

"She's probably been raped. That's what the doctor thinks. But she denies it and won't let them test."

Jasmine swallowed away the anguish. "I'll see if she'll talk to me." As an at-risk women's counselor, she'd faced this situation many times, but it never got any easier.

Leaving Banner and his partner outside, she walked into the room. Misty lay on the hospital bed, shivering, her arms pulled tight against her chest. She stared out the window but didn't appear to see anything. The rails of the bed were up, reinforcing the appearance of her helplessness.

"Hi, Misty." She moved around to the other side of the bed. At least they'd given the girl a private room. Jasmine put her hand on Misty's shoulder, causing her to jump. "It's okay, it's me, Jazz."

"Jazz." Misty focused on Jasmine for the first time. They'd met when Jasmine visited the jail a year ago. Back then, Misty appeared older, more sure of herself. Today, without the hardened look in her eyes and gaudy makeup, she seemed much younger than her eighteen years. Tears streamed down her bruised cheeks and over her split lip.

"It's okay, you're safe." Jasmine held her tight, feeling Misty's body shake in her arms. "You're going to be okay."

Misty nodded and pulled away, accepting the tissue Jasmine handed to her.

"Do you know who hurt you?" Jasmine waited, hoping for the best but fearing the worst.

Misty's face paled, and she hesitated before answering. "I don't know. One minute I was outside our building, waiting for a friend, and the next I woke up here."

Jasmine was an expert at reading people, but this time, she couldn't tell if Misty was giving her the full story. "If something comes back to you, let me know. You'll stay here for now. Get some rest and I'll check in with you in the morning. If you need me, you call."

Misty nodded and absently stared out the window again. After dropping her business card on the bedside table, she gave Misty's stiff form another hug and left the room.

Jasmine needed to get back to her apartment, away from there, to gain a little perspective. And a lot of sleep. As she headed out of the hospital, she heard footsteps behind her and tensed. Didn't that guy ever quit?

"Can I walk you home?" Banner called. He caught up to her and shot her a confident grin. He was probably in his thirties, too, but even with his difficult job as a police officer, they were years apart in life experience.

"What about Gerry?"

"Our shift is about over. She's heading back to the department."

"I don't need an escort. I can handle myself. Besides, the creep that did this won't be hanging around our building."

"I'm going that way anyway."

Jasmine shrugged and kept up her original hurried pace heading for Broadstreet House. The image of her cozy flat and fluffy comforter danced before her eyes even as the rain fell on them in sheets. One of these days, she'd have to actually buy an umbrella. Wasn't that the sign of a true Portlander? Do your best not to acknowledge the rain. Liquid sunshine. Complete denial.

They walked in silence for a few blocks; the only sounds to meet her ears were their shoes hitting the rain-soaked pavement and water droplets bouncing off the awnings they dodged under. Businesses hadn't opened, and it was too wet and early for most people to be out yet. She didn't mind. At moments like these, she'd pretend the streets were clean and safe. That the homeless didn't exist, and the runaways, loved and protected by their families, were fed and warm in their beds. Really, though, that didn't make her any better than most people who chose to look the other way.

Banner finally broke the silence. "I'm sorry I scared you."

"Scared me?" She glanced at him.

"Yeah. When you grabbed me in the hospital. I must have startled you."

11

Jasmine didn't reply right away. She had been on her own for the better part of her life, and she didn't need anyone trying to look out for her. She hadn't been afraid—she was on autopilot.

"It's cool."

Banner nodded. "I'm glad you left it at home."

She frowned. "Left what at home?"

"Whatever it was you were reaching behind your back for. If not, I think I'd still be at the hospital." He rubbed at his throat, trying to joke with her, but she was sure he didn't realize how true it was. Instinct forced her to reach for a knife she'd given up carrying. She hadn't had to use it in years, but there was a certain comfort in having it handy.

"Sorry." The skin around her neck and face warmed, and she knew if it had been lighter out he would see her splotching. He'd probably assume she was embarrassed. Hardly.

"No apologies necessary. I should know better than to grab someone who's asleep."

They agreed on something.

When they arrived at the complex, Banner opened the gate to the atrium and escorted her to the stairs of her flat. The building was an early 1900s Victorian, divided into studio apartments, with a central garden. She and Brandi had made sure each unit was clean, with updated carpet and paint. Even though all the furnishings were donated, it was the nicest place Jasmine had ever lived, and she hoped to stay there a long time. After a day like today, it was heaven. When Misty returned, they'd talk about taking more precautions when out at night.

Banner moved to walk Jasmine to her apartment, but she put up a hand to stop him. "I've got it from here." She never invited men into her apartment, cop or no cop.

"Get some rest."

"Thanks." She climbed the stairs to the second floor, closing the door behind her without bothering to say good night. She turned on the nearest lamp, lighting the room with a warm yellow glow. Going to her knees, she looked under the bed, stood and checked the closet, pushing past all the shirts and pants. Heading to the bathroom, she flicked on the light, eyeing the clear plastic shower curtain and empty shower stall. When it was apparent no one was hiding inside, she flipped the locks on her apartment door and finished by sliding the desk chair under the handle.

Jasmine kicked off her shoes and caught her reflection in the oval mirror near her bed. Her green eyes were haggard and rimmed in dark circles. Tonight was close to home. Too close. She pulled her black hair into a ponytail and slipped out of her jeans, exchanging her T-shirt for an oversized nightshirt. After brushing her teeth and washing her face, she climbed into bed and turned out the lamp. The sodium orange street light filtered through the cracks of the curtains on her window, giving the room a hazy look.

Her mind wandered, remembering the evening's events. The thud and scream outside her window. Finding Misty in a bloodied heap. Her own screams for help. It was like reliving history, all those years ago when she was on the street. She'd been the bloodied heap, and someone else had screamed for help.

She curled into a ball, pressing the pillow against her eyes, and refused to think about it anymore. Tomorrow life would go on. It always did. Even if she didn't want it to.

Her thoughts shifted to Misty and what might become of her. Did she know the man who had attacked her? It wouldn't surprise Jasmine. Victims on the streets often knew their attackers. It might have been her shiftless drug-selling ex. And she'd probably leave the hospital before morning and take off with him. Unfortunately, she might not see Misty again. People like her were good at hiding their trails and erasing their existence. If you survived more than a few months out there, you got good at it. Or you were done.

An ache behind her eyes pulled her attention away. Jasmine pressed her cold fingers to her lids and held them there. The pain built ever so slowly, with a sneakiness she always associated with cat burglars. She reached inside the desk that served the dual purpose of her nightstand, and pulled out her prescription. On the street, living in back alleyways, she had to suffer through the migraines, lying underneath cardboard boxes, or hiding in dark corners that smelled of urine and garbage. She didn't miss those days.

Jasmine popped a little white pill into her mouth and let it melt under her tongue. Getting up, she closed the blinds behind the curtains. Darkness enveloped her, easing the pain. She closed her eyes as she sat back down on the bed and willed the pill to work.

The sour smell of her forgotten dinner dishes wafted from the sink to her nose, swirling around her like a tightening noose. Searing pain shot through her head, visible and hot like a blast of lightning. She moved her thoughts away and tried to think of something else. Had she locked the door? The chair was there, and she never put the chair under the handle unless she'd locked it. But she'd been distracted and tired. Maybe she'd forgotten this time. Jasmine made a move to check, and nausea stole her breath away. Shuffling over to the door, she checked the lock, the latch and the dead bolt. All secure. She hated when her mind played tricks on her. She took several deep breaths to release the stress building in her body.

That was a mistake.

She rushed to the bathroom and lost her dinner and most of the pill. Strangely enough, throwing up took the pressure away from her head. Exhausted, she crept her way to bed and climbed between the cool sheets. Tomorrow she'd go and check on Misty—if she could find her.

Two

Incessant knocking woke Jasmine from a deep, dreamless sleep. The curtains blocked out most of the daylight, making it hard to tell the time. As her eyes adjusted, she focused on the clock. Eight AM, which normally wouldn't be such a big deal, but she'd only been asleep for three hours.

"Who is it?" Her voice croaked as she yelled toward the door.

"Ned Banner."

Seriously?

Groaning, she climbed from the bed, pulling on a pair of sweats as she went. She cracked the door, leaving on the chain, staring at him through the slim opening.

"You do realize I've only been asleep a few hours here?"

"Sorry to wake you. I was just at the hospital. Misty snuck out sometime in the last hour."

A growl of frustration escaped. "I'll keep an eye out for her. If she shows up, I'll let you know." She began to close the door.

"So, I was thinking," he started, and stuck his shoe into the opening of the doorway.

Irrational fear made her skin prickle. "What?" Her hand tensed on the door knob.

"One of these mornings as I'm going off shift, and you're heading to work, we should get together and have breakfast. What do you think?"

Nonplussed, she stared at him.

"I mean, it makes sense. We make a great team out here, helping youth. We should take it to the next level."

Next level? Team? "Listen, Officer Banner, I appreciate that you think sticking your foot in my doorway and offering a nice girl like me a good time is your way of inviting me into some sort of relationship, but you are way out of line. I have tried, in no uncertain terms, to put you off. We aren't a team in any sense of the word, and never will be. Now, kindly remove your foot from my door before I hurt you." The realization that she was threatening a police officer came only after she'd finished her tirade. The shocked look on his face almost made her regret her harsh tones.

She got over it when he snorted and said, "It's not like you're getting any younger, Jazz."

"Good-bye." She shoved against the door. He pulled his foot free before she smashed it. Setting the dead bolt, she climbed back into bed. As she was about to fall back asleep, there came another round of knocking on her door.

"Go away!"

"Uh, I can't," came an unfamiliar voice.

She got up and went once again to the door. Leaving the chain on, she peered out, seeing a delivery person. "Can I help you?"

"I've got a registered letter for Jasmine Reynolds."

She hesitated. "That's me."

The befuddled delivery boy slipped a clipboard through the opening. "Please sign and print your name."

She did as requested, handed back the clipboard and accepted a manila envelope before closing the door. She'd never gotten a registered letter before. Really, the only mail she ever got was bills. And they never came to "Jasmine," they were always addressed to "Jazz." She gave up using Jasmine as her name her first year away from home. It gave her an edge. Jasmine was a lost, abused, helpless girl. Jazz was a tough street kid no one would mess with if they were smart.

She climbed back into bed, pulled the covers up, and looked over the package. The return address belonged to Sampson and Benson, Attorneys at Law, Bright River, Oregon. Her hands went cold. She pulled the covers tighter and stared down at the envelope. She hadn't voluntarily thought of Bright River in years. For some people, the name of their hometown would bring warm, fuzzy memories, but she had none of those. At fourteen, she'd left with Fiona and the carnival and never looked back. At least, she'd never gone back.

Her fingers lifted the clasp on the back and slid under the flap, opening the letter. She pulled out a slip of paper with the same name on the letterhead as on the envelope, scanned it, then re-read it. It slipped from her hands to the floor as she lay back against her pillows.

Her mother was dead.

Her father had died ten years ago, and now her mother was dead as well. They would have invited her to the funeral if they'd had her contact info at the time, but they only came across it in an old file her mother had. Dead and buried for a week. They requested she come for the reading of the will. It'd been her mother's last wish. Why?

There was no way she could go there. That life didn't matter now. She had a meaningful job and good friends. Well, she had Brandi, anyway. And her little apartment and peace. The very last thing she'd ever imagined doing was going home. The girls here needed her. She couldn't run off and abandon them. Besides, her mother clearly had her address. If she'd really wanted her to come home, wouldn't she have contacted her before now?

Jasmine let out a long breath. The weariness from the previous day sank down upon her. A tear slipped from her eye. She always advised her clients to get back in touch with family when it was safe to do so. It gave them closure. She hadn't taken her own advice, and now it was too late. Jasmine turned over and hugged a second pillow to her chest. She closed her eyes, hoping exhaustion would take over and chase her thoughts away, but instead her mind clicked awake.

She leaned over the side of the bed and picked up the letter. Her eyes focused on the signature at the bottom. Tim Able. Timmy? It had to be him. She read it again for any sign of the friendship they had once shared, but found none. The letter read cold and businesslike. Considering Tim had once been her best friend, it was startling. Then again, she'd never told him what was happening at home. She couldn't have faced him again if he'd known. Had he ever forgiven her for running away and never saying good-bye? From the tone of the letter, it didn't appear so.

She'd always told herself that running away was the best thing she could have done. At least she had someone to run to. A second tear slipped down her cheek as she remembered Fiona. She was the first adult Jasmine had ever really trusted. Sure, she had "gypsy blood" as Fiona had called it—the urge to travel and the inability to stay in one place too long. But she was trustworthy—a new concept at the time.

Hadn't Fiona and Brandi been her inspiration to reach out and help girls just like she'd been?

Conviction settled over her like a heavy, dirty blanket. What kind of counselor was she if she couldn't face her own issues? She gave good advice; maybe it was time she took some of it. Brandi had been encouraging her to face her issues for years. Her parents were dead now—they couldn't hurt her any more. She knew what she had to do. Jasmine picked up her phone and called her mentor.

"What's up?" Brandi's sunny voice wavered through to her ear.

"I'm going to need to leave town for a bit." She walked to the closet and pulled down her suitcase.

"I sure hope you're taking a vacation."

"No."

"I should have known better. You've never taken one before—might as well stick with a clean record."

"Ha ha." She paused, drawing in a controlling breath. "Listen, I just got word that my mother passed away."

"Oh shoot, I'm so sorry, Jazz. Are you going to the funeral?"

"No, missed that I guess. They want me there for the will reading." She stood in front of the open closet, befuddled by the situation, not knowing what to pack.

"Are you okay?"

"Not really." She moved to the opposite wall, slid down, and sat on her floor, staring at her clothes.

"Do you want me to come with you?"

Did she? Part of her wanted to say yes, but the rest desired the familiar comfort of her self-imposed isolation. "No. But will you keep an eye out for Misty?"

"I heard about it."

Jasmine sighed. "Banner."

"Ned's a good guy. A little in your face, but basically good."

"Whatever you say, just keep him away from me." She folded a cable knit sweater and a couple pairs of jeans—leaving the ones with the holes in the knees in the closet.

"Ask you out, did he?"

"How'd you know about it?" Jasmine felt her neck go hot.

"I could see it coming."

"He said, and I quote, 'It's not like you're getting any younger.'" The ire from yesterday washed over her.

"Did you deck him?" The grin was audible in Brandi's voice.

"In my mind. You know I don't have time for men, and even if I did, it certainly wouldn't be Ned."

"I know."

Jasmine could hear Brandi's disappointment but didn't take the bait to go down that path of the conversation. All that needed to be said about that had been said. "Are you going to kick Misty out?"

"No, not until I know the whole story. If someone attacked her, that's no fault of her own. If she was meeting with her ex and he beat her, then she's broken her word to us. You know the rules. The apartments are for girls who want to really change their lives and get off the streets for good. They have to make that choice; we can't force them into it. She signed the contract, and she knows what will happen if she breaks it. We can't make an exception for her, because the next one will walk all over us."

"I know. She's got such promise. I hope she's okay." She started packing her toiletries case, making sure to stow her migraine prescription inside.

"Me too. I'm not in the habit of giving up on my girls." The sentence carried a double meaning for Jasmine.

"I know. And I'll be grateful to the end of my days." She hoped Brandi knew how grateful she was.

"When do you leave?"

"Tomorrow."

"Call me when you get settled."

Jasmine smiled at Brandi's mothering tone. "As my friend, my counselor, or my boss?" She bit the side of her lip, waiting for Brandi's classic comeback.

"Any one will do."

Jasmine swiped her phone off. It wasn't any good. No matter how much staring she did at her wardrobe, nothing jumped out at her to pack. Her two business suits were somber and responsible looking for court. But most of her wardrobe was composed of jeans and T-shirts. Overdressing put off people on the street. Maybe she'd go buy some new clothes.

No, like Brandi said, why break her record? She'd figure something out. Somehow.

Three

Jasmine drove through the valley from Portland to Bright River, alongside the mountainous range and snow-fed river. Rolling down the window of her early nineties Corolla, she let the cool morning air blow inside. The aroma of spring grass and fir trees filled her car and washed away the stench of exhaust and fast food that always seemed to linger.

As she cruised down the winding road, she passed apple and pear orchards, their straight rows flitting by. The orderliness of it all filled her with a sense of peace.

Before she knew it, she was pulling into the sleepy town of Bright River. Traffic surprised her—she hadn't remembered any. Within a four-block radius, she counted two Starbucks, and one Dutch Brothers coffeehouse. A mom-and-pop diner, The Getaway Cafe, sat on the corner of the main street. It might have been the same one where she and Tim would grab fries and sodas after school. Where was the school? All the additions to town turned her around. She hadn't driven back then, so being in a car disoriented her.

Jasmine pulled over to the side and decided to walk to get her bearings. She'd been dreading her arrival but now felt compelled to take a closer look around. Climbing from the car, she pulled on her navy suit jacket and headed down the street. Between that or the brown, she thought it looked slightly more approachable. She glanced down at her high heels, wishing for tennis shoes. It didn't matter how nice they looked, those things were torture devices.

Since she didn't need to be at the law office for another hour, she'd figure the town layout, find her hotel, and then go to the reading of the will.

Jasmine passed by men and women in professional attire, most likely on their way to work. Some were about her age. Did she know any of them? Besides Tim, there weren't any names that popped into her head. You had to think about things for them to stick in your mind, and she'd pretty much stopped thinking about this place as soon as she'd left it.

On the corner, she peered into the window of a drug store she thought she remembered. Next to it sat a pet store, old-fashioned toy store, and several office buildings. She spied the law office across the street and moved on, not wanting anyone to notice her. Rounding the next corner, she found Central Park with its aging statue of one of the city founders. The statue was in great condition and tulips had begun to bud around the base of the trees. The trees seemed much larger and the playground equipment much smaller. And rustier.

Down the street sat a grocery store and gas station along with the hotel where she would stay. It didn't look as nice in person as it did in the ad, but it was the only game in town besides the bed and breakfasts—and sharing a bathroom with strangers was not something she was willing to do. As she walked into the motel office, a warning chime alerted the desk clerk.

"I'll be right out," a gravelly voice called. A rumpled woman came from a back office. She barely looked up to acknowledge her.

"I'm checking in."

"We usually don't check in folks until eleven." She clicked some buttons on the computer in front of her, and the monitor buzzed to life. "What's your name?"

"Jazz Reynolds."

The woman's fingers paused, and her eyes shot up and scanned her. "Don't you look professional?" Her voice sounded anything but complimentary.

"Thank you?" What was her problem?

"Didn't expect you until later today." The woman gave her another accusing glance.

"I got in early. I can come back later if it's a problem."

"No, I'll check you in." Glossy red nails clacked on the computer keyboard. "You don't remember me, do you?"

Jasmine stared at the woman, taking note of the cut of her face, the faded gray color of her eyes, and the stocky build. "I'm sorry, no."

"I used to sit behind you in English class. Marcy Stumps. My name's Buchard now," she said with emphasis.

Jasmine waited for the light to dawn, but nothing came to her in the darkness. "I'm sorry; it's been a long time."

"It certainly has." She looked over Jasmine, as if appraising her for sale. "Life been treating you well?"

"Sure," Jasmine lied.

"I'm good friends with your sister," she said significantly.

"That's nice." So Lily was still in town. Would she be at the will reading? What about Sweet William?

"Do you remember my husband?"

"I'm sorry?" Jasmine's eyebrows knitted together. This game of twenty questions was getting old.

"Dave Buchard. He was on the basketball team. He gave you flowers in the eighth grade. He told me you wouldn't accept them."

The temperature seemed to rise in the cramped office.

"You acted like you were too good for him." Marcy folded her arms over her chest.

"I really have no idea what you're talking about." Jasmine adjusted the collar of her jacket and fiddled with the buttons.

"We got married right after high school."

"Good for you."

The woman's eyes glared at her. "What's that supposed to mean?"

"Nothing. You sound like everything is going really well. I'm glad you're happy. Can I have my room key now?"

Marcy Buchard grabbed the slide card key, programmed it to her room and slid it across the counter toward her. "How long are you staying?"

"Not long."

"Here to see what you got left in the will? If you were my kid, I wouldn't have left you anything at all." Marcy spun away from her and went back through the same doorway she'd entered.

Stunned, Jasmine turned and walked out, tucking the room key in her pocket. She decided not to introduce herself to anyone else in town.

Turning left out of the parking lot, she glimpsed a section of the old fairgrounds in the distance. From this vantage point everything looked quiet—but in the fall, it would be covered in campers, tents and people for the harvest festival carnival. It was the most anticipated event for the kids in town, almost equaling the excitement of Christmas.

She couldn't remember what had planted the idea to run away with those people. But after working it two summers in a row, she had a good sense of what their lives were like. And Fiona, dear kind woman. Jasmine had gotten to know her over those two years.

Of course, working a carnival for fun and working for a living were two different things. By the time she'd been to her second town, the luster and excitement of being on the road with a carnival wore off, and it was pure hard work. But she'd been safe. Jasmine could almost smell the aroma of the carnival at night—popcorn, stale beer and the chemical scent of portable toilets. All the newer workers would go around and pick up the smashed paper cups and discarded food littering the fairgrounds in the dim glow from nearby street lamps that mixed with the winding down rides.

And there was Fiona's brightly colored knit sweater that carried the aura of two packs of cigarettes a day. The years of smoke acted like glue, keeping it together. Fiona carried herself with pride, even though her joints were rusty and she needed a cane. Actually, now, Jasmine wasn't too sure if she had only pretended to need the cane, limping and acting helpless. She remembered one time Fiona had used it on another carny who had made advances toward Jasmine. She never forgot the rage in the old woman's eyes, and the sense of love she had for her when the altercation was over. Fiona held her to her chest and let her cry and cry. She promised her she'd always take care of her. Too bad that hadn't worked out.

Death didn't respect promises. Fiona had died in her sleep about a year later. Jasmine's ride with the carnival lasted another year, but it got too hard to fight off the unwanted advances without Fiona around. When the carnival went through Olympia, Jasmine left for what she hoped were greener pastures. They weren't.

The girls she mentored had the same problems. They would run away from one situation and find themselves inexplicably reliving the same drama where they landed. Nothing ever changed for them until they faced their pasts and learned they had worth. Much more worth than to be traded in an alley for cash or, in her case, drugs.

Glancing down at her watch, she saw she still had a half-hour. She headed back along the other side of the street, past bushes and lawns with permanent paths worn through them by generations of children racing and hiding. She gazed up a street that looked familiar, and an involuntary shiver coursed through her. Her house was up that road. She'd run past these bushes, and cut that same corner countless times in her childhood. She could almost hear her younger self panting, racing home in time for dinner, her tennis shoes hitting the steaming pavement at the end of a hot summer day. Sometimes her family would sit outside and eat, hiding in the shade away from the heat of the house. Her dad would make homemade ice cream and invite the neighbors. He'd often do free electrical work for folks in town going through hard times. Everyone loved her dad.

She continued walking, not wanting to go there, but knowing she would have to at some point. *You can't hide for the rest of your life.* At this point most of the young women she counseled would say, "Why not?" Right now, she didn't have a good answer.

Deciding to go in the opposite direction, she found herself standing in front of The Getaway Cafe. It was as if her feet knew where she needed to go. She entered and grabbed a table in the back, against the wall. For some reason it felt safer to see who was coming—even if she didn't recognize them. She ordered coffee. Her instinct was to add fries to her order, a throwback to the old days, but she stifled the words.

As she watched people outside pass by, she heard her name. She didn't recognize it at first—it'd been over twenty years since she heard it, not counting the delivery boy whose envelope brought her back to this place.

"Jasmine."

She looked up to see a man with light brown hair, a sprinkle of gray around the temples, and deep blue eyes with gentle crinkles at the corner. He wore a tweed coat with worn leather patches on the elbows, a blue dress shirt, open at the collar, and black jeans. Against all common sense, she immediately trusted him. And that never happened.

"Yes?" She reached out her hand and met his in a friendly shake. "You'll have to do me a favor and tell me your name."

She saw what she imagined must be hurt in his eyes. "Tim. Tim Able."

The years melted away, and he was Timmy, her best friend, and they were about to get into some marvelous trouble. He was taller than the fourteen-year-old she remembered. He had shoulders now.

"Do you mind?" He motioned to the seat across from her.

"Not at all." She really didn't.

He scooted the chair up and arranged the silverware, straightening it before turning over his coffee cup. The waitress arrived and filled it immediately, giving him a warm smile. He nodded his thanks before turning his attention to Jasmine.

"Did you have a good drive?"

Being at a loss for words was an understatement. From the businesslike tone of his letter, she hadn't expected any kind of a reception, let alone a warm one.

"Actually I did. I'd forgotten the orchards. And the river. I don't know how, but I did."

His eyes showed amazement. "It surrounds everything here."

"I know." She couldn't explain. Suppressing memories for twenty-two years was bound to do some permanent damage. She couldn't remember the trees and the river and still forget the ache and shame. It didn't work that way. The eraser wasn't discerning and took out wide swaths of memories. She was lucky she remembered how to get there at all.

"What have you been doing with yourself?"

"This and that."

"You're in Portland now. I was surprised when I found your address. So close by. I'd imagined you ran off to California."

"California? Why?" She had gone to California with Rob once, to pick up a drug shipment. That didn't need mentioning.

"I thought maybe you wanted to become an actress or something. You used to love old movies."

Had she? Yes, she had loved old movies. They'd been a great escape. She and Tim would watch old re-runs of classics every summer at the theatre. For hours they'd sit and laugh and eat popcorn. What else had she loved?

"No. I didn't become an actress. I ended up in Seattle for awhile, and moved to Portland about seventeen years ago."

His eyes showed surprise. "And you never came home."

"No."

He went quiet for a moment. "We came here nearly every day and shared fries. Do you remember Elsie Thomas?"

Jasmine's brows knit in concentration. "Was she rather small and had blond curly hair?"

Again, that look of disbelief filled his eyes, but only for a moment. "Remember sometimes we'd go and play in her tree house up on the hill? Or go fishing?"

"Oh yeah," she lied again. How much more lying would she have to do before she escaped back to her real life?

"Remember the time we forgot the fish under your back porch and they rotted in the sun? Your dad couldn't figure out where that awful stench was coming from." Tim chuckled.

She looked at her watch, having grown tired of the memory-lane game. "It's getting to be that time." Her voice sounded much angrier than she expected. How could he have known her father made her pay for forgetting the fish?

"I suppose it is." He looked out the window for a second, and she could almost see him pull on the demeanor of his position like pulling on a stiff pair of jeans.

"So, did you marry Elsie?" She didn't know what made her ask, but she suddenly had to know more about him. The look in his eyes confused her.

"No. I never married." He looked away. "Bill and Lily will meet us at my office. It should only take an hour or so."

Bill didn't sound familiar. "Did Lily get married?"

"Oh, I think she must have been at some point, her last name is different. But she's not now. I didn't know her very well; she and your brother were several years ahead of us in school. She's been back in town for a few years now, taking care of your mom."

"Oh. Who's Bill?"

"Your brother, Sweet William. He started going by Bill

when he followed your dad into the electrician business. I guess Bill sounds more responsible than Willie."

Her mother had named all her children after her favorite flowers. Her father hadn't liked the theme. It was probably the only time her mother ever stood up to him about anything. She tried to imagine Sweet William as Bill and couldn't do it. She pictured him working alongside her father and couldn't imagine that either.

"Did Willie, I mean Bill, marry?"

"Yes, he's got a nice little wife. He married Elsie."

It became clear why she would have been expected to remember Elsie. She didn't remember ever seeing Elsie and Bill together. They must have been eight years apart in age. "When was that?"

"After your dad died, ten years ago now I guess. As soon as Bill took over the business he asked Elsie to marry him." He smiled as if in approval.

"Is my brother a good man?"

If Tim thought that a strange question, he didn't act like it. "Yes, he's a good man. Even more well liked than your dad."

That didn't mean much.

Tim stood. "I've got to head over and get all the paperwork in order. You've still got twenty minutes. You might want to grab something more substantial than coffee—especially with that coffee." He pushed his hand against his stomach for effect, and she felt the sensation he was warning her about. He waved and she watched him as he headed out, across the street and up the block.

"Tim's a nice guy. Is he your lawyer?"

Surprised, Jasmine looked up at the waitress. "In a manner of speaking."

"Well, whatever you've hired him for, he'll win. He's got a nice way about him. Although we can't seem to marry him off. He's dated just about every female in town between the ages of twenty-five and fifty." She topped off Jasmine's coffee.

"Oh?"

"Yep. Dates them twice and they turn into great friends, but that's where it ends."

Jasmine thought about that for a second as her stomach wrenched. "I think I'd like to order some fries."

Four

The law office sat inside a late 1800s brick building, taking up most of the top floor. Jasmine rode the modern elevator up to the fourth floor and stepped out in front of the antique walnut receptionist's desk. There was a comforting smell about old buildings. You could almost taste the age in the dust in the air. Two-hundred-year-old dust. The carpet appeared updated, but they still used the original brick walls—many owners would have drywalled over them. Ceiling-high partitions made up offices, but the main part of the space contained open cubicles. She counted eight desks. Their business must be doing okay.

The receptionist hung up the phone. "Can I help you?"

"Yes, I have an appointment with Mr. Able."

"And you are?"

"Jazz Reynolds."

The receptionist looked over her ledger. "Do you mean Jasmine Reynolds?"

"Yes." The use of her old name made her flesh crawl as if someone raked sandpaper over a scab.

"Please come with me." The receptionist stepped out from behind the desk and led Jasmine to the back left of the building.

As Jasmine walked past the cubicles, she sensed several sets of eyes upon her. Did she know any of them? Or rather, did they know her? The woman opened the conference room door for her and ushered her inside, motioning toward a chair sitting at the oblong conference table. Apparently, she was the first to arrive.

"Mr. Able will be with you in a moment; he's on a phone

call. Your brother and sister should be here shortly."

Again, the mention of family took her by surprise. She'd been an entity unto herself for so long, this was like wearing someone else's skin.

"Would you like some coffee? Or tea?"

"No thanks." The two cups of coffee she'd downed at The Getaway had long since disintegrated the French fries and were boring holes in her stomach as she spoke.

The woman left, and a minute later Tim entered, followed by a man and a woman. Their eyes were familiar, but if she'd seen them on the street, she would have passed them right by. Bill turned and took his seat. When he cocked his head at her, she saw her dad in his expression—she'd never forget that face. Bill had brown curly hair and wore a black striped logger shirt and faded blue jeans. Lily had gray-blond hair, pulled back into a loose bun. She wore a tan pantsuit and carried a notepad with her. Her fingernails were painted a glaring fire engine red.

"To start with I think introductions should be made." He glanced at Bill and Lily. "Bill, Lily, meet Jazz."

Jasmine smiled when Tim used her name—it was the first time in hours she'd felt like herself. Her comfort lasted only seconds.

"Jazz?" Lily broke the ice. "How do we know she's our sister and not some scam artist?"

"You sound like mom." Jasmine hadn't meant to say it aloud. Their eyes locked on her for a moment, and they continued asking for proof.

"Ask me something only your sister would know?" Jasmine suggested.

Bill spoke directly to her for the first time. "What was I most afraid of when I was a kid?"

Jasmine had to think a moment. Sweet William had been afraid of a lot of things when he was a boy. She knew the thing he feared most though. It was the thing they all feared, but for different reasons. "Sleeping alone."

Bill's eyes softened. "Jasmine is the only one I ever told that to." He got up and came around the table to hug her. Lily stayed seated.

The hug lasted only a moment, but it felt real, and

comforting. He went back to his chair.

"So she answers one question and you've been bought? I want more proof than that." Lily crossed her arms and gave Jasmine a scowl.

"Actually, I had her checked out fully before I sent the letter inviting her to the reading of the will. Jasmine is indeed your sister." Tim spoke with an authority that apparently carried weight with Lily, because she backed down.

"Now that her identity is established, I'll go get the file. Excuse me." For the first time she realized that maybe all those questions in the coffee shop weren't genuine curiosity. Maybe he'd been testing her.

"I'm sorry I wasn't at the funeral."

Lily coughed. "You weren't expected, trust me. You missed Dad's, why would you be at Mother's?"

"Oh." Jasmine shifted in her chair.

Bill shot Lily a look but said nothing.

"How've you been, Sweet William?" Jasmine asked, changing the subject.

His eyes softened again. "I've been good. I got married, have a couple kids. I know they'd like to meet you."

"That'd be nice."

"Don't do it." As Lily spoke, bitterness dripped from her tone.

"Why? They deserve to know their other aunt," he answered back.

"What for? She's not going to be here long. They'll get attached to her and she'll leave. Do you really think she's back to stay? Tim said she's lived four hours away for seventeen years and never stopped by. How likely do you think it will be that she'll keep in touch?"

Tim came back into the room. "So, are you guys getting caught up?"

"Something like that." Jasmine forced a smile.

"Good, good." He took his seat again and opened the file on the table. "Well, I've taken a look at the will, and it's all very straightforward. The property has been split in three. Lily, you get the apple acreage and small house. Bill, you get the hunting property, and the business will be entirely in your name now." He glanced over the papers again. "And Jasmine

31

gets the house in town."

The house?

Lily exploded. "What? Why does she get the house? She lived there for fourteen years, ran off, and never looked back. I grew up there and took care of Mother until her dying day. All my things are there."

Tim put up a hand to slow her down. "I can arrange movers for you, and they can move your things to the apple property. The tenants moved out last month. The orchard is leased, and you'll get a share of the profits every year."

"I don't want the apple property. I want the house."

"I'm sorry, but the will is very clear."

Tim passed the papers to Bill, who read them over with care. "I'd forgotten the hunting property. There's a nice little cabin up there. It'll be a good place to take the kids camping." Bill seemed content with the way his mother had handled things.

"So that's it? I invest the last six years of my life taking care of that house and our mother, and I'm evicted."

"I don't want the house." Jasmine's voice sounded otherworldly to her.

All three of them stared at her.

"I don't care who gets it. I don't want it."

"Please don't speak too hastily, Jazz. The house is all paid off. You'd make quite a profit if you sold it. I did some research, if you'll forgive me, and I know you live in a very small apartment in the city. The money could help you quite a bit."

"Help her? Why should anything or anyone help her? All she's good at is running away." Lily got up and grabbed her purse.

"Where are you going?" Bill stood, putting a hand on Lily's arm, but she wrenched away.

"To pack."

Tim held a pen out toward Lily. "Before you leave, please sign the papers as evidence you were here. I'll contact you about getting the property legally transferred in the next few days." Lily grabbed the pen, scratched her name loudly on the page, and left.

Jasmine watched her storm from the room. Tears came to her eyes, but she blinked them away.

"I'm sorry about that, Jasmine. She's had a hard time." Bill's voice broke the tension in the soft way he'd always had. Jasmine knew too many women who could probably top her sister's hard time. "I don't know why she's so angry. I don't want the house."

"Tim's right. Don't give it up. Sell it." Bill spoke with such conviction they both looked at him. Did he know what the house meant to her?

"If you'll both sign here, we'll call it done." He slid a set of keys across the table to Bill and another to Jasmine. She stared at them as they lay cold and familiar in her hand. How could she remember their color and shape, but not remember Elsie?

Bill stuck his hands in his pockets. "Come home with me for dinner, would you, Jasmine? You too, Tim. Elsie's been cooking all day, hoping we'd hit it off and you'd come home with me." He had such optimism in his eyes, she couldn't say no.

Bill lived within walking distance, so after the papers were signed, both Tim and she followed him there. They walked along the street, catching glances from people who knew the men, but whose eyes questioned who she was. Most of them offered warm greetings.

"You both seem to know everyone in town."

"Small town." Tim shrugged.

"Not as small as it was. But we've all grown up here together. Once you've been back awhile, they'll greet you too." Bill spoke as if it were a done deal. She looked sideways at Tim, who was biting his lip. He used to do that when they were kids, when he was thinking hard.

They turned a corner and walked up to a restored Victorian with a chain link fence, lined with trellising roses, surrounding a well-kept yard. Here and there were toy dump trucks, a tricycle, and a scattering of dolls. As they entered through the gate, a petite, blond-haired woman came out on the porch. She squealed and hopped down the stairs, grabbing Jasmine in a tiny bear hug.

"You look the same!" She squeezed her again. "I can't believe you're here." She held Jasmine away from her and looked her over—but it wasn't the same once-over everyone else had given. Elsie was making sure she was okay, and the concern in her eyes brought tears to Jasmine's for the second time that day.

"Come in and meet your niece and nephew." Elsie wiped at her eyes with the dishtowel she was carrying.

Jasmine followed her and Bill inside, and Tim followed close behind. She thought she felt his hand on her lower back a minute, like an usher. Or maybe he was making sure she wouldn't bolt. The strangeness of it all got to her. She was a sister and now an aunt. Three days ago, she was no one.

Two young children with curly blond hair came shuffling down the stairs.

"Hey, are you our Aunt Jasmine?" This came from the boy. The girl, the younger of the two, was silent and sucking the first two fingers of her right hand. The other hand clasped a half-dressed teddy bear.

"I guess I am. Who are you?"

"Jason. I'm seven."

Jasmine looked at the little girl who shied away from her. "And who is this?"

"That's Rose. She's three. Show her."

Rose held up three fingers from around the bear.

Jasmine looked up at her brother quickly, caught the twinkle of pride in his eyes, and back down at Rose. "Rose is my middle name."

"Yep," came out around Rose's fingers.

Bill's hand on her shoulder was heavy and warm. He gave her a squeeze and motioned for them to move into the dining room. Inside the room lay a vintage carpet, an antique farmhouse dining table set with floral china, and a matching hutch in the corner, full of floral teacups and matching saucers. Jasmine stared at them intently through the glass.

"They was Grandma's cups. Mom said one day they'll be Rose's." Jason spoke with authority beyond his years.

The cups, like the keys, seemed burned into her memory. She was never allowed to touch them, not even to dust them. They were the most fragile thing in the house, the thing her mother ran to and protected first when her father came home in a drunken rage. She never ran to the kids, just the hutch. She could almost hear her shrieking now, "Please, they're all I've got."

There they sat, behind the glass, untouched and whole.

"Is there anything there you'd like to have, Jasmine?" Elsie's sweet voice brought her out of her reverie.

"No. I think Rose should have them. All of them." She looked at Bill, but he kept his glance outside, through the rounded windows, on something in the yard.

"Well, let's sit down and I'll bring in the roast." If Elsie sensed anything amiss, Jasmine couldn't tell. This was going to be a long meal.

Five

Dinner went by in a haze of conversations, most of which Jasmine didn't feel capable of commenting on. She sensed the tension concerning her sudden reappearance and knew they must want to know where she'd been and what she'd done. But they didn't ask, and she didn't offer information. Instead, they discussed the challenges of Bill's business, the intricacies of Tim's work, and Elsie's many projects in town.

As soon as the children finished eating, they cleaned up their dishes. Rose gave her father a sticky kiss on the cheek, but Bill didn't grimace or wipe if off. He gave her a hug and tousled Jason's hair before sending them upstairs to play. She could see their love and trust of him mirrored in their faces. Tim was right; her brother was a good man.

"So, Jasmine, what do you do in the city?" Elsie broached the subject as soon as the kids were out of earshot.

"I work as a counselor for homeless and at-risk young women."

All eyes focused on her now, filled with more than a bit of surprise.

"That sounds like a good job." Elsie gave Bill an encouraging smile.

"It pays the bills."

"So, when you say counselor, what do you mean?" Elsie's eyes seemed to hold an authentic sparkle of interest no matter who she spoke to.

"I hold a doctorate degree in mental health and have been working for ten years. I worked under a mentor for a long time, and still work in conjunction with her on many projects."

"What do you help these women do?" Tim's face showed genuine interest.

"I counsel them when they find themselves in tough situations, mostly those escaping sexual trafficking, the abused and homeless. I help them find safe housing and work."

"How meaningful." Elsie spoke with an edge of the romantic to her voice.

"It might be meaningful, and good work, but there isn't much to be idolized. These girls have suffered a great deal, often at another's hands. It's my job to show them they don't have to live that way and give them courage to depend on themselves." She hadn't meant to sound so harsh, but it was true.

"We need something like that here, don't we, Tim?" Bill said. "Our church has an outreach to battered women, but we don't have any on-staff counselors. The only thing we can do is give them a safe place to stay, feed them, and pray."

"Yeah." Tim didn't sound enthusiastic.

"Maybe you can advertise for someone. There might be someone who needs an internship your church could hire." She wanted to shut down any discussion of her helping at their church. Church was about trusting in God. It hadn't worked for her. She couldn't pretend that God would be anyone else's solution. Being self-sufficient was the best way.

"I thought if you moved back home, there'd be a job." Bill smiled hopefully at her, but she didn't return it.

"I'm sorry, I won't be moving back, Bill. I don't think I could ever stay here again. Besides, as soon as I take care of all the property stuff, I have to head back. I have young women depending on me."

Bill looked away and dropped the conversation.

"Will you be staying with us, or at the house?" Elsie asked.

Jasmine didn't want to see the house, let alone stay in it. "I have a hotel room in town. I'll be fine there. I might have to spend time on the phone with clients, and it's better that I have a private place to do that."

Tim stood and nodded to Jasmine. "I'd better get going. I'm sure we'll see each other again before you leave town." He offered his hand to Bill. "Thanks for the invite. Wonderful food as always, Elsie."

Bill walked him outside.

"Tim's a real nice guy." Elsie began clearing the table and Jasmine started gathering silverware and platters.

"He seems that way. How's his dad doing?"

"Jim? He retired as sheriff a couple years back, and moved to some property outside of town to spend his days fishing. Sometimes he leads fishing tours. He's got some whopper fish tales to tell."

"Must be nice." Jasmine remembered Tim's dad as a kind man.

"Are you sure you want to stay at the hotel?"

"Why shouldn't I?"

"Well, because of Marcy."

Jasmine put the stack of plates down she'd been hauling to the kitchen. "What is that about anyway? She obviously hates me."

"Her husband's got some problems. She's very bitter about a lot of things." She paused. "Not to mention she's really good friends with Lily. Marcy used to come and help her with your mom."

"That explains a lot more than you know. But I still don't understand Lily."

Bill walked back in with a thoughtful look on his face.

"Bill, what's with the women in this town being so bitter? Like Lily, what did I ever do to her?"

Bill sighed. "You've got to see it from her side."

"What's her side?"

"Mom started having trouble about eight years ago. She'd forget things."

"Alzheimer's?"

"That was our first guess, but when we took her to the neurologist, he did a CT scan. He said if he hadn't known better, he would have thought the scan had come from a veteran boxer."

Jasmine shot a look to Elsie and back to Bill. He put up his hands as if to calm the situation. "It's okay. Elsie knows about Dad's drinking problem, and the violence. That's why I've never taken a drink in my adult life. I don't want to go there." He took a deep breath. "Mom had progressive brain damage. The tissue started to die off, and it first affected her memory.

Then it affected her body."

Jasmine sank into the chair. "So Lily's mad at me because I wasn't here to take responsibility?"

"I really don't know. I offered to help, and she refused. Mom's insurance would have paid for some help, but she wouldn't take it. When Mom got real bad, I thought we should put her in a home, but Lily wouldn't let me. If she hadn't passed in her sleep, I would have gotten Tim involved and tried for power of attorney to do it."

"So if that's not it, what is it?"

"That's something you're going to have to ask her yourself. Are you sure you don't want to stay here? I hear Marcy's an old bear."

"No, I'll be fine." Jasmine needed downtime. She'd been on her own for so long, she'd forgotten what it was like not to have time to think.

"I'll help you tomorrow." Elsie gave her a warm smile.

Jasmine looked up at Elsie. "Help with what?"

"Clean the house out. We'll get boxes and movers and we'll get it done in record time. I've got a lot of good friends who love this kind of thing."

"How bad is the house?" Jasmine shot a look at Bill.

Bill and Elsie looked at each other before answering. That couldn't be good.

"Well, before we organize anything, I think I'll head over there and check things out. Okay?" She wasn't looking forward to it and didn't want any witnesses. She needed time to clear her head.

"Sure. As soon as you're ready, we'll get to work." Elsie stepped away into the kitchen. Jasmine watched her go.

"You don't remember her, do you?" Bill asked point-blank.

Jasmine tried to hide her surprise. "What do you mean?"

"Whenever you talk to her, it's like you're talking to someone you're trying to place. You play along, hoping something will tick a memory."

"I remember her."

"But you don't remember spending time together. You don't remember playing dolls, or running all over town."

Dolls? "I guess not." She looked intently at him. "Please don't tell her, she seems so nice."

"She already knows," Elsie said, as she stepped in from the kitchen. "Don't feel bad, Jasmine. It's been a long time."

"I'm sorry. You seem like the kind of person I'd remember." A helpless feeling washed over her.

"You and Tim were always the leaders. I was the tagalong. That's probably why."

"Maybe."

Jasmine moved into the living room, passing by the china hutch with great care—stomach tensed, feet cautious, as she had when she was a child. Bill followed her, and they sat in silence for awhile. Just as she thought she'd make an easy exit and escape, Bill broached the subject that'd been in the room all evening.

"You want to tell me where you've been all this time?"

Gentle, but direct. He'd been like that growing up. She looked over her shoulder to see where Elsie was.

He could read her then, too. "She's gone to give the kids baths. We're on our own."

"I don't know how much you want to know."

"I know Lily and I ran out on you. Why don't you take it from there?"

Her eyes locked to his. "What do you mean?"

"I mean, as soon as we were old enough to leave, we did, and we didn't look back."

"You always checked in with me."

"Yeah, but I didn't come back. I didn't offer to get you out of there. I didn't ask anyone for help with Dad's drinking."

She watched her hands as she rubbed the tension building inside her out through her fingers. Bill kept mentioning the drinking. Maybe he didn't know. Maybe no one did. "I got myself out of there."

"I know. I'm sorry." He had tears in his eyes. "I felt so awful when we all thought you were dead."

"Dead?" Her head snapped up.

"Yeah. They found your bike at the bottom of Green's Slough. They dredged it and searched for days looking for your body."

Her mind drifted back to the night she left. She'd waited for her parents to fall asleep. They turned off their bedroom light, and she knew they'd be asleep about an hour after that.

She'd been spending her nights in the camper, door locked. Packing everything she dared to in her backpack, she watched the time carefully. When all was quiet, she dressed warmly and left the camper, locking it after her. By the light of the stars, she walked her bike quietly down the gravel hill to the main road. Once she was out of earshot, she got on her bike and rode it hard toward the creek. When she got there, she tossed her bike down into one of the deep pools. It had been raining earlier in the day, and she knew the waters were muddied It glinted in the moonlight before sinking beneath the slow running stream. After that, she headed toward the carnival, taking every backcountry lane she could.

"I left with the carnival. I thought if Mom and Dad believed I was on my bike they'd watch the roads for me."

"They didn't suspect the carnival for months. At that point, there wasn't a good record of where the carnival had headed. The next year, a different one came, and we never did find out if you'd gone with them or not."

"I stayed with the funhouse crew."

He nodded.

"Sorry you thought I was dead." Guilt cascaded over her in waves.

"It must have been difficult to be away from home like that."

Not really. "I got used to it."

"So, you were a carny for awhile and ended up in Portland?"

"Something like that." She rubbed her forehead, willing the tension away. The last thing she needed was another migraine. She needed to go rest and be alone. "That's enough for tonight, okay?"

"Still get those?" He winced in sympathy.

"Sometimes. I need to take a pill and be quiet for awhile. That usually works nowadays."

"I'll walk you to your hotel." He got up with her.

"I can take care of myself." She patted his arm. "I'll come by tomorrow afternoon and we'll visit some more."

He took her dismissal well, something that other men were not too good at.

"Count on dinner tomorrow night. Every night you're in town, okay?" She heard a desperate tone in his voice.

41

"Don't worry, Bill. I won't leave without saying good-bye, I promise. I'm not running from anything anymore."

His eyes told her he didn't believe her.

Jasmine pulled on her coat and headed down the block and toward the hotel. The night air held a chill, and she wondered if it would frost. For the farmers' sakes, she hoped not. The trees were in bloom; if they got damaged, it could carry over into the fruit crops that made or broke the town every year. Breathing deep, she caught the whiff of wood smoke intermingled with the still sweet air of spring blossoms. The aroma tugged at her mind, drawing out memories she couldn't quite grasp, like a dream forgotten once she'd been awake for a minute.

By the time she reached the hotel, her headache had disappeared. Grateful, she moved her car to the hotel parking lot, and let herself into her room. She checked the closet and bathroom before hanging out the Do Not Disturb sign and bolting the door. Her routine was always the same, no matter how old she got, no matter that no one had ever jumped out of her closet. A peace of mind settled in when she knew she was as safe as she could be.

It helped her sleep to know she was alone.

Six

Jasmine awoke to the ear-splitting sound of the hotel room phone ringing next to her head. She answered in a blurry haze and met an acidic-sounding Marcy on the other end.

"It's six AM."

"I don't remember requesting a wake-up call."

"The sooner you clean out the house, the sooner you can clear out of town." Marcy slammed down the phone.

The angst of this woman was getting on her last nerve. She made a mental note to unplug the phone before going to bed that night. Maybe she'd take Bill up on his offer. Jasmine didn't want to be at Marcy's mercy while going through everything else.

It bothered her that no one seemed to realize what she faced. At the same time, she was having trouble fighting the temptation to keep hiding the secret and leave town without facing her past.

Groaning under the weight of her conflicting emotions, Jasmine turned over and hugged her pillow to her chest. Somehow, she'd thought Bill must have known about her abuse. When she was a kid, she thought everyone must have known. When everyone laughed at a joke, when they celebrated birthdays, whenever they were together as a family, she was pretending. Put a better word on it, Jazz. Dad lied, and you were a liar. Her whole life she'd hated lying. It left a sour feeling in her gut and laced her tongue with a bitterness no amount of drink could wash away.

Should she tell Bill? He already thought of their father as a drunkard and abuser. But sexual abuse brought her father even lower. That could devastate him. The counselor in her knew that in order to heal, sometimes the wound had to be exposed. But she didn't want to take anyone down that path with her unless she had to.

They weren't called family secrets for nothing.

After dressing, she grabbed a cup of coffee and a bagel to go at The Getaway, skirting the hotel's free continental breakfast and Marcy's lancing remarks. She sipped the coffee and tucked the bagel into her jacket pocket. In the other pocket, she carried a small notebook to organize whatever mess she was about to find. As she walked, she pulled out her phone and called Brandi. She answered quickly.

"Hey, how's it going out there in apple town?" Brandi always put a happy spin on everything—she could be annoying that way.

"Weird." Jasmine followed the street up the hill, trying to ignore the looks of passersby. Didn't people talk on cell phones in this town?

"What's on the agenda today?" Jasmine could hear Brandi flipping through pages of notes and could imagine her getting ready for another busy day.

"I'm about to find out what kind of mess the house I inherited is."

"You got the house." Brandi's serious tone told Jasmine that she understood her dilemma.

"Yep. Lucky me."

"How do you feel?"

"Can we cut the counseling jargon here for a bit?" Jasmine took a stumbling step down the curb crossing a street. Maybe she couldn't walk, talk, and drink at the same time.

"Sure, sorry. Really though, do you want it?"

"No, but apparently it's in my best interest to have it." If she had her way, she'd drive the keys over to Lily and give the whole mess to her.

"Do they know?"

"No. I don't think anyone knows. All my childhood I felt like a spectacle, like they were letting it happen to me because they hated me or something. Come to find out, they had no idea."

"Sorry, Jazz."

"I'm okay."

"No you're not." The conversation went still. After a moment, Brandi changed the subject. "I saw Misty today. She asked about you. I told her you were called home for an extended period. I let her know I could help her if she'd let me."

"How'd she take it?"

"I think she'd prefer you. I told her she can go back under your care when you return."

"Thanks, Brandi."

"I've been praying for you, kiddo."

"Well, that's nice." Jasmine balanced the phone between her shoulder and her ear while she took a bite of bagel.

"You don't really think so, but it is. Trust me."

"Sure thing."

Brandi laughed. "Don't forget to call if you need help."

"Why do you think I'm calling? Get your rear out here and help me pack."

"I'm not into boxes."

The inside joke brought a smile to Jasmine's face. Not long after Brandi met her, Jasmine had threatened to leave and head for the streets again. Brandi said if she really wanted help she had to stay in the shelter—she wasn't into visiting boxes.

"Oooo. Okay. Take care, Doc." Jasmine slipped the phone into her pants pocket and came up short in surprise. She blinked a few times to clear her vision. Somehow during the conversation she'd arrived at her childhood home. Her feet seemed to know the way.

The bushes were much larger, no longer neatly trimmed like her mother had always kept them. The big oak tree in the front yard was gone, a wide stump the only evidence of its existence. The two-story home, once pristine white with blue trim, was a tan, peeling mess. Yellow spots covered the front lawn in a crazy polka dot pattern. The roof tiles were curling up in age, surrounded by thick moss. Some were completely missing. If she'd seen this house on any other block, she would have never guessed it was her childhood home.

Jasmine sat on the stump, pulled out the bagel again along with her notebook. After taking a couple bites, she flipped the notebook open and began writing down her to-do list.

New roof. New paint. Seed grass. Trim bushes. Luckily, all the work she and Brandi had done on Broadstreet House prepared her for such a task.

The front door screen slammed open against the house, catching her by surprise. Lily came outside, carrying a box overflowing with items.

"I'm out of here." Lily's eyes blazed in anger.

"Wait." Jasmine stood, not sure what to say. "I don't want things to be like this."

Lily's eyes reddened as tears filled her eyes, and a look of defeat crossed her face. "Jasmine, I don't know why you had to come home."

It was an idea that had run through her mind more than once since she'd left Portland. Still, hearing it aloud was another matter altogether. An unexpected ache built in her throat.

"What did I do to you?" Jasmine put out her hand to her sister, but she backed away.

Lily took a gulping breath. "You left."

"I had to." The conviction in her words rang true, resounding throughout her body. She really had.

Lily shook her head, tears flowing down her face. "You always got what you wanted, didn't you? Always invited to parties, always popular with friends. You've still got Tim somehow wrapped around your finger. Just like Daddy."

"Okay, what?"

"Daddy's girl. He always called you that. He never said it to me. He never told me I was pretty, or smart, or even necessary."

"You don't know what you're saying." Jasmine's stomach roiled.

"Yes I do. You were the favorite. Nothing was the same after you left. He drank more, beat Mom more. You left and he went crazy." Lily wiped at the tears on her cheeks.

"Lily, listen."

"No, you listen. You can have the house, and whatever is left in there. I took what was mine and a couple things I know Mom wanted me to have. Bill's already taken all of Dad's stuff. It's your turn to take what's left over." Lily threw the house keys on the ground at Jasmine's feet. Storming past Jasmine, she shoved the box inside the trunk of an ancient Oldsmobile, jumped inside, and drove away.

Jasmine leaned down and picked up the keys. She sank back down on the stump and stared at the house. Lily didn't know what she was saying. Jasmine would have given anything to be ignored by her father. Because she didn't know what else to do, she picked up the notebook again, pen poised, but her mind went blank where repairs were concerned. Forbidden memories flitted through her mind. Moments in the kitchen when he cornered her and whispered in her ear how pretty she was. When her mother came around the corner, he'd start joking with her. Afraid, ashamed, she'd played along.

Jasmine rubbed her ear, as if his hot breath still lingered there. When would the ugliness ever go away? Twenty-two years, and she still carried it with her like an old tattoo. She willed her mind to go blank, losing all track of time.

Footsteps behind her jarred her back to the present. Her heart thumped in her chest as she got her bearings.

"Hey stranger." Tim sat down next to her on the stump, patting the bark on the side. "I miss the old tree, don't you?"

"I guess so. Although it makes a nice stump." She smiled sideways at him. "So, what brings you up the hill?"

"Lunch. I understand they haven't seen you at Bill's, or the cafe, so I suspected you probably hadn't eaten." He held out a sandwich.

She stared at it.

"Don't worry, it's a Club. Turkey, bacon, and loads of mayo. Nothing healthy in there."

"It's kind of early for lunch, isn't it?"

He looked baffled. "It's twelve—how long have you been sitting out here?"

"Since Lily took off." Jasmine blinked. "Probably about eight?"

"Doing what?"

"Taking notes."

Tim removed the mostly untouched notebook from her hands. "Not much to show for four hours of work."

She'd lost four hours. Nothing like that had happened to her in years. The dew from the old stump had seeped into the back of her jeans, numbing her, but she hadn't noticed until now. "I guess not." She laughed nervously, but he didn't smile back.

"Are you okay?" He touched her arm, concern etched

across his face.

"Compared to what?" Her joke-like tone fell flat.

"I know we haven't spoken for a long time."

"Twenty-two years." She glanced down at his hand, still holding her arm.

"Even so, I'm still your friend. If you need to talk, I'm here."

Tears welled, but she blinked them away. "I'm okay. It's a lot to take. And Lily tore into me." She glanced at the house.

"I'll go in with you." He held his hand out to her. Now it wasn't only Bill reading her like the old days, Tim was too. She'd always considered herself to be a good poker player until now.

Her eyes locked on his outstretched hand. "I'm not a child, afraid of imaginary monsters hiding in the dark "

"Sometimes the monsters in the dark are real."

Her eyes darted to his. "Sometimes they are." She put her hand in his and they entered the house. The first thing she noticed was how much smaller the rooms looked. The next thing had to be the stench. Tim let go of her hand and went around the bottom floor, opening windows.

"What is that smell?" She pulled her shirt up over her nose to block the odor.

He wandered off into the kitchen and came back. "Rotting food. The sink is full of dirty dishes, the garbage is full, and the cat box is over flowing."

"A cat?" Her father had never let them have pets. She never suspected her mother to be an animal lover.

"Your mom had a couple cats. I don't see them around right now."

"Maybe they'll come back later." She pulled out her notebook and wrote "rental dumpster" in big block letters.

Tim read over her shoulder. "I know a guy who can get one for you—he's in construction. In fact, I think we might be able to get him in here for demolition."

"Demolition?"

Tim motioned toward the moldy wall near the window, and pointed out the stained and rotting hardwood flooring.

"I can't afford this."

"I didn't mention it earlier, but there was a bit of money left to you from your father's will. He had a life insurance policy, and you were on it. It's not a lot, but it will help. I didn't want to say anything in front of Lily."

"I don't want his money." Tim couldn't know what it meant to her, to take her father's gifts. That he'd left her something even after she'd run away opened up old wounds. He was still bribing her for her silence.

"If it will help you get the house off your hands, take it."

She swallowed down the resentment and guilt building inside. "Okay. I'll trust you to help arrange everything."

He grinned at her, and they went upstairs to open more windows. She passed by her old bedroom but didn't open the door. Instead, she went to her parents' room. Inside, she found the bed unmade and sheets covered in black cat fur. "More kitty signs." She brushed it aside and took in the room. The unnatural quiet seeped into her. When she was a kid, there was always a television on in this room. Even if they were busy with other things, the TV stayed on. Tim leaned against the door frame, watching her.

"For what it's worth, I know your mom loved you. She told me so not long before she died."

"I guess she loved me in the only way she knew how."

"What do you mean?"

Jasmine shook her head. She crossed her arms over her chest and took mental stock of all the repairs needed on the second floor. So far she'd counted three leaky windows, stained carpeting, and water stains on the ceiling, probably from the missing roof tiles. "This place is overwhelming."

"We'll take it one step at a time."

Her eyes showed disbelief. "You'll help?"

"Of course I'll help. What are friends for?"

He motioned her out, and they headed downstairs, past her room again. She wasn't tempted to go inside. In fact, it repelled her like opposite sides of a magnet.

Once they were downstairs, they heard a soft meowing.

"Oscar!" Tim lifted a very fat, black cat from behind the sofa. "Jasmine, this is Oscar."

"My mother named the cat Oscar?"

"Yeah. I can't remember why." Before he could put Oscar down, the black form hissed, dug his hind legs in—leaving

49

dark red gashes on Tim's arms—and raced to freedom. "Now I remember." He raced to the sink, pushing dishes aside to wash the wounds.

"What?" She followed behind him, looking for a clean towel to press to his wounds. There didn't seem to be any.

"The Grouch. Oscar the Grouch." He gritted his teeth against the pain.

"Great." Jasmine grabbed a paper towel instead and patted his arm dry. Blood seeped through the towel. "I'll go get the Band-Aids." As if she'd never left home, she went into the front bathroom, opened the lower cabinet, and pulled out the first-aid kit. She brought it back to the kitchen table and bandaged the open sores with gauze and tape.

"You might need to get a shot."

"A shot?"

"Yeah, cat scratches get infected pretty easily, even clean cats. His litter box is pretty gross. You've probably got all kinds of bacteria in there."

"Super." His faced paled.

"Are you still afraid of shots?" She laughed.

"Of all the things you remember about me, you remember I'm a coward when it comes to needles. Great."

Jasmine went over to the sink and found the trash bags. She made quick work of the litter-box and poured in clean litter. She hauled out the garbage to the back, leaving it in a stockpile of ancient, bulging sacks.

"I found more of the odor. I think the garbage service must have been cut off months ago from what I see back there."

"I wondered if Lily was making good decisions or not."

"I'd guess not. I wonder what she was thinking."

He cradled his arm. "It's still really hurting."

"Let me put out new food and water for the cat, and we'll head to the urgent care. I'll even hold your hand so you won't be afraid."

"In that case..." He put out his hand toward her.

Despite her better judgment, she took it.

Seven

True to her word, she held his hand. The years melted away; Jasmine felt more like herself than she had in a long time. After his antibiotic injection to kill off the infection, and a new set of bandages, Tim took her to the cafe for a cup of coffee.

As they sat down, his cell phone rang. He looked at her apologetically. "I'll be right back, I need to take this." She nodded and watched him walk outside the restaurant.

The waitress delivered their coffees. As she stirred hers and thought over the day, she sensed a presence.

"Hey." The voice, deep and smooth, startled her. She looked up at a half-open shirt, pulled tight over a pudgy stomach, adorned with a gold chain. Looking further up, she took in the bad dye job of a thirty-something-year-old man. His cheap cologne wafted down over her.

"Can I help you?"

"It's me, Dave. You remember, Dave Buchard. You're staying in my hotel." He ran his hand across his chest, and stretched his arms, flexing what must have been steroid-enhanced muscles. Not as old as he appeared to be.

"Oh, right. Marcy's husband."

"Remember me from school?" He sat down uninvited and slid Tim's coffee aside. "So, where've you been keeping yourself?"

"Here and there." She pulled her jacket tighter around her. "How's Marcy?"

"I'm sure she's fine. She was this morning. She stays pretty busy at the front desk. My hotel is the most successful in town." It was clear from the pride in his tone he thought a lot of himself. He leaned closer and leered. "Look, I've got this room I keep for poker nights and such. You want to get out of this dive and catch up?"

Sweat broke out across the back of her neck. "I'm afraid I don't remember you, so it'd be hard to catch up. By the way, you are sitting in someone else's spot."

His eyes narrowed. "Tim again. Always Tim. Listen, he's never been right for you. If you would have come around more often, you could have gotten to know me better."

Baffled, Jasmine said nothing. Her eyes darted toward the door, hoping to see Tim return.

"I've thought of you a lot over the years. Have you thought of me?"

The man was obtuse. "Listen, if I don't remember you, how could I think of you?"

He reached toward her hand, but she backed away from the table, her back pressing into the booth. "I'd like you to leave now." If she'd been in Portland, she'd have grabbed his hand and bent it back until he cried "Uncle." What was wrong with her?

"I can't believe you don't remember me. I used to bring you flowers, stick little notes in your locker, that kind of thing. You would flirt with me in gym class. Don't you remember?"

Jasmine had never more wished she did remember. She had no idea if this creep was telling the truth or not.

"Hey, Dave, how've you been?" Tim's commanding voice broke the tension at the table and filled Jasmine with instant relief.

Dave didn't look relieved though. His bushy eyebrows creased together, creating a ledge of fur over his eyes. "Tim, my man. Keeping busy?"

"I am indeed. Thanks for keeping my seat warm." He stepped back as if to make room for Dave to depart. Dave did, but not without a final proposition.

"So, what about that get-together I mentioned?" He was nothing if not persistent.

"I said no. That's final."

"Sure, sure. If you change your mind, it's room two-fifty." He winked at her and left.

"He actually winked at me."

"You're a pretty lady." Tim tried to hide his smirk.

"That is not helpful. He was inviting me to who knows what. I kept telling him I didn't remember him. He wouldn't back off."

"You really don't, do you?"

She shook her head. "Was all that stuff he said about putting notes in my locker and leaving me flowers true?"

"Yeah. He was basketball team captain, and whatever he wanted, he got. But he never got you."

"That's a relief. He kept acting like he did. My memories are scattered, but I thought I'd remember an encounter with him." She shivered.

"I really think you should move into Bill's guest room. I don't like the idea of Dave hanging around, hoping you'll show up at the love shack, and Marcy hunting you down like a cougar after a chicken."

The whole situation was absurd, but she didn't find anything funny about it. Dave had really spooked her. "I'll think about it."

After coffee, they drove to Bill's house and sat outside talking in Tim's car.

"I think I can have that dumpster there by tomorrow."

She rubbed at her temples, something she did much too frequently these days. "This is a much bigger job than I ever expected it to be."

"You didn't know you were getting a house."

"No." She changed the subject. "Why wasn't I contacted when my dad died?"

"Your parents weren't my clients then. I inherited them when our head partner passed away about three years ago."

"And you just found my address?"

"Your mom's file had a report from a detective agency. They first discovered your whereabouts fourteen years ago. From that point on, whenever you moved, your mom got a message. All the reports were mailed to a P.O. box, so I don't think your dad was privy to the information." He let the implication hang in the air but didn't ask more.

"She knew where I was all these years?"

"And apparently she told no one except her lawyer. Your brother and sister were quite surprised that we had been able to contact you."

Jasmine looked out of the car window, up at Bill's house, and watched the indoor lights switch on inside. The warmth and glow misted out toward her.

"It's a beautiful house." The wistful feeling in her heart came out in her words.

"They're good people."

"And Bill goes to church with you? Do you still go to the same one?"

"Yep. The same one my family has always attended. Bill started coming right after Elsie invited him to lunch. The next thing we all knew, he was coming to church with her. Her daddy said he wasn't welcome to court her if he wasn't a church-going man." He laughed. "I think he was pretending to be one for a long time, and one day it clicked with him."

"Religion wasn't something we spoke about at my house."

"I remember."

When she was twelve, Tim had asked her to church with him. She'd enjoyed herself. She'd never heard anyone talk about God besides Tim. The preacher read from the Bible and people prayed and it was all very sincere and honest. But when she got home, no matter what she said, her parents would have none of it. They said all church people were money-grubbing hypocrites and liars. She figured her dad to be an expert on that.

"It's for the best."

"What is that supposed to mean?"

"God doesn't want me. Trust me." She reached for the handle of the car door. "They're expecting me for dinner; do you want to come in?"

Tim looked a bit blindsided but managed to nod his head. She knew it wasn't fair to shut down conversations like she did, but there was a lot he didn't need to know, and even more she never wanted to think about. It was true, counselors made the worst patients. She was ignoring her own advice left and right.

Tim followed her inside. Elsie had already set the table.

"Come on in and have a seat." Her smile warmed the chill from her skin.

She and Tim sat down; Bill came in next with the kids.

54

Then he did the unexpected—her brother prayed. She didn't hear a word he said; her surprise blocked her ears.

"So, how was the house?" Bill managed to ask in-between bites of casserole and salad.

"I can't speak of it over food." Jasmine wrinkled her nose. "I thought so. Mom got really set in her ways and very upset if Lily moved anything. She even made Lily promise not to have the garbage taken in case she threw something important away. More than once she had Lily out in the garbage digging for something that they'd find the next day sitting on a table somewhere."

"It's pretty bad. I'm surprised the neighbors didn't complain."

"They did. Believe it or not, the garbage has been hauled more than a few times. Lily hadn't gotten to it before you arrived."

"Did you get a good look around at the inside?" Elsie interjected.

"Found the cat." Tim held out his arm for inspection. "Had to get a shot."

"Yeah, don't suppose you want Oscar?" Jasmine put on her hopeful face.

"No, I've got no use for that useless grump. Sorry he got you, Tim." Bill shook his head. "The only one he could ever tolerate was Mom."

"What's the plan?" Elsie asked.

"Tim knows a builder, and he's going to bring by a dumpster, hopefully tomorrow. I'll call and see if the garbage service will come by for a special pickup, and I'll start going over things. There's a lot of antiques in there. Did you want any of it?"

"The only piece I ever admired was the hutch, and your mom gave it to me before she died. She said she knew I'd take care of it, and it'd be safe with Bill."

"And I have everything I can use from Dad's shop," Bill added.

"When did you start working with Dad?" She hoped her inquisitive tone hid her disgust.

"When he couldn't hold his own anymore. I was doing odd jobs, working construction, but after doing some side jobs, I realized I liked the idea of being an electrician. So I went to school for it. I was going to move away, but Dad told me he couldn't keep up and asked me into the business. And pretty soon, I was going out on most of the calls and he was doing most of the paperwork. It was a year later he had his heart attack."

Jasmine took thoughtful bites of dinner.

"Even when the doctors told him he was killing himself with booze, he never quit." Bill shook his head. "I'm sorry he never had peace here on earth. But, if any of what I told him soaked in, I'll see him again someday. I hope so."

Jasmine's stomach turned. "I can't say I feel the same." Her eyes leveled at Bill.

The table went silent.

Tim changed the subject. "So, tomorrow I'll come by the hotel and we'll grab a hearty breakfast and get started on the house."

"Am I your new special project or something? Don't you have other clients?"

He put his fork down. "Sure I do. I want to help."

"Sorry. I didn't mean to sound so snippy. I'm worn out after today and the very idea of going back to that place tomorrow fills me with dread."

"Which is why I'm going with you." He grinned openly at her, and she could almost see the boy he'd been.

Again the temptation to shut him down fluttered. But this time she pushed away the impulse. "All right. Thanks." It was totally out of character…and yet the tension in her heart eased a bit. "Just remember, you asked for it."

His grin told her he would.

Tim drove her back to her hotel after dinner. Again, they sat in front of the hotel, talking in the car.

"Are you sure you don't want to move to Bill's place?"

"I like my privacy."

"So tell me about your friends in Portland? Who do you hang out with?"

"I don't hang. I go to work, I help young women, and I go home."

"Not even a pet?"

"I might have to take on Oscar, if that makes you feel any better."

"Not much." He rubbed his arm. "You seem so alone. I was surprised you'd never married."

She thought about that for awhile. "There are a lot of worse things in life than being alone." She paused in thought. "What about you?"

He looked startled.

"Turnabout is fair play and all that. Every single woman in town has her eyes on you like buzzards over carrion."

"Carrion? Thanks."

"Sorry, bad metaphor. But they are just hoping you'll glance their way."

"Maybe I haven't dated enough?"

"Hardly. From what I hear, you've worked your way through the town—the two date maximum?" She expected he'd be embarrassed, but instead he spoke openly. "I guess at first I was looking to date because all my friends were. I was afraid to let anyone get close."

"Why?"

"When you left, Jasmine, it broke my heart."

She didn't know what to say to that.

"I know now from listening to Bill that you had good reason. But back then, all I knew is the girl I'd told all my secrets to, who was my very best friend for my whole life, left me. And she never told me good-bye."

"I'm sorry." Tears formed in her eyes, and the skin on her neck heated. She was glad it was dark in the car.

"It's okay now. As I grew up, I realized that it was wrong. Dating because I was lonely wasn't fair to the woman, or me. But I still wanted someone. So I'd go out to coffee or lunch. By the second date, I knew they weren't right for me."

"Right for you?"

"Sure—marrying material. I'm not really into being a bachelor. But I can tell from conversations with these women that even if we got to know each other better, it wouldn't be going anywhere, so I'd cut it off."

"And now?"

"Now that I've exhausted my options, I realized I'd gone about the whole thing the wrong way. I told God I wanted to marry, but he was going to have to bring her to me."

The atmosphere in the car went still.

"You'd better get to bed. I'll pick you up with breakfast and boxes bright and early at eight, okay?"

"Okay." She climbed out of the car, wished him good night, and entered her hotel room. She peeked through the curtains. Tim had waited until she was inside with the lights on before driving away. After all these years, it was unsettling to have someone watching out for her. And nice.

Jasmine did her room check and locked the door. As she pulled her shirt over her head to get ready for bed, she caught a whiff of her old house's smell imbedded in the fabric. Tears started. Alone, she no longer had to hold them away. Going home for some people was hard, facing all those good childhood memories. But all she had were bad ones. Lily's accusations hurt, because she couldn't tell her that being Daddy's favorite wasn't fun, or good. The thought that she would have traded places will Lily flitted through her mind. She realized though, as soon as it did, that no one deserved to change places with her.

Her phone rang.

"Jazz, is that you?"

Relief flooded through Jasmine. "Hello, Misty."

"When are you coming home, Jazz?"

"I've got a big mess on my hands here. It could be awhile. Weeks even."

"Oh."

"You doing okay?"

"I'm pregnant."

Jasmine's head spun. "How do you feel about it?"

"I want to keep it. The baby."

"Good." The line went quiet for awhile. "You still there, Misty?"

"I'm surprised you want me to keep it."

"Why?"

"I don't know. You are always talking about staying independent, not depending on anyone. And I don't think you like anyone to depend on you. I guess I expected you to tell me to get rid of it."

"Misty, I've learned the hard way that that doesn't take care of the problem, it makes more."

"Oh."

"Have you told Brandi?"

"Yes. She was happy for me. She's going to help me get baby things."

"What about the dad?" Jasmine was almost afraid to ask. If he was her ex, he wouldn't like the idea of Misty being pregnant.

"He doesn't want it." Jasmine could hear there was more to the story, but Misty had to let things come out on her own—there was never any pushing for info with her.

"I'm sorry. You keep talking to Brandi about it."

"She's been praying for me." Misty sounded hopeful.

"Do you like that?"

"Yeah. It's nice. I don't feel like I can pray for me, but I feel like it's okay to have someone else praying for me."

"I know what you mean."

"Do you want me to pray for you, Jazz?"

For the second time that night, Jasmine went speechless.

"I don't think I can ask God for anything for me, but I can ask Him to take care of you. Is that okay?"

Jasmine envied her faith. "That's nice, Misty. Thanks."

After Misty hung up, Jasmine lay back against her bed and thought back over the conversation. There was a broken girl in Portland praying for her. If only there was someone she could tell everything to. If only she could pray and believe it would matter.

Eight

    Jasmine and Tim shared breakfast sandwiches in silence on the stump while they waited for the dumpster to arrive. It was nice not having to talk, and Tim didn't seem to mind the quiet. Despite her job, Jasmine wasn't much for idle conversation; most of what she thought went on in her head, not with others. Maybe that was one-sided, but it worked for her. She did okay.

    The dumpster arrived, as did a large moving truck with Salvation Army written on the side.

    Tim motioned toward the truck. "I thought of that early this morning. They said we can fill it with anything we want, and they'll haul it off and evaluate it later. They only ask we don't put soiled or broken items inside."

    She gave him a grateful look. "You're pretty good at all this. Maybe you're in the wrong job."

    "I like being a lawyer. Helping people feels good."

    "You're not like any lawyer I ever came across in the city." She'd had several run-ins with uncaring lawyers. Her clientele didn't always inspire altruism—they could be rough around the edges. The good lawyers didn't always like working for state wages. Jasmine tried to kept tabs on the ones with kind hearts.

    "Maybe it's the small-town lawyers you need to see more of." His dating hints were like extra-wide speed bumps in the road. They slowed the conversation, but only for a moment. She steered him away expertly.

    "Well, let's attack the living room first, and we'll make our way on up. Sound good?"

    Two hours later they had the living room, dining room, and

her mom's bedroom furniture loaded. Her arms were throbbing and numb. She wasn't used to hard labor. She collapsed on the stump, downed a Gatorade, and watched Tim keep going. He brought out dresser drawers, one at a time. None of the clothes inside looked familiar to her. He poured the clothes out of the drawers into boxes. She started to help, but when she approached a drawer with her dad's old T-shirts inside, a whiff of his cologne made her gag and she had to walk away.

"You okay?"

"I'll be fine. You take care of the clothes, okay?" She stayed away until he had sorted them all.

Tim glanced worriedly at her but said nothing. She appreciated his instincts. After the job was done, he brought out a nightstand and opened the drawer in the sunlight. Jasmine went through it and found nothing but a couple old photos and a handful of change worth saving. He loaded it and brought out the other. Inside were more photos, old school reports of Jasmine's, and handwritten notes she'd left for her mother telling her she loved her. She didn't remember writing them, but there they were in her own little girl scrawl complete with signature. Her mother had kept them all these years.

"You want them?"

She was about to say no, but he gathered them up and slipped them into an old envelope he'd found and handed it to her. "Keep them. Throw them away later if you want, okay?" She took the envelope to the car and dropped it inside on the seat. As he loaded the second nightstand, he called out.

"Hey, I found something weird here."

She came around to the back of the truck. He had the stand upside down, and was peeling yellow, crackling tape off something on the underside. He held it up to her. It was a key.

"Why would your mom tape a key to the bottom of her nightstand?" He stared at it, and his eyes went wide. "It's like the one you used to wear on a chain around your neck." He held it out to her, but Jasmine didn't take it. Her stare locked on to it, and her knees went out from under her. Tim caught her and lowered her to a sitting position.

"Put your head between your knees and breathe slowly." She did as instructed, and the world came back into focus.

"What does this go to, Jasmine?"

Her shaky hand took it from him, turning it over and over in her palm. "The camper. It goes to the camper."

"I didn't know your folks had a camper."

"We did, when I was a kid, remember?" She stood and headed to the extensive and overgrown backyard. Nothing. In its place was an overgrown weedy mess covered in rotting tires and garbage sacks.

"It's gone."

"I'll call Bill and see if he knows what happened to it." The sense of urgency in his voice told her he realized how important this might be to her. Moments later, he was back.

"Bill said it might be up at the old hunting property. It's only about an hour away. Why don't we go take a look? It'll give us a chance to take a lunch break."

Jasmine didn't feel like she could eat anything at all. A burning urgency to see the camper filled her.

The drive was a quiet one, with Jasmine keeping her eyes on the road ahead and Tim glancing between her and the road. He handed her the cold case with sandwiches inside.

"Eat."

She obeyed without thinking, eating the sandwich, and handing him his drink now and then. An hour later, they pulled onto a long dirt road. The overgrown road was bumpy, and he had to take it slow. They pulled around by a cabin and got out.

Tim glanced over the property and back at her. "Have you ever been here?"

"No, they didn't have this property when I was a kid." Her eyes were darting here and there, hopeful and afraid at the same time. She knew he must think she was crazy, but for some reason finding the camper meant more to her than anything else.

They walked around to the side and headed to the back. Near a bunch of old oaks was a large rectangular shape, covered by an old green tarp. She walked toward it, her legs leaden. Tim took her hand, but she couldn't feel it, all she could see was the shape.

He pulled the tarp back, revealing an old cream-colored, ten-foot-long camper with a green stripe down the side. Jasmine held her breath a moment. It looked awful, covered in mold and dirt, but it was like finding an old friend.

"The windows are all shot out." Tim motioned to gaping holes in the glass.

She hadn't noticed. Indeed, they were all broken. On purpose. She could almost feel the anger in it. He'd done that. He took the only place she'd ever been safe and shot it full of holes, but it was too late. She'd escaped.

"My dad's handiwork."

"Why would he do that?"

Jasmine rubbed her hand over the door, feeling the cold roughness under her palm. She started sliding the key in the lock, but saw it wasn't necessary. The door had been pried open, the lock broken. She wrenched the knob open past rust and age. The door swung back with a metallic squeak, and she stood facing the interior.

She went inside and looked around. Her shoes crunched through the broken glass, and she wiped the table clear of dirt. The familiar manufactured smell mixed with the oaks and pines outside. The wild printed dining seats were moldy and soggy with rain from a leak in the tarp. She walked through the galley kitchenette and opened the cabinet door to find a mostly empty jar of grape jelly and peanut butter mixed in gray moldy fuzz. Next to it sat an open box of crackers. Rodents decimated them long ago, leaving droppings behind as a thank you. She opened a drawer, found an old lighter and tucked it into her jeans. Reaching under the mattress, she pulled out a knife. Funny how knives were a theme in her life.

A footstep behind her raked over the glass and she turned, startled, brandishing the blade.

"It's me." Tim, pale, had his hands up in a submissive move.

Jasmine took a ragged breath and reached under the mattress again and pulled out a diary, encased in a plastic sack. She'd cut a hole up inside the mattress and hidden it. There it was, as if she'd left it there yesterday.

"A knife and a book."

She nodded. "I didn't think I'd need the diary. But, over the years, I've wished for it."

"What was this place to you?" He looked around, lifting up a pile of old papers, and peeking inside cabinets.

"Sanctuary."

"Why did she hide the second key?"

"She bought the camper when my father was off on a binge one weekend. She gave me one key from a set. She must have hid the other under her nightstand all these years."

"To keep you safe?"

Tears welled in her eyes. "I think it was the only way she could think to do it."

Tim took a controlled breath. "Why didn't she ever call the police?"

"For the same reason I never told you I needed help, Tim. For the same reason any abuse lives on in families—because of shame and the horrific feeling that there's no escaping any of it."

"How long did you live in here?" His voice was barely a whisper, afraid to ask, but needing to know.

"I think about a year. It was the week he declared he would change the locks I knew I had to run. There wasn't another solution for me, do you understand?" Her voice implored him.

"I'm trying to. Was it scary to be out in the camper alone?" He looked around as if searching for some sign of comfort and found it lacking.

All she could see was security and protection.

"Sometimes. But he gave up trying the door. He ran out of excuses to come out and check on me. After awhile, this was the only place I felt safe, besides at school or your house."

She could see the meaning of it all sinking into him. She saw shock and anger play over his features. He turned away from her, stepping outside. She followed a moment later, not sure what he'd say, or how he'd feel about her now.

She found him a few feet away, standing in the sun, angst and tears in his eyes.

"I should have known." He took her hand in a tight grasp, but still didn't look at her.

"How? No one knew."

"Your mother knew, and she didn't do a blasted thing about it." Bitterness laced his words.

"She did, she kept me safe. It's important for me to understand that. It's important for me to know that in some small way she tried to be a mother to me and love me." Jasmine held up the key. "I can't tell you what that means to me." Tears streamed down her face.

He pulled her into his arms, where she cried for several minutes. The warmth of his embrace and the spicy scent of his cologne wrapped around her like a blanket. His arms were a safe place to be. If she could have picked anyone to be there at that moment, she would have chosen Tim.

After he released her, they found a pair of old folding chairs. Tim set them up in the sun and they sat together, looking at the shattered shelter. Squinting at it, she could almost imagine it was twenty-two years ago. The immediate feeling of safety she'd experienced when her mother placed the key in her hand settled over her. She'd moved in some clothes and stored an old coffee can under the table in case she had to use the potty. She'd stocked the cabinets with snacks and hooked the hose up for water.

And to think, some kids played fort for fun.

Jasmine shook her head, bringing her back to the present, focusing on the damaged camper, the sound of the wind rustling the towering pines, and the smell of sunbaked earth. She stretched her legs and kicked the package at her feet. Picking up the diary, she slid it from the plastic sack. Tim breathed easily next to her, waiting.

"I didn't dare take this with me. I thought one day someone might find it and they'd know the truth and why I had to leave. I wondered if you would find it one day." She opened it, ready to step back in time. Instead, to her horror, she found the pages cut, scored with a knife, each one. Her hands shook so hard, she dropped the book.

Tim picked it up and turned each page. "It can be repaired."

Jasmine shook her head. "He defiled it. It wasn't enough to ruin the camper, he had to do that" —she motioned to the damage— "and leave it for me. He hoped I'd be back someday—counted on it." Her body trembled, a shuddering that moved through her like the rumble of a newly tapped oil well about to erupt.

"I never knew what kind of man your father really was, Jasmine. I'm sorry."

She didn't know what to do next. She'd hoped to read about her life and remember. But those memories were slashed in the book as they'd been from her mind.

Tim took the diary and slipped it into the plastic. "Can I

take it? I'll have it fixed."

"I don't want any strangers reading what's in there."

"We'll fix it together, okay?" He folded the bag gently, as if wrapping a shroud over a guarded artifact. He put an arm around her, trying to calm her nerves, settle her shaking, but it wasn't working.

"I want to burn it."

His head snapped to hers. "You want to do what?"

"Burn the camper."

"Why?"

"I don't know. I feel like I should. It was my shelter, but he's ruined it. He ruined everything. I want to purge what he's done." She got up and searched around the cabin, tipping over rocks, turning over buckets, and checking under the doormat. "Do you have a key?" Tim shook his head. She tipped over a log by the back door and found one lying in the dirt. She opened the door, and the smell of gun oil, soap, and his cologne poured out. She backed away, gagging, unable to enter.

Tim rubbed her back in slow circles until the spasms stopped.

"What did you want in there?"

"Lighter fluid." She had one goal.

"Jasmine, we can't set fire to it without taking precautions. It's a hazard. Let me call the fire department in town. They'll haul it away and use it for training."

"I have to do it."

"I'll make sure you're there, okay?"

He shifted her away from the camper, away from the cabin, toward the car, speaking in low, soothing tones like one would to a traumatized child. The numbness in her hands worked its way up her arms as she walked along. She hadn't seen her father for twenty-two years, but he still controlled what she did.

He still touched what wasn't his and soiled what could never be cleansed.

Nine

Tim and Jasmine sat together in his car, in front of her hotel room. This had become a habit with them. She didn't want to go to Bill's, and the unspoken rule of not inviting anyone inside her apartment—or hotel room—stood fast. Night had fallen as they'd returned to Bright River. Darkness seemed to cover every thing and every thought she had.

"Please come to Bill's with me," Tim insisted.

"I said no. Not tonight. I need to process everything." She stared down at her hands, not moving to get out of his car but not willing to stay either.

"Bill doesn't know?" His voice broke the stillness of the car.

"No one knows."

He took her hand. "I do."

She pulled her hand free of his and wiped the tear from her cheek. She'd expected her comfort level to dip with Tim, to feel dirty and ashamed in his presence, but she didn't. Still, she didn't want him to touch her. She didn't want anyone to touch her.

"I should go." She reached for the door, but he put a hand on her shoulder.

"I don't want you staying here with Dave on the prowl. I think it's a mistake."

She smiled halfway at him. "He can't hurt me, Tim." She climbed from the car, and he stepped out, following her to the room.

"If you need me, call." He handed her his card with his private cell number written on it. "I mean it."

"Thanks. I'll be fine. I'll be cleaning out the house tomorrow."

"Why not take the day off? We'll go for a picnic."

She shook her head. "Everyone keeps forgetting I have a life to get back to."

"Maybe we don't want to remember." His eyes held hers, and she found herself involuntarily holding her breath. She knew what was coming. He took her hands in his, moving closer.

"I can't." Jasmine pulled away, swiped her key, and entered the hotel room, closing the door before she thought about what she was doing. She couldn't face him. She knew what he wanted, maybe what he always wanted, even back when they were younger. That's why she could never tell him about her father before this.

She peeked through the peephole and watched him stand there outside her door for a moment before turning to leave. She couldn't read his expression in the dim lights, but she knew he was hurting. She needed to get out of town before anyone else got hurt.

Picking up the phone, she called Elsie.

"Hi, I can't come to dinner tonight."

"Why not? We were looking forward to seeing you."

"Long story. Hey, can those friends of yours come over tomorrow? Or is that too short of a notice?"

"I'll make some phone calls." Elsie's tone told her she should have called sooner.

"Okay, we'll see you about nine, okay?" Jasmine knew she should explain, but that wasn't a possibility.

"We'll do our best. Did today go okay?"

"The place is pretty messy."

"Are you sure that's all?"

Had Elsie always been so curious? "Look, I've got to run. See you tomorrow." She hung up before Elsie could pry any further. In a couple days, she'd be out of there and back helping women get off the streets—a much safer place than Bright River.

She headed into the bathroom and took the hottest shower she could stand, trying to wash off the smell of her house, of the camper, of her childhood, but it clung to her with long, unyielding tentacles.

After climbing into bed, she set her clock and unplugged the phone to keep Marcy or Dave from intruding on her life. She flipped Tim's card over and over between her fingers, before tucking it inside her phone cover.

The next morning she met Elsie and her friends, a team of ten, on the front lawn of her parents' home. They all looked to her for direction. For once in her life, she wished someone else would take control.

"Thanks for coming. If anyone sees the black cat, don't touch him." The group laughed, as if everyone in town knew what a menace Oscar was. "I can't pay any of you, but if there's anything in the room at the top of the stairs on the right that you'd like, please take it."

All the women smiled, and headed inside, chatting and visiting. Elsie came alongside Jasmine after everyone was out of earshot.

"Your room's at the top of the stairs."

"Yep."

"You're giving away all your things? Your mother kept that room pristine." Elsie's tone chastised her, but Jasmine let it go.

"I don't have any attachment to those things."

"But they're all expensive collectables and dolls. You must want some of them."

"No, I don't." Her hands shook, so she stuffed them in her pockets.

"Well, maybe I'll take some of them for Rose. She might like one or two things."

"No." Panic rose in her chest. "Please don't do that. I'll buy something special for Rose, but I don't want anyone in the family having any of that." She rocked back and forth on her heels. The urge to run shot through her.

Elsie looked confused. "I don't get it. You used to try to give me your toys when we were kids. I don't understand why you don't want anything your parents gave you."

Tim walked up behind her, putting a comforting hand on her back and the shuddering stopped, her feet stilled. "It's a long story, Elsie. Please honor what she says, okay? She's got her reasons."

Elsie's eyes held in incredulous look. She opened her mouth

to respond, but closed it again as Tim shook his head. "Okay."
She headed inside the house and Jasmine released the breath
she'd been holding.

She turned to Tim. "Thanks for that."

"Sure. Are you sure you don't want to see your room one
last time?"

"There's nothing there for me."

"Okay." He picked up a stack of boxes and some tape and
headed inside. "I'll take care of whatever's left behind for
you."

Jasmine's legs went weak and shaky as her heart rate
slowed. She wasn't sure how she'd handle this today, but Tim
stepped up again, taking it on for her. She shouldn't depend on
him so much. Wandering around to the back, she looked at the
yard as if for the first time. The flowerbeds were overgrown
with weeds and looked as though they hadn't been attended
to for years. The trees and shrubs were in similar condition.
Her mother used to love her garden; she'd called it a place of
solitude. They weren't supposed to bother her there, dig in the
beds, or play in the trees. The side yard was okay, and even the
front, but the back, that was a protected reserve.

Jasmine heard a mewling from one of the bushes. She
leaned down and saw a fat, black cat peering out at her, orange
glowing eyes formed into inquisitive slits.

"Hey there, Oscar." She put out a hand, and Oscar came
forward. He rubbed on her hand and wrapped around her legs.
She squatted down in the grass, and he climbed in her lap,
purring and rubbing. His sun-warmed fur and accompanying
purr comforted her.

"I see you made a friend." Tim stepped out of the back door
with a sack of garbage.

"Seems that way. Are you sure this is the same brute who
sliced you open?"

"Oh, it's him all right. He seems to like you fine, though."

Oscar's purring increased as he kneaded her legs and curled
into a sleeping position.

"I guess that's a good thing, if I'm taking him home with
me."

A shadow passed over Tim's face, but he said nothing.

"I wonder where the other cat is." She looked around her

but didn't see any sign of a friend.

"Bill said he was mostly an outdoor type. A gray tabby with a missing ear. I don't think your mom was the only one feeding him, so don't worry too much over him."

She scratched Oscar between the ears and under his chin, and the purring continued. "Cat therapy."

"I supposed I can leave you safely in his claws, er, paws." Tim headed back into the house.

"Well, Oscar, we're a pair. No one in their right mind would take us on, so we'll have to stick together, okay?" She reached inside her pants pocket and dialed The Getaway, ordering sandwiches and drinks for the team. It was the least she could do.

Surprisingly, they had what was left of her room packed and loaded onto the Salvation Army truck by noon, and everything else cleaned inside by three. They all stood outside visiting like old friends, exchanging e-mail addresses with her. Rarely had she experienced this kind of kindness. They hugged Elsie good-bye, waved one last time at Jasmine, and drove away.

"Well, I've got dinner in the Crock-Pot." Elsie walked away, fully expecting them to follow whenever they were ready.

Jasmine sat down on the stump, and Tim joined her.

"It's over."

"This part is, anyway." He kicked the toe of his shoe in a dirt mound nearby.

"Do you know someone who can put it on the market for me?"

"I'll call my realtor."

"I'll retain you as my lawyer, of course."

"Sure, purely business, nothing personal," he teased her and bumped her shoulder with his.

"You know what I mean. I don't want you thinking I've taken advantage of our friendship. It's a lot of work trying to get a house ready for sale."

"Oh, speaking of, I got my builder friend to give me an estimate on fixing the drywall and floor. He said it'd be about two grand. The roof will be another seven. To replace the carpet, another three. He contracts out for painters, so we'll have to wait for the rest."

She choked. "Is that good?"

"Very fair. Don't worry, you can afford it."

"I guess I'll trust him to do a good job."

"Frankly, I wouldn't do that. I think you should stay and oversee the job."

He was getting good at throwing out those speed bumps.

"You know I need to go."

"You keep saying so, but I don't see the need myself. There's a lot for you here."

"There's a lot to stay away from here, too."

"I thought we were taking care of that? I got the fire department all lined up to burn the camper on Monday."

Monday was three days away. Could she stay here three more days? It had already been nearly a week.

"Thanks for that. I guess I'll stay through Monday." She heard him exhale. "Please don't ask me to do something I'm not capable of, Tim."

"You know I can't identify with what you've been through, Jasmine. I can't even begin to imagine it. But at the same time, don't you think you've run from this long enough?"

"It's not for you to say when it's been long enough."

His eyes flashed at her. "I guess I want everything to be the way I hoped it would be."

"How's that?"

"I used to imagine you'd come back, and we'd pick up our friendship where we'd left off." She knew it cost him to say it, but she couldn't let him think that way.

"I quit imagining when my childhood was stolen from me."

"I can't fix that." He stood up and paced. She could see the lawyer coming out now.

"No one can."

He stopped. "God can."

She shook her head at him. "It's too late for that—it was always too late. I lived a lie when I attended that church. I lived a lie the whole time I was here in Bright River. But I don't where I live now."

"Tell Bill what happened."

"I can't do that. I can't take his idea of who our dad was and break it. He's come to terms with what his damage was. He's doing okay. I have no right to take that from him."

"Do the people back in Portland know?"

"One of them does." Brandi knew everything. She'd been there for her night terrors, for her anger, for her grief.

"Well, what's the difference? You'll still be living a lie."

"So I should move here, start going to church, and life will all work out right?" Jasmine stood up, tired of being preached at.

"I'm not saying that it will all disappear, but at least you won't be alone anymore. I can't stand the thought of you living your life all alone like that. That's not who you are supposed to be."

Her anger built. "Who I was supposed to be was stolen from me a long time ago."

"Maybe. Maybe she's still in there, dreaming and encouraging others not to lose hope."

Jasmine could see the life he wanted her to have. He wanted her to act as if nothing was wrong, that life was all going to be okay.

"Do you want to really know me?" She asked the question like a threat, and he backed away from her.

"Yes."

"I'm not someone to be trifled with. I lived with a traveling carnival for a year, lived with a drug seller for a year, lived on the streets for two years. I can use a knife to defend myself, and have. I will never marry. I will never have children. Is that someone you want to spend time with? Go care about someone else, Tim." She tried to walk away, but he pulled her back to the stump.

"Don't leave." She knew he didn't mean right then, he meant don't leave town. Ever.

"Why not?"

"Because I think God wants you to figure something out."

"God again."

"Why do you think you're still alive? Luck? Street smarts?" She shrugged.

"Think about that, will you? How often does a fourteen-year-old runaway grow up at all? How about grow up and become an educated person? Add a professional to that."

"What are you trying to say?" She stuck her hands in her pockets.

"I think God has a purpose for you. And you owe it to

yourself to figure out what it is."

"What could He want with me? I've never done a thing right in my life. My life is all about making up for mistakes."

"What happened to you wasn't your fault."

Tears stung in her eyes as her throat constricted. "I've done a lot of things that were wrong, didn't you hear me?"

"True. But the catalyst—your father's abuse—that wasn't your fault."

"I should have stopped him." Even as she said it, she heard a hundred other women's voices at the same time, saying the same thing. And she heard her own voice telling them that was a lie. That they didn't have control over that.

He took her hand. "You did your best. You were a kid. You moved into that camper and locked him out. And when he tried to get in again, you ran—you ran hard and did the best you could, Jasmine."

"My best didn't cut it. I've done things I can never forgive myself for." Never.

"So you think God can't forgive you either." It wasn't a question.

"There's no reason that I'd matter to God."

Tim shook his head at her. "I can't convince you of that, Jasmine, so I won't try. But I hope you'll give it some thought. I hope you'll take the time and ask God why you are still here on this earth." It was at that point she realized he hadn't let go of her hand, and she hadn't tried to get away.

"Let's go eat." He pulled on her arm, trying to get her to follow him.

"Just like that?" The way his brain shifted gears kept her off-kilter.

"You're hungry, aren't you?"

She wiped the angry tears from her eyes and followed him to his car. No matter what he said, she wouldn't stay here past Monday. Once that was done, she was done.

Ten

After working all day at the house, Jasmine needed a bath. She convinced Tim to take her back to the hotel. She'd walk over to Bill's house after she'd cleaned up, and they'd share whatever wonderful concoction was stewing in Elsie's Crock-Pot. Once she'd showered, she pulled on clean clothes and ran a brush through her hair.

About to leave, she heard a knock on the door. Tim was probably worried about her being on her own. Somehow she'd have to convince him she could take care of herself. Without checking the peep hole, she whipped open the door to try to surprise him. "I told you I'd be there in a bit."

The laughter in her voice died. Dave.

"Where's that?" His eyes looked her over, making her skin crawl.

"I've got dinner plans at my brother's house." She stepped out past him, pulled the hotel door closed and headed toward the street and Bill's house.

"I'll walk you there."

"I know the way." She moved several paces ahead of him but sensed he still followed.

"I heard you were cleaning up your old house to sell. I might have a buyer."

She didn't want to get into a conversation with him, but if he really knew a buyer, she couldn't miss a chance. They were by the park, out in the open. It looked safe enough, so she stopped.

"Who's interested?"

"I am. Marcy and I have been looking for a place of our

own. Living out of the hotel saves us money, but she's wanted to start a family for awhile now. You really can't raise kids in a hotel."

"No, I suppose not." Too bad they were bringing kids into their mess.

"Once she has the kids, she'll be too busy to worry about what I'm up to." He winked at her, and it set off a cascade of uneasiness inside her.

"Well, once you have a serious offer, you can contact Tim."

"But I'm contacting you. How much do you want?"

"I'm really not up on the market." She stepped past him, but he shifted in front of her again, pulling her up short.

"That's fair. Listen, why don't we go somewhere and I can educate you?" He brushed his fingers down her arm. Unexpected feelings of anger and anxiety washed over her. Her legs wanted to run. As she fought for control, Jasmine swallowed down the fear and let it harden to rage as she spoke through gritted teeth. "Not ever." She whirled away from him, looking for avenues of escape. Through the park would be the fastest way to Bill's, but trees would block them from public view.

Dave grabbed her shoulder and wrenched her back around. It happened so fast, she didn't have time to think. On the streets of the city she'd have an answer for him, but here in her hometown, she felt like Superman surrounded by Kryptonite—her powers had faded and she was alone and unprotected. Her heart raced.

"You too good for me, is that it?"

"What about Marcy?"

"What's that to you? I know all about your life, Jazz." He pulled her in closer, whispering with menace, "Come back to the hotel, we'll talk."

She pulled out of his grasp and started to run. Cars drove by, conversations carried on between the strangers she passed. No one noticed her erratic breathing, her racing feet—she was invisible. She heard his footsteps behind her as she rounded the corner to Bill's house. As she reached the gate, his hand grabbed her arm. She screamed, came around with her fist clenched and socked him hard.

Instead of Dave, Tim lay at her feet, sprawled on the ground, groaning and holding his left eye.

She gasped. "Oh no!" Kneeling down, she helped him into a sitting position. "Are you okay?"

His good eye watered as he stared at her in disbelief. "What was that for?"

"You caught me off guard."

"I beg to differ."

"What I mean is I thought you were someone else." She pulled him to standing and moved his hand away from his eye so she could take a better look at it, cradling his face in her hand. He swayed, and she supported him.

"Who?"

"Dave."

"Dave? He's harassing you?" He squinted his good eye at her, checking her over.

"You could say that."

"I'll call the cops."

"Who are you going to call the cops on?" Bill arrived at the fence with Elsie following. When she saw Tim's discoloring eye, she ran back inside. They headed toward the house in her wake.

"Dave's harassing Jasmine."

"Then why is she hitting you?" Elsie handed him an ice pack as she joined them on the porch.

"Mistaken identity."

"Let's go inside, and we'll call the police right away." Elsie led Jasmine to the door.

Jasmine's head started spinning. "Please, don't."

They all looked at her and nearly in chorus asked, "Why not?"

She sighed. "I'm only going to be here a couple more days. The last thing I want to do is press charges and have the whole town come down on me for it."

"Who's the whole town? The whole town, as you put it, knows he's a womanizer and he deserves to be brought up on charges if he's acting inappropriately toward you."

She shook her head. "Can't we go in and have dinner?" She had moved past them but looked back in time to see Tim's incredulous look past the ice pack. They all moved to follow her, though slowly. Elsie served dinner at the kitchen table, having put the kids to bed already.

Tim put the ice pack on the table. "How's it look?"

Bill grinned. "Well, she's got power in that punch."

Jasmine put up her hand to block the red patches she knew must be appearing around her throat and chest. Tim's swollen eye was ringed with a purple tinge.

"Don't feel bad. It's an honest mistake. And don't worry, I believe you now." Tim gave Jasmine a wink and winced because he'd used the wrong eye.

"What do you believe?" Elsie asked.

"That she can take care of herself."

They all chuckled, but she wanted to tell them it wasn't so. Something in the air there stole her strength and turned her back into normal, everyday Jasmine. Jazz was nowhere to be found, and she didn't like it one bit. She hadn't been a victim for years now, but in Bright River reminders lurked around every corner. It was stamped across her forehead.

Bill interrupted her thoughts. "I want you to get your stuff and move into the guest room. It's very private, and we won't wake you at strange hours, or expect you to spend every moment of your time with us. I won't have you staying there anymore. Dave's a creep, and I don't want you at risk."

She nodded. "I think I'll take you up on that."

Elsie smiled a warm, broad smile at her. "The kids will be so excited. They really want a chance to get to know you better."

"That'll be great." Being Aunt Jasmine for a few days would be nice before she had to leave. They ate in silence awhile longer until Bill said something that made the food go stale in her mouth.

"So, Tim was telling me you want to burn the camper."

She turned an accusing glare on Tim.

"I had to ask him, it's his property." Tim put up his hands.

"Oh." She hadn't considered that.

"It's fine with me. It's a huge rattrap right now. I'm surprised you want to burn it though. We could replace the windows, dry it out, and donate or sell it."

Jasmine didn't offer any explanation but kept eating. Bill took this as a challenge.

"Maybe I'll keep it after all. I like hunting. I could use it as a base camp." She knew Bill was baiting her, but she couldn't take the chance.

"I can't explain it, but I really need to do this, okay?"

Bill exhaled slowly. "Okay. Do you think you'll ever tell me why?"

"No."

"You know, Jasmine, our whole lives we've had to live with secrets and lies and act like everything was okay. I told Elsie when I married her I wanted no more of that. I need my house to be a safe place, an honest place. I don't want to come home and tiptoe around someone else's expectations. I don't ever want to enter this place and pretend everything is or isn't okay."

Jasmine laid down her fork and stared at her plate. "I know what you mean, Bill."

"Good."

"I'll go." This was his house—he had a right to set the rules. She stood, unwilling and unable to share the burden she carried; the only thing left for her to do was leave.

"Jasmine." Bill's voice commanded her to sit, but she moved off through the living room and headed to the door. He followed her and pulled her gently to the couch. She refused to look up at him.

"If I didn't know you better, I'd think you were carrying on the drama-queen act like Lily. But that's her gig. You need to tell me something, and you need to tell me now. No more lies, no more secrets, little sister."

The shaking inside built slow in her extremities, like a coal stove catching light, filling her legs, her arms, and settling into her stomach.

"I can't." Her voice quivered.

"If you were counseling someone in this spot, what would you say?"

"That's not fair." She pressed on her temples to calm the pounding.

"Maybe not."

"It's all too much, too fast, Bill." Tears fell from her eyes in great drops, making dark blue blotches on her jeans.

"Okay. I won't push. But, before you leave town, you and I need to talk."

She nodded, and he pulled her into a big bear hug. When

she pulled away, Tim entered the room. She could see in his eyes that he'd overheard the conversation.

"Give me your hotel key. I'll gather your stuff and bring it back."

"I should go too."

"No. I'll take care of it. I'll settle your bill. I don't want you ever going back to that place again."

Jasmine reached into her back pocket, pulled out the key card, and handed it over to Tim. Her fingers were stiff and achy from the punch.

"You want company?" Bill asked him.

"No, I'll take care of it." He headed out the door, shoulders squared, on a mission.

Elsie came into the room. "Can I show you your bedroom?"

Jasmine nodded and followed Elsie upstairs, down the hall past the kids' rooms to one adjacent to Elsie and Bill's. She held her breath, worried she'd see some other artifacts from her childhood inside, but there wasn't anything. It did, however, look familiar. The door opened into a small room with a full-sized white-framed canopy bed. There was a small white roll top desk near it, a matching bedside table and floral hurricane lamp sitting atop a circular doily. A full-length standing mirror took up one corner, and a wardrobe stood in the other. The furniture left enough space to walk a u-shape around it. The door to the immediate right opened into a small private bathroom.

Elsie pushed the door open wider. "This used to be a closet, but the kids' bathroom is on the other side, so it was easy to gut it, share the plumbing, and turn it into a third bathroom. We thought that one day maybe one of our mothers would end up living with us, and we wanted it all set already."

"It's very nice." She turned back and looked at the bedroom, trailing her fingers over the desk. "This feels very familiar to me."

"It's my old bedroom furniture from when I was a kid."

Jasmine frowned. She could remember furniture, but not people. What was wrong with her? She remembered Tim, and her family, and places. Why not hanging out with Elsie?

"I'm sure I'll be very comfortable here, thanks." She sat on the bed and tried the mattress.

"You can hang your things in here." Elsie opened the wardrobe and showed her the floral padded hangers. The smell of lilacs filled the room.

"I remember that smell." Jasmine walked over and pulled one of the hangers from the closet, rubbing her thumbs over them. An image of a little blond girl laughing at one of her jokes flashed through her mind. It was a gentle memory, without much substance, but it didn't fill her with dread. "You had something like these in your room." It wasn't a question.

Elsie squeezed her hand and smiled, her eyes sparkling with unshed tears. They heard a door close downstairs and voices talking.

"Tim must be back. I'll send him up with your things."

"Thanks. Thanks for all of this." She gave Elsie a hug and let her leave. In moments, Tim was at the door, knocking for admittance.

"Come on in." She motioned for him to come in. "How was Marcy this evening?"

"Calmer than I would have expected. Which could be bad, or good. Either way, your bill is paid, and your things are safe." He put down her suitcase, purse and a paper sack of items he must have scooped from the bathroom.

"Thanks for that. Add it to my tab." She couldn't imagine Tim keeping a list of all the kind things he'd done for her since she'd arrived—but the scales seemed very one-sided. She gave her things a cursory once over. Everything was there.

"Absolutely." He gave her a mock-serious look, and changed the subject. "I won't see you tomorrow—I have to be in court all day."

The disappointment surprised her. "I hope you win."

"Me too." He scrunched his eyebrows together like he used to when he was a kid and was working up to say something. "There's a town picnic planned for Saturday. Do you think you'll be up to attending?"

"The annual spring picnic?" She grinned, remembering the festivities from when she was a child.

"That's the one."

"I'd like to go."

"Good. I'll see you there." He smiled and winced, putting a hand up to his bruised eye.

81

"Sorry about that."

"Oh, it'll be okay. Makes me look tough. I'll scare the defendant's team. How's your hand?" He lifted her right hand under the lamp light and turned it over, inspecting it. There were light purple bruises on her knuckles. As he brushed his fingers gently over them, a tiny jolt of electricity raced up her arm. She didn't feel like running when Tim touched her, that was certain.

"I guess I hit harder than I thought." Her words came out almost in a whisper.

"Should have had you ice it." He let her go, looking self-conscious, and took a couple steps back, shoving his hands deep inside his pockets. "Take some Advil or something or it will stiffen up."

"You speak from experience."

"I've been in my fair share of fights. Not since I became the respectable lawyer type, mind you." He stood taller, looking impressive and proper.

"Can't have the town hero beating up folks." She laughed.

"I can't claim hero, by any standard of the word. But one does attract more business being congenial." He tipped his head to her. "I'll see you Saturday."

Jasmine watched him go, and gently closed her bedroom door. She got ready for bed and climbed in, sighing in contentment under the heavy down comforter, her form sinking into the thickly padded mattress. Lovely. She needed to get a new bed when she got home.

Within moments, she was fast asleep. It hadn't occurred to her to check the bathroom or lock the door.

# Eleven

Sunlight beamed into Jasmine's room, past lace curtains she hadn't noticed the night before. It was another beautiful spring day. Somewhere down the block, someone was mowing their lawn. Jasmine picked up her cell phone and saw it was nearly noon. She hadn't slept like that for as long as she could remember. She got dressed and headed downstairs to see if anyone was around. She found Elsie in the kitchen.

"Good morning." Elsie beamed at her.

"Sorry I slept so long." Jasmine sensed the red flush on her neck and pretended it wasn't there.

"That's okay. I sent the kids over to our neighbor's to keep things quiet on purpose. I didn't think you'd gotten much rest since you've been here."

"No, I guess not." She moved to the coffeepot and took a mug off the wall. She inhaled the aroma—Elsie knew how to make coffee.

"It's pretty strong."

"It smells really good. Not like that stuff at the cafe."

"Oh, don't drink that. We've got a Dutch Brothers right around the corner from them. They're much better—it's a bit like drinking a candy bar. Still, not as good as mine, though."

Jasmine sat at the kitchen table, taking in the kitchen and its bright, clean feel. A vase of cut daffodils sat central on the old farm table. Pictures the kids painted or drew with bright colors and exaggerated sizes adorned the refrigerator. The cabinet doors were made of framed farm glass, and held a variety of nice china, everyday dishes, and a huge selection of cookbooks.

"You and Bill have made a nice home together."

"Thanks."

Elsie stopped what she was doing at the counter and brought over two plates holding sandwiches. She opened a jar of homemade pickled asparagus and another of applesauce and sat down. She bowed her head and asked for the blessing. Jasmine didn't join in but found herself watching Elsie, like someone watched a nature program.

"Tim called earlier. He's got your house listed, but the realtor needs to meet with him and do a walk through on the repairs later today at three."

"That was fast."

"Tim knows a lot of people in town."

"I'm gathering that." She might too, if she'd stayed around. "So, am I supposed to know this realtor?"

"I don't think so. She's new." Elsie didn't add anything to that.

"Even if she wasn't, I probably wouldn't." Jasmine took a bite and pretended it didn't matter. But it did. Every day it mattered more.

"Don't be so hard on yourself. I don't know how many people I would remember from when I was fourteen if I hadn't seen them every day." She passed her the jar of applesauce. "It's from our trees in back."

Jasmine smiled. Everyone in town, even if they weren't official fruit farmers, boasted apple, plum, and often cherry trees in their backyards. And theirs were always doing better than the neighbors'. She tasted the tangy-sweet preserves and nodded.

"Very good." Jasmine took another bite and sighed.

"Thanks. Bill and I made that last year. He loves to cook with me." Elsie got up and pulled a few various jars of things from a cabinet and set them next to Jasmine. "For you to take home."

"Thanks." Elsie appeared to be the only one not in complete denial that she had a life outside of Bright River. "Bill cooks? I didn't know that."

"He was on his own as a bachelor a long time, and he likes good food. He had to do something. That's where we met again, actually, in a night cooking class at the high school."

"Really?" Jasmine couldn't picture Bill being self-motivated to attend a class like that. Something to do with construction or electricity—things where you could permanently maim yourself—but not cooking.

"He kept doing better than I did at every dish, and it made me so mad. One day he invited me to his house for dinner. I was really surprised, because we were in such a competition in class. But he claimed he needed help with pie making—and that was true, he really couldn't do pies. So I went over, and he made this elaborate chicken dish, with roasted vegetables. It was so good. We made a pie together and visited while it baked. We had such a nice time talking, I forgot to be mad at him. And afterward he cleaned the whole kitchen—it was a mess, let me tell you. He's still the messiest cook I have ever seen. But he wouldn't let me help."

"Sounds nice."

"You don't know how nice. No one had ever taken care of me like that before. It might sound like a small thing, that one dinner, but that's when I started looking at him differently."

"Does he still do dishes?"

"He does. And he helps with the kids, and works hard on the yard with me. He's a very hands-on guy. We're a team."

"How did he learn to do all that?" Jasmine was self-taught at everything. And from counseling others, she knew it was hard to break out of old molds and begin life new. Frankly, if Bill was a raging, abusive alcoholic she would have been less surprised.

"He said he watched your family and knew that it wasn't right, knew that he wanted different. So he did everything he could not to be like that."

"Just like that?"

"As Bill says, with God all things are possible. He knew he couldn't become a better person on his own, so he turned to God to tutor him."

Jasmine took a bite of her sandwich and shifted the conversation. "It's good."

"Thanks."

They sat quietly for awhile. "So how are your folks, Elsie?"

"My dad is okay. My mom passed away about three years ago."

"I'm sorry."

"She had cancer. No one seems to be immune from that, you know? It ravages so many families."

"I guess so." Jasmine didn't have experience with cancer, but she did know about things that tore families apart. Substance abuse topped her list.

"Bill and my dad are really close. They go hunting together and have long talks on faith. He baptized Bill."

"I thought pastors had to do that."

"Nope. He and my dad talked many times about faith. For awhile I got kind of jealous, because he was seeing my dad more than he was seeing me."

Jasmine laughed along but couldn't picture it. The Sweet William she knew didn't like authority figures.

"One day he showed up, said he'd accepted Christ as his savior, and wanted my dad to baptize him at the church picnic."

"I'm having trouble picturing all that. My parents were not supporters of religion." Understatement of the year.

"Bill told me that."

"It surprises me he took an interest in God."

"I think he realized that God always had an interest in him, and that made him want to know more and want to know why."

Jasmine went quiet again. God didn't have an interest in anyone she'd ever met, but it wasn't for her to say. Maybe she ran in the wrong circles. "Well, I should probably call that builder and work out the details so I can pass on the information to the Tim." Jasmine took her dishes to the sink, washed them, and put them in the drainer.

"Jasmine?"

"Yeah?" She turned toward Elsie.

"Some people equate God's love with how they feel about themselves, or how they were treated by others. That's not how it works. God is a constant. What the broken people on this planet do or don't do isn't an outward sign of His love or lack of love for anyone."

Jasmine stared at Elsie. Outwardly, her small form hardly commanded anyone's notice, but right now, she had all of Jasmine's attention.

"Elsie, if He's God, and if He loves us, why do all these bad things happen? Couldn't He stop them?"

"He could. Sometimes He does. Sometimes He doesn't. And only He knows why."

Jasmine shook her head at Elsie. "I'm not okay with that."

"Think of it this way, we're not puppets and He's not the puppet master—He's our loving Father who wants a relationship with us." She walked over and hugged Jasmine in a quick embrace. "All the phone numbers you need are on the notepad in the den, to the left of the living room. I've got to go and pick up the kids next door. If you leave, here's a key to lock up. It's an extra. Bill and I want you to keep it." She handed her a key painted in apple blossoms. "We want you to know that no matter where life takes you, you can always come here, come home." Elsie walked through the back door without another word.

Jasmine looked down at the key in her hand. A feeling that couldn't be described any other way than regret filled her being. This woman she could hardly remember, who had no reason to accept her into her life, was taking her to a place she'd never experienced before. And she'd almost missed it. Jasmine wandered through the living room to a set of curtained, glass-framed double doors. Pushing them open, she let herself into the den. Inside was a plank oak desk with a small pile of papers and a computer. To the left was an old oak filing cabinet and two bookcases. On the wall opposite hung framed pictures of the children, and photos of Bill and Elsie, of them with a couple that must have been Elsie's parents. There were gaps in the display, where nails still stuck, but pictures were down. Maybe Elsie was redecorating?

Sitting down at the desk, she found the list of phone numbers she needed to tackle. After making her calls, she sat back in the chair and looked at the photos. If she had come home sooner, she might be in some of those.

Regret wasn't a feeling she often delved into. It was a negative emotion that brought most of her clients down. It was best to think of the positive things in life, or what could be, rather than look back too deeply. But here she was, wondering what might have been. There wasn't a way to know when it was safe to come home.

It always came back to that. Protection. Bill and Elsie were all about that. Jasmine looked back at the photos of her brother and his wife, and realized what was missing. The pictures of her parents. They must have taken them down. She poked behind a stack of papers up against the wall. She looked inside the closet and found a small stack of frames covered with a towel. After she unwrapped them, she laid them out on the desk. Her eyes searched for her mother—what had she looked like toward the end? Truthfully, she wanted to know if she would have recognized either of them. Her hand shook as she lifted one after another. Most of them were pictures of her mother and the kids. Lily looked so much like her mother. In one picture of Lily and her mother, their eyes were slanted in identical skepticism. As she lifted the next photo, her breath caught. There he was. Sitting with Bill on a bench in front of their electrical shop. Bill wore a slight smile. Their father, though, had a deadness in his eyes. Jasmine shivered. The deep brown of his eye blended into the black of his pupils. The aura of anger glowed from the photograph, but Bill appeared immune to it. As if it were hot to the touch, she put it back on the cover, wrapped the photos up and placed them back in the closet. Bill had taken them down, to shield her, without really knowing why.

She drew their house key from her pocket and hooked it on her key chain. Bill and Elsie cared enough to protect her even if they didn't know what they were protecting her from.

When she'd first arrived, she had never intended to return. Now, ties to this place grew. But instead of feeling tethered and trapped, she felt...loved.

Twelve

As picnics went, the Bright River Spring Festival was pretty calm, but it brought together all members of the town prior to the working season. There were booths set up for seasonal workers, and another for teens looking to fill a summer saving cash for a new car or college. Most of the booths were for fun and games. An array of colorful tents attracted children to water games, throwing games, and that sort of typical hometown fair feel.

Jasmine wandered through, watching kids have their faces painted, win goldfish, or pop balloons with darts. Tim walked at her side, watchful but quiet. She didn't remember her last Spring picnic with any particular memory. At fourteen, she had been in between adulthood and childhood, lost in an area that had little support in the small town. She watched the teens on the edge of the park, standing aloof and arms crossed, but still with a touch of wonder in their eyes. She knew how that felt.

"Hasn't changed much, has it?" His voice broke into her thoughts.

"No, I guess not. The young ones still having fun, the adults still gossiping, and the teens at a loss for what to do."

"The Fall Festival is the one we really get into, you know, with the carnival and all."

"The carnival." A contemplative smile crossed her face.

"Tell me about it." He motioned for her to sit at an empty table.

"Remember that year we worked the carnival together?"

"Best fun I'd ever had."

"I got to know the funhouse lady a bit."

"I didn't remember that. I was busy working the ring toss, and sweeping up horse manure after shows."

"Her name was Fiona. She looked at me, really looked at me. She asked probing questions, wondering why I wasn't off chasing boys, or hanging out with friends, rather than spending time with her at the funhouse."

"Did you tell her?"

"Not right away. The funhouse seemed like a good place to lose myself. I pretended I belonged there. I wore makeup and a wig, so even when kids from school came, they didn't recognize me, and I put on an accent and they never knew. I think that's when the idea began to build in my mind."

"Two years before you left?"

"It built and built, and I knew when my dad threatened to change the locks on the camper what I'd do. It was fall again, and Fiona was here with the funhouse, and I went to her and confessed all that was happening. I told her I needed to leave, and she took me on like that."

"Really, it's kind of criminal." Tim's voice carried a hint of resentment.

Jasmine thought about that a minute. "I suppose so. Hiding a youth who'd run away. But you see, she left home for the same reason."

"Or she told you that."

Jasmine's temper rose. "She wasn't like that. She shared from her heart, long before I said anything. I think she suspected when I asked to work later and later, that I didn't want to go home very bad."

"You'll have to forgive my suspicious attitude. My being the son of a police officer and now a lawyer—I've learned to ask questions."

"Being a counselor puts me in the same spot. But, you know, when I work with those girls, I try to mimic Fiona. I listen first, don't judge. I help them understand that no matter what, I'll stand by them. Some of those girls never have heard that in their whole life."

"Fiona wasn't the first person to tell you that." He gave her a knowing look.

She smiled at him. "No." She squeezed his hand. "But she was the first adult. There's something in a young person that craves adult approval, and if they can't get it from their parents, they go looking places they probably shouldn't."

He nodded. "How long did you live with her?"

"A year. She got very sick that winter and never really got over it. All the traveling around was rough. Carnivals try to stay ahead of the weather. Ours broke for a month in the worst of it, so I stayed with Fiona in a trailer park as her granddaughter. One night, a few months later, she died in her sleep."

"What'd you do?"

"They said if I could handle the funhouse, I could keep her spot. I tried for awhile."

"Did they know how old you were?"

"People don't exactly ask your age when you live like that."

"It got to be too much for you?"

"The men got to be too much for me." Jasmine watched the anger flash in Tim's eyes at her words. "Without Fiona there protecting me, they started coming around, harassing me. I knew I didn't want that again. So one day, this good-looking guy came through and asked me to lunch. He had a lot of cash, which interested me greatly—and he wasn't afraid to lavish it on me. We hung out for awhile, and I thought I could trust him. So I told him I wanted to break free of the carnival, and he offered me a job."

That's what sex traffickers did. They bought girls clothes and food, told them how wonderful they were—things no one else had ever said. And then they asked the girl to do them a favor and go with a friend of theirs. Then another. And before they knew it, they were trapped, broken, and there was no getting away.

"You took it?"

"It seemed like a good idea at the time. As I got to know Rob, I realized it was probably the worst mistake I could have made—but I didn't have anywhere else to go."

"You stayed with him for how long?"

"Nearly two years."

"He was the drug dealer."

She measured him with her eyes. That wasn't all Rob dealt in, but she didn't feel comfortable telling Tim. Not yet. "You remember things pretty well."

"Lawyer." He tapped the side of his head with his first

91

finger.

"Yeah, he was the dealer. He got arrested, and I got evicted onto the streets of Portland." Best thing that ever happened to her.

"And you ended up where?"

"In alleyways. Boxes. Under bridges. In bushes. Hiding in buildings before they closed and sleeping under clothing racks or in bathroom stalls. I'd bathe in sinks, the best I could, and dry off on paper towels."

"Wow."

"One day I came across a shelter for women, so I went in— not expecting much, mind you. But they fed me, gave me a place to shower and sleep, and I met Brandi."

"She's the one who got you interested in counseling?"

"Yeah." She's the one who saved her life.

"I owe her a debt of gratitude."

Jasmine wished he'd quit saying things like that. It wasn't so much what he was saying—it was how he was saying it.

"I'll tell her."

"Maybe I'll meet her one day. Portland's not that far away, you know."

It's farther than you think. She looked off in the distance, not sure how to respond.

"You've got to know I don't intend on losing contact with you again, Jasmine."

She knew. She wasn't sure what to do with the information. He wanted their relationship to go places she would never let it.

"We'll always be friends." Her voice wavered.

"Friends. Absolutely." Their eyes locked a moment, and she looked away.

"Hey, I heard you were in town." A female voice came up alongside them. Jasmine glanced up at a red-haired woman, about her age.

"Jasmine, right? I'm Mary Tessler. We went through school together."

"Oh, yeah. How have you been?" She felt Tim's incredulous stare. He knew she didn't remember this woman.

"Good. I heard you were here, but it came as such a shock. I mean, we all thought you'd died."

Jasmine swallowed hard and forced a smile. "No, not dead."

"Jasmine moved to Portland," Tim added.

"Oh, Portland."

The conversation went silent at that point.

"Hey, let's get something to eat, okay? Will you excuse us, Mary?" Tim lifted Jasmine by the arm and started leading her away.

Mary wandered off the other direction.

They headed to the ribs stand and got in line. "How come everyone in this town thinks I owe them an explanation?"

"A lot of kids liked you. And you were the first kid to disappear like that. A lot of parents were afraid, mine included. No one knew if you'd died in an accident, or if someone took you. It was a scary time in our existence. Try not to take it too personally."

"Okay."

"And I think you should quit lying." He gave her a pointed look.

"Lying?"

"Yeah. You don't do it well. Your neck gets all red and splotchy, like when we were kids. Tell them you don't remember them. It's the truth."

It wasn't the lying—it was being put on the spot like that. "It's hard to admit."

"To them? Why would you care what they thought, you don't remember them."

"No, to me. Why can't I remember them?" She hadn't meant to sound so desperate, but she was.

"I don't know." He put his hand on her shoulder. "Maybe it'll all come back. Maybe not. But quit being so hard on yourself."

She was about to open her mouth when the man at the counter asked for their order. They started walking toward the craft booths, gnawing on the ribs as they went.

"You got a little something on your chin." Jasmine motioned to Tim with a napkin. He swiped at it a couple times, but kept missing the largest glob of barbeque sauce and spread the smaller splotches further across his cheek.

"Here, let me." She laughed as she held up the corner of her napkin. "Spit."

"What? That's gross."

"It's either that, or I do it."

Tim quickly spit on the napkin and scrunched up his face as she wiped off the sauce.

"This is humiliating." Tim glanced around, hoping no one was watching them. She grabbed his chin in one of her hands to hold him still.

"You eat like you did when we were kids."

"Thanks."

As Jasmine looked up into his eyes, all the laughter died away. She felt that pull toward him once again, and dropped her hand. Her heart raced as he reached up and tucked a strand of loose hair behind her ear, brushing his thumb down the side of her face as he did. His eyes softened as he leaned toward her.

"Jasmine," Tim started, but was interrupted by a businessman walking past.

"Jasmine? Jasmine Reynolds? I heard you were in town." He put out his hand. "I'm Paul—remember? from P.E.?" He laughed as if they shared a good joke.

"No, I'm afraid I don't. Sorry."

"Really?" Paul shifted from one foot to the other. "Not even that time we hooked all the tetherballs up in the basketball nets and drove Mrs. Langly crazy? She was so short." He stopped when he noticed that Jasmine wasn't playing along.

"Sorry." She shook her head at him.

"Oh. Well, welcome home anyway." He nodded to Tim and sulked away.

She sighed. "The truth isn't exactly going over either. I think I want to go home." She looked down at the remainders of the rib wrapped in wax paper in her hand, her appetite gone.

"Not yet. If you leave, you'll miss several boring speeches people are going to make about the impact of the orchards on Oregon. And we'll sing some town songs and be bitten by a bunch of spring mosquitoes."

"Oh, I sure wouldn't want to miss that." They moved to a nearby bench and waited for the town band to quit playing. The mayor and several staff proceeded to make speeches. Afterward, the band played the National Anthem. She put her hand over hear heart. Years dropped away and she was back in her schoolgirl days. A sting on her leg brought her back to the present. As Jasmine reached down and slapped a mosquito from her leg, she instantly got the giggles.

"Shh!" A little gray-haired woman sitting near them hushed her.

Jasmine leaned close to Tim and whispered, "Was she our librarian?"

"Shh!" The gray-haired lady glared at them both.

Both she and Tim shook with laughter. "Come on, let's get out of here." He pulled her up and they headed away from the grandstand.

As they broke free of the crowd, they laughed aloud, tripping over their own feet. She tossed her half-eaten rib into the garbage, and ran up an old side trail. Her feet had an instinct of their own, leading her deeper and deeper into a part of the forest nearby she'd forgotten about but instantly knew. She heard his heavy footfalls behind her, and kept laughing as she ran. The forest opened into a clearing with rotting logs tipped here and there. It wasn't what she'd expected to see.

"Our tree house, it's gone." A deep sense of loss settled in her chest.

Tim caught up to her, gasping for air. "It's been gone a long time. Blew over in a bad storm. The town said good riddance; it'd been unsafe for awhile. But I mourned."

Jasmine picked through the underbrush and found an old metal cup, dented and filthy. "Do you think it was one of ours?"

"Hard to say. Might have been. I never came back here after you left. Everything we had pretty much stayed here."

There it was again, the heartbreak in his voice.

"I guess I let down a lot of people." She sat on the wood stack and stared up at the dim sky, stars beginning to shine.

"Don't think of it that way. I don't mean to make you feel bad. Facts are facts. You left, and everything changed."

That was true enough. "I couldn't have stayed."

"I know." He put his arm around her shoulder and pulled her toward him. They sat like that for a long time, watching the stars appear. He had been her one faithful companion. She was glad to have his friendship back, glad to be able to talk openly with someone, more than she'd ever been able to talk to anyone she'd known. At the same time, her guilt increased.

She knew he had hopes for their relationship. Most of her knew she should cut it off with him. The rest of her hoped he'd be willing to stay friends for the rest of their lives.

"We'd better get you home. Bill saw us run off—but I don't want to get in trouble for keeping his little sister out past curfew."

"I didn't see Bill."

"He was up on stage, getting ready to make the next speech."

"Oh, no!"

"Don't worry. He'll understand. He didn't want to give it any more than anyone else wanted to hear it."

She laughed loud and slapped his arm. "Don't be mean."

"It's true. Ask him."

"But still." She stopped.

"Still nothing. For a counselor, you're awfully co dependent."

"Gee, thanks."

"I'm just saying." He gave her a nudge in the arm. "Jasmine, I meant what I said earlier. I don't want us to lose touch again."

"I don't either. I can't tell you what it means to have you here, beside me, through all this. I don't know what I'd do without your encouragement. Thanks" —she cleared her voice— "for your friendship."

He nodded slowly at her. "Sure." But there was something familiar in his eyes that made her want to ask him who was lying now.

Thirteen

"So the house is all listed?" Bill passed her a bottle of soda as they sat on the front porch watching the kids play.

"Thanks to Tim. His guys have really worked the old place over—paint even."

"Shouldn't have any trouble selling it right now. A lot of people are trying to get out of the city." He said it in such a leading way Jasmine had to laugh.

"One, I can't drop my life there and run here. Two, there's no way I'd ever live there, Bill." She counted her reasons off on her fingers. "Three, you can't go home again. Not really."

"Right. Memories. I understand all about that, you know?"

She nodded, knowing he really didn't.

"So after the effigy, are you leaving town?" It was the first time he'd mentioned burning the camper since dinner that night.

"That's my plan. Brandi didn't expect me to stay away this long. I've got a client waiting for me."

"Does Tim know your plan?"

She leaned back against her chair. "I've tried to tell him. Despite being a brilliant lawyer, as he keeps reminding me, he's not listening."

"Sometimes we only hear what we want to hear."

"Maybe so." A ball bounced up on the porch, and Jason dashed up after it.

"Aunt Jasmine, wanna play?"

"Sure." She went out on the grass with Rose and Jason to play catch. Bill put down his soda and joined them.

"Can you stay with us forever?" Rose asked, innocent blue

eyes peering up at her.

"No, sweetie, I can't. But I'll be back to visit."

"We can come see you, can't we?" Jason asked.

"I don't have much room in my apartment, but there's a hotel not too far away. We've got a zoo and a huge rose garden and lots of parks."

"I've been to the zoo, when I was little." Jason spoke with the tone of the aged.

"I never been to the zoo." Rose's eyes widened dreamily.

"We'll do that when you come." She was grinning as she looked up and caught her brother's serious glance. Maybe she was speaking out of turn. But she hoped not.

Elsie came out on the porch and called the kids in to wash for supper.

Bill continued to throw the ball back and forth with her. "You coming to church tomorrow?"

"I hadn't thought of it."

"It'd mean a lot to the kids." He grinned.

"Low blow."

"What do you think?"

"It's not my thing." She tossed the ball to him.

"It's not like it'll hurt you."

"I know that. I went before. I don't like pretending." She threw the ball back to him a bit harder than she meant to. He shook his hand from the sting.

"I know. I've been there. What's there to pretend about?" He tossed it back, lighter than before, as if to make a point.

Jasmine didn't know if she could put it into words. It was the same thing that kept her from flirting with Tim, or allowing herself to think of a relationship with anyone. It was the thing that kept her aloof from most people around her.

"I won't ever make that commitment, so there's no reason for me to go and make people think I will."

"You know that for certain?"

"Yes." She lobbed it to him and he caught it with ease.

He held on to the ball, searching for words. "I used to feel like that. Like when I did go, that no one understood who I was, how I felt, or what I'd survived. Especially God."

"And?" She had wondered when Bill would tell her about

this strange new part of his life.

"I realized that God knew. He never was far away from me my whole life, but I was so busy looking at the bad I couldn't see Him."

She caught it again. "If he was so close by, why didn't He keep us safe, Bill?" There was no accusation in her voice—only honest inquisition.

"I don't have an answer for everything. But I know He was there. There's no other reason I can think of that I didn't turn out like Dad." He headed back up on the porch and sat down. She followed. "And there's my family. Everything about Elsie and the kids are a good thing—and I've never done much good to deserve them, so I know they're from God too."

"I'm glad you're happy. I don't see that God has that much to do with it."

"He's got everything to do with it. I mean, do you consider me a fool?"

"No."

"If I'm not a fool, and I follow Christ, maybe I've got something going on here."

She laughed. "I'll give you that."

"So, will you come?"

"I can't, Bill." A sorrowful tone laced her voice.

"You sound like you want to."

"I guess I want to have the faith you do. But there's been too much that's happened for me to go there."

"Are you ready to talk about that yet?"

"No."

"You leave the day after tomorrow."

"Then tomorrow." She looked away from him.

"It can't be that bad, Jasmine."

"You don't know." Her eyes filled with tears. He was forcing her hand, and she didn't want it. "When I tell you, everything will change."

"I can't walk on eggshells around this any longer, Jasmine. Remember the rule? No phoniness here. I can't take it. Faking it makes a rotting feeling in my gut. I'm your big brother. Let me help you carry whatever it is you've got. Tell me about the camper."

She couldn't believe she was going there, not now. She'd

hoped to leave town before Bill noticed they'd never talked about it. And the years would pass, and pass, and there'd never be a discussion. The busyness of life would keep the ugliness away forever, and holidays would come and go and no one would have to feel bad.

It wasn't to be.

"It kept me safe."

"I gathered that."

"After you left, and Lily left, I had nowhere to hide. There were fewer witnesses, and everything got worse."

"His drinking and beating you and Mom?"

"No, Bill. You didn't ever notice did you? He never beat me." Her voice was barely a whisper.

Bill's eyes narrowed, trying to follow where she was going.

"Mom bought the camper when Dad was off on a binge. When he got home, I'd moved my things inside, and stocked it with food. She told him it was for fun, but it was to keep me safe."

"Safe, from Dad?"

"I guess she didn't know any other way to help me, Bill."

The meaning of what she said sunk in, and his face went pale.

Bill swallowed hard. "He'd hurt you, that way?" He couldn't even say it.

"Yes."

Bill got up from the porch, eyes blazing. "How long?" His words were heated, but she sensed the anger wasn't at her.

"I can't honestly remember when it started. It feels like it was like that always."

Bill turned away, looking out over the yard, hands white-knuckled on the rail. "How could he?" He looked up at the sky. "Oh, God, how could he?"

She hoped the question was rhetorical, because she didn't have an answer. She ached in empathy for his pain. She shouldn't have told him. Everything—every sweet thing was gone now.

"How could Mom let it go on?" He paced on the porch for several seconds before sitting down heavily in the chair next to her. "That's why he gave you all those presents. That's why you'd never take any of them." He shook his head. "I found a bunch in the garbage one day. I was so angry at you for being ungrateful." He gasped. "And jealous. He never gave Lily or me presents." He cried. "I'm so sorry. I'm so sorry." His body wracked with sobs as he pulled her into his arms.

For some reason, she couldn't cry. Jasmine looked up and saw Elsie at the door, a look of horror in her eyes. It was too much.

"I didn't mean to overhear." Elsie wiped the tears from her cheeks with a shaky hand. "I came to tell you about supper."

Jasmine shook her head to dismiss her worry at intruding. She looked into Bill's pain-filled eyes. "It's not your fault. I never blamed you."

As Elsie came out and stood near Bill, Jasmine gently pushed out of his embrace, and let Elsie take her spot. As Bill sobbed in his wife's arms, she walked down the steps, down the path, and out the gate. She started to run. Fast. She had to get away. She should have put him off for another day.

Jasmine's feet slapped a rhythm out against the road to match her heart beat. Before she knew it, she'd arrived at the bridge over Green's Slough and stood looking down at the snow-fed creek rushing under her feet. She stared out at the hole she'd tossed her bike into so long ago. She'd hefted the bike over the edge and tied her memories to it that night, letting the ugliness and fear sink with it. She remembered back to that night, when she'd promised herself she'd never come back, never look back.

She'd done a pretty good job of it. Maybe too good. If she could go back to that night, would she wish all her memories away again?

Footsteps came up behind her. She smelled Tim's cologne and felt the comfort of his arm around her shoulder. Most people's touch made her edgy, but not his, not ever his.

"I saw Bill." The gravity in his voice told her how well Bill was taking the news.

The dam holding back her emotions broke, and she turned into his shoulder, sobbing. He held her tight, his arms supporting her. The sound of the river surrounded them, the rush of white noise blocked out the world.

Jasmine wasn't sure how long they stood there, him holding her, her crying. She pulled back, and he handed her a handkerchief to dab her tears.

Jasmine held it up before she wiped at her face and blew her nose. "I didn't know people carried these anymore." She gave him a half-hearted smile.

"It's new. I didn't want a repeat of the spit-cleaning incident." He kissed the top of her head and she moved to the rail of the bridge. Night had fallen, but the moon sparkled up at her from the water, its reflection dancing on the rhythm of the ripples below.

"I don't know if I can go back there."

"You have to." He rested his chin on top of her head.

"I suppose so." He wrapped his coat around her shoulders.

"Bill's a strong man. He'll face this, like you are, and you'll both move on."

"It'll never be the same."

"No, it won't. It'll be better, because you'll both be on the same page. It might be uncomfortable for awhile, but that will pass."

"I thought I was the counselor here." She wiped at her eyes with her shirtsleeve.

He noticed her wiping with her sleeve again. "Where's the hanky?"

"It's kind of yucky." She tipped her head up, narrowing her eyes. "Want it back?" she dared him.

"Uh, no. It's a gift." He gave her a grin. "I've always heard that doctors shouldn't treat themselves. I think that covers counselors too."

"And you're so smart?" She rocked back into him.

"Not always. There're some things I'm really lousy at. But I'm good at being your friend."

She smiled at his honesty. "I suppose I should head back."

"Not yet. He and Elsie need time to talk. Can I take you out to dinner?"

The last thing on her mind was food. "Sure." They made their way up the hill, back into town. Cars passed them by as they strode along the gravelly road. Walking in silence, they ended up at The Getaway and headed toward a back booth.

Tim ordered and Jasmine excused herself to the bathroom. Inside, she washed her face, taking notice of the dark circles under her eyes, and her disheveled hair. She ran her fingers through her hair and pulled it back, secure in her ponytail once again. The lights made her face look gaunt and severe. She pulled out the ponytail and shook her hair free. That helped.

Once back at the table, they ate in silence. There wasn't much left to say. Tim glanced at his watch.

"Do you think it's been long enough?" She rubbed her temples to release the tension building. The last thing she needed was a migraine.

"The kids should be in bed by now."

Her shoulders slumped. "There's so much collateral damage."

"That's not your fault."

"I could have found a better time."

"Bill told me he forced your hand. I wish you'd stop. You're here blaming yourself and we've got Bill at home blaming himself. The only one to blame here is your father, and he's dead."

"Convenient of him."

"And your mom." She understood the tinge of betrayal in his voice.

"You know, this trip has been good in that respect. My eyes have opened a bit. I never felt like she loved me at all, but I think she did. In her own way, she did. She wasn't any good at it, but she did."

"I can see that. I wish she'd had the courage to do more for you."

"Sometimes people are so broken, they can barely take care of themselves." She stared down at her empty plate and realized she didn't even know what she'd eaten.

"Was it any good?" She motioned toward her plate.

"Yeah. It was good." He laughed, breaking the tension. "You ate a Monster Burger and a side of fruit. What do you do for food in Portland?"

"Salads, sandwiches. That sort of fare. I cook on occasion. Usually, I'm too tired to eat a full dinner."

"Well, when I come for a visit, I want you to find a really nice place, my treat."

"Tim," she began, but he put up his hand and stopped her.

"I know you think you're going home and won't ever see me again. But it's not true. And if you won't see me for anything except a friend, that's okay with me, Jasmine. Don't shut me out because you're afraid I might abandon you."

"I'm not used to people wanting to be with me."

"Get used to it." He waved the waitress over and paid for their meal. They got up and walked toward Bill's house. When they reached the gate, she hesitated. He took her arm and led her up the path, to the door. It opened, and Elsie welcomed them in. Bill sat on the couch, staring at his hands, looking more lost than she felt when she first arrived.

Jasmine went to her knees, like she did when she was a little girl, and leaned on his side, her hands wrapping around his arm. She was too big to crawl into his lap now. He put an arm around her, and Tim and Elsie move into the kitchen.

"We're going to be okay, big brother." Jasmine felt him nod, and she closed her eyes, hoping she was right.

Fourteen

Jasmine awoke the next morning to a storm raging around her. The wind rushed and screamed about the house. Hail pounded down, and rain streamed from the rooftop, pouring down the window in rivulets. It seemed late. She activated her phone, and it showed it was ten-thirty. She pulled on her sweats and headed downstairs. The house was dark. She heard noise in the den and pushed open the door, shielding her eyes from the ceiling light. Bill sat at the desk, going through the stack of photos, ripping out the ones with their father in them.

"Where is everyone else?"

"Church. I didn't want to leave you alone, so I stayed home."

Lightning crashed overhead and the light in the den flickered.

"That was close." She peered out the window, trying to see where it might have touched down.

"It's been doing that on and off for the last hour." He kept pulling out photos.

"I was dead to the world up there. What are you doing?"

"I'm getting rid of him."

"You made peace with him a long time ago." She'd never seen this side of Bill—angry and focused.

"I made peace with who I thought he was. He was never more than a food provider for us. He used us all, abused us all. I would have let my kids spend time with that man." He shivered and tore another photo from a frame. "I can't have his face in here. I can't see him. Maybe one day, but not now." He pulled out a paper sack and poured the photos into it.

"I'll keep their wedding photo, but the rest, they were all fake."

She knew what he meant. Her father had pretended to be a father, and like her, Bill couldn't tolerate carrying on the lie.

"What are you going to do with those?"

"I'm going to stick them in the camper." They locked eyes. "I'm selling the hunting property. I'll buy something else someday, but I don't want anything that was his. I don't want my kids going near anything he touched."

"That's how I feel about the house." There was something comforting knowing he understood. A thought flitted through her mind. "What about Lily?"

A grating sigh filled the room. "I haven't a clue. She's lived in her own dream world for so long. She's so full of hate and anger; sometimes I can't bear to be in the same room with her."

Jasmine swallowed. "She thinks I was dad's favorite."

"I know. I know what she's said and what she's thought. I've been her sounding board too long. I'll tell her if you want."

"No. Not yet. One of these days."

"Okay. But don't expect me to wait on you. If the moment presents itself, I'm telling her. I've had enough of her bitterness to last me forever."

Bill pulled apart the last frame and tossed the picture in the sack. "Tomorrow will be quite a day. Anything else you want to burn?"

"I can't think of anything." The rain pounded outside, and she thought she heard a knock on the door. Bill went to check. Outside stood a young woman, soaking wet.

"Can I help you?"

"I'm looking for Dr. Reynolds. Someone at the cafe said she might be here."

Jasmine came up behind Bill and caught her breath in surprise. "Misty?"

"Jazz, there you are. I've been all over town."

Bill opened the door and led a dripping Misty inside. Within moments he had towels and a blanket for her.

"I've turned on the kettle." Bill stood nearby, looking helpless, as Misty sat wrapped in warmth on the couch and rubbed her hands together.

"What are you doing here?" Jasmine asked her.

"Brandi told me you'd be here." Misty's teeth chattered so hard it was hard to understand her. The kettle whistled.

"Let me get you some tea." Jasmine left and made a cup of mint tea. As she handed her the cup of tea, she waited for her to drink and calm down before starting the rest of the story.

"Feeling better?"

"Yes, thanks." Misty kept her fingers wrapped tight around the cup. "This is good."

"Are you hungry?"

"No, I grabbed a sandwich at the diner. Not bad."

Jasmine smiled. "Just don't try the coffee."

Bill pulled on his coat. "I've got to check on Elsie and the kids. I think we're in for quite a storm here." As if on cue, the lights went out, and stayed out. "Jasmine, there are candles in the first cupboard in the kitchen, matches too."

He went over to the wood stove in the living room and tossed another log in the stove. "Keep this going, okay? Power takes awhile to come back on out here. We might all be sleeping around this thing tonight."

Jasmine nodded and watched him leave. After lighting a candle in the kitchen and one in the living room, she came back and sat next to Misty.

"Why don't you grab the last warm shower for awhile? I don't want you catching a cold. We'll talk when you're done." She led her upstairs and showed her the bathroom, situating a candle on the sink counter. Misty thanked her as she closed the door.

After Jasmine went downstairs, she heard a knock on the door. She moved the curtain and saw Tim's familiar form in the shadow on the porch. She smiled and opened the door.

"I saw Bill leaving and thought you shouldn't be on your own in the dark." He held up a bundle of hamburgers and fries. "I thought when everyone got home from church, we'd have lunch all ready."

"That's great. Come on in." She led him into the kitchen. He put the food on the table.

"Power is out all over town. There's a run on candles."

"Bill's got quite a good stock in here." She motioned to the cabinet.

"Good." They heard a thump upstairs and he started toward

the noise.

"Wait. It's one of my clients. I'm not sure why she's here yet, but I sent her upstairs to warm up in a hot bath. She showed up dripping wet."

"Oh." He glanced down at the food. "I hope I got enough food."

Misty came around the corner, drying her hair on a towel. "I don't eat much." She was wearing a pair of old sweat pants and an oversized sweatshirt. "I took a fast shower in case anyone else needed one when they got home. I'm warm enough now."

"Tim, this is Misty."

They shook hands. "I got tired of waiting for Jazz to come back to Portland, so I came to her." She had a light tone in her voice, but her weary eyes told another story.

"Why don't you guys go warm up in the living room, and I'll set out the plates for lunch. Bill and the family will be back soon." He shooed them out to the living room.

Jasmine didn't know if it was his lawyerly instincts, or being a good friend that made him so sensitive to others around him. Either way, it was a good quality to have. Misty followed her into the cozy living room and watched her check the fire before joining her on the couch.

"I told Brandi I'd be home in a day or so."

"I had to see you. I told you about the baby." Misty put a hand to her already growing stomach.

"Is the baby okay?"

"For now. I want to keep it that way."

"What do you mean?"

"Jed. My ex-boyfriend." Misty took a deep breath, and the story poured out. "Jazz, I didn't know who attacked me. I really didn't. But that's why I didn't want the exam at the hospital. I didn't want anyone to find out about the baby." Tears formed. "Jed knows and wants me to end the pregnancy. I told him it was his, but he doesn't believe me."

Jed was a rough-looking drug dealer and pimp, who often had more than one girl on his arm at a time. Never around Misty, but Misty wasn't so foolish to think she was his only girlfriend. After all, three years before he'd taken an interest in Misty, she'd been one of his girls—not his girlfriend. And now he'd made it clear that he expected to be her only boyfriend.

He didn't like it one bit that Misty lived at Broadstreet House now and had to stay away from him.

"You know you're not supposed to be in contact with Jed, or you could lose your place at the house."

"I know. But I figured if he knew about the baby, maybe he'd give up his ways. I figured it'd be okay to tell him—since he's the father." She started to cry. "I think Jed might have even sent that guy to beat me up. To scare me, and maybe make me lose the baby."

Jasmine took Misty's hand in hers. "Are you sure the baby is okay?"

"Yeah. The next morning I asked the doctor to take a look at me. They did some tests and as soon as I knew, I got out of there. I figured if I hung around, word would spread and I'd be kicked out of the house."

"We wouldn't have done that. You shouldn't have hooked up with him again, but this is different." Jasmine sighed. What would they do with her now? "Tell me the rest."

"A couple days before the attack, he found me at work and handed me a wad of money with the address of an abortion clinic. He said he wasn't ready to be a father, let alone a father to the baby I carried. He demanded to know what other guy I was sleeping with. I told him there wasn't anyone else. And then he said I got pregnant on purpose to trap him."

"Is it true?" Sometimes it happened. It never worked out well, but that didn't keep desperate young women from trying.

"No. I know I'm not ready to be a mother, Jazz. I don't have a proper home. I'm not married. I'm not decent enough to be anyone's mother. The last thing I wanted was to get pregnant." She put a protective hand over her stomach. "But now that I am, I want to do what's right. I want to have the baby and give it up for adoption."

"Adoption?"

"I think so. Unless someone can help me get settled and get a job. I want to live a good life, Jazz. I don't want to live on the streets anymore. I don't want to raise this baby with a drug dealer for a father. It doesn't deserve that. I want it to have what I didn't." Tears streamed down her cheeks.

Jasmine handed her the tissue box. "How did you get here?"

"I told him I wanted to keep the baby, and he said if I tried,

I'd regret it." Misty shuddered. "So I said I'd changed my mind and took the money. I packed my suitcase, bought a bus ticket, and came here. He doesn't know where I've gone."

"He might follow you." Jasmine knew men like Jed didn't like losing their property. Ever.

"Maybe. I don't think I'm worth the trouble."

Her statement created an ache in Jasmine's chest. More young women than she could count had said that to her.

"Where do you want to go?"

"I want to stay here."

Jasmine frowned. "Why?"

"Because you're here." Misty's hand tightened on Jasmine's.

"But I'm not staying here." Panic seized her chest.

"But you'll be back to visit. I can't go back, Jazz. He'll kill us." Misty put a protective hand over her stomach.

The back door into the kitchen opened and the family poured inside, the loud voices of Jason and Rose excitedly telling every bit they could about the storm. As they filtered into the living room and saw Misty, they went quiet.

"Everyone, this is Misty." They all greeted her. "Misty is going to stay here for awhile—here in town. Misty, this is my sister-in-law Elsie, my niece Rose, my nephew Jason."

"Nice to meet you."

"Lunch is ready." Tim called them back to the kitchen, where they shared the hamburgers and fries in the light of the candle.

Afterward, the kids moved upstairs and Elsie and Bill cleaned up the kitchen. Tim asked the question on everyone's mind.

"So, where will you be staying, Misty?"

"I didn't know Jazz was staying here. I thought I'd stay at her hotel for awhile with her, and find a job and a place of my own."

Glances shot around the table.

"Can I see you in the other room?" Bill motioned for Jasmine to follow him, through the double doors into the study. He shut the doors behind them.

"Tell me her story."

"I can't. There's a doctor/patient confidentiality clause."

"Okay. Tell me if she's safe to have around the kids."

"Yes, she is. Her ex-boyfriend isn't, and that's why she's here."

"Okay. The church has a halfway house she can move into."

"Do they have any rules about pregnancy?"

He hung his head a minute in empathy, the whole situation dawning on him. "No. They take all kinds of young women there."

"I'll let her know. Could she stay here tonight?"

"I'll have to check with Elsie."

"Of course. I'll leave it to you to invite her if it's okay. And if it's not, give me a signal, and we'll head to the shelter."

Bill nodded. "Sounds fair. Poor kid."

"She's a sweet girl, she doesn't know how valuable she is."

"Sounds familiar." He squeezed her shoulder and headed back into the kitchen.

Fifteen

The entire family, Misty included, spent the night in the living room around the wood stove. Morning dawned without power, so they ate a breakfast of cold cereal. Bill went to the store and brought back several pounds of ice and packed the perishable foods from the refrigerator inside camping coolers. Jasmine and Misty headed toward the shelter. Today was Monday. Hopefully, even with the power outages, the camper burning was still a possibility.

Tree limbs and leaves littered the pathway as they walked through a quiet little neighborhood, past the church her brother attended, and up a long driveway. At the top of the drive stood an old Victorian, in great need of paint, but sporting a new roof and new railings. Jasmine recognized a work in progress.

Misty stood to the side, looking every bit like an orphan abandoned on the porch. Jasmine tried to brush off the feeling. Part of her wished Misty would be going back to Portland with her. She could pretend that nothing had changed, and life would go on as it did before.

Bill was right, pretending didn't get anyone anywhere, but it could be comforting for awhile.

Jasmine used the heavy iron knocker on the door and waited. An older woman with graying hair, a cotton floral dress, and a white apron met them at the door.

"You must be Dr. Reynolds. I'm Mrs. Craig." She put out her bone-thin but warm hand and took Jasmine's in a grip that surprised her.

"Nice to meet you, Mrs. Craig. Please call me Jazz." She moved aside and motioned for Misty to come forward. "This is Misty."

"Oh, my dear. You are most welcome here." She put out her hand to Misty, and Jasmine could see tears in the old woman's eyes. "You come in and lay off your things in your room. We'll have a nice lunch and get to know each other."

Jasmine had never had a grandmother that she'd known. But if she had, this woman would have met all the criteria she'd imagined. As she showed them around the house, Jasmine felt safety and comfort, as she had at Bill's house the first time she entered.

The house had four large bedrooms. Misty was one of two boarders. The rules were simple—stay clean, try to get work, help with the house chores, and attend church.

As they sat around the table, she passed Misty a contract. She'd signed a similar one when she moved into Broadstreet House.

"How does that look to you, Misty?"

Misty, mostly silent until now, smiled. "It sounds really fine. How long can I stay here?" She scribbled her name.

"Until we think you're ready to leave."

"I'll have a baby in November." Misty seemed to wait for Mrs. Craig's disapproval, but got none.

"That's what I understand." Mrs. Craig patted Misty's hand. "The rooms are large enough for cribs, so don't you worry."

"I don't know if I want to give it up yet or not." Misty dared Mrs. Craig to be shocked.

"That's your decision. If you decide to put the baby up for adoption, Mr. Able can help us find a nice couple that you approve of. If you want to keep the baby, we'll do our best to support you."

Jasmine patted Misty on the back, sure now they were making the right decision. Misty might have a chance here in this small town, more than in Portland. She'd be away from many of the risks. Not that a small town was isolated. Sometimes the drug and alcohol use in small towns was much worse than people ever imagined. But she'd have support here and be away from the old influences.

"We attend a small church. You probably passed it on your way here. You'll be expected to attend every Sunday."

"Oh, that's fine. I've always wanted to go to church." Misty paused. "But do you think they'll want me there?"

"Yes, dear. They sponsor this house. You'll be accepted by most. There might be the handful that is doubtful at first. Please don't let that bother you, if you can."

"I'll try." Misty yawned.

"Why don't you go take a rest?"

Misty nodded and moved to the stairs. She came back and hugged Jasmine before going up to her room.

Mrs. Craig broke the silence first. "I'm glad to meet you, Jazz. You know, we have a great need for someone who can counsel the young women that come here."

"I've heard that." Jasmine suddenly felt she'd been set up. Looking at Mrs. Craig's warm hazel eyes, she knew it wasn't true.

"I know you are settled there in Portland. But if you ever feel the need to leave the city, please think of us here. I'm often at my end with these girls."

"You mentioned another boarder. Who is she?"

"She grew up being abused by her aunt and uncle. She ran away and somehow ended up in our little town. She's very angry at times, and I don't know how to help her."

Jasmine nodded. Even with years of training, she often didn't know either. "I'll give you the best advice I ever got. Listen and be there for her."

Mrs. Craig smiled at her. "I do that. And I spend a lot of time on my knees. Our Lord is the healer of broken hearts."

Jasmine didn't have an answer for that. Mrs. Craig seemed to think she went to church, and she wasn't about to dispel the idea. There wasn't any reason to get into it. If prayer helped Mrs. Craig, fine. Jasmine stood, and they shook hands again. Mrs. Craig gave her a business card. "The number to Bright River House of Hope is on here, if you want to call and speak to Misty. And we'll keep an eye out for that bad fellow of hers."

"Don't hesitate to call the police if you see him."

"We won't."

Jasmine walked back to Bill's house, feeling unsettled. She was supposed to drive back to Portland today but found herself dreading it. It was like she was two different people, and she didn't know which life she was supposed to live. Two paths, converging for a moment, like the rails switching under a train. Should she stay on, or jump off?

As she approached the house, she saw Tim sitting on the porch, head back against the rail, enjoying a sun break. She stepped over the limb of a fallen oak tree—more signs of yesterday's storm—and approached from below.

"You might burn if you sit there like that."

He cracked his eyes open a bit. "I'm sure I will. It's nice sitting here though. Will you join me?" He pulled his legs around to make room for her.

She climbed the steps and sank down beside him on the topmost one. "So what are we pondering today?"

"I'm trying to think of ways to get you to stay." His honesty always took her by surprise.

"You know I can't."

"So you say."

"Please, Tim." She shook her head. "One week of partially good memories can't make up for a lifetime of bad. Over time, I'm sure I'll feel more at home here, but please put aside any fantasies you have about me picking up and moving here. It won't happen."

"Can't blame me for trying, can you?"

She shifted her weight and knocked shoulders with him. "No, I suppose not." She closed her eyes and tipped her head to the quickly disappearing sunshine.

"Bill will be home at noon, we'll head over to the fire department when he gets here. They've got the camper there."

The gray clouds moved across the sun, blocking out the warmth and bringing with them a chilling wind.

"Sounds good."

"Then you'll pack up and leave?"

"I'm already packed."

She saw him bite the side of his lip, thinking hard. "Do you have your phone on you?"

She handed it to him. He flipped it open and typed. "There's my cell number, my home number, and my work number. And my address." He glanced over at her with a distant look in his eyes. "I've never even showed you my house."

"We've run out of time."

The front gate slammed, and they looked up to see Bill

coming up the path. "I'll be right out, and we'll do this thing."
The seriousness of the day settled on her. He walked past them,
eyes intent and dark. She heard the phone ring inside and Bill
answering.

"How long will it take you to drive home?" Tim handed her
back her cell.

"About four hours."

"Four hours." Their eyes locked for a moment before Bill
came up behind them, startling them.

"Bad news." They both jumped and spun around on him.

"What?"

"The fire department called. They've got the camper moved
and set, but they can't spare the men after all. The storm has
their resources pulled tight. Out here they have a lot more to
do than fight fires. There's a bunch of trees down, blocking
the roads. Some power lines are down, and they had a fire this
afternoon that's got them tied up."

Jasmine's shoulders sagged. *But I'm all packed.*

"Well, we'll make do. When will they be ready?" Tim's
voice sounded light, at ease.

"Not for three days."

"Thursday?" Jasmine knew she sounded angry, but didn't
care. She needed to get home.

"Sorry. Look on the bright side, the kids will like having
you around longer." Bill smiled at her, and she realized that
she was the only one unhappy about her delay.

"The kids, huh?"

He shrugged at her. "I've got to head back to work. I'm
going out to help some of the places where the lines are down."

"Be careful."

"I will." He patted her back. "I'll let Elsie know to expect
you to stay a few more days." He turned and went back into
the house.

"If I didn't know better, I'd think he stalled those guys."

Tim made a chuckling sound. "He wouldn't do that, but if
he did, could you blame him? He's missed you. We all have."

Until that moment, she couldn't have put her finger on the
exact thing making her want to run away. It wasn't only the
bad memories with her parents, though those surely played
a part. Or other people's expectations of her. Or people

assuming she knew them. Or even her own forgetfulness. As his hand touched her arm and she heard the hope resonating in his voice, her chest tightened and she knew what it was.

Her eyes locked on his hand, refusing to meet his glance. She couldn't let him think of her that way.

"Want to help me unpack my car?" Jasmine pulled away and headed down the porch steps. He didn't follow her right away, and that was fine. They needed distance. Had she known, all those years ago, that he cared for her so? Her focus had always been on escape and survival—not relationships.

She sensed his presence behind her as she unloaded her bags and handed them back to him. He followed her in silence inside the house and set down her bags in the living room.

"Here okay?"

"Yep, that's fine." She carried an unnaturally happy tone in her voice. It sounded fake and forced, but it was the best she could do.

"Well, I'd better get back to the office." Tim turned toward the door.

Elsie came into the living room. "Will we see you for dinner tonight?"

Jasmine felt his eyes on her again but kept her attention on the magazines on the coffee table.

"No, I can't. I've made other plans. Maybe tomorrow?"

"Sure, that sounds good."

Tim walked out without saying good-bye. Jasmine let out the breath she'd been holding and met Elsie's accusing glance.

"Why are you so hard on him?"

"I don't want him to care for me." She sank down into the couch.

"Why not? He's the most eligible guy around. He's a good man, and your brother's best friend. What more could you want?" Jasmine could see the confusion in Elsie's eyes.

"Look, I made a pact with myself a long time ago that I wouldn't get involved with anyone. I don't believe in dating to keep loneliness away. It would lead to somewhere I can't go. I won't ever get married, Elsie."

Elsie sat down next to her. "For heaven's sake, why not?"

"I can't trust myself. It's not as though I haven't dated. I did. Losers, every one. I know the statistics of abuse victims choosing poorly—and I meet all the criteria."

"Surely you can see Tim's not like that. You've known him your whole life."

"I knew the boy. I don't really know him now." It was a lame excuse, and she knew it.

"Well, we can attest he's not like that."

Jasmine shook her head. "I'm not really worried about Tim. I'm sure he's nice. And he'll make someone a wonderful husband someday. But not mine. I'll never make anyone a good wife. He deserves better."

To her chagrin, her eyes filled with tears. Crying wasn't something Jazz would do, but Jasmine did little else these days. Grabbing her suitcases, she headed upstairs before Elsie could talk to her anymore. She closed the bedroom door and lay down on the bed, wiping the tears from her eyes and swallowing her grief.

Turmoil filled her, urging her to grab her bags and leave town. Let them burn the camper and send her a picture. She instantly knew that wasn't what she needed. Somehow, she'd have to avoid Tim for the next three days. In a town this small, it didn't seem possible.

Sixteen

The noisy voices of the children downstairs clued her in to the dinner hour. She'd go down and eat with them, make small talk, and go for a walk. Being alone seemed her best bet right now; she was used to thinking things out for herself. Having others around so much drained her.

As she entered the kitchen, though, the grinning faces of her niece and nephew stopped any thoughts of escape. Their eyes adored her as they hung on every word she spoke. They were hungry for a relationship with her. Elsie motioned for her to sit down as she put out the platters and bowls of food. Fried chicken, mashed potatoes and gravy were on the menu tonight.

"I'm sure glad you're staying." Jason passed her the rolls. "I didn't get a chance to show you all my toys yet."

"Or my dolls," Rose added.

"Yeah. Her dolls. She's got a lot of dolls." He rolled his eyes. "I've got cars, and a rat."

Jasmine put down her fork. "A real rat?"

Bill came in from the back door and washed his hands at the sink. "It's a pet."

Pet. "I forgot about Oscar. I'll have to head over to the house and feed him tonight."

"Do you want to bring him here?" Jason asked, his eyes welling with hope.

Both Jasmine and Bill said no in unison. They laughed. She ruffled Jason's hair. "He's not the family type." As soon as she said it, she realized she fit into that category as well. She went back to eating, listening as the kids told stories on each other. As soon as they had finished dinner, she excused herself to leave.

"I'll go with you," Bill insisted.

As much as she wanted to be alone, being at the house in the dark didn't really appeal to her. She agreed and let Bill escort her. They walked in silence up the hill, stopping in front of the darkened home. It looked like any other normal house, sitting there in the dark, with a For Sale sign in the front yard. You couldn't see the new paint or neatly manicured yard. Or the memories.

"It should sell pretty fast." He held his hand out for the key. She passed it to him and watched as he unlocked the door and turned on the entry light. She heard Oscar's meowing right away.

"Poor guy." She knelt down and petted him as he wrapped himself around her.

"He never gave mom that kind of attention. They survived on mutual respect."

Bill leaned down to stroke Oscar but stopped when he was met by a deep guttural warning.

"He seems to like me." She shrugged at the split personality of the cat rubbing his face on her palm. She walked into the kitchen, cleaned the cat box, and opened a can of food for him. She gave him fresh water and sat by him as he ate.

"It's probably lonely in here without all the furniture."

"I left a box for him with blankets in it over in the corner." He motioned toward the back door, to a large box there.

"Thanks. I guess I'm not used to caring for anyone but myself."

"That's understandable. How long have you been on your own?"

"A long time. I think it'll take some getting used to, having him around."

"I'm glad you'll have him."

After scratching Oscar's ears for a few more minutes, they turned on the sink light and left the house. They walked down the hill, the four blocks into the business center of town. A movie was letting out, and the normally angst-ridden teens stood outside the theatre making jokes.

"Want to grab a cocoa?" Bill tipped his head toward The Getaway. A vivid picture of her holding Bill's hand and walking to the cafe for a special treat flashed her in mind.

"Sounds good, big brother." Jasmine flashed him a grin. "You know, I still want to call you Sweet William."

"I'll let you do it, but not when anyone else is around," he whispered to her conspiratorially.

"You never said where you got the money to buy cocoa with." She put her hand around his arm as they walked.

"Odd jobs. Lily never wanted to come—but you always did. For some reason, it felt like I was making up for how we lived." He leaned over and kissed her head. "Sometimes I was more like a dad than a big brother."

A tear rolled down her cheek. "To me, too."

They entered The Getaway, took a middle booth, and ordered two hot chocolates. The waitress brought their cocoas, complete with whipped cream and a cherry. So much around them had changed, but this place seemed trapped in time.

She ate the cherry first and fiddled with the stem.

"Still good." He wiped the whipped cream from his upper lip.

"Do you bring the kids here?"

A shadow passed his eyes. "For lunch here and there. But not for cocoa." He gave her a knowing glance.

"I'm sorry." She'd spent little to no time thinking about what people must have thought after she'd run away. But now there were daily and sometimes hourly reminders that she didn't run away from the bad—but sacrificed many things that were good.

"Don't be. I can bring them now." Tears filled his eyes and he blinked them away. "Sorry." He took a sip and stared into the mug, trying to hide his emotions from her. "I'm not usually so emotional."

"Believe it or not, neither am I."

"I keep thinking I'm used to having you back, and then some little thing you say or do will trigger a memory and it's twenty-two years ago." He looked out the window, watching the occasional car drive by.

"It's okay. I was so busy leaving him behind, I didn't think about all the other people I left." She took a sip of cocoa to build her courage. "I had to go."

He turned toward her. "I know. I don't blame you. Secrets

and lies eat at you, you know? Not knowing if you were alive or dead some days would steal my peace. I would blame myself. And one day I realized I could pray for you."

"Pray for me?" She put down her mug.

"Sure. I mean, I didn't know where you were, but God did. So Elsie and I would pray for you, that you were safe and that we'd see you again one day." He reached over and took her hand. "And here you are."

She wasn't sure what to say. "Are you still going to pray for me?"

"Yep. Every night."

A week ago, that might have made her resentful, but tonight it filled her with a sense of comfort. She didn't think she mattered to God, that wasn't it. But that her brother and his wife would think of her every night, that comforted her.

"When I go home, I'll stay in touch. Don't worry, okay?"

"I won't. I know you'll keep your word."

If she hadn't intended to before, she would now. She watched his gaze out the window shift. She followed it and saw Tim walking with a woman down the street. They were laughing.

"Who's that?" Her chest tightened as he put a hand to the small of the woman's back and she looked up at him and smiled.

"Jenny Clifton. She's new in town and attends our church."

Despite her best efforts, her stomach tensed. "I didn't know he was seeing someone."

"Oh, he's not. It's the coffee date." Everyone seemed to know Tim's bad habit.

"He told me he was done with that. He's waiting for God to bring a wife to him."

Bill suddenly found new interest in stirring his cocoa. "Well, like I said, she's new in town."

They moved closer to the diner. *Don't come in.*

The bell over the door chimed and Tim and his date entered the cafe. Tim waved to them, his eyes not registering any surprise at seeing her there. In fact, he looked resigned for a moment before putting on a larger smile. She watched them sit down at a far booth and order coffee. And fries?

"She's nice." Bill's words cut into her thoughts. She had no business caring.

"Good. He deserves someone nice." Her hair color couldn't be natural. No one had that shade of auburn.

Bill's eyes narrowed on her in an expression she couldn't quite make out.

"Yes, he does." He took another drink.

She heard Tim laugh and took a larger slug of cocoa than she intended and wiped the whipped cream from her nose. "So, ready to head home?"

"If you are."

As they passed by Tim, he motioned for them to stop.

"Hi you two. Hey, Jasmine, this is Jenny Clifton. She's new in town. Jenny, this is Jasmine Reynolds. She's in town visiting her brother, Bill."

He introduced her as Jasmine. Fine.

"So nice to meet you. Is this your first date?" She tried not to look at Tim. Unfortunately, that meant she had to focus on Jenny's perfect completion, shapely figure and designer clothes.

Jenny avoided her question. "I hope you enjoy your visit. Isn't this town perfect? I wish I'd grown up here." She smiled warmly at Tim. Jasmine fought the urge to dump the discarded plate of fries sitting next them in her perfectly pleated lap.

"It's a good town." *It's a good town?* "What do you do, Jenny?" Was it her imagination, or did Tim just squirm?

"Oh, I'm a realtor. I've been looking for the right place to settle for a long time and fell in love here." Jenny drew out the word love in a way that made Jasmine's skin crawl. "In fact, aren't you Tim's client who's selling that cute little place on the hill?"

Realtor. This was Tim's realtor? Jasmine shot a pointed look at Tim who'd found intense interest in a menu he knew by heart.

"Why, yes." Jasmine's voice lilted in a way she'd never imagined possible. "Are you the helpful realtor Tim told me about?"

Jenny laughed. "What a wonderful coincidence. I know after you've made all those repairs we shouldn't have any trouble selling. I'm working very closely with Tim on this—don't worry."

Jasmine opened her mouth to find out just how closely, when Bill interrupted their conversation.

Bill forced a laugh as he took Jasmine by the elbow and hustled her to the exit. "We'd better get going. See you later, Tim."

"Sure." Tim got up and walked them outside. They stood on the corner while Bill moved off to get a newspaper from the bin. Her eyes were still locked on Jenny and her hair.

"I thought I'd come by tomorrow. Since you're going to be in town a couple more days, I'd like you to see my place. What do you think?"

Jasmine looked back through the window. "I think you should finish your date."

Tim followed her gaze. "She's a business acquaintance."

Jasmine suddenly saw outside herself. She had no intention of sounding jealous. She did mean it—Tim deserved someone wonderful. Not that woman, but someone. She changed her tone and looked up into his eyes. "If you ever want any of these women to be more than friends, you're going to have to get better at dates."

"We'd had this night set weeks ago. And really, she's just a friend."

"You certainly don't owe me any explanations—although she doesn't seem your type." She cleared her throat. "I do have a suggestion though."

"What's that?"

"Quit dating until you're ready, Tim. You're a nice guy. Nice guys are hard to find—so when you take a woman out, they get their hopes up. You've got the entire single female population of this town holding their breath in anticipation."

"I hardly think…"

She put her hand on his arm. "Trust me on this. I used to be your best friend. I've always given it to you straight, haven't I?"

"Sure."

"Find the one you want, and go after her in earnest. Pursue her. Give the rest of them a break."

Tim's jaw dropped open as a hundred emotions played over his features.

Before he could respond, Bill joined them with the paper

folded under his arm. "Ready to go?" He gave them both a curious look, but neither of them filled him in on what he'd missed.

"Good night, Tim." She pulled Bill away, not waiting to see if Tim went back inside.

She and Bill began the short walk home. The streetlights guided them past the park, up the street, toward his house. Even though the blooms on the trees were closed, the sweet aroma from their flowers lingered in the air.

"Are you sure you want to leave town to get away from just the memories?" Bill looked at her sideways, waiting for her answer.

"That's not the only reason. I have a life in Portland. My job is important to me. And I owe it to Brandi to help her out. She put her neck out for me all those years ago. I like to repay my debts."

"Okay."

"I know that tone. What are you getting at?"

"I wonder if you are running toward something, or away from someone."

"Someone?"

"Tim."

Her shoulders drooped. "Why would I be running away from Tim?"

"Because you care for him. I could see it tonight when you locked eyes on Jenny, the way your neck turned red and splotchy."

She pulled up her collar. "I'm tired. Besides, I gave him dating tips tonight. I think he should settle down and get married."

"And you hope he does it really soon so you won't feel what you're feeling anymore. But it's not going to go away. If he does marry, you'll be three times as miserable as you're feeling now."

"I'd take my feeling miserable over his any day."

Bill stopped walking. "What do you mean by that?"

"Tim needs a wife. He's meant to be married and have children. I'm not that person, and I know it."

"You mind explaining that?"

"I'm not marrying material. Plus, he needs a woman to

share his life with, his faith with. We both know I'm not that person."

She knew Bill was thinking that she could be. But he didn't know about her past, the choices she'd made.

"So you plan on living the rest of your life alone?"

"I have Oscar." She tried to laugh, but it sounded hollow. "And now I have you and Elsie and the kids."

"When you see Tim and his wife and kids at my house on Christmas, you'll smile and laugh and act like everything's okay?"

"Yes." Her confident answer didn't match the twisted feeling in her heart at the visual image Bill described. It didn't matter. She knew she was right. It was for the best.

Bill shook his head. "More pretending."

"I won't be pretending, Bill. I'll mean it." Her voice cracked. "I'll mean it."

His arm came up around her shoulders. "Okay, little sister." They walked that way up the path, up the porch steps.

As soon as they entered the house, she went straight upstairs to her room. There wasn't a way to explain to Bill without telling him everything. She changed into her nightshirt and climbed in bed. Her eyes locked on the closet as she realized she hadn't checked under her bed or in the closet once since she'd moved into Bill's house. Lifting the corner of the sheet, she wiped the tears from her eyes. She'd never known safety before. Living with Fiona was as close as she'd gotten until now, and Fiona had slept with a gun near her bed.

Turning over, she flicked off the lamp and watched the shadows from the maple tree outside her window play over the ceiling. She listened to the house shift and heard footsteps creak on the stair. In the background there was the murmur of Bill and Elsie's voices. She could imagine Christmas here, the kids opening packages, screams of joy and amazement. Laughter.

She'd borrow their laughter and store it up in her heart. That would never be for her.

Where Misty protected the life within her, Jasmine had succumbed to Rob's pressure. Within three months of her abortion, Rob had been arrested. When she found herself on the streets, she convinced herself she'd made the right decision.

The streets were no place for a baby. After she'd moved into the shelter, and saw the women with their children, she told herself again that she'd made the right choice. Even when she saw the love the women had for their children, and the help they received, she told herself she'd been right.

The first night in her own apartment, only two years later, it hit her. The child would have been two. In retrospect, she could have made it for two years with the baby. She'd survived worse. The baby wouldn't have known her worries, the danger it was in from time to time. They would have been together.

Not long after that, she'd gotten an infection. During her checkup, the doctor informed her she'd probably never have children because of damage from the abortion. The bitterness she'd felt for Rob, for herself, for the life she'd made for herself burned inside. After she mourned, she made a pact never to marry, never to be in a relationship again. She chose Rob, she sold herself, drugs, she had an abortion, and in doing so she gave up any rights to children she might have one day. She didn't deserve to have them. The odds weren't good for her. She might not go back to Rob, but someone like him was always around.

He wouldn't be a drug dealer or pimp. He'd be something more respectable now. But he'd still treat her like property, like he owned the rights to make all her decisions. Never again.

Bill was right about Tim. She could trust him, but that was a different set of problems. He didn't deserve to be saddled with her. He needed someone trustworthy, someone whole. No matter how much time passed, she'd never be that person.

Seventeen

The next day, Jasmine sat on the back porch and flipped through her notebook, making a list of things she needed to do when she got home. She made a few phone calls, checking in with Brandi and the shelter. She told them about the Bright River House of Hope and gave them Mrs. Craig's contact information. And Jasmine let Brandi know Misty had moved in. Now they had an apartment open again at Broadstreet House. The other two young women were Brandi's clients. She would miss Misty.

The warmth of the sun called to her. She walked down the steps to the hammock set between two tall pines swaying in the breeze. Climbing in, she lay back against the flexible mesh and let the wind lull her into a much-needed nap. Some time later, a familiar voice woke her from a dreamless sleep.

"If I didn't know better, I'd think you were taking a vacation or something."

She opened one eye, taking in Tim dressed in a formal suit. "Did you win?"

"I did indeed. I'm heading home for lunch and wondered if you'd join me in celebration."

Jasmine sat up from the swing, resigned with meeting his expectations for now. The sooner she went, the sooner she'd be back. "Sure. Let me put these things away." Gathering her papers together, she headed inside the house to put them away and met him by the front gate. He led her to his BMW.

"Not within walking distance?"

"Some days. Today, I'm tired." He opened the door for her, and she slid onto a leather seat.

128

"Nice ride."

Tim shut his door and started the car. "Thanks. It's not practical in the wintertime, so I also have a truck. But on my fancy days," he flipped up his tie, "I drive the good car." He drove through town, past the gas station and up the other side of the hill. Here the houses were set back from the road, with plenty of trees around for privacy.

After driving down a long gravel road, he stopped in front of a two-story dark blue farmhouse with white trim. The customary fruit trees grew along the left side. On the right was a feshly plowed garden, framed in the back with grapevines. Past that was a long hedge of raspberry bushes. Lining the other side of the property were newly budding honeysuckle bushes. As she climbed from the car, she filled her lungs with the scent of spring.

She walked up the front porch and spied a large pink-tinted flowering bush. He smiled as she ran her fingers over the delicate blossoms.

"Your namesake." He plucked some of the jasmine buds and handed them to her. "They'll flower again in winter. Some people overlook their delicate flowers for something flashier, but you won't find a sweeter aroma, or a more beautiful reminder of God's providence in winter. If you come back for a visit, you'll have to come by. It's like a promise that winter will one day be over, and spring will come again."

Tucking the blossoms into her purse, she followed him into his house. Inside sat a dark brown leather Craftsman couch and rocking chair. A pair of wing chairs flanked the fireplace, and a large television hung on the wall. To the left was a huge DVD collection of old movies.

"Still a movie buff?"

"Yep. I'm going upstairs to change. I'll be back down in a second."

She glanced over the titles and wandered on through into the kitchen. It reminded her a lot of Elsie's kitchen. Built-in storage met her everywhere. Behind the glass doors of the cabinets sat dishes and books and all matter of things. Okay, it wasn't as well organized as Elsie's, but the style was the same. It must have been from the same period.

On the kitchen table sat a bouquet of tulips in an old glass pitcher. Tim called down to her.

"There's a sack with sandwiches inside the fridge. And there's a salad in there someplace too. I'm going to grab a quick shower."

"Okay." She opened the fridge and pulled out everything for lunch. He'd obviously been home to drop off food and betted on her agreeing to come for a visit. She went to the cupboard and got out the plates and glasses. When she heard the water turn off, she hollered up to him from the foot of the stairs. "Did you want a soda?"

"I think there's iced tea in there. I'd like that."

She pulled out the pitcher and decided she'd have some as well. As she poured their drinks, he came down wearing a sweatshirt and jeans. His dampened hair stuck to his forehead, and she fought the urge to push it back.

"Feel better?"

He sat down across from her. "Yes. I like the suit, but after sweating it out for the last five hours, I needed a change."

"Do you get a lot of big cases around here?"

"The occasional one. Most of what I handle are wills and such. But we have our share of excitement. A nasty divorce, robbery, murder. There's no statute of limitations on ugliness in a small town."

"No, I suppose not."

"On occasion I take other cases too, some even in Portland."

Jasmine glanced at him when he said that, wondering if he was getting at something. Instead, he bent his head and prayed over their food. Besides Bill, he was only the second man she'd ever seen do that.

"So how's your day?" He scooped some potato salad onto his plate.

"Good. Got caught up on my phone calls. There are three new girls at the shelter I help at. I'm hopeful one of them will be a candidate to take Misty's spot. And the fire department called. We can burn the camper tomorrow."

Tim stopped mid-bite. "Tomorrow?"

"Good thing, too." She hurried on, keeping the conversation moving. "Brandi is overwhelmed with paperwork. I'm going to be up to my eyeballs by the time I'm back at work." She kept her voice even. What she didn't say was that she'd fought tooth and nail to get the fire department to agree to tomorrow. "Well, that'll be good." He'd stopped eating.

"You said it." She took a hearty bite of her sandwich. "This is very tasty."

"There's a new deli around the corner from my office."

"Well, they're talented." She sipped her tea. "How did your date go after we left?"

His eyes measured her, but she kept her cool. "Good. I'm thinking of asking her out again."

She swallowed her tea in a lump that ached all the way down her throat. "Good."

"Have you told Bill about the camper?"

"No, I'll tell him tonight at dinner."

"Do you mind if I join you at the burning?"

"No. I'd like to have you there." There was no sense in pretending she didn't want or need his friendship. She did, badly. "So how long have you lived here?"

"I bought the place about five years ago. I've been fixing it up ever so slowly. A country lawyer is a lot busier than people think. This spring I'm working on the garden. The plots and most of the plants and trees were already in from the last owners. But it's still a lot of work."

"I remember how hard my mom worked in her garden. She'd be out there for hours every week." It was her mother's favorite place to hide—out in the open where no one would suspect anything.

"Hopefully, it won't take me that long. I've hired a local kid to mow every week, to make sure the place looks respectable."

"I think it looks great already. You've got most of my favorite plants growing."

"Do I?" He smiled and went back to eating.

She raised an eyebrow in question at him. "There's an atrium outside my apartment. The bulbs are getting ready to bloom."

"Sounds pretty." He didn't look up at that, so she dropped the subject. Whenever she spoke of her apartment or leaving, both he and Bill shut down. After picking at her sandwich awhile longer, she realized she'd lost her appetite. She wrapped it back in the paper and took her plate to the sink, washing it and setting it in the drainer. She turned around to face Tim, who had a strange look on his face, like someone had gut punched him.

"What is it?"

He shook his head and brought his plate over and put it in the sink. "You don't know what it's like to see you there. Sorry." He gave her a slight smile. "I'll do mine later." He walked into the living room and sat down in one arm chair. Jasmine followed and sat in the other.

"Your house is very comfortable. Based on your BMW, I expected fancier." As she changed the subject, the uneasy look in his eyes faded.

"Are you disappointed?"

"No, not at all. This suits you well. It's a beautiful home. I imagined a stately manor."

He smiled. "A wise man once told me to put my first checks into my car, my suits, and my briefcase."

"Why?" As she spoke, a chill passed through the room and she pulled the throw behind her over her shoulders. Again a lost look crossed Tim's face, but as soon as she noticed it, it was gone.

"Image. People are more likely to hire a lawyer who looks successful than one who drives a beater pickup truck."

"Sad but true."

"So I rented a long time, lived in some real dives, but I drove an awesome car and had two really expensive suits." He laughed to himself. "I even lived in a barn with my car for awhile. I took the loft, and my car stayed on the first floor."

"So you two are really close," she teased.

"Sadly, it's probably the closest relationship I've got." He laughed, but it fell flat.

"That's not true. You're close to Bill and Elsie. And you have the respect of the town."

He ran his fingers over the arms of the chair and locked eyes with her. "It doesn't make coming home to an empty house every night any better."

"Do you want a cat?"

"No. I certainly don't want a cat." He smiled at her, the crinkles around his eyes deepening. "Well, this turned into a morose conversation. Let me show you around the place."

They got up, stepped out on the porch, and from there

headed past the garden and up a slight incline. Behind the house a grove of fruit trees towered, and through them sat a stack of boulders at the top of a hill. He invited her to sit. The view before them was picturesque. The river wound back and forth below on the other side of his property, silver glimmering in the sunlight, meandering around the bend.

"Lovely." She breathed deeply, the cutting aroma of budding oaks and damp evergreens laced the cool afternoon air.

"I like it here." He picked up a twig and chipped the bark off it with his thumb. "Do you think you'll be back?"

His question caught her by surprise. A week ago, she would have said no, but now everything seemed different. "I will. I don't know when, and I'm sorry I can't make any promises about that. My life is rather erratic, depending on my clients." She sighed. "I'd love to come back for Christmas. To see Bill's house all decorated for the holidays." Her eyes misted. "That sounds silly, doesn't it? Why should I care about such a thing?"

"Why wouldn't you?" He picked up a piece of bark and splintered it apart with his fingernail.

"I don't know. I'm not a sentimental person. Those kinds of traditions always seemed so fake. But, I can picture their home, dusted in snow, the Christmas tree peeking through the front window, all lit up with color and homemade ornaments; the kids playing in the living room with their new toys; the smell of turkey and gingerbread in the house." Again tears came, and she looked away, ashamed of her weakness.

He gently took her hand. "Don't be embarrassed. It's okay to want those things."

"I've never wanted them before. I never needed them."

"You did when I knew you. Remember we'd go to the toy store and imagine what we were getting? And we'd always go watch them decorate the Main Street tree. And we'd talk about what it would be like when we grew up."

She could see Tim thinking about those things. But had she?

"I'm not that person any more, Tim. I haven't been for a long, long time." Her voice sounded more regretful than she'd expected. Embarrassed, she pulled her hand away, got up and started through the trees, back to the house. She fixed her gaze on it, also picturing a life for Tim. She saw a woman in the kitchen window, making things homey for him, washing dishes, cooking. She imagined children playing in the yard, climbing the trees, calling for his attention.

He came up from behind and put his hands on her shoulders. "Jasmine, it's not wrong to want those things."

Jasmine wiped at her eyes with her sleeve, wishing she could confide in him, but knowing he would dismiss her worries and say something romantic and foolish. She shouldn't have come here, letting him think they'd have more together than they did. "I'd like to go back to Bill's house now, okay?"

"Okay." His hands dropped. Tim walked past her, toward the car, and opened the door for her. He climbed in the other side, and they drove the short distance back into town, pulling up in front of Bill's house.

"Thanks for showing me your home." She made the mistake of glancing into his eyes and saw her own pain mirrored there. "I'll see you tomorrow."

"See you tomorrow."

She let herself inside, using her own key and, after checking and seeing no one else was home, headed upstairs and lay on her bed. It was hard seeing Tim every day. It was hard seeing his home and imagining his life there.

The worst part, though, was when she imagined the woman in the kitchen window, she had seen herself.

Eighteen

"Ready?" Bill met Jasmine and Tim on the porch and walked out into the yard. He carried a box of photos and papers under his arm.

"What do you have there?" Tim asked him.

"Lies."

From the grave look on Tim's face, Jasmine knew he understood.

Bill turned to Jasmine. "All set, sister?"

"I am." She took Bill's other arm, and Tim followed behind them as they walked to her car. He climbed in the backseat, next to her things. She'd spent the morning saying good-bye to Elsie and the children. Explaining why she had to leave was harder than she'd imagined—the reasons she'd clung to for so long sounded flat. She put the key in the ignition and saw the house key dangling there. They'd meant it. They wanted her to feel like this house was home. And it had been, more than she'd ever felt anywhere before.

"I'm buckled up." Tim's muffled voice came from behind her.

She suppressed a smile as she caught his reflection in the rearview mirror, encased by her things, knees up around his ears and looking rather like a little boy. He forced a smile, but she could see the serious look in his eyes.

"You could have ridden with Bill."

"I can ride with him any time."

"Why didn't you sit up front?"

"Have you seen your front seat?"

She glanced sideways at the stained seat, littered in snack

bags and stacks of books and papers.

"It's like my second office. Sorry."

"I hope your apartment is cleaner than that when I come to visit."

Jasmine's stomach clenched around his words. Her apartment was very neat and tidy, but she doubted he'd ever see it. Pulling out, she followed Bill up the road a mile outside of town.

The camper sat central in an otherwise empty field with the fire chief standing to the side talking on a radio. They climbed from their cars and walked over. Bill headed straight to it, and motioned for her to follow him. Jasmine opened the door, and Bill put the box inside. She smelled the familiar smell and was once again transported back in time.

"You sure about this?" He put a hand on her shoulder.

"Yes." She motioned to the cardboard box that now held a variety of items, including the photos in the paper sack and a baseball. "How about you?"

Bill answered in a nod. She made a last walk though, opening and closing all the cabinets. Convinced she'd already found everything of value, she headed out and moved over by Tim, far back from the camper. After shutting the door behind her with finality, Bill joined them and signaled the chief.

The chief motioned to a couple of men, and they headed over to the camper, pouring fuel inside, around, and on top of it. They took a lighting can around and set it ablaze. The chief lifted the radio to his mouth and made the call. Within seconds, they heard the scream of sirens tearing through the town, growing louder as they approached. Two trucks pulled in, flanking the camper. They readied their hoses but waited.

Blue and red flames built and rose, flicking into the sky. The acrid smoke billowed and carried the ugliness she'd lived with up, high into the sky. She watched the smoke thicken, the rising black puffs play on the currents of heated air, thin to wisps, and disappear. Tears streamed down her cheeks. Bill took her hand and held it tight in his safe grip, but no sense of closure filled her soul.

Within minutes, the fire gutted the camper. The firefighters turned the hoses on, taking turns in this bizarre training mission. Bill, Tim, and she were forgotten.

The blaze was out, and the men were congratulating themselves on a job well done. Bill, Jasmine, and Tim moved toward their cars.

"Join us for lunch before you go?" Bill's hopeful tone broke her heart.

She wiped her eyes. "I can't." The pull to stay in the safety of her brother's house called to her. She felt her resolve slipping and knew she had to go. A forced smile crossed her lips as she looked into their eyes. "I'll be back."

She had no idea if she were lying or not. She would need time to heal from this trip.

"I gave Elsie my contact information."

Bill and Tim looked as lost as she felt.

"We'll drive into Portland one day soon. I'll call you, and we'll make plans." Bill patted her back.

"Sounds good." Jasmine let herself be pulled into her brother's comforting embrace. The warmth in his hug gave her strength. He let her go and walked to his car, not looking back.

She met Tim's eyes. "Keep an eye on him for me, would you?"

"I thought he was the big brother?"

"Even a big brother needs someone to look out for him. Will you?"

"I will." He leaned over and kissed her cheek, and the spicy scent of his cologne wisped around her. "Good-bye, Jasmine."

Tim's words sounded final in her ears. She realized that neither of them ever expected to see her again. Despite her responsible job, and seemingly good character, all they saw when they looked at her was the girl who left. And here she was, leaving again.

She glanced into Tim's eyes, regretting it as soon as she had, seeing the longing and worry there. It'd be for the best if she did stay away, at least from Tim. She'd never be the woman he imagined her to be.

"I'll call you." She tried to sound reassuring.

"Sure." She could tell from Tim's tone he didn't believe her. He used to know her better than she did herself. Maybe that was still true. She moved toward her car, climbed in, and drove away. To cap off all the mistakes she'd made since she'd arrived, she looked back and watched him standing there, watching her drive away, hands in his pockets, shoulders slumped. She knew the image would haunt her.

Jasmine passed orchards and farms and found herself slowing in front of one on the edge of town. Back in the trees sat a familiar one-story farmhouse. She turned down the lane and, without thinking, climbed from her car and approached the door. It opened.

"Leaving town, are we?" Lily stepped out on the porch, arms crossed over her chest.

"I wanted to say good-bye."

"Of course. This time you'll say good-bye. Were there a lot of tears at Bill's house?"

Jasmine didn't have a clue what she was doing, standing on the porch of her sister's home, taking abuse she didn't deserve.

"Take care, Lily." She turned and headed back to her car When she looked up, the porch was empty and the front door closed. She didn't know what she'd expected. When they were kids, Lily had always been unapproachable. She was the middle child, often feeling left out. This seemed to go much deeper than that. What Lily didn't know was how lucky she'd been to be overlooked by their father.

Driving down the lane, she felt the heaviness of a life of secrets pressing down on her. Bill understood what it meant to have everything in the open. The freedom honesty brought was healing. Even if she'd told Lily her perspective of their childhood, she didn't think Lily would believe her. She pulled past a shed and spied a barn cat in the grass. Cat.

Oh no, Oscar.

For the first time in her life, she had someone else depending on her—and she'd left him behind without a thought. She turned back into town and drove up the street to her childhood home. The key was under the mat, and she went inside.

"Oscar!" she called.

Oscar sauntered out of the kitchen, his green eyes showing expectation as if he'd been waiting for her. She dumped his cat box out and packed up his food and dishes. She found a cardboard box and cut holes in it. After she loaded everything, she approached him with an open can of food. He came to her and allowed himself and the can to be loaded inside. She folded the flaps shut. She grabbed a notepad on the table, and scribbled, "I've got Oscar. Love, Jasmine." It was the first time she'd written her given name in over twenty years. She stared at it, focusing on the loops and swirls of her handwriting. She didn't know if it even belonged to her anymore, or if she should leave it where she left the rest of her childhood. She looked up at the ceiling, knowing above the kitchen sat her room. Before she realized what she was doing, she found herself standing outside her old bedroom door, her hand on the cold metal doorknob.

Jasmine pushed the door open onto an empty, newly painted room. They'd even replaced the carpeting. She closed her eyes and imagined the room of her childhood: a twin bed, a small desk and over-filled bookcase. A foot below the ceiling ran a line of shelves covered in stuffed animals and collectables she'd never asked for and secretly wished she could throw away. They'd mocked her; looked down at her. She'd never played with them. Not once.

Going to the window, she looked out onto the backyard—the debris was cleaned up and garbage hauled away. The yard looked much as it once had, with the exception of the well-tended flowerbeds that grew there when she was a kid.

"Why?" She asked the question aloud, the only response a resonant echo from the empty room. Her shaky legs collapsed, and she slid down the wall, staring at the open door, reliving all the ways she'd imagined blocking him from entering. The trapped feeling, the panic rising. She sobbed, crying louder and louder. "Why?" She knew who she was asking, but God didn't answer.

Tim wanted her to go to church as a kid, and she had, because somehow, despite all the ugliness, she'd known God was real. She had prayed her prayer to Jesus. And that was what hurt her the worst on the loneliest of nights. She knew God existed, but He didn't seem to care about her. No matter how good she was in school, how nice she was to kids who were mean to her, how well she did her chores, her life never improved. Even going to church hadn't made a difference.

Tears continued down her cheeks unchecked. "Why didn't You do something?"

A vivid picture of the camper came to her mind. Not the burned-out wreck she'd seen this morning, but the new, shiny one parked in the side yard. And the bright new key her mother gave her. "Keep this close," she'd told her. "Don't give it to anyone."

Jasmine leaned her head back against the corner of the room. Another picture came to mind, that of Fiona, loving, dear Fiona from the carnival, her arms stretched out wide. Fiona holding her through hard nights; listening to her cry; her comforting pat on the back of Jasmine's head as she fell asleep. And Brandi. Brandi coming alongside her at the shelter, Brandi believing in her, mentoring her, and arranging her scholarship to college.

Jasmine let out a ragged breath and wiped her tears with her the hanky Tim had given her. She heard a strange yowling noise accompanied by frantic scratching and realized Oscar must have finished his food and wanted out. Pulling herself to her feet, she took a last look around the room. After making her way downstairs, she picked up the unhappy cat in his makeshift container.

"Come on, kitty. Let's go home." This time, when she drove past her sister's house, she didn't even look.

Hours later, she pulled into downtown. Portland bustled with noisy, pushy life as the work day ended. Food carts down the street were closing for the night, but she could still smell the aroma of every type of offering mixing on the breeze. Jasmine hauled her things into her apartment, ignoring her hunger pangs.

Once everything was inside, she checked the closet, under her bed, and the bathroom. Even though she'd only been out of the habit a week, it felt strange to pick it back up again. Certain they were alone, she locked her front door and let Oscar out of his cardboard prison. He bolted around the room once and darted under the bed. She set up his litter box in the bathroom and poured fresh food and water into his dishes in the kitchen. She sat on the floor, leaning back against the wall with a pile of mail on her lap.

By the time she'd sorted the junk from the bills, Oscar poked his head out from under the bed and wandered around, testing his new world. He walked the perimeter, nosed around in the bathroom, and, once satisfied, hopped on her bed and curled up in a black ball for a nap. She put the mail on her desk and wandered over to the bed, lay behind him and pulled a blanket over the two of them. From under the covers, a soft, lulling purr filled the room. Before she knew it, she was asleep. The phone woke her. It was Brandi.

"You home?"

"Got back a couple hours ago." She flipped the switch on her lamp and filled the dim apartment with light. Glancing at the clock, she saw it was seven-thirty. "I was napping with Oscar."

"Do tell, who's Oscar?"

"My cat."

"You inherited a cat?"

"He apparently only likes me."

"A loyal cat. There are worse things." Brandi snickered.

"True." They were quiet a moment.

"Jed came nosing around asking about Misty."

"You didn't tell him she'd left, did you?"

"No. He'll have to figure things out on his own."

"Bright River House of hope is a nice place. Actually, if you know of anyone, they could use an on-site counselor. I thought it'd be great for an internship, even. We could set it up."

"Let's keep that in mind. I want to meet for breakfast in the morning, to hand back over your client list."

"Sounds good. Have a good night." Jasmine ended the call and reached down to pet Oscar.

"Did you have a nice nap?"

He yawned at her.

"Me too." She got out of bed and pulled on her shoes and coat. "I've got to go to the market. I'll be back in a half hour, okay?" He put his head back down on the bed and closed his eyes. She took that as a sign of acceptance and headed out toward the local Safeway with her pull-cart. An hour later, she returned home with fresh groceries, cat food, and litter. She also got a couple cat toys. She'd never had a pet before and looked forward to some company on quiet nights.

As she entered her apartment, though, she found a huge mess of papers strewn all over the floor. The water dish was tipped over, and Oscar was back under the bed, growling.

"I'm home, Oscar. It's me." What got into him? She began to close the door, but it was ripped from her grasp as someone pushed it from the other side. An arm snaked around her waist and pulled her back against the closed door.

"Hey, Shrink, where's Misty?" Jed's menacing voice whispered into her ear, the stench of alcohol heavy in the air.

Her heart rate rose, but she kept a calm demeanor. "From what I understand, no one has seen her around." Her hand ached for her knife stored in the chest of drawers on the other side of the room. She really needed to start carrying that again.

"Yeah, and you were gone a few days too. You know what I think?" His lips rested against her ear, his scruffy beard scratching the tender skin of her cheek.

"What?" Jasmine took slow, controlled breaths. *Don't panic. Make a plan.*

"You took off with her and my kid."

"Your kid?"

"Yeah, she's going to have a baby. It's my kid. She's got no right to leave town with my kid."

"I see. Well, if you've asked around, you know no one knows where she's gone. I can't help you." She slipped her hand into her pocket and quick-dialed Brandi's phone. It was a maneuver they'd talked about and practiced over the years, but had never had the opportunity to try. She waited a minute. "Jed, I think you should leave my apartment. I don't want any trouble." Oscar's growls intensified. Jed shoved his free arm at Jasmine, and she saw deep bloody scratches and welts. "Your crazy cat attacked me."

"You should probably get to the hospital. Cat bites and scratches are highly infectious."

"Yeah, right. And you'd call the cops on me. No way, lady." He inhaled. "You smell real nice, you know that?"

Alarms went off in her head at his amorous tone. Nausea stirred in her stomach. *Everything's fine. Help is on the way.*

Jed started to nuzzle the back of her neck as he pulled her tighter and she felt a gun poking her in the ribs. "I'm down a girl. And look here, I've found a girl."

Jasmine moved her head aside. "Breaking and entering is a felony. How many strikes do you have against you, Jed?" She hoped her coaching tone didn't tip him off that there were others listening in. At least she hoped they were.

"I'm not worried about the law, but you should be worried

about me. I'll find Misty. And when I do, if I find out you knew where she was, I won't be so friendly."

"This is the police. Open up!" Ned Banner's commanding voice on the other side of her front door startled them both. Normally, she wouldn't have found that comforting, but she did tonight.

She called out to him. "Officer Banner, this man broke into my apartment and is threatening me."

"We know. We've got him recorded and we've got a witness."

At Banner's response, Jed's eyes went white with panic. He shoved her hard to the floor, ran past her, and broke through the window to her fire escape. As she rose, the sound of gunshots filled the air. She heard Banner yell, "Man down." The noise chased Oscar into the bathroom, where she closed him in for safety. Someone knocked on her door, and her heart jumped.

"Jazz, it's me, Ned. We got him."

She opened the door to find the grim-looking officer on the other side of her door.

"Is he dead?" She held her breath, waiting for his answer.

"No, just injured. He pulled a gun on my partner. We've got a load of evidence against him. Can we count on you as a witness?"

"Yes."

"Thanks." He looked around her apartment in disgust. "This is a lousy welcome home, isn't it?"

She realized she hadn't ever given Ned a fair chance. "Yeah." Her hands shook as she ran them through her hair, and she shoved them deep into her pockets.

"I know a glass guy close by. I'll give him a call, and he'll be right over."

"At this time of night?"

"We're good friends, it'll be fine."

"You don't have to do that."

"I know. But you won't sleep with that thing being broken. He owes me." He grinned at her as if that said it all. She accepted the offer. Two hours later, the glass was replaced, and he'd installed an iron gate, only able to open from the inside.

Banner stopped back by. This time, she let him inside. He inspected his friend's craftsmanship.

143

"He does good work, doesn't he?" He pulled on the gate. "That'll keep you safe. No more intruders." He smiled at her. "Jed's recovering from his gunshot wound and will be moved to the jail tomorrow."

"I'm glad you guys got him."

"That was a good idea, calling Brandi."

"She's on her way over." Jasmine knelt and collected the last few papers still strewn on the floor. Except for the new gate on the window, it would be hard to know anything had happened there that day.

"That's good, you shouldn't be alone. Well, I've got to get going. You take care, okay?"

"Ned?"

"Yeah?" He turned around at the door.

"Thanks."

He smiled, tipped his head, and closed the door behind him. Seconds later, Brandi was knocking. Jasmine let her in.

"You okay?" She pulled her into a hug and didn't let go for several seconds. Jasmine appreciated the support. Brandi was always good for hugs.

"Yes, I'm fine. Do you think I should let Misty know?" They sat down at her small kitchen table. Jasmine offered her a cup of coffee.

"Why wouldn't you?"

"I'm afraid that now Jed's injured and has been arrested, her sympathy for him will overpower her good sense."

"Do you think she'll be hurt someday to find out? Or do you think she'll be comforted knowing he's in prison?"

"Let's wait until he's convicted to tell her. I think it's better that way."

"We'll go with your instincts on this one." Brandi's brown eyes took in her new window.

"Banner arranged for that."

"Officer Banner's a nice guy." Brandi smiled knowingly at her.

"Yes. A nice guy." She took a sip of her coffee.

"Still no men on your horizon?"

"I can't go there, you know that."

"What about that guy at home?"

"This is home." The tone in her voice went low.

144

"Okay, in Bright River. Tim, wasn't it?"

"Tim's a nice guy."

"Seems like you've no end of nice guys around you."

"Seems like. Listen, you know my reasoning. It's sound. I'm not going there."

"Okay, okay." Brandi sipped her coffee. "So did burning the camper satisfy you?"

"Truth? Not as much as I'd hoped. I thought I'd have a deeper sense of closure. I'm glad we did it, for both Bill's and my sake. But I guess I have more questions than answers."

"Give yourself time." She looked around at the mess of papers on her bed. "Did Jed do all this?"

"No, Oscar did. When Jed tried to break in, Oscar gave him what for. Scared them both, I think."

"A true watch cat. Where is he?"

"Locked safely in the bathroom. You'll have to meet on another day. He's had quite a scare, and he's not friendly on his best days."

"No problem. Do you want to stay at my place tonight?"

"I'm fine. Jed's locked away, and I've got the attack cat." She smiled but knew it would be a long night.

Brandi handed her a stack of files. "There's a new candidate at the shelter. She's not local. I haven't been able to get a lot of information out of her yet. You'll probably have better luck. But she's a hard worker and has been clean for several months. The shelter thought she'd be a good fit for us."

"Okay." She laid the papers down. "Thanks for calling the cops for me."

"It's a good system. Glad it worked the first time." Brandi pulled her into another sisterly hug. "Take a couple days to get back in the swing, okay? And call me when you're ready to talk."

Jasmine pushed the door closed, locked it and sighed aloud. She opened the bathroom door, and Oscar gingerly walked out, jumped up on the bed, and pawed around at the papers there before lying down on top of them.

She poured new food into his dish and cleaned up the water spill. She finished organizing things before she heated up a frozen dinner. As she turned on her laptop and curled up on her bed to catch up with an old television show, Oscar tucked himself up next to her and she found herself petting him. "Thanks for watching out for me, Oscar." Even as she said it, she wasn't sure if it was only Oscar looking out for her today.

Nineteen

The next day Jasmine headed to the shelter, her new client file under her arm. She wore a yellow cotton shirt and comfortable jeans. Well-dressed people gained respect in most avenues, but if you showed up in a suit and heels at a shelter, you were suspect. As she entered, a settled and safe feeling covered her. It happened every time she came. This was the place, the turning point in her life. If they hadn't offered her a safe place to sleep, showers, fresh clothes and food, she'd probably have been dead by now. Or worse.

The kitchen staff waved at her as she walked by. She headed inside the main hall and saw a young black woman sitting by herself, reading a magazine. Her hair was cut close to her head, and a tattoo of an angel ran down her neck. She wore a loose-fitting sweatshirt and baggy jeans over her slender body. Jasmine walked up from behind her and cleared her throat.

"Veronica?"

The woman grunted but didn't look up at Jasmine.

"Brandi asked if I'd come and meet with you. My name is Jazz."

Veronica tipped her head, looking at her with the most skeptical look in her eyes that Jasmine had ever seen. "Jazz? What kind of name is that?"

"It's short for Jasmine."

Veronica snorted. "You're a doctor, too, like that Brandi? How come neither of you use doctor before your name?"

"People often feel more comfortable talking to the regular us than the doctor us."

She snorted again. "Whatever you say."

147

"You can call me Dr. Reynolds if you want."

Veronica lifted her eyebrow at that.

"Mind if I join you?"

Veronica looked to her left and went back to her magazine.

Jasmine sat down and opened her file.

"I see you've been clean for a few months now. How's that going?"

"Lousy."

"Why?"

"Because I still want to use."

"Like, if I offered you drugs, you'd take them?"

"You think I'm nuts? I'm not going back out on the streets. I said I want to use, not that I'm going to use. Who do you think you are, coming in here like that, offering me drugs?"

"I didn't offer you drugs. I wanted to see where you were at. I see that you've found a job too."

"Waitressing."

"You like it?"

"I'm getting used to it. People are real pigs in restaurants." She flipped the page of the magazine.

"I hear you."

"You waitress before?" She gave her another disbelieving look.

"No, I used to clean hotel rooms."

Veronica made a face. "That's gotta be way worse than food."

"Cheap hotels, too. Might be a tie. Brandi thinks you'd be a good candidate for our house."

"Live with you?"

"No, it's an apartment house Brandi keeps to help young women like you get a foot up. Do you think you can manage rent?"

"I got some money put aside. But I don't know if I'm ready." She glanced around at the place she seemed to disdain with a hint of worry. "I still need to talk to people. I still need help."

"You'll be expected to keep up on drug counseling. And you can take meals here for as long as you want."

"Where's it at? I don't have a car."

"About ten blocks from here. You can walk it, I do."

She put down the magazine and crossed her arms. "Can I

see the place?"

"Sure." Jasmine got up and started walking away. She looked back to see Veronica's wide eyes. "Are you coming?"

"You mean now?"

"Unless you're busy?" Jasmine shot a look at Veronica's magazine. Business 2.0?

"No. That's fine." She stood, towering over Jasmine. Veronica had to be five foot ten—at least. Veronica motioned toward the door. "Lead on, Doc."

Jasmine led her up the street, past the men's rescue mission, up a hill, and into a residential area. Veronica walked in silence, a woman of few words. When they arrived in the courtyard, Jasmine led her inside past the atrium.

"They got a garden?"

"I put it in. You can plant something if you like."

Veronica sniffed and turned down her mouth as if thinking it over. "That's cool."

Jasmine led her up the stairs nearest her own apartment and opened a door with her key. It was a mirror image to her place.

"It's small."

Jasmine expected that comment. But after a few minutes of opening cabinet doors and looking out the windows and running her hand over the furniture, Veronica smiled. When she did, her face lit up with a warmth Jasmine didn't expect.

"It's nice. How much?"

"Three hundred."

"A month? Three hundred? You might as well tell me three thousand. That isn't going to happen."

"No. That's the deposit. You can pay it over time, but you can't move out until it's done."

"Three hundred dollars and I can live here?"

"Until you're ready to move on. You also need to pay utilities and be putting money into a savings account for when you're ready to be on your own for good."

In the beginning, Brandi had considered letting women stay there for free, but they didn't have ownership of it and didn't grow from the experience. A free ride wasn't good for anyone.

"How much are your bills?" Veronica eyed her.

"How did you know I lived here?"

"You're real comfortable here. I bet that's your place."

She inclined her head toward the wall adjoining Jasmine's apartment. "How long you been here?"

Jasmine had to smile at her insight. "A long time. Brandi helped me get out of the shelter and onto a good path."

Veronica nodded, thinking. "You're a counselor now?"

"Yep."

"How long were you on the street?"

"Four years."

Veronica chewed on her thumbnail for a moment. "Okay."

"Okay, what?"

"I'll move in." She headed out the door and down the stairs. Jasmine locked up and joined her.

"What made your mind up?"

"You. You're honest, I like that." She smiled again, and they headed back up the street.

"How long have you been on the street?"

"Two years. My man left me here. I didn't know what else to do."

"Where did he go?"

"He got killed." She said it so matter-of-factly that Jasmine did a double take. "We were married for three years. He lost his job, and we moved here trying to find work. He got messed up with some bad dudes, and we started using. The next thing you know, he's dead."

"But you're only nineteen."

"My mom emancipated me to him. He was twenty-two. She got tired of having me around, so when I asked to get married, she said yes."

The stories Jasmine heard never ceased to amaze her. "I'm sorry you lost your husband."

"Yeah. Me too. When he wasn't using, he was a real decent man. Too bad drugs mess you up like that, right?"

"Right." Jasmine knew too well what drugs did. She'd never used, in all those years, because she couldn't afford to lose control. She'd seen Rob out of control enough to convince her of that. She had to be on guard, alert, ready to protect herself. Ready to run.

They turned the corner and were back at the shelter. "So when do you want to move in?"

"Tomorrow? I need to work tonight."

"Sounds good. Do you have a lot of stuff?"

"A couple bags of clothes."

"That's a start." Jasmine was about to say good-bye, when Veronica asked her a question that stopped her cold.

"You go to church?" Veronica narrowed her eyes at Jasmine, sizing her up.

"No."

"I go to chapel here on Sunday. You should come. I don't like sitting alone. We could walk together."

Jasmine frowned.

"What you got against God?"

"I don't have anything against God."

"Well, He sure don't have anything against you if you believe in his Son. So you should come, too. We'll come together."

Jasmine watched her walk away, past the kitchen to the dorms. Her mouth hung open.

"She's tricky," came a small voice.

Jasmine turned around to see who addressed her. A young girl played with toys at a nearby table.

"Tricky?"

"Yeah. That's how she got my mama and me to go to chapel. My mama didn't like it, but I like Sunday school. Teacher gives out cookies and tells about Jesus. I like Jesus." The young girl dressed her baby doll and left.

Jasmine headed to an empty corner and pulled out her cell phone to call Brandi.

"Hey. Veronica's on board. She'll be moving in tomorrow."

"Good. I think she'll be a good fit."

"She's an old soul." Jasmine picked at the seam of her jeans.

"Veronica's been though a lot. Oh, do you want to get together Sunday for lunch?"

"Sure. I'm not sure what time. I seem to have plans in the morning."

Brandi laughed. "She got you, too, huh?"

"What do you mean?"

"They've nicknamed her The Evangelist. She's invited more people to services at the chapel than anyone ever."

"I wish you'd have warned me." Jasmine got up and started pacing.

"Why? I've been trying to get you to go to church for years."
Jasmine sighed aloud.

"It won't kill you."

"I've already told you, Brandi, I don't like pretending."

"God doesn't want your pretending, Jazz. He wants your heart."

She sighed a second time.

"Quit all that huffing and puffing. Go once. If you feel like a liar, don't go anymore. That's it."

Could it be as easy as that? She didn't know if she was ready to feel like a liar, to wonder if God wanted her at all after everything she'd been through. After everything she'd done. Or worse, to feel nothing at all.

"I'm still thinking it over."

"Well, don't let Veronica talk to you again. Because one way or the other, she's going to get you there." Brandi laughed.

"I'm glad you find this so humorous. I'm done for the day here and will be catching up on things at home."

"Sounds good. See you Sunday."

Twenty

Jasmine shifted from one foot to the other as she waited outside the chapel, watching people enter and avoiding their glances. As she'd decided to leave, Veronica came up from behind her, blocking her way.

"Found it!" She held up her tattered Bible in victory. "I was worried someone walked off with it."

"Great." Jasmine watched more people walk past her. Some were dressed nicely; some still wore their homeless garb. Jasmine didn't know what to expect, so she'd chosen a sweater and black jeans.

"Doc, you look like a squirrel right before winter."

Jasmine's head snapped to Veronica. "What's that mean?"

"Hungry and hurried. Don't worry. Everything's going to be fine. Come on in." She put her hand out to Jasmine. Jasmine didn't take it because her hands had gone all sweaty. But she gave Veronica a smile to let her know it wasn't anything personal. Jasmine followed her inside, and they sat toward the back. The place was packed.

The worship leader stepped out and started to lead songs. Jasmine didn't know any of them, but she stood with everyone else and listened. She recognized the leader as a woman she'd helped about five years ago. The woman made eye contact with her and gave her a welcoming smile. As Jasmine looked around, she saw more and more familiar faces in the crowd. Some she knew from street corners, but she knew many of the young women from counseling sessions at the shelter.

The service was simple, one on the forgiveness of God. She didn't hear much of it; she was busy listening to the voice inside. After services were over, she tried to walk out ahead of Veronica. She didn't want to be trapped by anyone who'd recognized her. That wasn't to be. Multiple women swooped down upon her with welcoming smiles and pats on her back.

"So good to see you here, Jazz."

"I hope you come back, Jazz."

"None of us would be here without you, Jazz."

The others' comments could be dismissed as kind platitudes, but the last one surprised her. She caught the young woman's arm and pulled her aside.

"Becky?"

"Yeah?"

Jasmine leaned in closer. "What did you mean?"

"None of us girls, you know, would be in church if it weren't for you."

"I don't get it. I never told any of you to go to church." In fact, if anything, her directions to be self-reliant and independent rather went against the teachings of any churches she'd heard of.

Becky smiled at her. "But you loved us when no one else would. That's God."

Emotion choked her, but she swallowed it away. Jasmine couldn't think of anything else to say, so as Becky hugged her, she reluctantly let her, and afterward meandered out of the chapel hall and into the cafeteria where many people stood having coffee and chatting. If there was a phrase to explain how she felt, it'd be shell-shocked.

"So what did you think?" Veronica approached her with animated anticipation.

"I didn't feel like a liar," she said rather abstractly, lost in her thoughts.

"What?"

"Nothing." She cleared her voice and made eye contact with Veronica. "I think it was fine."

"Will you come again next week?"

"I don't know, but thanks for inviting me."

"Since we're going to be neighbors, we could walk together. That'd be good, wouldn't it?"

Jasmine had never been on the receiving end of such friendly manipulation before. Before she could answer, Veronica asked another question.

"Want to have lunch?" She motioned toward the kitchen where the cooks were serving up enchiladas.

"Sorry. I'm meeting Brandi. Maybe next week?"

"Sure, after church." Veronica tucked her Bible under her arm and gave her a rather triumphant grin before leaving.

Jasmine headed outside and walked toward the restaurant. Her mind whirled with ideas and emotions that were strange to her. She couldn't grasp what had changed, or what she was feeling. Inside the restaurant, she waved at the hostess, grabbed a seat at their regular table, and waited a moment for Brandi to arrive. The aroma of Italian food wafted around in the air as the servers exited and entered the kitchen. She watched the door swoosh back and forth, the busyness of servers entrancing her.

"Where are you today?"

Jasmine looked up from her glass, startled to see Brandi sitting across from her. "I'm sorry?"

"I've been sitting here a full minute and I don't think you've even said hi yet."

"Oh." When did she get there? Had Jasmine tuned out again?

"Are you okay?" Brandi's eyes narrowed in concern.

"Yeah. Let's order." Jasmine motioned to the waitress, and she ordered salad, lasagna, and an iced tea. She remembered the last time she'd had iced tea. With Tim.

"Okay, you've officially got me worried."

"What?" Her attention focused on what Brandi was saying.

"Something's up. You never eat more than a salad at lunch. And you've usually given me a rundown of new clients, suggestions for other candidates, and the weather forecast by now."

"I'm sorry. I've got a lot on my mind."

"Did Veronica say something upsetting?"

"No. Nothing like that. In fact, I really like Veronica. She's got a lot of spirit for someone who's lived through so much."

"Like someone else I know." She grinned at Jasmine.

"Thanks."

"What is it?"

"The chapel service." She paused, looking for the right words. "It wasn't what I expected."

"What did you expect?" Brandi's half-smile encouraged her to continue.

"To feel like a liar. To feel like I was a fake. That I didn't belong there."

"And you didn't?"

"No. It felt real." She picked at her newly arrived salad. "I didn't really hear much of the sermon. I was so busy trying to decide how I felt about being there I kind of missed out on that part. But the music was nice. And I saw a lot of women we've helped in the past." She loaded her fork, but didn't actually take the bite.

"That all sounds like good stuff, but you don't look happy."

"I guess confused would be a better description. I don't know what do to about it."

"Go again next week."

"Maybe." She put down her fork altogether. "Do you remember that little chatterbox, Becky?"

"Sure. How is she?"

"She seemed good. Doesn't she live on the other side of the river now?"

"Yeah, I think so." Brandi took a sip of her soda.

"So, what was she doing at the chapel at the shelter?" Jasmine pushed her salad away when her lasagna arrived, but she didn't eat that either.

"You'll have to ask her that one. What did she say to you?"

"That's the part that has me confused. She said she and many of our other clients were there because of me. Because I reminded them of God's love."

Brandi smiled.

"What's that look?" Jasmine narrowed her eyes.

"What? God works in mysterious ways. Even through reluctant ways."

"I don't see why He'd bother working though me. It doesn't make any sense." Jasmine crossed her arms.

"God uses the most unlikely vessels. Moses—he didn't want to be the leader of a people. Noah—he didn't want to spend years and years building an ark and be ostracized by his friends and neighbors. Joseph—he didn't want to be sold into slavery. But God used all of those folks to carry out His plan. Paul—one of the greatest teachers in the Bible. He persecuted

the Christians for their faith before God changed his heart."
Jasmine frowned at her. "I don't get it."
"It's not what they did; it's what God saw in them. Potential.
He used them to carry out His wondrous plans so He'd be
glorified. Who are we to say who He can and can't choose?
Only God knows what a person's full potential is. You have a
gift to love others without judgment. Do you know how rare
that is? That comes from the love of Christ, Jazz."
Reaching up to brush something from her cheek, she pulled
her hand away and saw it was wet with tears. Crying again?
She could easily count the number of times she'd cried in the
previous five years—and in the past week, she'd surpassed
that number ten-fold.
"Just because you can't see what God wants to do in your
life, that doesn't mean He's not doing it. You are loving others
for Him and not even knowing you're doing it." She reached
over and squeezed Jasmine's other hand.
"What am I supposed to do?" The sense of helplessness,
normally under strict control, rose.
"You know, the best person to talk to is God." Brandi
opened her purse and handed her a slim, ragged box.
Jasmine opened the box and found a new leather-bound
Bible with her given name engraved on the front. Near it was
an embossed flower—a Star Jasmine. She took it from its case
with care and flipped open the pages. Inside were little sticky
note tabs with verses scribbled on them.
"What's this for?" She flipped through the tabs.
"I've been saving that for you for a long time. I've marked
verses that have helped me over the years. I hope they'll bring
you comfort and give you direction."
Jasmine looked over the notes; some were quite tattered
and aged. "You've been carrying this around with you?"
"I've been waiting for the right time."
"How do you know this is it?"
"In all our counseling sessions, in all our long talks, I've
never seen you look out of control like you are now. I think
you're ready to admit you can't handle it all by yourself. I
think you're ready to find out if God really does want you
after all." She motioned toward the Bible. "Think of this as an
elaborate love letter, from your creator to you."

Jasmine flipped through the marked pages and read verses, one after another. Many of them she'd heard, but they'd never made sense to her. It was as if a light had turned on inside her head. An hour passed, then another. She asked Brandi so many questions that by the time they parted, her head was buzzing.

She slipped the Bible into her purse and headed home after lunch. She didn't even remember arriving at her apartment, but she climbed the stairs still wondering about what had happened to her that day. Inside, Oscar waited for her by his food dish with an accusing look in his eye.

"Uh oh. Did I forget to feed you? Sorry about that." She knelt down and poured out some dry kibble for him. He continued to glare. "Okay, okay. I guess you're right. That deserves wet food." She popped open a can and dumped the contents onto a small plate, placing it before him. Doing so elicited immediate purrs of appreciation, and Oscar wound his way around her legs three times before he settled in to eat. She leaned down and petted him as he ate, loving the company. She'd never realized how alone she was before. A thought played through her mind.

"You and Mom hung out a lot, I bet." She scratched his ears. "Did she ever tell you about me?" Oscar turned his golden-green eyes on her, blinked, and went back to eating. She petted him a few more times, wondering how her mother learned to live with what her father had done. Or if she ever had. Jasmine had seen a lot on the streets and knew people were capable of a great many desperate things. Instead of feeling contempt, though, compassion flooded her. She glanced at the ceiling, to a place where the younger her believed God hovered.

"God, if you see my mom up there, tell her..." She paused, not sure where to go with that. "Tell her hi for me." She got up and, making her way to the desk, laid her Bible down and pulled out a chair. Her cell phone rang. An overly stoic picture of Tim flashed on the screen, his mouth pulled into a near grimace. But his eyes held the twinkle she knew so well. She grinned. When did he get hold of her phone to do that?

"Hey."

"Hey yourself. How's life in the big city?"

Jasmine looked at her new window and her new Bible. "Interesting."

"I'm going to be in town a week from Friday for a meeting with a client. Can I take you out to dinner?"

So much for staying away from him. She seemed to be fighting a losing battle. "Sure."

"Really?"

"Why do you sound so surprised?"

"I expected more of a challenge."

"I could say no," she teased.

"No, that's fine. We'll stick with yes. You pick the place. I'll come by a bit early and you can show me around your apartment."

"It won't take that long." She glanced around her one room place.

"We'll catch up. What's a good time?"

"About five-thirty? Meet me at my office, I'll text you the address."

"Sure." Their conversation tapered off, and they were silent a moment. "Bill's doing really well. He's renamed the shop to Bright River Repairs."

"Good for him." She tried picturing the new sign. Someday, maybe Jason would want to take over. That was a family heritage she could support.

"Your sister is livid. She thinks Bill is being ungrateful."

"He hasn't told her yet?" She thought Bill would have done that by now. It'd been two weeks since she came back home.

"I guess not. I think he has to come to terms with it all before he does."

"Even when he does, I don't think she'll hear him."

"She might not."

Again the silence took over.

"Misty is working at the grocery store. I saw her yesterday. They've got her stocking shelves for now."

Jasmine smiled. "That's great. She told me she had an interview. Mrs. Craig really sticks to her word."

"Yeah, if Mrs. Craig had her way, the town would pay for college education for all the young women going through the house."

She flipped a couple pages and wondered where to start. The companionable silence drew out, and she could hear him doing something in his kitchen.

"Cooking dinner?"

"Cleaning up."

She pictured him at the sink. "I'm glad I got to see your house."

"Me, too." She heard some pots clanging. "Well, I'd better let you get back to whatever it was you were doing."

She smiled and flipped through the pages of her Bible. "I'm reading a letter."

"Enjoy."

"Thanks. See you in a couple weeks." They hung up, and she decided, as with all letters, it was best to start at the beginning.

Twenty-One

At her second chapel service, Jasmine began to relax. She had yet to feel like she was lying or pretending by being there. She kept waiting for the other shoe to drop, but so far, the experience was awakening a few good memories of attending services with Tim and his family. She never let her mind wander too far ahead, to the time her parents forbade her to continue. Or the difficult time she had explaining to Tim's parents why she couldn't go with them anymore.

It amazed her that she could fall so far, and that God's grace would still be available to her. The verse from Romans tossed in her mind. *For all have sinned and fall short of the glory of God, and are justified freely by His grace through the redemption that came by Christ Jesus.* It was a startling realization that there wasn't anything she could do to gain favor in God's eyes, but only through her acceptance of Christ as her savior could she approach Him.

As everyone in the chapel rose to their feet to sing, she smiled. Her favorite part of the service had always been worship. She loved the old hymns and the new songs. They expressed the longing she felt to connect to God, the need growing in her to understand Him better through His word, and the honor she felt at being chosen despite all she'd done wrong in her life. If she thought too hard about it, it made her dizzy.

There was still the one thing she wasn't sure about it. Her abortion. This wasn't something she spoke of with anyone. It wasn't even something she let herself think about often, but it was always there, hanging in the background. Mother's Day was the worst and her mind would play out the idea of who her child might have been. If she hadn't ended her child's life, he or she would have been eighteen. The other thought that nagged her was had she replaced her baby with these broken girls, or was she trying to make up for something?

Jasmine didn't think it was that easy. She glanced at the other young women around her, some young mothers, and realized she never wanted any of them to be forced to make that choice. It wasn't a real choice, but the clinics and laws made it sound like one.

They all sat down as the sermon started, and memories shifted in her head. She remembered when she'd found out she was pregnant, and the subsequent beating she'd gotten from Rob. He'd thrown cash at her and sent her out the door, telling her not to come home pregnant. She'd wandered around, not sure even where to go, but after flipping through a phone book, she'd found a clinic. They had taken her money and asked her to fill out a few forms. That seemed simple enough. There wasn't much in the waiting room, but it was clean—she'd been worried about that. She knew abortion was surgery, and she didn't want to get an infection.

Had that been the only thing on her mind? The pamphlets assured her it was only a ball of cells, growing and changing, but not a life yet. She'd wanted to believe them, to think it would be that simple—a quick procedure and everything would be back to normal.

It sure didn't work out that way.

The procedure wasn't quick. It hurt terribly, there were frightening noises, and right in the middle of it, she started to doubt her intentions. The doctor and his assistant were cold and unfriendly, although they gave her several forced smiles and patted her arm during the worst of it. The experience reminded her of when Rob forced himself on her. After it was over, they sent her on her way with a post-op treatment directive. As the door closed behind her at the clinic, she wondered for the first time what they would do with that mass of cells. Would they flush it, or throw it away? Had she thrown away her child?

A baby cried, nestling in her mother's arms, and Jasmine's eyes locked on her sweet round face. An ache grew in her chest that radiated out to her arms. She likened it to an amputee who had lost an arm or leg. The brain experienced phantom pains, as if it were still there. But there had never been anything there for her to hold. There never would be.

The pain on Mother's Day would never match the day she'd gone to the Oregon Museum of Science and Industry in Portland. She'd escorted a group of young girls from the shelter. They were off in all corners, having a great time, and Jasmine wandered through, keeping an eye on them. She came upon a gestation model of a baby. Around the corner was a larger display. When she walked inside the darkened vestibule, she thought for a minute that what she saw before her were models as well. But as she read on, she realized that the display boxes on the wall housed actual fetuses, real babies that had died at one stage or another of gestation. Like watching a car wreck, she couldn't look away.

Jasmine couldn't leave until she'd read each placard, and stared hopelessly in shock and shame at each specimen, each little life that had ended so prematurely. As she came to the end, a thought struck, and she hurriedly walked to the case of the nine-week-old fetus. She saw the "mass of cells" the same gestation stage her pregnancy had been. It wasn't a mass of cells. It was a baby.

She'd run from the display, turned the corner to the bathroom and barely made it before she vomited. Jasmine sat in the far corner of the handicap stall and cried until her phone rang. The girls were ready to go home, and they couldn't find her. She had pulled herself together and went out to wash her face. As she looked up into the mirror, she saw a look in her eyes, a hollowness that she'd never forget.

Someone jostled her as people moved around her, and she realized that once again, she'd missed the whole sermon. She stood on shaky legs and, instead of walking out the back, approached the worship leader. The woman had given testimony about her life the previous week. She'd been a drug addict, and she'd had an abortion. Somehow, despite her life, she'd moved on to a place where she felt she could lead worship. Jasmine wanted to know how she'd done it.

The worship leader, a Hispanic woman in her fifties wearing bright colors, turned around and saw Jasmine approaching. She smiled at first but must have noticed the grave look in

Jasmine's eyes, because her expression changed to one of seriousness.

"I'm sorry to bother you," Jasmine began.

"Sure, no problem. Have a seat."

Jasmine looked around, feeling exposed.

"Or we could go in the back, where it's more private?" The woman motioned to a door off to the side of the stage.

"That'd be nice. Thanks."

Jasmine followed her to the back of the stage, through a doorway, and found a couple upholstered chairs to sit in. The leader closed the door, and the noise and bustle from those leaving the service was silenced.

"So what can I do for you?"

Jasmine wasn't sure where to start, or even why she'd approached this woman. She'd tried to talk to Brandi before, but hadn't felt any kind of closure afterward. Why would this time be any different?

"It's about your testimony, last week."

"Yes?"

"How did you..." Jasmine paused, not sure of what she really wanted to know. "...come here and—"

"How did I ever approach God again?"

That was it. How could she approach God, knowing what she'd done—knowing He knew what she'd done? She nodded.

"It's not the same for any of us."

"Us?"

"Those of us who realize what we've done, what we can never take back."

Again Jasmine nodded. Asking for forgiveness for stealing, for doing drugs, for any of those things, paled in comparison to asking forgiveness for ending her child's life.

"And while it's not the same, we all start from the same spot. We have to believe God means it when He says that if we ask for forgiveness in Jesus's name, He will honor that request and grant us forgiveness."

"But it doesn't take it away." She knew, because she'd tried, and the ache still clung to her.

"No. The memories won't ever go away. But the intense pain and guilt will—with time."

Jasmine sat quietly with the woman. "My child would be

164

eighteen."

The woman smiled. "Mine would have been thirty-three. I might have been a grandmother by now." Tears filled her eyes, but she didn't try to hide them from Jasmine.

"Do you have other children?"

"I do. They are young adults now themselves, and they know they have an older brother or sister in heaven that they'll meet one day."

Jasmine had never thought about it like that.

"Sometimes, I pray to God and ask Him to tell my child how I miss him."

A sense of wonder and hope filled Jasmine's heart. She'd never considered that her child was anywhere, let alone in heaven.

"My asking God doesn't take away the ache I feel when I long to hold him, when I feel regret, but I know one day, I will gather him in my arms. The emptiness will end." The woman took a tissue from a nearby box and gently blew her nose.

"I can't have other children." Jasmine's shoulders slumped at her admission.

The woman reached out and took her hand, enclosing her cold fingers inside her warm palm. "I'm sorry. That can happen, much more often than they tell anyone."

They sat there like that for several minutes, together in the quiet of the small room. "I'm not sure what to do."

"Have you asked God to forgive you?"

She nodded. "Many times in the past few weeks."

"Have you forgiven yourself?"

Sobs wracked Jasmine's body. "How can I?" She swiped her tears away with her hand. "I don't deserve to heal." She'd felt that, deep down, but she'd never formed the words or let herself really think it.

"You want to be punished for what you've done."

"Shouldn't I be?" Anger swelled inside.

"How long will you punish yourself? Until you feel better? Until you never feel better?"

"I don't know." She shook her head, and tears fell onto her lap. She felt a tissue being pressed into her hands, and she wiped her nose.

"God has a plan for your life, but He can't use you to your

full potential until you accept the forgiveness He offers you."

There was that word again, potential. Brandi had used it, and now this woman.

"Why would He want me at all?"

"Because He loves you. You are a creation of the Lord, fearfully and wonderfully made. No one is worthless in His eyes."

The truth of what she said sank deep inside Jasmine. She had worth in the Lord, and He wanted her. There were very few times in her life when she'd felt wanted. Her father wanted her, but for the wrong reasons. Maybe that was why it was so hard to believe she had value to God. She'd never been of any value to her parents.

"Can I pray for you?"

Jasmine could only nod. The helpless feeling she'd worked so hard to box away escaped and filled her spirit, crushing her down.

"What's your name, dear?"

Dear. Fiona had called her dear.

She lifted her head. "My name is…Jasmine."

The woman closed her eyes. "Our Savior Jesus, we come here before You to pray for healing and for forgiveness for Jasmine. Help her to know she can approach the Father in Your name, and receive the forgiveness she so desperately needs. Help her to heal, Lord, from the pain of the abortion, from the guilt that she carries with her wherever she goes. Jesus, You are the Comforter. Come now and comfort the heart of Your dear one. She is so precious in Your sight. Help her, Jesus. Amen."

Wrenching sobs wracked her body. When she finally opened her eyes, she saw that the woman was crying with her. She leaned over and held Jasmine in a tight embrace for a few minutes, before leaning away, smiling through the tears.

"That's the first step of many. Whenever you feel your guilt well inside, whenever you feel regret build, you get to your knees and face the Savior. He will meet your needs, every time."

Jasmine nodded. "Thank you."

"Of course. We are sisters in Christ, walking with one another through the trials of this world."

"I don't even know your name."

"Charlita." When Charlita smiled, her face filled with a radiant glow, one Jasmine likened to surpassing joy.

"Thank you, Charlita."

Charlita nodded. "I was pretty sure I knew who you were. Many of the young women in the congregation credit you for their lives improving and getting off the street. You and Brandi have a wonderful ministry."

Again, the feeling of complete unworthiness washed over her. "How could I have a ministry? I didn't even like God."

Charlita gave her a slight smile. "He will be able to do so much more with you now. Wait and see." She squeezed her hand. "I have to get home and see to my family. Will we see you next week?"

"I'll be here."

"Good."

They left the small room, out into the main chapel, and found it completely empty. Lunch was well underway in the cafeteria.

"I'm sorry to have taken so much of your time."

Charlita made a clucking noise with her tongue and teeth, and shook her head at Jasmine, putting her at ease.

"This is why I share my testimony. I don't talk about it often, but when the Lord prompts my heart, I obey. Last week, he prompted my heart. Not a soul came, so I started to pray for the person." She smiled past her tears. "You were that person. Praise Him." She hugged Jasmine and left her standing in the chapel in the quiet and stillness, enveloped in a peace she'd never felt before.

Twenty-Two

Jasmine sat at her desk, staring at Veronica's file, trying her best to come up with a good scenario for her. To her right, Veronica perched on a chair, chewing on the skin around her thumbnail. Finding young women local jobs was more than a challenge. Once they were clean, their first response was often that they had to find an honest way to make money to survive. The shelter provided for their immediate needs, which often helped them see the love of Christ in action. But auxiliary programs brought in more support—the support needed to start a new life.

"So what do you have experience doing, Veronica?"

"I worked at a gas station for awhile. And I worked at a mini-mart. But I got married right away, so I didn't get much experience before we moved." She looked distressed until an idea popped into her head. "I baby-sat. And I waitressed. Until last week." She made a funny noise in her throat. "I can't believe they fired me to hire their worthless niece. All she does is sit and do her nails in the back, ignoring the customers."

"There's a job at a day care near here. They've hired our clients before. Do you think you could work there for a year?"

"A whole year?" Jasmine couldn't tell from her tone if she was happy about this idea or not.

"You need to find something you can do for an entire year, maybe more, to build up a good reputation."

A grin spread across her face. "I could do that. I like kids. I wanted kids, but that didn't work out for us." She'd stopped chewing her thumb and stared out the window at the people passing by the office. "I think I could do that for a year. Maybe

168

longer if they'd keep me."

"Do you have any references we can use for baby-sitting?"

"No. None of the people would be there anymore. They were folks in and out of the house we rented. I felt bad for their kids and took care of them while they were using."

"Were you using at the time?" That wouldn't work for much of a reference if she had.

"No. That didn't happen until later."

"Okay. Well, I'll try to spin it a bit, but basically they'll have to hire you on first impressions. We'll have to see." Jasmine typed up a letter of reference for her.

The door to the office opened and closed, and someone approached her desk and cleared their throat. Jasmine didn't look up, as she was typing away at Veronica's letter of reference. She wanted to get it done today, and get Veronica an interview before the job was taken by someone else.

"Please take a seat; I'll be with you in a minute."

"Sure." The familiar voice made her fingers freeze on the computer keys. She glanced up and saw Tim sitting down in the small reception area. Somehow, he looked even taller than he had the last time she'd seen him. She could hardly believe it had only been three weeks ago.

"He's hot." Veronica's whisper broke through her surprise.

Jasmine's eyes snapped to Veronica's face and saw her checking Tim over.

"Who is he? I'd work for him."

"He's a good friend. And a lawyer."

"He your man?" Veronica turned her gaze back to Jasmine.

"No." Jasmine felt her neck go hot.

Veronica turned back to her. "Does he need office help?"

"Uh, no, I don't think so. He works for a firm out of town. Okay, back to you. Here." She leaned back and took the page she'd printed from the printer and handed it to Veronica. "Tell me what you think."

Veronica read it over a couple times. "You mean all that?"

"Sure I do. You're a very smart woman. You're outgoing and motivated. I mean, you got me, of all people, to go to church. I think you'd do a wonderful job at the day care."

Veronica's eyes held a sort of wonder. Jasmine had seen it many times before. When someone finally believed in these girls, it made such a huge impact on them. Often, no one had ever told them anything good about themselves before. Reading it in print had a big effect on them.

"Thanks."

Holding out a slip of paper, Jasmine gave Veronica directions to the day care. "I want you to go home, put on something conservative and head over there today before someone else applies. If they need to, they can call me directly on my cell. I put that on the letter."

"No mini skirt?" Veronica pulled at the legs of her baggy sweatpants.

"No. Jeans and a nice top will do fine."

"Okay. Thanks." Veronica stood up and headed past Tim, giving him a long look. Tim's eyes locked on Jasmine's, his eyebrows up and that deer-in-the-headlights look all over his face. She grinned. Tim had no idea how good looking he was, or how kindness surrounded him like an aura. She motioned to him to come over, and he took Veronica's seat.

"What was that about?"

"She thinks you're hot."

He straightened his coat. "I get that a lot."

Jasmine snorted and checked her watch. "Hey, you're an hour early."

"I got done early and thought I'd chance it." He glanced around the office and took in the size and used miss-matched furnishings. "This is nice. I pictured something a bit more offbeat."

"Not us." She pulled on her jacket and called to Brandi, who was nose down in a file, taking notes. When Brandi didn't answer, Jasmine smirked and picked up the phone. It rang on Brandi's desk. She picked it up.

"This is Brandi."

"Brandi, this is Jasmine. Do you think I could leave a bit early today?"

Brandi sat up straight and looked surprised then began to laugh before she hung up the phone. "Showing off all our technology?" She stood up, walked over, and held out her hand to Tim.

"Sorry about that. I'm Brandi Monroe, you must be Tim."

Tim stood and took her hand. "Nice to meet you."

Jasmine could see Brandi sizing Tim up as well. Not in the same way Veronica was, but in more of a sisterly way.

"If you'd like to get out of here early, I think that'd be fine. In fact, I might pack it in early, too." She smiled at Jasmine and headed back to her desk.

"Well, that's settled. Want to show me where you live, and we'll head to dinner?"

"Okay." Jasmine turned off her computer and grabbed her purse. Tim was being overly congenial. She couldn't put her finger on it, but something wasn't quite right. They headed out of the office and up the street, toward her place. As they did, they passed several groups of homeless men and women. Many of them nodded to Jasmine.

"You have quite a following, huh?"

"No child looks at a homeless person and decides that's what they'd like to be when they grow up, but sometimes we don't have a choice. Sometimes, we have to get away."

"I know." His voice softened.

"It doesn't take much. Acknowledge them as human beings, and you are a step ahead of the rest of the human race." She hadn't meant for her tone to sound angry, but it did.

He put his hand on her arm to stop her. "You know I didn't mean anything like that. Did you have a hard week?"

She glanced sidewise at him. "In some ways, but it didn't have anything to do with my job." They walked along in silence, passing by more and more businesses until they crossed the street into a residential part of town. She came to a halt in front of her building.

"This is it." She opened the gate, and he followed her inside, past the garden, up the steps to her place. Once inside, she moved some things from one of the chairs and invited him to sit down. She'd always been happy with her place, but now, it was as if she saw it through his eyes. It was very small for company. Of course, besides Brandi, the repairman and Misty's criminal boyfriend, she'd never had any.

"I like it. It suits your needs, and you." She could tell he was being diplomatic. It didn't matter—what would she do with a whole house to herself? And Oscar.

"Thanks." She glanced back into the kitchen alcove. "Can I get you something to drink? Juice or water?"

"No, I'm fine. Listen, I have something I wanted to talk with you about before we went to dinner."

Jasmine's shoulders tensed, she knew something was up. She sat down across from him in her other chair. She'd hoped they would be on friendly terms tonight, and not pushing the relationship issue again.

"Okay."

Reaching inside his coat, Tim pulled out a package and handed it to her. Her eyebrows pinched together as she opened it, and recognition dawned on her face. Her journal.

"I had it repaired."

"You let someone read this?" The tension in her voice rose.

"Well, no. I mean, I repaired it. I did my best to mind my own business."

She flipped through the pages, meticulously taped and glued back together, before setting it aside. "I'll look at it later; do you want to go now?" She could tell from his expression that she hadn't given him the reaction he'd expected. "What?"

"I sort of thought you'd want to read it."

"I will."

"Today."

"Why? Do you want to have our dinner plans ruined?" Jasmine got up and put down more food for Oscar, who came sauntering out of the bathroom and gave Tim a cursory growl.

"No. I thought I'd be here for you while you read it. I don't think you should do it on your own."

"Why?" She started to get more suspicious.

"Because, well, it's probably hard stuff. Emotional stuff."

She could almost feel the walls she'd torn down rebuilding themselves. He had no business doing this, friend or not.

"I'll deal with it how I like, when I'm ready. I'm not ready. Quit pushing me." She grabbed a glass from the cabinet and got some water. She knew what was right for her, not him.

"I'm not pushing."

"The heck you aren't. You pushed me to come to Bright River with your official letter. You pushed me to tell Bill about our father. You came here early on purpose. I don't know what you expected, but I'm not into group therapy. I don't want anyone around when I go through my journal. Least of all you." She hadn't meant the last part, but he had her back up, and suddenly all she wanted him to do was leave.

"I'm sorry. I overstepped." He put up his hands in defeat. "I was with you when you found this, and I got the idea you'd want to read it with a friend nearby to lean on. I was wrong." He stood and straightened his coat. "I should probably go now." He headed out the door and started down the stairs before she realized he was leaving. She raced to the stairs.

"Where are you going?" She didn't want him to leave.

"I've got a long drive ahead of me."

"So that's it? You show up, expect me to spill my guts, and when I'm not willing, you turn tail?"

He pulled up sharp and stared up at her. "Turn tail? I'm not the one who left town before she had to. I'm not the one who hasn't called her family since she left. I'm not the one who hasn't called her friend even once to tell him not to worry. I'm not the one hiding from my past. You are."

Anger built inside her with each sentence, each word. "You've got no right." She started down the stairway toward him.

"I get that now, real clear. No worries. I'll keep my friendship to myself from now on." He met her eyes, challenging her. She knew if she said one more thing, there'd be very little chance of going back. She swallowed her anger, facing the truth. She didn't want to lose his friendship, not when she'd gotten it back after all these years. She was never one to back down, but there was a lot to lose here.

"You need to stop pushing me, Tim. I'll do this when I'm ready."

"It's always about you, right? What about me? I drove all the way here to be here for you." He groaned. "You act like it's the worst thing in the world to depend on someone else, Jasmine. Friendship is a two way street. You've got to let someone in some time."

Jasmine heard the reason in his argument. And she didn't want him to leave like this. Maybe he was right. She probably shouldn't be alone when she read it.

"I'm sorry."

His eyebrows knit together in confusion. "What?"

She almost laughed at his surprise. "I'm sorry. You're right, I'm wrong, and I'm really hungry. Can we at least order in?"

She turned around and headed back up the stairs. "Are you coming?"

"I'm not sure. Are you going to sic Oscar on me?"

"I might."

"Okay then." He followed her back inside and sat down again. She picked up the phone and ordered Chinese takeout. "We'll have to pick it up in about forty minutes."

"No delivery?"

"If you want to add twenty dollars to the order. Or we can walk about two blocks down and save the twenty bucks."

"Saving money is a good thing."

She sat back down and looked at the diary. She had no idea what was inside, or if she really wanted to read it. Glancing at him, she saw him chewing the side of his lip.

"Why is this so important to you?" She really couldn't figure out why he felt so pushy about the whole thing.

His shoulders sagged as if under a great weight. "I guess I feel like everyone deserves to know themselves, to claim their past, even if it's not what they want it to be. You seemed so lost when you were back home. All these people knowing you, and you not knowing them at all. I guess I hoped that something in there would click with you and give you back some of what you'd lost all those years ago."

"What I gave away, you mean?"

"What was stolen, I mean." Tim's voice deepened in anger as he drew himself up and she knew she never wanted to be on the opposing side of any court battle.

"Oh." She picked up the book and brushed her hand across it. The mildew smell was missing, having been replaced by a vanilla-scented deodorizer. "Did you have it professionally cleaned?"

"I did. And they didn't read it either."

He'd gone to a great deal of trouble to preserve her past. Something she had never done. Did she even want it all back? God was taking her down many detours the past few weeks, and she'd been facing some pretty hard things. The thing was, she didn't know if she was able to do this.

"You'll stay, no matter how long this takes?" Having been comfortable with being solitary, she was in a strange and foreign land not wanting to be alone for this.

"I've got a few days off."

He was a good friend. The best she'd ever had, besides Brandi. It was like with Veronica all over again. Only this time, she was the one hearing she was worth it.

"Okay." She took a deep breath, flipped open the front cover, and started to read.

Twenty-Three

The beginning of her journal held the innocent stuff of a young girl's dreams, daily events and happenings. But as she read on, she could see in between the lines. She often spoke of wishing she could disappear. Of wishing she'd never been born. Of wishing for different parents or circumstances. Of fear.

"I sure spent a lot of time being afraid." When her childhood passed quickly through her mind as an adult, she'd seen herself as a tough tomboy with a smart remark at the ready and fists balled, prepared to fight. But that's not what the dairy held.

"You had a right to be."

"Did you ever think I was afraid?"

"No."

Nodding, she flipped through more pages. Christmas came and went, and once again she was slipped unexpected and unwanted gifts from her father. She would find them under her bed. One time she got the courage to ask him why, and he told her it was because she was special. She'd never told her brother or sister, because she didn't want them to feel bad, but also because she was beginning to understand their true meaning, and she didn't want them to find out. She didn't want anyone to find out how "special" she was.

"I mention giving Elsie my Christmas present." Elsie was in her diary, as much as Tim was—why couldn't she remember her? Jasmine flipped several more pages before stopping. This entry held a poem. The pages were warped, but not from damage or repair. It had been from tears.

Closing the journal, she went and stood next to the window,

176

looking out through the bars. The timer went off on the microwave. "Dinner's ready."

Tim moved to the door. "Two blocks down?"

"I'll go with you. Can't have you getting lost." She glanced over her shoulder at the closed diary. The last thing she wanted was to be alone in her apartment with it. Jasmine grabbed her coat, and they headed to the Chinese restaurant for their takeout. They arrived at the restaurant, paid for their meal, and were back in her apartment before she realized they'd left. She knew this fog.

"Are you okay?"

"I feel myself slipping away. I used to tune out, sometimes for hours."

He brought her plate over to her. "Don't worry, I won't let you go far." He scooped up a forkful of food and held it out to her. She ate a few bites, continuing to look out the window, her thoughts askew.

"Can I read the poem?"

Wincing, she nodded her consent. She heard the pain in his voice and knew this cost him, too.

"Betrayer. Liar. Hider. Sneaker.

All of these I am. All of these you made me.

Daughter. Friend. Trustworthy.

All of these things I was. All of these you stole from me.

Give it back. Take it back. Save me.

All of these things I beg of you. All these things you keep from me."

Tim looked up at her, uneasy. "Do you remember writing this?"

She nodded.

"When?"

"One night, when my mom came looking for him. For some reason. I don't know. I don't remember what happened when she walked in and saw him. I had my face hidden, I was crying. I heard her voice, full of hate. I thought she hated me. I stayed at Elsie's for several days after that. When I came home, she gave me the key. I thought she was throwing me out."

"You remember staying with Elsie?" Excitement rose in his voice.

"I do. Isn't that funny? I remember the white bed and the

177

scented hangers. Not much else." She shook her head, hoping for more but coming up empty. An idea formed in her head. She did remember this, clearly now, and she was beginning to understand why Elsie was boxed in a special way from everything else.

"And then you wrote the poem?"

"I think I finally felt free to write my feelings down, if he couldn't read them. They were private thoughts, my own feelings. Up until then, I wasn't allowed to feel anything about what was happening."

"What do you mean?"

"He didn't want the guilt. When I locked him out, he had to face what he'd become. He didn't stop being that man though. He just stopped hurting me." Until one night he'd rattled the door handle until she thought it'd break off. That was when she knew the key wasn't enough.

Tim's eyes held a dark expression. "I need to go for a walk." He got up and headed out, walking down the street past her window. She thought she heard him talking to himself.

Jasmine lay down on her bed, pulling her pillow to her chest with one hand, the journal up with the other. She continued to delve into her past. Some entries she read like a friend, some like a counselor, some like a sister. This girl, this sad, alone, damaged girl exposed on the pages before her needed her.

The cupboard opening and closing, the sound of a metal lid being pulled from a can of cat food, woke her from her nap. The journal, closed, lay in front of her; a blanket had been pulled up over her. It was dark outside.

She rubbed her eyes, focusing on Tim's back at the counter, silhouetted in the light over the stove. "You came back."

"I needed some air."

"Sorry you lost me. I don't remember falling asleep." She sat up on the bed and watched Tim feed Oscar his supper. "Canned food is for special events."

"I'm especially trying to bribe him." He lifted a hand as if to pet Oscar but pulled back, changing his mind. Oscar ignored him and kept eating.

"Mmm. Good luck with that." She stretched and peeked at the clock. Midnight. "Wow, where'd the night go?"

"You needed to sleep."

"I guess so." She saw him stretch his back and pop his neck. "Do you have a hotel?"

"Do you want me to leave?"

"No." She snuggled down in the blanket, trying to remember when she last felt so exhausted, and fell back to sleep. When she awoke six hours later, she saw Tim sprawled on the floor, a blanket over him, his coat wrapped up for a pillow and Oscar at his back. Progress for Oscar.

As she tiptoed past him on the way to the bathroom, she caught a glimpse of the boy she knew in his features. She trusted that boy, and now the man he'd become. He'd given her reason to. She knew she held back from people until they'd shown her proof they could be trusted. She didn't mean to. Everyone was suspect until they'd passed a waiting period.

After her shower, she came out to the sounds of cooking in the kitchen. The blanket Tim had used lay folded neatly on the chair, and his coat hung over the arm.

"Tonight, you can have the bed, I'll take the floor." She sat in the other chair, watching him cook.

Oscar wrapped his furry form around his legs, first one way, then the other. "But Oscar will miss me." He grinned down at the cat, and she thought she saw him wink conspiratorially.

"What's for breakfast?" Something smelled wonderful.

"Omelets. Best I could do—you don't exactly have breakfast food filling the shelves."

"I'm not a breakfast kind of gal. I like leftovers for breakfast."

"You said you mostly eat salads. You eat old salad for breakfast?" He stuck his tongue out.

"Or a bagel."

"Ick." He plated their food and brought it to the table with a flourish. "Madam."

"Very professional."

"Worked my way through college waiting tables and even subbed as a short-order cook."

"Wow. I'm keeping you around." She said it without thinking, but if he heard her, he didn't show it. She quickly took a bite before her mouth betrayed her again.

They ate in silence, and she watched him clean up before speaking. "I finished the diary."

"I wondered if you had. How do you feel?"

"It's hard to put into words. I'm glad you brought it, but I think I'll have to read it again at another time, too. There's so much there in between the mundane things." There were nuances to understanding a teenage girl's mind—even if it was her own.

"I think I know why I've blocked so much about Elsie now." Tim's eyes widened. "Go on."

"Jealousy." She put up a hand before he could interrupt her. "She had two parents who loved her. Her father really was a good man—he didn't pretend to be one for the public. That's why I felt so relieved whenever I gave her my toys—she really did deserve nice things. But at the same time, I wanted to be her—sometimes so bad it hurt." She held up the diary. "I couldn't resolve those feelings, so I forgot them."

Tim got up and hugged her. "I wish I'd known."

"You couldn't have done anything. I still would have run away. Reading this solidified that in my mind. If you'd found out, it'd have been quicker is all."

He sighed in frustration and sat back down. "Did it bring back any good memories at all?"

She shook her head. "Isn't that nuts? I wrote mostly good things in there. But when I read them, it's like they happened to someone else. If it weren't for the names, and the bad experiences sprinkled here and there, I don't think I'd even realize that was my diary."

"I was hoping you'd remember more." There was something in his voice she couldn't read.

"I know. How much does it suck that all I can remember are the bad things from my childhood?" She had started to say it as a joke, but her voice cracked, and with it released some of the pent-up emotions inside. She got up and paced.

"You will." He sounded more sure than she felt.

"I think I know why I can't remember other people or events very well, though."

"What'd you figure out?"

"You know that night, standing on the bridge before I threw my bike over?"

Tim sat taller. "Yeah?"

"I thought about throwing me over, too. I considered it for

a few seconds. One jump and it'd be all over. But there was a stronger part of me that wanted me to go on living. So I threw my bike and decided everything was new. I walked away from it all, and my head did a pretty spectacular job of shutting down everything else."

"Too bad you don't have that key."

"Maybe one day I will." An edginess built inside her, and she itched to get out of that room and get some fresh air. She wrapped and unwrapped her arms across her chest.

"Are you all right?"

"No. I'm not all right." Jasmine grabbed the journal and held it up to him. "She's a stranger to me."

"Give it time."

Heat crept up her throat, and Jasmine put up a hand to hide it. "Let's get out of here, okay?"

"Sure." They grabbed their coats and headed out into the early spring morning. "Where are we headed?"

"I know a place. It's peaceful."

A twenty-minute drive later, they were entering the Japanese garden. There were clusters of people here and there, but it wasn't very crowded. She flashed her membership card, and they wandered about the pristine greenery, down pea-gravel lanes, past small maples and giant conifers. The cherry trees were ending their bloom; loose soft petals rode the breeze and swirled around them like pink snowflakes. Jasmine took a deep breath of the floral and evergreen-scented breeze and relaxed, feeling the strain of the last few days begin to leave her system.

They walked in silence down to a large koi pond and sat on a bench facing a twenty-foot-high waterfall tripping and trickling over bright green ferns and moss-covered rocks. Lily pads shifted with the passing of huge coral, white, and yellow spotted koi.

"It's beautiful here." Tim took in their surroundings.

"I come here when I need to clear my head." A group came by pointing to the fish and taking photos. They moved on, and she relaxed even more.

"People make you tense."

She smiled halfway. "I suppose they do. I've been on my own for so long, being around others is stressful, even if they are nice others."

"I hope my being here doesn't stress you out."

She thought a moment. "No, you don't." Now that Tim had quit pursuing her, she actually felt like she could be herself around him. He'd always been the one person she could feel at ease with. He reached over and caressed her cheek. Leaning into his hand, she saw his eyes darken, wanting. Her breath caught as she moved away.

So much for that idea.

"I'll stay at my hotel tonight. It's paid for, and I'm pretty sure the hotel bed will be better for me." He rubbed his hand over the back of his neck.

Jasmine tried to lighten the mood. "That's probably best. I think sleeping on my floor another night would give Oscar the wrong idea."

Tim's eyes locked with hers.

"What do you do on Sunday?"

She'd forgotten today was a Saturday. Last night blurred her sense of time in more than one way. "Actually, I've been attending a church service lately."

That got his attention.

"Could we go together?"

"Do you think you'd feel comfortable? It's at the shelter's chapel."

"Sure, why not?"

"Homeless people."

"I'm not afraid of homeless people."

"Good thing."

Rising, they walked through the garden and found another secluded spot with a bench overlooking the sand and stone garden. The lack of color mixed with intentional pattern and texture changes in the rocks brought another kind of peacefulness. The gardens were a blend of complements and contrasts.

"So how is Misty doing?"

Tim shifted in his seat, taking longer than she thought he should to answer. "She's fine."

"What's up?"

"What?"

"You're chewing your lip. You only do that when you're

trying to find the right thing to say, or thinking too hard."

His teeth released his lip. "She's having a hard time making a decision about the baby."

"I thought she was pretty sure she'd keep it."

"Her emotions and logic are fighting with each other. She's got an opportunity to go to school and finish her education. But she doesn't think she could do that with a baby. She'd miss out on the first four years of its life; it'd be in day care. At the same time, she feels a closeness to the baby."

"I hope she makes the right choice."

"What would you have done?"

Her stomach knotted at his question. She'd made another choice altogether. At least both of the choices Misty pondered would honor her child's life.

"I'm the wrong person to ask." Jasmine got up and walked down the wood plank way to the next section of garden. She paused at an overlook to take in the view of the city below. From up there, everything looked clean and clear. Down in the middle of it all, people were struggling and making choices every day, choices they might later regret.

"I didn't mean to upset you."

"I was pregnant once." She wasn't sure why she chose that very moment to divulge something so private.

"Oh."

"I didn't choose either of the options that Misty has." She swallowed hard. "I'll regret that until the day I die."

Tim put his arm around her. "I'm sorry you were put in a position where you didn't feel like you had another choice."

"That's the easy way out." She pulled away from him.

"What?"

"Making an excuse for me like that. I chose wrong. But I've done my best to share with every girl in Misty's condition that they really do have choices, and none of them have to entail killing their child." She heard the vehemence in her voice and felt her face and neck flush. "I'm sorry."

Tim shook it off. "The other reason I'm in Portland is to look into an adoption option for Misty."

"What?"

"I was sent to interview a perspective parent."

"You mean parents?"

"Well, right now there's only one."

"Well, I hope you give them the once over." Thinking about Misty's baby created a sense of protection in her.

"I will. Trust me." He chewed his lip again.

"Spill it."

"That's really unfair." He rubbed his lip, hiding it with his fingers.

"I'd suggest never playing poker with me, either."

"I'm not sure how to approach this."

Jasmine hated when people hedged. "You aren't winning bonus points with me here."

He stopped pacing. "Is that what I've been doing?" He grinned at her, hope sparkling in his eyes.

"It's an expression. If you don't want to tell me, don't." She shrugged and stared out at the city skyline.

"She wants you."

Jasmine had heard plenty of things that had shocked her over the years, but this one beat out the others by far.

"What do you mean?"

"She wants you to adopt the baby."

"Why in the world would she want that? I can't raise a baby!"

Tim's head hung low for a moment. "I was afraid you'd say that."

"Of course I'd say that. Is she nuts? I barely have a private life. There's no room in it for another person, let alone an infant. And don't get me started on my apartment."

"I thought you liked your life and your apartment."

"I like it for me. There's no room for a child. I'm no parent. Trust me. I have no right to even hope to be a parent."

"Why not?"

She rolled her eyes at him.

"I mean besides the small apartment and demanding job. You have a lot of patience and compassion, why couldn't you raise a child?"

"Great, you're nuts too." She stormed off, not caring if he followed her.

"Jasmine, wait."

She heard his footsteps grinding on the gravel to catch up with her, but she didn't slow down.

"Where are you going?"

"Away from you."

"Why are you mad at me?"

She spun around on him. "You pick this weekend, when I'm going through a difficult time, to bring me that journal. So I gave in and did the memory lane thing. Now you follow it up with how Misty wants me to adopt her baby. What kind of friend are you?"

He grabbed her arms. "I'm someone who cares about you. I'm someone who thinks that no matter how you feel about it, you deserve a second chance at happiness in life."

Her brows furrowed. "And being saddled with someone else's baby will help me how?"

"Misty needs your help, and I remember you used to want kids."

Wrenching out of his grasp, she stormed away, yelling at him over her shoulder. "You know, it really ticks me off that you remember more about me than I do."

Twenty-Four

As Jasmine got ready for church, she heard a knock on her door. Opening it, she found Tim on the other side, looking hopeful.

"I thought you'd left."

"Church, remember?"

She narrowed her eyes at him. He wore a cable-knit sweater and jeans. At least he hadn't overdressed. After she'd stormed up her steps last night and slammed the door in his face, she hadn't expected to see him. A huge part of her hoped she wouldn't.

"I'll be out in a minute."

"I'll be here." He turned and walked down her steps, sitting on the last one.

Part of her felt guilty for treating him badly last night, but the other part was still angry at him. No, angry wasn't the right word. She took a deep breath to clear her thoughts, gave Oscar a pat and joined Tim downstairs. He gave her a hopeful smile that she didn't return.

Livid. That was the word.

She swallowed it down. It was Sunday, after all.

They walked the few blocks in silence until they arrived at the shelter. She expected Tim to feel uncomfortable, but he didn't seem to. He nodded to those who appeared friendly, and didn't take offense from those who glared suspiciously. They entered the chapel together and found a seat in the middle.

"Hey, Jazz. You recruiting now, too?" Veronica came around and sat next to them. "Oh, it's you." Her eyes lit up when she recognized Tim. "How you doing?"

"Hi, Veronica. Good to see you." He put his hand out to her. Veronica took it and giggled.

Jasmine frowned, moving closer to Tim. "He's visiting."

Veronica gave her a sideways, knowing glance. "Oh sure. Visiting. I come here to visit all the time." She gave them both a grin and motioned for Jasmine to come closer as she whispered in her ear. "Don't worry, hands off. You make a cute couple."

Jasmine's mouth dropped open, but the music started before she could respond. Jasmine offered to share her hymnal with Tim, but he didn't need it. Of course he knew all the right words. Jasmine tried to let go of whatever was eating at her and enjoy her favorite part of the service, but the more she listened to Tim sing, the more his voice resonated near her, the more the unpleasant feeling grew. She suddenly wished she'd never mentioned her attending church to him, let alone inviting him along.

The pastor took the stage and introduced an older man. He appeared ragged, but clean—and very nervous.

"Mike wants to share about his life."

Mike took a spot central to the stage. He nodded to everyone. "I don't know why I'm up here, talking to you, but it felt like something I was supposed to do. Pastor Jim said sometimes God nudges our hearts. Maybe that's what He's doing to mine." He lifted a shaky hand and ran it over his beard.

"A lot of years ago, another life ago, I survived an abusive home. Just when I thought I was free of it, it caught up to me. My dad would go on a binge and beat us and such. When I was about ten I drank one of my dad's beers. I noticed the calming effect it had on me. When I drank, his beatings didn't seem so awful, you know? By the time I was fourteen, I was a full-fledged alcoholic." He gave a ragged cough, and the pastor handed him a cup of water.

"I left home and never looked back. I got a good job and found a beautiful girl and married her. But I never stopped drinking. Things were fine until the kids got old enough to mouth back at me, and this rage" —he choked on his words— "built in me. I didn't know where it came from. I hit my son." He wiped at his eyes. "I started to beat my wife and sons, and I felt justified when I did it, but I'd go and throw up afterward.

See, I knew, deep down, I'd become the one I wanted to run away from my whole life. My dad, he'd taken up residence in me, and I'd never even seen it happen."

A sob built and broke. The pastor came and put a hand on his shoulder. "So I left 'um. I ran away. It was the most loving thing I could make out to do. Now that I'm sober, have been for four years, and have a job, I went looking for them. They needed to hear how sorry I was." At this point, his eyes locked on a woman in the crowd. "My oldest son, he doesn't want to talk to me yet, but my wife is giving me a second chance."

Jasmine watched the woman take the stage and put her arms around him, tears streaming down her face. A knot of anger twisted in Jasmine's gut.

"I'm in counseling, and I might be for the rest of my days. And I'm not moving back in yet, not for awhile, maybe not ever. I'm leaving that to God, because nothing's too big for Him, but I'm an awful broken man." He pulled his wife into his arms. "I wanted to thank you all for praying for me. I didn't deserve it, but He's given me a hope. Thanks for showing me God's love."

The audience was on their feet, cheering. Tim rose and clapped his hands, but Jasmine stayed in her seat. As the pastor dismissed them, Tim put his hand out to her to follow him. She did but didn't take his hand. People milled outside, drinking coffee and eating donuts. Veronica caught up with them.

"Wow, now that's something. What can't God do?" She clapped a friendly hand on Jasmine's shoulder, making Jasmine jump.

"You okay, Doc?"

"Sure, I'm fine. Thanks." Jasmine lifted her cup to take a sip of coffee and saw it shaking in her grip. She knew Tim saw it, too.

"How about lunch? It'd be my pleasure to take both you ladies."

"I never turn down a free meal." Veronica laughed. "Let me get my coat."

"I'm not very hungry." Jasmine set the cup back on the table.

"Well, come along anyway. I have to leave in a couple hours. And I don't want to be alone with Veronica." He winked at her, trying to make light of the situation. He always did that. Even when they were kids, he'd spin whatever was going on to the happy edge, to an uplifting moment. She didn't have the talent to pretend like that. Pretending made her sick to her stomach.

"I said I wasn't hungry." Jasmine pulled on her jacket and headed out of the building, up the block. She heard running footsteps behind her, and then a hand touched her shoulder. She wrenched away, grabbing his hand, twisting up. It was all instinct, so much a part of her, it never went away.

Tim wrenched out of her grasp. "Ow. Hey, what was that?"

Her hands shook, all the way up to her shoulders, down into her stomach. Every once in awhile, she lost control and fear took command. At least she hadn't hit him this time. Instead of owning up, she acted angry.

"Don't sneak up on me."

"I didn't sneak, I called to you. I came up here running and puffing." His face carried several layers of hurt.

"That's it." It all made sense to her now.

"What's it?"

"Me. I can't get away from me. That man, he got away from his family, but he was still who he was. Even now, his wife should run like hell. He'll never get away from who he is, who his dad made him into." She shoved her shaking hands into her pockets.

"You don't believe that. You give young women hope every day of a new, brighter future."

"Maybe it's false hope." She turned away from him, past crowds of shoppers, the homeless on the sidewalk begging for cash, groups of rough, tattooed kids. She pressed on until she got to the park and collapsed on a bench. As she felt his presence sit down next to her, she groaned.

"You don't take a hint very well, do you?" She wanted to be alone.

"Hint?"

"For a lawyer, you're kind of slow. I keep walking away."

"And I keep following." He took her hand. "I'm here for you, Jasmine."

She pulled away from him. "But I don't want you to be. I want everything to go back to being the way it was two months ago. I want to get up every morning and go to work, and come home and eat dinner and go to bed and do it all over again the next day. I don't want to think about myself, or who I've become, or what I've lost." She swallowed back the emotion building in her throat.

"And my being here does that?" He pulled his hands together in his lap and slumped on the bench.

"Your contacting me did that. I'm sorry, but it's true."

"Knowing you have friends and family who love you, that's a bad thing?"

"Yes," she admitted in a whisper.

They sat there in silence for a long time. Across the lawn a squirrel darted back and forth, foraging and fighting off the jays for his store of food. Most everyone in the park walked by, missing the conflict.

"I'm sorry I can't be who you want me to be." She didn't look at him when she said it.

"Wait a minute. Who do you think I want you to be?"

Turning her head, she attempted a slight smile in his direction. "You want me to be that girl again. You want me to be happy and carefree. But I was never her. Never. You made her up in your head."

"That's not what I want."

"You want me to love you."

"I want us to be friends again. I've missed you my whole life. You were the one who always understood me."

"We all want that to a point." She dismissed his feelings with a wave of her hand.

"You don't. You don't want anyone to try to understand you. You want to be left alone."

"It's easier that way, Tim." She shook her head. "It's ironic, though. I can't go back to living in isolation. As much as I want to. There's this gaping hole in my life now."

"That I put there."

"Yes." That was it. He'd put his finger right on the sore spot and pushed. "I think that's why I feel so resentful toward you. You keep holding up who you thought I was, and I keep screaming that she was a lie. She never existed. But you aren't hearing me." She took in his crestfallen face. "Please hear me, Tim."

190

"So that's it then." He leaned over, still clasping his hands, arms resting on his knees. "I'd hoped..." His voice trailed off. He glanced to the side. "Fine. I'm going to go, but you need to hear something first."

He would leave. She wouldn't see him again, and that'd be for the best. Nothing he'd say would matter. She'd let his words come and go and not keep them with her. She waited.

"I want to tell you who you are."

She took a deep breath, willing herself to block out his words, not to listen.

"You are the same person you were when we were kids. You haven't changed. Your circumstances changed. How you look at things changed, but the core of you, it's the same. You love deeply, but you don't want anyone to know. You are compassionate to a fault for those who are hurt. You are trustworthy, and although you've let yourself down a lot—you don't let those girls down, ever. When we were kids, you were the first person I'd turn to for advice. You kept my secrets, shared in my confidences, and cheered me when I tried and failed."

Despite telling her subconscious to block her ears, she was hearing every word. And each one cut her, chipping away at the hard exterior she had spent years building around her heart.

"You've been used, mistreated, abused beyond belief, and you survived. I'm sure sometimes you didn't want to, but I think God has a plan for you, something you haven't even thought of yet. I hope you don't shut Him out when He's getting your attention. That, more than anything else in your life, would be a loss you will not get over. You don't want to be around me, fine, I get that. You don't want to be around your family, I get that too. The memories are painful and hard to deal with. The loss of memory even more so. But don't you dare shut out God now that He's got your attention."

The demanding tone in his voice caught her by surprise. She locked eyes with him.

"Promise me, Jasmine." His eyes were pink from unshed tears.

"What?" Her voice croaked.

"That you'll pray and listen to Him. That you won't shut Him out."

Before she realized what she was doing, she nodded. "I promise."

Tim paused, taking a deep breath. "I'll miss you." He pulled her into his arms and held her. She'd never felt so safe, so protected in her life. Tears spilled down her face, onto his jacket. She could hear his ragged breathing as he held back his emotions.

"If you ever need me, you know where I am." He kissed the top of her head, pressing his lips against her hair, breathing her in. After giving her another squeeze, he let her go.

Emptiness surrounded her as she watched him walk away. It wrapped around her, bound her feet, wheedled into her chest. He didn't look back, he didn't waver in his steps. He was gone.

Instead of the relief she'd imagined she'd feel once he was out of her life, she felt more miserable and lost than ever.

Twenty-Five

The next few months passed in a stumbling haze of incessant phone calls and piles of paperwork growing exponentially. September was half over, and colder days were on the way. The girls who thought it'd be a good idea to run away from home in the summer were figuring out life wasn't all they'd dreamed it could be on the streets. A select few would outlast the heat, and by winter they'd be in pretty poor shape. Anyone could survive on the streets in temperate weather, but when the temps dropped, they'd see another story.

"You doing okay?" Brandi's voice broke into the haze of her existence.

Jasmine looked up into her kind but worried eyes. "I'm a bit overworked lately. I'll be fine."

"Hmm."

"I know that sound. What?"

"I think you need a vacation."

"I just had one."

"That was five months ago, and I hardly think attending a will reading counts as a vacation."

Jasmine pushed away from her desk, leaning back in her chair. "I didn't realize so much time had passed." Her eyes locked on a stack of pink phone message slips. Several were from her brother.

"I know you want to think you're invincible, but you're a person like the rest of us."

Jasmine gave a hollow laugh. "Hardly."

"Hardly a person, or hardly invincible?"

Before Jasmine could answer, the door to their office opened, and a young woman wearing a dirty hoody and soiled saggy jeans entered. Her dark eyes darted around before settling on Jasmine. She walked forward with a slip of paper clutched in her grubby hand. An aroma of sour rot wafted around her.

"You Jazz?"

Jasmine nodded and offered her a chair as Brandi moved back to her desk, giving them privacy. As the woman sat down, Jasmine saw the bulge of pregnancy under her shirt, made more apparent by her emaciated form.

"What can I help you with?"

"This girl, she gave me your name." She held out the crumpled paper, and Jasmine could see her own name and the office address under the smudges. "She said you'd help me." The door opened, the mailman dropped off the mail on Brandi's desk. Jasmine didn't miss the edgy expression in the young woman's eyes—she was ready to run.

"Who are you hiding from?"

"My old man."

"Father or boyfriend?"

The woman's eyebrows furrowed together. "My boyfriend." She gave a harsh laugh. "'Cept it's been a long time since he was any kind of a boy."

Jasmine waited.

"Look, I don't want to work anymore. I been working for him for a long time. So long, I don't even remember who I am anymore. Not that it matters, but I have my baby to think of." The way she said it, it sounded like she was repeating someone else's advice, not her own thoughts.

"I'm not sure how I can help." Jasmine pulled out a pad of paper and wrote directions to the shelter on it.

"Look, I already been there. That's who sent me."

"The shelter sent you to me?"

"No, Ronnie did. She's real cool. She said if anyone could help me, it'd be you."

Jasmine searched her brain for someone named Ronnie. "Oh, you mean Veronica."

"I don't know any Veronica. I know this nice black girl with short curly hair. She's way into God and stuff. She said to come here."

Jasmine's eyes bounced to Brandi, and she saw her nod in

approval.

"What did Veronica think I could do for you?"

"Hide me."

"Pardon me?"

"I'm tired of working, like I said. I need to get out, but he'll kill me for sure. He won't put up with my running off. He's looking for me already." She glanced over her shoulder when the wind rattled the office door behind her. "I got this baby to think about. If he finds out I'm pregnant, he'll do us both."

"He doesn't know yet?" Jasmine couldn't hide the surprise from her voice.

"I been keeping real busy. As long as I'm bringing in money, he doesn't pay me much mind. I'm not as pretty as I used to be, so he doesn't look my way too often. But if I leave, I'll be setting a bad example, and he won't put up with that."

Jasmine put the papers she'd been shuffling down on her desk. "What's your name?"

"Destiny."

"Is that your real name?"

She looked up at Jasmine, clearly surprised by the question. "No. No one uses my real name."

"I'd like to. What is it?"

The girl hesitated. Jasmine knew that street names were like superhero names, they brought protection and anonymity. But she wasn't about to help this girl if she wasn't willing to drop her guard a bit. Trust had to be on both sides. "I know you want to keep yourself safe, but I have to know some things if I'm going to be able to help you."

"My daddy named me Doris, but everyone used to call me Dee." At this admittance, she picked at her sweatshirt and looked in any direction except at Jasmine.

"What did you love best when you were a girl?" This tact might or might not work on Dee.

"I loved to ride horses, a real cowgirl, you know. I was always dirty." She glanced down at her grimy clothes. "Not like this, though."

"Sleep in a dumpster last night?"

"Wouldn't call it sleeping, but that's where I spent the night."

"And if you go to the shelter?"

"He'll look there. That's where he found me in the first place."

Jasmine shot another look at Brandi who looked equally alarmed. "He picked you up at the shelter?"

"Yeah."

Anger pooled in Jasmine's veins; she felt the heat of it on her cheeks. "And how old were you?"

"Fifteen. My daddy died, and my stepmother really hated me. She did everything to remind me she didn't want me, that I was a charity case in her eyes. I didn't need that, so I came to the city to find a job." She shook her head and whispered, "Didn't know what kind of job I'd get, or I would have stayed put." Her body tilted to the side in her chair, and she righted herself with shaky hands against the arm rests.

"How long since you've eaten?"

Dee looked down. "I can't remember."

"Come with me." Jasmine walked to the back of the office and opened the door to the next room. Inside was a bathroom that housed a tiny shower. She walked in and opened the cabinet, revealing several sets of clean sweat pants and shirts. There was a shelf with underwear and socks as well. "I'm sure you can find something in here to fit you." She glanced at Dee, whose eyes were wide in disbelief and a bit of hope.

"I don't know what we'll do yet, but the first step is to get you cleaned up, and the next is to feed you. You can't make any decisions until that happens. Come out when you're done."

Shutting the door behind her, Jasmine went out and sat at Brandi's desk, knowing she'd overheard. "So what do you think?"

"I don't think we can send her back to the shelter, that's certain. I also don't think she's ready to live in one of our rooms." Brandi flipped through her Rolodex.

"If he's got eyes on the shelter, then I'm not sure what to do."

"I am." Brandi looked up at Jasmine. "That home out in Bright River."

"The place Misty is at? What makes you think they'll take her?"

"What makes you think they won't?"

Jasmine swallowed down the panic rising in her chest.

"There's got to be a closer solution."

"I don't know if closer is a good idea."

Jasmine ignored her last statement and went to her computer to search for one, anywhere but in Bright River. She made several calls, even going up into Washington, but no one had any room. A sinking feeling settled into the pit of her stomach.

"Do you want that number in Bright River yet?" Brandi gave her a look that said enough was enough.

She replaced the receiver and stared at the notepad on her desk covered with rejected possibilities. "No. I have it."

"Call it." When Jasmine faltered, Brandi locked eyes with her. "What are you afraid of?"

"I'm not ready to go back there."

Brandi came over and sat by Jasmine's desk. "This isn't about you."

"I know." She did know it in her head, but the rest of her was breaking out in a cold sweat.

"Are you worried Misty will try and force her baby on you?"

"I'm not sure what I'm worried about. Just thinking about going there makes me shaky. I can't face it again yet."

"Get back on that horse."

"Come again?" Jasmine massaged her temples, clenching her eyes closed.

"When you fall down, get right back up and keep trying."

"I didn't fall." She gave Brandi a look. "Don't you think we're way past platitudes and clichés at this point?"

"Not if they work." Brandi patted her arm. You faced it once, you can do it again. Every time you do, it'll get a little easier."

"So that's the point? Keep subjecting myself to bad memories and I'll grow a little more numb each time?"

Brandi looked at her with thoughtful eyes. "Hiding from your problems doesn't make them go away, you know that."

"I know. I wish I could convince my heart of that." Jasmine leaned back in her chair, staring at the ceiling.

"You know what's best for this girl. Interview her, get a feel for her, but make that call first and see if they have an opening." Brandi left for her desk as if the issue were solved. Jasmine knew an order when she heard one.

She didn't call right away. Instead, she went four doors down to a small cafe and ordered breakfast for Dee. While she was in line, waiting for her order, two men entered, and one bumped her shoulder. She tried to slide out of the way, but the other man stood behind her.

"Don't I know you?" A sly voice questioned her. He wore a scruffy haircut and faded black leather jacket. His near black eyes carried a glint of satisfaction.

"I don't think so." She stepped closer to the counter, ignoring him.

"Of course, there's a lot of pretty women around. Maybe I don't know you. You could give me a call."

"Why's that?" She tried to sound disinterested.

"So we can get to know each other."

"No thanks."

"Might be a good idea. A lot of girls are going missing these days." He leered down, breathing his hot breath over her. "I could protect you."

"I don't need anyone's protection." She glanced his way and turned, intently focusing on the woman serving her meal into containers on the other side of the counter.

He shook his head at her, and she sensed his eyes scanning her body. "My buddy Jed was looking for his lady a while back, worried for her, you know. Got himself shot." He sucked on his teeth. "There's a lot of unsavory folks on the street, and he wanted to be sure she was okay. Do you know that some weak-minded woman had him arrested?"

Jasmine's skin crawled, warning signals blaring in her mind, but she swallowed the panic down.

"I think he's right. You should be very careful." The other man's breath carried the hint of cheap liquor. He drew closer, grabbed an apple from the counter and squeezed it in his hand. "My girl's gone missing too. Rumor has it she got a better offer from someone." His knuckles went white as his fingers dug into the skin of the apple. "Skinny little thing. Maybe you've seen her?"

"No." She kept her eyes locked on the counter.

He leaned in close. "If you do, you send her home."

Jasmine took a side step, her heart beating rapidly in her throat, trying to move away from them both. The man with the apple wore an old brown London Fog raincoat that came to his knees. She looked into his eyes and met a cold, hard stare. She did her best to keep her fear tamped, her face blank.

"Here's your order." The waitress avoided using her name, and Jasmine looked at her with grateful eyes.

"Excuse me." Jasmine moved past the men and collected the sack. As she left, she went the long way back to her office, down side streets, in one business and out the back door into another. When she was sure they weren't following her, she headed back.

By the time she sat down at her desk, there wasn't any avoiding anymore. She knew what she had to do. As much as she hated the idea of returning to Bright River, she knew Dee's life was on the line. Jasmine dialed Mrs. Craig on her cell. She explained the situation.

"Oh, this is providential," Mrs. Craig's excited voice startled Jasmine.

"How's that?"

"Our other young woman left to live with some cousins."

"So you have room."

"Not only that, but many of us at church are feeling led to make this into a pregnancy outreach house."

A small thrill ran through Jasmine. An idea long dormant in her mind stirred. "When did you decide to change your focus?"

"Well, when Misty came. Not only are we helping her, but we're helping her baby. No matter what she decides to do with her child, we'll be here for her, coaching her. We feel like we're saving two lives, not one. We've had a huge outpouring by the community. They've donated four cribs and diapers and baby clothes. Our women's group is making blankets and knit hats. You don't know what a blessing this has been to our church. We've lost our focus over the years, getting wrapped up in ourselves and our own problems. Now we'll have two young women to love."

Emotion welled in Jasmine's chest. "Can you take her by tonight?"

"Yes. I'll get her room all ready."

Five minutes later, Dee exited the bathroom looking and smelling much improved. Her brown hair was pulled up into a ponytail, and Jasmine noted she was a pretty woman when she wasn't covered in filth.

"Have a seat." Jasmine motioned toward a small table in the back corner where she and Brandi would often eat their lunch. On it were several Styrofoam containers full of eggs, pancakes, and sausages. Dee sat down in wonderment, and bowed her head and prayed.

When she was done, Dee dug into the food with abandon. Jasmine pulled up a chair next to her and watched her eat, smiling. "You have to keep up your strength for that baby, don't forget." Dee nodded at her. "I have some questions to ask you. You have to be honest with me, or I can't help you at all. Keep in mind, I've been lied to by the boat, so please don't try and put me on."

She nodded again, taking bite after bite of food.

"Do you know who the father of the baby is?"

Dee shook her head.

"Are you now, or have you ever been addicted to any illegal substance?"

Speaking past her food, she said, "I've used here and there. But not since the baby. And I don't like drinking. My stepmom drank something terrible, and I could never stomach the smell."

"Are you wanted for any crimes, or have you ever been convicted of any crimes?"

Dee put down her fork. "God knows I've lived a horrible life. If the police knew what I've been doing these past five years, I'd go to jail for sure. But, no, I've never been arrested."

"Would you be okay living in a place that had a Christian influence?"

"Really?" Her eyes brightened, but then a strained look passed over Dee's face. "Shouldn't you be asking if they want a prostitute living under their roof?"

"Are you still a prostitute?"

"No." Conviction settled over her face.

"Why?"

Dee took a deep breath. "It started off being because of the baby. But I met Veronica, and she told me about Jesus. My dad believed in Jesus. But I never understood it until Veronica explained it to me. It was like a light came on in my head, and it shone all over inside, showing me all the ugliness inside. And when I prayed to Him, all the dirt washed away, like when

I took that shower earlier. I was clean inside, and I knew I could never dirty myself up like that again. It's like I could see His eyes looking at me, loving me, and I didn't want to let Him down."

Jasmine didn't know exactly what she meant, but she believed she was telling her the truth. Dee wouldn't go back to her old life if she could help it. Determination filled her, pushing aside the fear of returning to Bright River. Jasmine was going to make sure Dee could help it.

"There's a home about four hours from here, sponsored and run by a church. They've recently started to support pregnant moms. I called them, and based on your answers, they'll want you there. There's one woman living there now, and a live-in resident. She's a dear woman named Mrs. Craig."

"You told her all about me?"

"Enough. You get to tell her the rest when we get there."

"When's that?"

"Tonight." Jasmine felt her stomach tie in knots at the thought. She didn't want to scare Dee off by telling her about the men at the cafe. "Why don't you go lie down for a bit while I get stuff together?" She watched Dee head into the back room and lay on the cot. Within seconds she was snoring away.

When Jasmine looked up, she caught Brandi watching her.

"That was a fast change of heart."

Jasmine walked to Brandi's desk and spoke softly. "Her pimp is searching for her; I crossed paths with him. We need to get her out of here, fast."

"Do you want to call Officer Banner?"

"Would you, and fill him in? I think her pimp has an idea she's been in contact with me."

"Is everything okay?" Brandi gave her a leveling look.

"I'm pretty sure it is. But I'd rather be on the safe side. I'll be back in awhile to pick her up. I'm going to go pack."

"Be careful."

"I will. You'll take care of Oscar for me?"

"That beast? Will he let me in the apartment?"

"Come in with an open can of cat food."

"You're not teasing, are you?" The expression in Brandi's eyes conveyed her worry.

Jasmine shook her head. "No, I'm not teasing."

Five hours later, they pulled into the driveway of House of Hope. Jasmine gently nudged Dee awake. "We're here."

Twenty-Six

The sinking feeling still lingered in Jasmine's stomach, but she pushed it aside and willed herself to get her head together. She'd been careful on the drive and was sure no one followed them there. Glancing at the clock on the dash, she saw it was eleven-thirty. As she led Dee up the steps of the old Victorian to knock on the door, Mrs. Craig opened it, a soft smile on her lips. Her eyes looked over Dee like a long lost child.

"You come on in here." She gently took her by the arm and escorted her into the living room. The couch and chairs were in a U-shape, facing a gas fireplace. She motioned for Dee to sit down and handed her a clipboard of papers to fill out.

"I'm Mrs. Craig."

"I'm Destin...I mean, friends call me Dee." She stared down at the papers.

"You don't have to do that tonight, but it'd be best if you had it done by lunch tomorrow."

Dee nodded.

"I've got an appointment with the doctor for you tomorrow afternoon."

"Doctor?" Dee's eyes filled with worry.

"Prenatal care. Don't worry, it won't hurt, and you won't have to pay for it." She came and sat down next to her. "But you will be expected to help with chores here in the house. And we'll be looking for a job for you in town."

"Who's going to hire a pregnant woman?"

"Oh, don't sell yourself short. There's a lot of jobs out there."

Jasmine heard a noise in the kitchen and watched as Misty

came into the room, carrying a tray of steaming cups and a plate of cookies. She smiled broadly at Jasmine as she set down the tray on the coffee table. There was no missing her pregnancy now—her stomach ballooned out away from her body.

"This is Misty. Her baby is due in November."

"Hey." Misty nodded to Dee; Dee returned the nod and both women sized the other up. If they recognized each other, they didn't say so.

"Well, I'd better get going." Jasmine stood to leave.

"Are you heading back tonight?" Misty asked her.

"No, I'll be at my brother's house." She'd called Bill as she packed. He and Elsie were thrilled she was coming. "I'll check in with you tomorrow."

Misty walked her to the door. "I'm glad you're here."

Tension grew in Jasmine's stomach. She'd never called Misty to tell her no about the adoption idea.

"Don't worry, Tim told me you didn't want to adopt my baby."

"It's not that easy, Misty. I don't think I'm the right person for the job." She gave her a weak smile.

"You might not be sure, but I am. I'm praying you'll change your mind." She hugged Jasmine and left her at the door, feeling cold and insecure.

As she drove up to the house, she saw the porch light on, and felt a sense of homecoming she'd never experienced before. Coming home to her house as a girl had never stirred cozy, warm feelings. Quite the contrary. But here she was, grateful, tired, and thinking of nothing more than the quiet room Bill and Elsie saved for her.

Climbing the front porch, she pulled her keys out of her pocket, flipping to the house key they'd given her months before. Smiling, she slipped it in the lock and opened the door. There was a note on the coffee table and instructions for food she'd find waiting for her in the refrigerator if she was hungry. She realized she hadn't eaten for much of the day, and now that both she and Dee were safe and sound, her hunger kicked in. She dropped her bags at the end of the stairs and headed into the kitchen. The light was on over the sink, creating a warm glow over the kitchen table. She opened the fridge and found a plated, wrapped sandwich and pre-poured glass of milk.

Sitting down to eat, she unwrapped the sandwich and realized if anyone else in her life tried to mother her like that, she'd resent it. Another note met her at the table. It was a drawing of her, Jason and Rose playing with toys in the yard. Her normally straight black hair was scribbled lovingly with a licorice-smelling swipe of black crayon. She sniffed the picture, picking out the smell of strawberries and chocolate as well as grass. Scented crayons rocked.

On the other side of the kitchen, she saw the shelves covered in baskets of apples, preserves and four pies. Fall in Bright River. Jasmine heard a creaking sound on the stairs. A moment later Bill patted her back in welcome, came around, and sat down by her at the table.

"I thought I heard you come in. How was the drive?"

"Uneventful."

"That's good." They sat in silence together a moment.

"Is the apple harvest good this year?" She nodded toward the baskets.

"One of our better years. Elsie got the plums and cherries put up last month, but it's nothing compared to the apples. Lily's orchard will bring in a lot of extra money for her this year."

"How is she?"

"She's keeping to herself. Elsie has seen her in town, but Lily acts like she doesn't see her." If her behavior angered him, he didn't show it.

"So you haven't spoken."

"No."

She didn't go any further, or ask about Tim, not wanting Bill to think she cared more than she did. There'd been enough misunderstanding already.

"The Harvest Festival Fair is opening tomorrow."

As soon as Bill mentioned the festival, a dizzy feeling washed over her. She gripped her glass and put it down with care, trying not to drop it. Bill didn't seem to notice.

"Elsie is entering two pies, and some applesauce. She earned a ribbon last year, but not first place. She wants that big blue ribbon pretty bad—but she won't admit it to anyone." He grinned at her. "I thought we'd go as a family."

Her first instinct was to tell him she had to leave early and couldn't attend, but that would be a lie, and Brandi's voice was echoing in her ears. She didn't want her accusing her of running away again.

"That sounds like a good plan." At least she wouldn't be going on her own. Bill patted her shoulder again as he got up from the table.

"I'm off to bed. Get the lights on your way up."

"Sure. Good night, big brother."

He gave her a wide grin and headed up the stairs as she took her dishes to the sink and turned off the lights. She walked past the back door, looking out into the yard. In the dark she couldn't see the change of leaves, but she knew in the morning she'd see a blaze of orange and red blowing in the breeze.

The scent of ripened apples and cinnamon wafted up from the counter. The aroma brought back memories of what felt like a hundred falls, all celebrated the same way: Picking apples in the hot sun. Bees swarming madly around, searching for their last meal before the first freeze. Peeling and washing and paring until her fingers ached. Canning and juicing and mashing until the skin of her hands were smooth from the acid of the fruit.

A good memory filled her mind, shutting out her worries for a moment. Her brother, sister, and she on the porch peeling apples, laughing and flicking seeds at one another. Nothing bad happened, nothing stole the memory from her. For the first time since she'd returned home, she felt a semblance of control back in her life. She'd remembered, and it hadn't been awful, it hadn't triggered something painful. A slight tear escaped from the corner of her eye. Maybe attending the fair wouldn't be such a bad thing after all.

Twenty-Seven

The next morning Jasmine awoke to the sounds of hushes and giggles. She cracked one eye open and spied her niece's face, the sweet flowery aroma of plum jelly on her breath.

"Mama told you not to wake her, Rosie." Jason whispered the unheeded warning at his sister with his raspy, all-knowing tone.

"Hush. I'm not wakening her. I'm watching her until she wakes up." Rosie reached up a tentative finger and touched the end of Jasmine's nose.

"No touching."

"Her nose is cold." She pulled the blankets up and tucked them under Jasmine's chin. A case of the giggles was building in Jasmine and finally broke loose.

"Oh, sorry Aunty, your nose was cold."

Jasmine reached down and pulled Rose up into the bed with her. She patted the other side and Jason climbed up.

"What are you two monkeys up to this morning?"

"We have to leave for the fair soon. Mama made you breakfast and told us to let you sleep."

"What time is it?"

Jason leaned knowingly to the side and read the clock. "One-zero-zero-nine."

"Ten already?" She glanced out her window at the gray day. "Pretty cloudy out there."

"Mama said it might rain by tonight, so we should go soon and enjoy the day. And we have to drop off her energies." Rose stuck two fingers in her mouth and sucked away.

"Her entries. The pies and stuff." Jason clarified on Rose's behalf. "I'm all dressed." He stretched out so that Jasmine could inspect his orange plaid shirt, blue jeans, and cowboy boots.

"You look very handsome."

Rose giggled. "I have a pretty dress." Jumping off the bed, she twirled for Jasmine to see all the ruffles.

"Girls have to be really uncomfortable," Jason informed her.

"Maybe she likes it?" Jasmine glanced at Rose, who nodded with enthusiasm.

"You don't wear frilly stuff like that, do you?"

Jasmine gave her wardrobe some thought. "No, I don't think I've ever worn anything that could be called frilly. But that doesn't mean I don't appreciate it when I see it." She gave Rose a big smile, and Rose rewarded her with a kiss on her cheek. Elsie came into the room.

"I'm very sorry." She glared at the children, but Jasmine could see a twinkle in her eye. "You kids go use the bathroom, and get your coats. I'll meet you by the back door."

They both chimed a "Yes, ma'am" and raced from the room.

"I'll be up in a minute if you can wait for me." Jasmine sat up in bed and stretched.

Elsie smiled. "No rush. We can meet later."

"I'd like to go with you."

"Sounds good. What about breakfast?"

"Toast is fine."

"I've got some on the table already. I'll meet you downstairs."

Jasmine came down wearing a bright pink T-shirt under her gray and blue plaid flannel. She wore tennis shoes and jeans. Jason gave her an approving look, until he spied her shoes.

"You need boots."

"I'll have to work on that, I guess." She tousled his hair and took a piece of toast. "I'm ready to go when you guys are."

"I'm waiting for Bill. He's going to take the rest of the day off." Elsie checked her watch.

"How long has he been up?"

"Since five. He's already been to four jobs."

Bill came stomping up the steps of the back door. "You guys ready, or what?"

The kids pushed out past the screen door and clambered into the king-cab truck, hollering with excitement. Jasmine couldn't help grinning as she climbed in the backseat with them. As she did, she caught Bill's eye in the rearview mirror.

"You okay, sis?"

"You bet, Sweet William."

The kids snickered hearing his given name. "Thanks." He gave her a wink and they pulled out, heading up the road to the fair.

Despite not being open to the general public yet, the fairgrounds were bustling with activity. Most of the trailers had been there for two days, getting their animals used to the grounds—the noise, the smells, and the other animals. The carnival rides were running as their managers did last-minute safety checks. The booths were up, selling wares of all sorts to the newcomers. The first thing Jasmine noticed as she entered through the gates was the sweet smell of fried food—elephant ears to be exact. Even after being a carny for a year, she never tired of the smell or taste of the donut-like treat.

Bill led their group, carrying a large box of Elsie's entries to the staging area for food contestants. After filling out paperwork, Elsie set out each item at the correct display. Judging for perishables was that afternoon. She looked with pride on her pies, but followed with a loud sigh.

"Don't worry so much. I know you're going to win." Bill gave her a kiss on the side of her head, and they left the building, heading toward the animals. Jasmine's heart warmed at the gentle, encouraging ways Bill had with his family.

"I want to see the bunnies," Rose begged.

"I want to see the horses," Jason followed, sounding as important as he could.

"I'd like to see the cows myself." A familiar voice from behind startled Jasmine. She turned to see Tim standing there, attired with a cowboy hat, jean jacket, jeans, and boots.

"Are you riding?" She'd never remembered him as the cowboy type, but things changed. Lots of things.

"Oh, no. I like looking the part." He tipped his hat to her. "Nice to see you. Are you all having a good time?" He didn't seem surprised to see her there, so she surmised Bill must have filled him in on yesterday's escape out of Portland.

Jasmine couldn't seem to catch her breath to answer, so she smiled.

"Not yet." Jason crossed his arms, grousing.

"Tell you what, partner. I'll take you to see the horses, if you go see the cows with me."

"Why do you want to see them old cows for?"

"I'm looking to buy one for my place. And some chickens, too."

"You have a farm?"

"I'm working on it. What do you say? Will you help me out?"

"Okay."

"I've got my cell with me if you need us farmers." Tim patted Jason on the back.

Bill nodded and handed five dollars to Jason. "If you see a ride or two, go ahead." He gave Tim a curious look. "Make sure to take Mr. Able on the roller coaster."

Tim's face went ashen. "Yeah, we'll be skipping that."

"Please!" Jason went into full-on hopping. "Come on, they're fun."

"Not for me. And not for you if you're sitting next to me." Tim put a hand to his stomach and glared at Bill who started chuckling.

"You listen to Tim, now." Elsie admonished Jason, trying to get him to calm down. She sent an equally scathing look at Bill.

"Sorry." Bill chuckled. "Be nice to Mr. Able, Jason," he called as they wandered down the Midway.

Jasmine watched them walk away, an uneasiness in her stomach. Her first meeting with Tim had been painless, but for some reason she felt disappointed by the distance he kept between them.

"Can I escort you three lovely ladies around the fair?" Bill put out his arms for Rose and Elsie. Rose gave a deep giggle and pulled on his arm.

"Bunnies." Rose spoke as if directing her private chauffeur.

"Yes, ma'am. Bunnies it is."

Jasmine walked a few paces behind, soaking in the fair atmosphere, letting her mind drift. From the game stands, she heard the callers tempting folks to try their luck. She looked up the Midway, curious, but continued to follow Bill and the girls through the animal displays. Within two hours, they'd exhausted all their options—everything from bunnies to goats were discovered and giggled at. Rose was a joy to watch. She begged to pet everything, but only asked once to buy a rabbit. "Please, Daddy? I'll take really good care of him."

"When you're older, sweetie. You can join 4-H and raise him right."

Her lip stuck out as she put on a good pout, but as soon as Rose saw the baby chicks, she was off on another tangent. By lunchtime, they were out sitting at the tables enjoying hotdogs and soda. Tim walked up with Jason, who had a large bag of kettle corn.

"We already ate. I hope that's okay." Tim handed a second bag to Elsie. "This is for Princess Rose after she's had her meal."

Rose ate more earnestly, keeping her eyes locked on the bag of kettle corn.

"That's so thoughtful of you. Did you find what you were looking for?" Elsie handed Rose a napkin.

Tim sat down next to Bill as Jason slid in next to Jasmine and Rose, holding out the bag of sweet popcorn to her. It'd been years since Jasmine had eaten any. The caramel, salty flavor tasted as good today as it had when she was a kid.

"I think so. I learned a lot, anyway."

"I didn't know you were looking for animals." Bill seemed curious.

"It's a recent idea." Tim didn't elaborate.

"Are you going to get chickens? Can I name them?" Rose grew animated at the idea. "I could come feed them every day."

"Tell you what, Rosie, if I get chickens, you can help name them, and when they start to lay eggs, you can even help collect the eggs."

"Wow."

When Tim spoke to the kids, Jasmine noted how sincere he sounded. He needed to find the right person and settle down. He'd make a terrific father. An idea flitted through her mind.

As the rest of the crew wandered off to the judging, she and Tim lagged behind, walking slowly through the Midway. He cast a glance her way.

"I didn't expect to see you here."

"I had to come. There was a young woman in trouble, and Mrs. Craig opened the doors for her."

"Bill told me. I didn't think you'd stick around." His tone was level, not accusing, really. But it also didn't reveal how he felt about it. She changed the subject to avoid an argument. "When did you decide to farm?"

"I felt like I needed to throw myself into something new that had nothing to do with the law. I thought some animals around the place would be good—and I'd donate the milk and eggs to the women's shelter."

They walked on, ending up at the Ferris wheel. "I've got a pocket full of tickets, want to ride?"

Had it been over twenty years since she'd been on a Ferris Wheel? She gave him a nod and they stepped up, waiting their turn. They'd ridden one like it many times as kids. She watched the wheel come around, and the carny opened the bucket for them. He closed the bar over them and the bucket lifted up, going around to the top, halting to let off, then on, other riders. As they waited, they rocked in the breeze.

"Sure is pretty up here. You'll have to ride it again tonight when it's dark. I love all the lights." His eyes were taking in the view.

"Everything looks easier up here, cleaner, happier." Below them, a pair of children clamored after the cotton candy their father tried to hold out of their way.

"Like taking off on an airplane. You look down and all you can see is the clear lines of houses, roads, and trees. The people are miniscule, if you can see them at all. There's no garbage, no mess, no problems."

"I used to think that's how God saw us. That He was so far up there, He didn't really see us or know us anymore." She tucked a strand of escaping hair behind her ear.

"You don't feel that way anymore?"

"No. I've been thinking—about the bad times, since that's mostly what I've got—and I can remember, sometimes, not feeling so alone. I didn't know it was Him, but now I think it was."

They rode around the loop in silence as Tim pondered her words.

After the second loop, the ride slowed to let passengers off, one after the next. They stepped off when the gate opened to them, and headed up the path. As they passed the fun house, she stopped and stared at it.

"Do you think it's the same one?" He leaned over the metal crowd control rail.

"No, it's a different model. The sound, the feel of it is the same though." Jasmine moved to walk through it, and Tim gave the attendant tickets, following behind her. She walked past the bendy mirrors, watching her reflection shrink and grow.

The night before she ran away, she'd stood before the same spot in Fiona's funhouse. Her reflection went thin, fat, and blurry. Looking in a real mirror had never been pleasant for her—her eyes always showed a different person on the outside than she felt like on the inside. But, before those mirrors, she could look and not feel condemned.

Tim moved on around the corner. Jasmine reached out and traced the outline of her face, her eyes, against the cold panels. Even past the distortion, she could see who she really was now—at some point, it'd gotten easier to look. They continued on through the maze of mirrors, up some stairs, over some spinning discs and down a long slide. At the end she felt like part of her had been spun off and left behind.

"I remember that being more fun." Tim shook his head to clear the dizziness.

"I liked it better this time than ever." She glanced back, lost in thought.

"Bill said you might be expecting trouble with this new girl."

"I call them girls, but they seem like girls because they're young and have been taken advantage of so often. She's nineteen."

"That's a girl by my estimation."

"By the time they reach nineteen, they've seen more of life than most people ever want to." For some reason, she needed to explain the hardship these young women had to endure to make it to nineteen.

"One of them is being followed?"

"Technically, they both are. One of the men is in jail for

213

breaking into my apartment. The other let me know clearly that I'd been in contact with her and gave me a stern warning. It'd be great if you could give the authorities a heads up. They don't know me well enough to trust me at this point."

Tim stopped short and put his hand on her arm. "Come again?" His eyes looked her over for sign of injury. "What happened in your apartment?"

"Misty's ex broke into my apartment, thinking he'd find her there. He's in jail."

"Did he hurt you?"

"No." She frowned at him.

"Quit looking at me like that couldn't happen. I know you're tough and all that, but you are alone, facing some pretty rough customers."

"I have Oscar," she joked. She'd never admit how afraid she'd been to him.

Tim growled. "You are either in major denial, or you're a fool."

Jasmine's jaw tensed. "I've faced a lot worse than that guy. I can take care of myself." She pushed past him, heading into the ever-growing crowds around the fairgrounds. He followed her closely, keeping pace.

"You keep telling me that."

"When are you going to start listening?"

"Just because you survived this long doesn't mean you should push your luck." His voice rose with tension.

Jasmine stopped walking, her head hung down, wishing she'd never said anything at all. "Don't worry, I'm not going to do anything stupid."

"I want you to be safe."

"I will be."

He seemed to accept her answer.

"Let's go see how Elsie did." She motioned toward the building where they'd left Elsie's entries. He followed her up past the rest of the rides, to the food arena. They walked past several groups of women, and found Elsie standing proudly by her pie. She had a blue ribbon in her hands.

"Hey, congratulations." Jasmine gave her a hug.

"I knew she'd do it." Bill beamed with pride. "No one can match her apple pie."

Elsie's face flushed.

Jasmine was still grinning when movement to her left caught her eye. Marcy and Dave were moving past them, Marcy prattling on about how the ribbon was stolen from her in the applesauce competition. Dave looked past his wife and gave Jasmine a leering look and a wink. She backed up, bumping into Tim. He put a comforting hand on her arm and pulled her toward him, a protective measure she didn't entirely dislike.

"Let's get some coffee." He didn't wait for her to answer but continued to pull her away, heading to a vending booth nearby, in the opposite direction of Dave Buchard.

Twenty-Eight

"Wait a minute, where are we going?" Jasmine tried to wrench her arm away, but Tim kept a tight grasp until they were out of the densest part of the crowd. He handed her a cup of coffee, and she was surprised to see her hand shaking as she took it. That was happening too much lately.

"Drink it."

She took a sip, but her eyes blazed in anger at him. The shuddering in her arms and hands calmed—but she wasn't about to admit it to him. "Fine, I drank some, now can we go back and be with my family?"

"What happened back there?" The intensity of his eyes startled her.

"What do you mean?" Jasmine glanced away from him.

"I mean not thirty minutes ago you were giving me this speech on how tough you were, and how you could handle yourself, but one wink from Dave Buchard and you fall apart."

"I did not fall apart." She took another swig of coffee. "It's only…"

"What?" The intensity dimmed to deep concern.

"It's hard to explain. I'm going to sound stupid."

"Unlikely." A comforting warmth seeped through her at his compliment, but she did her best to ignore it.

"I don't know how to put it. When I'm in Portland, I'm streetwise, tough. I'm Jazz. Not fearless, but certainly not intimidated. When I come back here, I'm…" She trailed off, not sure how to put it.

"Little Jasmine Reynolds?"

Her eyes brightened, grateful he understood. "Yes. Exactly.

I lose all my confidence, and I feel stripped down, helpless."
Tim's countenance fell.

"What is it?" She put a hand to his arm, worried.

"I guess it's hard for me to accept, that's all."

"What?"

"That you're not coming home for good."

Tim finally understood.

She nearly looked away from the pain in his eyes. She hated hurting him. He was lonely—but he deserved someone so much better than her. Maybe now was the time to share her plan with him. He didn't have to be alone.

"Listen, I've got an idea. You're going to think it's silly, but hear me out, okay?"

"I wish you wouldn't do that."

"What?"

"Degrade your ideas. Call yourself stupid or silly."

"Whatever. Do you want to know my idea or not?" If she didn't get it out now, she'd lose her nerve.

"Okay, shoot."

"Misty's baby."

"You want to adopt her baby after all?" His eyebrows rose in excitement.

"No. I think you should." She waited for the idea to sink in, for his acceptance and joy at her insight.

When his eyes locked on hers, all the sounds around them— the talking, the noises of animals, the venders hollering for attention—were blotted out. To say he looked incredulous was an understatement.

"I'm sorry?"

"You're rattling around in that huge house of yours all alone. The place was made for kids. I don't know, but it seems like the perfect fit."

Definitely not joyous.

"I don't believe you." The anger in his eyes took her aback.

"I don't want you to be alone." Her voice shook as she spoke, and she saw his eyes soften for a moment at her response. It was quickly replaced by frustration.

Bill, Elsie and the kids walked up. Elsie held up two fingers. "I got two blue ribbons. One for my pie and one for my apple butter."

Neither of them spoke.

"Everything going okay out here?" Bill asked, worriedly looking back and forth between them.

"Yeah. We saw Dave Buchard inside, and I thought Jasmine could use a breath of fresh air and a cup of coffee." He glanced over his shoulder as if checking on something. "Actually, you know, I've got to get going." He gave Elsie a smile that didn't quite make it to his eyes. "Congrats on the wins."

"Thanks. Will we see you at church Sunday?"

"I'll be there." He tipped his hat, avoiding Jasmine, and walked away from them, not looking back.

"I'm going to take the kids to the junior rides." Elsie led the kids away and gave a knowing look to Bill. Jasmine sensed a speech coming on.

"You want to tell me what that was about?"

Jasmine was still staring after Tim, even though she could no longer see his back.

"All I did was suggest he adopt Misty's baby instead of me. I mean, he's lonely, he's got that huge house, and he's got the money he'd need to care for the baby."

"Didn't like that idea much?" His tone let her know he didn't care much for it either.

"What?" Jasmine didn't see what was so wrong. Two problems solved with one solution.

"Let's go find a spot and talk." Bill walked through the crowd to an open bench, back away from the commotion of the ever-increasing crowds. She pulled her shirt closed against the cooling fall air as she took a seat next to him.

"I think Tim's got this idea about the two of you."

"I know, I wish he'd let that go." She waited for Bill to agree—he didn't.

"Easier said. Listen, when you left town, you left a lot more people than Dad."

"I know it was hard on Tim and you and..." She was about to add Lily, but she wasn't sure about that.

"Hard isn't exactly right. Tim's dad was a deputy at that point. The whole town panicked when they didn't find your body. They suspected foul play."

"Kidnapper?"

"That's right. Every kid in the neighborhood was suddenly

being escorted to school. No one played on the streets after dark. The parks went empty. The schools brought in counselors to help your peers deal with your loss. The town was on high alert."

Everything started to make sense. "And Tim was caught in the middle."

"Tim overheard the officers talking about your chances of coming back alive. He was your best friend. He and Elsie were questioned. Some of the kids blamed Tim."

"What? Why would they?"

"Who knows what goes through teenagers' minds? He lost you and most of his buddies at school at the same time. Elsie was the only one that kept talking to him. Over time, things went back to normal."

"But not for Tim."

"No. He'd take long rides on his bike, searching for clues. He never gave up."

As the weight of what she'd done settled on her, she sank back against the bench.

"I didn't know."

"No guilt. That's not what I'm telling you this for. You did the best a fourteen-year-old could do. I don't know if I could have done any better. I'm relaying the facts."

"I should ease up on him."

"Try to see things from his side." He leaned forward, resting his elbows on his knees. "When he found your address in those old legal files, the first thing he did was call me, ecstatic."

"I guess I've been pretty unfair."

"I'm not saying to pretend to return his feelings, I want you to know where he's coming from. And the last thing on his mind is raising a child by himself."

"That goes for two of us."

He put his arm around her shoulder.

"Tim's a good man. I'm lucky to count him as my best friend. Whatever happens, I hope you two can stay friends."

"Me too." They sat in quiet, watching the people passing by on their way to rides and booths. She really did. But every time they were left alone together, it all went south.

"Back to Dave Buchard. If he says word one to you, I want you to tell him you'll press charges against him for harassment."

"He hasn't done anything."

"If he does, do it. He'll be afraid of the public pressure. He cares an awful lot about that hotel and his perfect-looking life. If you threaten to go to the authorities, the chance that it could get out should be enough to stop him."

"Okay." She really didn't like the idea of stirring up trouble. She wished Jazz were here, her knife-wielding alter ego, to protect her from herself. Maybe if she got a super suit, things would even out. What would a streetwise super hero wear, anyway?

"Are you hungry?" Bill interrupted her thoughts.

"Yeah, actually." The aroma from one of the booths enticed her. "I want an elephant ear."

"You'll ruin your appetite." Bill used his fatherly tone, and for a moment, Jasmine heard her dad, but she shook it off. Bill's eyes held only kindness and compassion—looks that never entered her father's. Not once.

"And I want to ride the rides." She spoke in high, whiny tones, playing along.

"Do you have money?"

"You didn't give me my allowance." Jasmine bumped him in the side as they walked arm in arm to the food booths, laughing.

Three hours later, Jasmine stood to the side of the Tilt-A-Whirl, watching Bill and Jason in one cart, Elsie and Rose in another. Each time they whipped by her, she could hear them screaming and laughing. She sighed, feeling contentment seep into her for the first time that day. If only things would smooth over between her and Tim.

"I love the carnival, don't you?" The sound of Dave's voice in her ear made her skin crawl. She didn't look at him, didn't acknowledge him, but continued to smile at her family. She wished Bill were at her side, instead of trapped on the ride.

"Did you hear I'm buying your daddy's house? Marcy wants it."

A sick feeling roiled in her stomach. "I didn't hear anything about an offer."

"Oh, you will. I've been in contact with your lawyer."

She still wouldn't look at him. If he'd spoken to Tim,

wouldn't Tim have said something?

"I don't know if you knew this, but your daddy and I were friends. It makes me feel good knowing I'll have his old house. I'll take real good care of it for him. You could come visit." He ran a finger down the side of her arm, and she flinched away.

"Don't touch me."

"I know what you like." The angry, controlled emotion that laced his voice made the hairs on the back of her neck stand up. This man was ten times more dangerous than Jed or any of his cronies back in Portland. "I'll keep your old room ready for you."

Turning, she looked him full in the face. "If you think I'll sell my house to you, you're nuts. If you touch me again, or even speak to me, I'll press charges."

"Sure you will."

"Try me." Her fist clenched, ready to strike.

"I'd like to," he whispered, his face drawing nearer to hers. The sour smell of beer and hotdogs met her nostrils and turned her stomach even more. She took three steps back, panic rising. She tried to picture herself like she was in charge in Portland, but all she could do was pray.

God, help me.

Her eyes darted to the side, but Bill and Elsie were both so caught up in the ride, spinning and whipping around, that they didn't see what was happening. Lightning bolted over the Midway as rain sprinkled down. Dave didn't appear to notice.

"I hear your girls at the home are looking for work."

She didn't look at him.

"I could use a couple maids. I'll scratch your back and help them find gainful employment, and you can scratch mine." He stepped closer. "Maybe they could scratch my back, too. They are professionals, aren't they?"

That did it. "Get away from me and stay away from my girls." The rain started coming down harder. People raced away from the rides, seeking shelter, but the rides hadn't shut down yet.

He laughed at her. "I know all about you and your daddy." His eyes roamed over her body, invading her privacy. Everywhere he looked, her skin burned. "I'm sorry he's not here to welcome you back home. I'm here though." He reached out a hand to touch her face, and she slapped his hand away, turning to escape. Anywhere. Dave grabbed her arm, wrenching her around to face him, pushing his hot mouth up against her ear. "Now that I know what kind of girl you were, I can guess at the kind of woman you are. I don't mind. Trust me."

Jasmine tried to push him away, but his grip tightened. "You don't know what you're talking about."

"Don't play dumb with me. I got the word firsthand."

Adrenaline rushed through Jasmine at his words, like someone had poured boiling water over her. With strength she didn't know she had, she shoved Dave away. In horror, she raced off, through the crowd, every part of her screaming for her to hide.

Jasmine's back crawled with tension, sure he was right behind her, but panic told her to keep moving, to get away and not look back. She pushed past the mobs of people at booths, playing games, the music blaring and spinning new tunes with every ride she passed. Thunder rumbled overhead, barely heard above the sound of the rides. Her eyes darted everywhere, looking for a safe haven. Spying the craft barn, she drove through the crowds toward it, but everyone else had the same idea, trying to get out of the rain. Bodies blocked every avenue of escape.

The deluge continued, and icy water streamed down her face, blurring her sight. There had to be someplace she could go.

"God, I really need some help here," she whispered. She moved ahead, struggling past people, not sure if she should cry out for help, not sure if anyone would hear her.

Dave caught up to her, stubby fingers digging into her upper arm. She yelped in pain. "I never was good enough for you to look at in high school." Lightning crackled overhead, lighting up his face and wild eyes. "I know why, though. You needed a grown man. Well, now you got one." He yanked her to the side, past the people, and through the bushes, toward the carny trailers. Jasmine screamed for help, but it blended in with the melee, and no one took any notice of her. He pulled her, dragged her back past the portable toilets, toward an empty horse trailer. She stumbled and slipped in the mud. He grabbed her by the back of her rain-soaked shirt and wrenched her to standing.

"Get up." It was the same tone her father used with her when he was drunk.

Jasmine jammed her heel onto his foot, kicked his shin, and twisted out of his grasp. She ran, full speed ahead. Despite his size, Dave was fast. He tackled her to the ground, flipping her over to face him, pinning one arm down by her side with his knee. Her elbow felt like it would snap under the pressure.

"Get off me!" she screamed, shoving him with her free hand.

"I like the out of doors, don't you? It's romantic." Jasmine felt his fingers dragging at the waist of her jeans as his body pressed down on her. Everything seemed to slow down. Lightning flashed overhead, and she caught the look of seething malice reflecting in Dave's eyes. She swung and struck his face; he retaliated and slapped her cheek with the back of his hand. Her head exploded in pins and needles. Grappling at the golden chain around his neck, she tightened the noose, gagging him. He struck her again. She felt herself go limp a moment and fought hard not to blackout.

"You're gonna learn to love me, sweetheart." Spittle flew past his clenched teeth.

The strong stench of manure drew her attention to a darkened mass by her head. She grappled after it with her free hand. Getting a handful, she smeared it across his face, pushing it into his eye socket. He cried out in rage, loosening his grip, and she clamored away, crawling, racing on all fours, trying to get her feet under her. She came down hard on her knee in a gravel-lined puddle, and the pain shot up into her hip. Her head screamed to get out of there, and her body was doing its best to obey. Once on her feet, she ran hard, but the muddy, grassy ground made it hard to gain any traction.

Behind, she could hear his heavy, labored footsteps racing after her, and curses spewing as he gave chase. A tall dark shape raced past her, almost knocking her to the ground, then another came tearing through the bushes. Both shapes leapt onto Dave, and they landed with a wet thud by her feet.

"Let me up, let me go!" Dave's screams were drowned out by threats from the two men. Searchlights came shooting through the bushes, carried by dark figures. Jasmine thought she saw the glint of a badge.

She heard slams, punches, yells. All she could do was stand by and shake uncontrollably as rivulets of rain ran down her body.

"Okay, boys, let him up." The sheriff's officer shone his light on Dave, and Jasmine could see Bill and Tim, covered in mud and muck pulling Dave to a standing position. His nose bled down his front, mingling with the mud on his shirt. His eyes were caked in manure, but what she could see blazed in anger at her. Two more officers arrived and handcuffed him, hauling him away, ignoring his threats to press charges.

"Are you okay, miss?" a kind voice near her shoulder asked her as a flashlight passed over her body and a blanket was wrapped around her shoulders.

Jasmine couldn't speak but felt herself pulled into a warm embrace. Bill held her tight against his chest. "I did it this time. I kept you safe." She could feel him sobbing under her, his chest shaking with emotion. "I saved you this time." His arms wrapped around her, holding her.

She felt herself trembling, crying, in a detached kind of way. Everything was separate from her. Darkness closed in, her head filling with a strange whirring sound. The last thing she remembered was someone softly calling her name.

Twenty-Nine

Warmth and comfort enveloped Jasmine. She opened her reluctant eyes, wanting to stay in the safe, dreamy place. When she did, she wasn't too disappointed; she was lying in her bedroom at Bill's house. She shifted her body and felt wracking pains up and down her back. Her arm throbbed. She lifted it above the covers and saw multiple black and blue marks running down it, many in the shape of Dave's fingerprints. The memory of what happened seeped into her consciousness, and she sobbed.

Elsie came rushing in to the room. "It's okay, everything is going to be okay." She wrapped her arms around Jasmine, holding her close, letting her cry. "He's been arrested, he can't hurt you anymore."

Jasmine knew what she was saying was true, and she wasn't afraid of him anymore—it was the feelings he'd awakened in her, released from the locked-down place in her mind, that threatened to overwhelm her now. And the pain.

Bill came in, carrying a tray with tea and toast on it. He sat down next to her, looking helpless as she sobbed in Elsie's arms. She reached a hand out and took his, gripping it tightly. Within a few minutes the tears subsided. Wiping her face on the sheet, and blowing her nose in the tissue that Elsie offered, she lay back, breathing deeply. She locked eyes with Bill.

"Thank you."

Tears welled in his eyes. "I wasn't too late." He went to his knees, bending over her and hugged her. "I got there in time."

She nodded into his shoulder. Unable to speak, tears rolled again. There was a knock on the door. Elsie looked at Jasmine.

"It's Tim. He's been waiting downstairs all night. Do you think he could come in for a second?"

Jasmine gave her a slight nod.

"Come on in, Tim."

Tim stuck his head around the door and gave her a gentle smile, but she could see the hurt and worry in his eyes. She must look awful. "I've got to get going, but I wanted to see if you needed anything."

"I don't think so." The rasp in her voice surprised her, and she remembered the screaming. "Thank you both for saving me. I didn't know what to do, so I prayed, and not long after, you two came blazing out of the bushes." She felt tears streaming down her cheek. "After that, it's all a big black hole."

Bill spoke. "I saw Dave next to you by the ride. I started motioning the ride guy to stop us, but he didn't see me at first. Thank God it started to pour, that made him turn it off. By the time we got off, all I could see was Dave's back, chasing after you. He's a big guy, and I didn't think I could take him, so I ran to get the police. On the way, I saw Tim." He gave Tim a grateful look. "We told the police which direction you were headed, and we ran as hard as we could to where I thought he might be taking you." Bill swallowed hard. "I was so worried we'd be too late, but you held your own, little sister. You gave him a good fight." He cradled her hand in a gentle embrace.

She looked at Tim and saw the pride in his eyes. "I'll say. He'll be washing horse manure out of his eyes for weeks. And I'm pretty sure you broke his toe."

Despite the situation, Jasmine smiled. A wave of dizziness washed over her, and she leaned into Elsie. "I'm awfully tired." She closed her eyes a minute, lay back on her pillow, and waited for the room to quit spinning.

"I need to know if you're pressing charges." When Tim spoke, she heard the lawyer kick into action.

"Yes."

"I'd like to represent you."

"Absolutely." She opened her eyes and gave him a weak smile.

"If you'll excuse me, I have a trip to the police station to make." He tipped his head and left.

Elsie handed Jasmine her cell phone. "You call me

downstairs if you need anything. The doctor said it'd be best if you rested."

The last thing she remembered was the downy covers being tucked under her chin and around her. She was asleep in her cocoon in seconds.

The next day, as Jasmine reclined in the chair near the wood stove, dosing off and on, a knock on the door brought her to attention. She was about to get up and answer it when Bill came in from the kitchen.

"You stay put; I'll see who it is." The protectiveness from the past two days hadn't lessened any.

Past the open door, she saw Lily standing on the porch. Her first thought was that Lily had come to check on her.

"Lily, come in." Bill opened the door and stood back for Lily to pass by. She came and stood in front of Jasmine, her eyes hard, her mouth drawn into a taut line.

"Would you like to sit down?" Jasmine motioned to the sofa. Elsie came out and offered her a cup of coffee.

"No, thanks, I'll stand. It'll only take a minute to say my piece."

"Your piece?" Any idea of loving concern disintegrated in the steely gaze of her sister's eyes. Jasmine felt a tense knot grow in the pit of her stomach. Bill came and sat down on her right, Elsie sat on her left, and they all looked up at Lily.

"I've come to ask you to drop the charges against Dave Buchard."

The shock from her statement roiled through the room. Bill jumped to his feet.

"You've got to be kidding." Bill looked back and forth between Lily's tense expression and Jasmine's ever-reddening neck and face.

"I assure you, I'm not. I'm here on behalf of Marcy and the child she carries." She took a controlled breath. "If you drop the charges now, Marcy and Dave might be able to save what semblance of a reputation they have left."

"You're worried for their reputation?" Bill stood aghast, his eyes locked on Lily.

"Marcy is my best friend. They don't need a thing like this hanging over their heads, especially with a baby on the way."

"Lily, maybe you don't understand what happened," Elsie

began. Lily put her hand up, stopping her from continuing. "I'm perfectly aware of what happened. Dave had been drinking too much, and Jasmine tempted him in his weakness. He's always cared for her. When she led him on, it was too much for him." She sounded like she was repeating a speech.

It was Jasmine's turn to feel outraged. She sat up, but Bill put his hand on her, keeping her still.

"You listen to me, Lily. This is the second time he's acted inappropriately toward our sister. Jasmine refused to press charges last time, and I wonder if she'd be doing much the same this time if it weren't for all the witnesses." Lily's eyes widened in slight surprise, but she held her ground. "It doesn't matter what anyone says."

"Well, it matters to me. I saw exactly what happened, so did Tim and three police officers. You can't ignore the witnesses."

"I'm not saying things didn't get out of control, I'm saying we should lay the blame on the right person."

"You're saying it's my fault?" Jasmine's voice shook with emotion, hardly believing what she was hearing. Her worst nightmare was coming true.

"If you go and tell them how you teased and tempted him, how you led him on, I think they'll go much lighter on him."

"He's in jail for attempted rape and assault. You can't ignore Jasmine's bruises or her emotional state." Elsie's attempt to gain Lily's sympathy failed.

"If she learned to stay out of the way, she wouldn't be getting into things like this."

"That's enough." Bill spoke through gritted teeth.

"No, it's not. She's come home like a wounded lamb, waiting for us all to take her back into the fold. She's brought those women into our community. They're prostitutes."

"They're survivors of sex trafficking. Our church is helping those women to start their lives over. Jasmine is trying to keep them safe." Elsie's voice was almost lost in the din of emotion swirling in the room.

"Nothing you can say will change my mind. I want her to go to the police station today and drop the charges. The damage that's been done can't be entirely undone, but she doesn't have to ruin everything all over again."

"That's nuts. What are you talking about?"

"I'm not crazy. I know what she did."

Jasmine looked up at Bill sharply, and back to Lily. "It was her."

"What do you mean?" Bill's eyes filled with questions.

"Dave knew about the abuse. Said he'd been given the info firsthand. I couldn't imagine who would betray me like that." She turned to Lily. "You told him." Jasmine stared up at Lily, still not quite believing it was true. "You knew all along what Dad did to me." The words choked off in her throat. "Instead of coming to me, you told that creep and his wife."

"I didn't mean to tell him, he overheard me telling Marcy. She was sharing with me how Dave had a crush on you in school, how she was worried with you coming back for the reading of the will, and I didn't want her feeling badly about it. I told her you had most of the boys wrapped around your finger from a young age. How you kept Tim on a short string, and even now that he pined away for you. I told her how you manipulated Daddy. How you got everything you ever wanted, even the house." She choked on her emotion. "I saw him touching you, saw you leading him on. I know the truth." Lily put a hand to her mouth to stifle her crying.

"I was a little girl, how could you think that?" Jasmine's stomach rolled with nausea.

"It had to be that way. He wouldn't have done it otherwise. He couldn't have." Lily's sobs punctuated each word.

Voices in her head chimed in, agreeing with her sister's assumptions. A weakness washed over Jasmine, stealing every ounce of strength she had. The room started spinning, and she clenched her eyes closed.

"You need to leave." Bill's voice cut through the tension in the room as he stood between Lily and Jasmine. "I won't tolerate lies in my house. Don't come back until you're ready to hear the truth." He advanced on Lily, and she took several steps back. "Our father was a wretched alcoholic; he was a broken, sinful man who abused us, beat our mother, and misused our sister. Anything good about him was a complete lie."

"If that's how you're going to be, fine. I won't be back." She headed toward the door.

"You're going to pick that lecherous man and his spiteful

wife over your own sister, over your family?" Bill's voice shook with anger.

"Marcy's the one who helped me at all hours when Mom got so bad. She and Dave have been more supportive to me than you and Elsie ever have." She turned on Elsie with a look so heated that Elsie rocked back away from her. "Jasmine bought you off all those years ago. It should come as no surprise to me at all that you'd take her side."

Jasmine sat, helpless to stop the ugly accusation from scratching new wounds in her soul, still raw from the attack. Poor Elsie—she'd do anything for anyone. Jasmine reached up and took her hand, trying to let her know she was there for her, unable to find the words.

"We offered to help you any number of times. You never accepted." Elsie's voice cracked with emotion.

"I really didn't except anything I said to matter."

Bill strode over to the door and opened it, his tolerance of Lily gone. "You've made your choice."

Lily walked out and the weight of another division in Jasmine's life crushed her down. When would the damage of her father's sin stop hurting the ones she loved? When would all this end?

Thirty

Through a sleepy haze, Jasmine heard her phone ringing on the bedside table. Daylight streamed in through her window, but she had no idea what time it was, or what day it might have been. Her life had become a blur.

Grappling for the phone, she answered without checking to see who it was. "Yes?"

"Jazz, is everything okay?" Brandi's concerned voice filtered through to her ear.

"No, not really." She rubbed her eyes, trying to clear the sleep away.

"Your brother called me and told me what happened. Do you want me to come?"

"What day is it?" Her mind spun on a bumpy axis.

"I'm coming. I'll be there by tonight. Is there a hotel I can stay in?"

Jasmine felt a laugh build. "Hotel? No, I wouldn't stay in the hotel. Yeah, that'd be a colossal bad idea."

"Let me talk to your sister-in-law, okay?"

"Why?" Nothing made any sense to her. She wanted to sleep. Elsie walked in, carrying a tray with food on it. "It's for you." She handed the phone to Elsie and rolled into a ball on the bed.

"Hello?" Elsie listened and made some suggestions for places to stay in the area. When she hung up the phone, she turned to Jasmine, pulling the tray table by the bedside.

"Your friend is coming. I think you need to get up and get showered. You'll feel better."

Feel better? The only thing that made her feel better was

slipping into unconscious sleep. She didn't dream, didn't think, didn't wonder. The best part was that the voices in her head didn't torment her.

"Come on." Elsie uncovered her, pulling her to a sitting position. She was in no shape to fight her. Her back ached, her elbow was swollen, and her legs screamed against the pressure. She hadn't felt this bad since she was mugged and left for dead in the alley that time. And what did they get? Her jacket. All for a jacket. She shivered.

"I've got the bath ready for you. Do you need me to help you undress?" Elsie's voice floated around her.

"No, I've got that." Jasmine felt the closed toilet lid under her, but she had no recollection of being walked down the hall.

"Okay, I'll check on you in a little bit. You climb in and soak, warm yourself up and relax. Afterward, you'll eat something and take a nap."

Once again, Elsie was mothering her. She'd never been mothered, and here was this woman, her own age, loving and caring for her.

"Elsie?"

"What is it?" She came and put an arm around her, sitting on the edge of the tub.

"If you weren't here, I don't know what I'd do."

"I know it doesn't seem like it right now, but everything is going to be okay."

Jasmine didn't respond. She didn't think anything would ever be okay again. All the memories she'd kept locked down, all the feelings she'd kept under control were bubbling to the surface of her life, and she had no way to stop them. They rushed at her, taunted her, until she didn't think she could take it anymore.

Elsie gave her a hug and closed the door, leaving her on her own. Jasmine undressed, peeling off her leggings and T-shirt, clingy with sweat. She turned to the tub, but caught sight of herself in the full-length mirror. Her body was mottled with yellow and purple blotches in a pattern that reminded her of a giraffe. But it was the gaunt look in her eyes that scared her the most.

"Elsie said you're going to be okay." Her plaintive voice echoed in the bathroom, cracking with emotion. "God, help

232

me." She leaned her head against the mirror, trying to comfort the cold form of her reflection. "Take it all away. I don't want to remember. I don't want to feel." Her shoulders shuddered, and she sank to the floor, leaning on the mirror, sobbing.

The ache of loneliness that had chased her the past four days subsided. Somehow, she sensed she was not alone, that God was there, in that place with her. He'd protected her, through the desperate strength she'd used to beat off Dave, through her brother and Tim, through the rainstorm.

"What am I supposed to do now?" She had to face Dave in court soon, but that wasn't what scared her the most. She no longer knew what the focus of her life should be. She couldn't think straight about any of it. Lily's accusations screamed in her ears, echoing off the walls of her soul.

"Could I have stopped him?"

No.

"Did I tempt my father, or Dave, or any of them?"

No.

The answers sang in her heart, giving her a sense of hope inside the bleak well where she swam. The accusing voices faded. "I've never asked for healing, Lord. I've always tried to do it all on my own. I can't do it anymore, though. I'm all used up. I don't know what to do next, or what You want from me. But I'm giving that to You. Whatever You want for me, God, that's okay with me."

She cried until the tears would no longer come. When the well of sadness dried up, she felt something else filling her, overflowing. A warmth and a sense that life would go on—that the days following this would not be easy but would be easier—gave her hope. She stood and turned on the hot tap to warm the tub. Climbing in, a determination not to give up covered her like the warmth of the water, washing her inside out, not just cleaning out the dregs, but replacing the ugliness with His goodness.

Maybe that was what Dee had meant.

After her bath, some food and a long nap, she sat on the side porch, watching the sunset. Brandi's car pull into the driveway and her dearest friend climbed out and walked straight toward her. Jasmine waved to her as she approached.

"Well, you look better than you sounded earlier."

"Were you praying for me?"

Brandi gave her a kind smile. "I have been ever since I heard of the attack."

"Thanks." She patted the seat next to her. "We're on our own here for a bit. I convinced Elsie to go to bed; she's been caring for me nonstop for days now."

"She sounds like a special woman."

"She really is."

"I hear the regret in that statement."

"I wish I could remember her completely, instead of in bits and pieces. We did a lot of things together." If anyone deserved to be remembered, it was Elsie.

"I think you need to let go of that and appreciate one day at a time."

"I think you're right. I've been so angry. I didn't know I was, but I was."

"You're finally grieving." Brandi took her hand. "I've been praying for that a long time."

"I thought I'd already gone through this. But I hadn't. I'd stuffed it away." Funny how easy it was to put grief aside and let yourself get busy with things and never think about it. But it grew and lingered there in the darkness, always ready to be released.

"It's part of the process." She hugged her sideways. "It's letting go of your hopes and dreams of the past and looking forward from today on. It's mourning what can never be, but hoping for the best in the future."

"I've been trying to do it on my own, on my own terms for a long time now. It wasn't until I gave it all up to God that I had any relief. I wish I would have done that a long time ago."

Brandi hugged her sideways. "God is patient. He's been using you where you are. You might be surprised where He takes you next."

"You know, for the first time, I've got a sense of peace about that."

"Peace is a lovely gift." She held on to Jasmine's hand and looked around her. "Well, seems to me I didn't need to come out here after all." She made as if to leave.

Jasmine laughed. "Don't you dare go. I've got to go to court tomorrow for the initial hearing."

234

"I'm not going anywhere. I want to meet all these people I've been talking to on the phone." She grinned. "And I thought I'd stop in and see the house where Misty and Dee are living."

"It's a really neat place."

"I hear another regret in your voice."

Jasmine sighed. "Not regret. Maybe a sense of discomfort."

"Misty?"

"Yeah. She's praying I'll change my mind."

Brandi didn't say anything.

"You think she's right." She pulled away from Brandi.

"I never said that. I think that instead of listening to Tim, or to your own fears, you might want to listen to God."

"Do you know how crazy an idea it is that I should be a parent?" Super crazy. Impossible.

"Because you're single?"

"That's not even at the top of my list."

"What is?"

Jasmine fell silent.

"Is it that promise you made to yourself?" Brandi shook her head.

"Yes." She hated to admit it.

"Don't you think you've punished yourself enough?"

Jasmine didn't say it, but she knew Brandi could read the answer in her eyes.

"I see. Well, if God is big enough to forgive you, maybe you should start thinking about forgiving yourself."

"Even if I can, it doesn't change anything. I don't deserve to have a baby."

The door on the porch opened, and Elsie stepped outside, carrying a tray of tea and scones. She sat it down on the low table nearby them and held out her hand to Brandi.

"I thought I heard someone out here. You must be Brandi?"

"You must be Elsie. That looks yummy."

"Plum butter and scones." She shivered. "Why don't we move this inside?" She glanced up at the darkening sky. "We're going to have more rain tonight." She picked up the tray, and they followed her inside to the living room. She stoked the fire. "Did you find that bed and breakfast okay?"

"I did. Thanks for the recommendation. The owners are very sweet."

"They are. They've done a lot for the House of Hope, too."

"The place Mrs. Craig runs?" Brandi took her tea cup.

"Yes. Now that they've decided to take care of young women in trouble, it's given the community something to really strive for."

"It's all run on donation?"

"Yes. Is that how you run your business?"

"I get some government monies, but mostly it is by donation. The big shelter supports us, too, as we come alongside some of their women and help them get jobs and reestablish their lives." Brandi's eyes sparkled.

"What are you thinking, exactly?" Jasmine asked her.

"What makes you think I'm thinking something?"

"I know you." When Brandi got a look like that in her eyes, something was up.

When Brandi didn't answer, Jasmine changed the subject. They were talking about the ribbons Elsie won at the fair when they heard a knock on the door. Tim stuck his head in the window and Elsie motioned him inside.

"I didn't know you had company." He closed the door and took a seat. "Brandi, right?"

"That's right. We met in my office."

He took Brandi's offered hand in a gentle shake before sitting down next to Jasmine.

"I'm glad you're here, you can be a support to Jasmine in court tomorrow." Tim turned to Jasmine, all business. "I wanted to prep you on the arraignment. You won't be required to say anything at this point; we're months away from a trial. This is about establishing that he's a danger to the community. We want to make sure he stays in jail where he belongs."

"How can you do that if I don't testify?"

"His record will speak for itself. I'd like for you to be there, so the judge gets the sense of the seriousness of the situation, and it becomes more personal if he sees you. But after that, I have seven affidavits from other members of the community that he's acted not only inappropriately, but made threats against them."

Jasmine felt the floor rock under her. "There are others?"

"Those are the ones who have come forward in the past two days. I have a feeling there are many more. In fact, I'm going to make sure that his college-town paper gets wind of the story, and see if there are any women from his college days that want to come forward for the trial."

"I can't believe you've done all this."

"We're going to put him away, Jasmine." His eyes held a steely glint.

Brandi laughed. "If I ever need a lawyer, I'm calling you."

"Can you stay for supper?" Elsie offered.

"No, I've got to get everything prepped for tomorrow." He shifted his gaze to Jasmine. "Don't worry, and get a lot of rest."

"Yes, sir." Her stomach was in knots, but having Tim in her corner made everything seem manageable.

As he headed out the door, Elsie made the same offer to Brandi.

"I'd love to, thanks." She followed Elsie into the kitchen, and the two of them were chatting and fixing dinner like old friends. Jasmine couldn't hear exactly what they said, but she could hear Brandi laughing, and the sound cheered her spirit.

Jasmine closed her eyes and tried to relax. Lily would be there tomorrow. She could handle someone's justified anger. But this? The unfair, untrue accusations Lily hurled at her burned in her stomach like hot coals. There wasn't anything she could do about it—she and Lily would never bridge this gap.

"Whatcha thinking about?"

Jasmine opened one eye and saw that Brandi had rejoined her in the living room.

"Dinner cooking?"

"Elsie's a pro. I made a salad and she shooed me out." She picked up her tea cup and took a sip. "It'll be a bit yet. Want a scone?"

"Not hungry."

"Too busy chewing on your worry?"

Jasmine frowned at her. She could cut to the heart of a matter faster than anyone she'd ever met. Really annoying.

"You could say that."

"This Dave guy really got to you, huh?"

"You know, I can handle the Daves in this world. It's my sister."

"It's something all abuse victims have to be ready for—

misplaced blame. It doesn't make sense, and it's horribly hurtful and damaging, but nonetheless, you'll have to learn to deal with it somehow."

"I know. Don't I tell that to our clients? Knowing all the facts doesn't give them a personal connection to me. I never realized how hard this was. It's like I'm being victimized all over again."

"How's that make you feel?"

Jasmine's eyes refocused on Brandi. "What?"

"Sad? Depressed? Morose?"

"Angry. Really angry. It's unjust, unfair, and..." Jasmine paused, not knowing what else it was.

"All those things." Brandi took a bite of her scone and sat quietly for a few seconds. "I'm going to tell you something that's going to stretch you, but you need to do it. You need to forgive her."

"I am not going there yet."

"You can hold on to it for as long as you want. But picture this—that anger you're feeling, it's just. And right now, be angry. But if you keep that anger around, carry it with you day after day, it's going to start eating away at your soul, like it's made out of acid. The longer you carry it, the more holes it's going to make."

"Yeah, yeah." Jasmine picked up a scone and dismantled it on her plate, crumbling it to dust.

"Listen to me. Those holes don't disappear once you've forgiven her. They take time to heal. And sometimes the wounds we make for ourselves take twice as long to heal as the ones others give us."

"The list of people I gotta forgive is getting longer by the hour here."

"You remember what I said." Brandi sat back and continued sipping her tea as Jasmine took stock of the holes in her soul.

Somewhere around thirty, she lost count.

Thirty-One

The next day dawned bright and shiny. It had rained in the night, leaving a slick gloss on the remaining fall leaves, giving the impression that they were pieces of bright colored material. Bill drove Brandi and Jasmine past Central Park, past the town square, to the courthouse. People milled around, all wearing their Sunday best.

"I didn't expect so many people to be out this early." Tension flew through her.

"This is big news. Don't worry, they won't be allowed in the courtroom."

Jasmine caught his eye. "Who will be in the courtroom?"

"I'm not exactly sure." His answer didn't instill great comfort.

Inside the courtroom were more milling people. Some of the women gave her encouraging smiles, but most people looked at her suspiciously. Tim sat at a table at the front of the room, with his back to her. He studied his notes, flipping through page after page of yellow legal pad. An intense feeling of gratitude filled her. What would she have done without him?

As if he sensed her gaze, he turned and gave her a warm, encouraging smile and once again she glimpsed the young man she used to know. As the judge entered, they went through the routine of standing and sitting. A sheriff's officer brought in Dave Buchard. At that moment, a woman started to sob. Jasmine turned to her right and saw Lily comforting Marcy. She handed her a tissue and whispered comforting words. Jasmine's stomach clenched in a bizarre twist of jealousy.

Brandi squeezed her arm in support, and she turned back

around to watch the proceedings. The charges were read. They sounded cold and impersonal. It made sense why Tim wanted her to be there.

Tim approached the bench with a stack of letters. The judge, a woman of about fifty, took their measure. She looked at Jasmine before her eyes focused back on Tim and finally shifted to the defense.

"Mr. Moore, you've heard the charges, how does your client plead?"

"Not guilty, your honor."

Jasmine knew to expect that, but hearing it stirred her ire all over again. She caught movement from the corner of her eye. Dave turned, giving her a leer. She couldn't believe his nerve to do so, even in the courtroom. She pressed back in her seat, as if to get away from him, and glanced at the judge, hoping she'd seen it.

She had.

"Proceed."

"We request my client be released on bail, your honor."

"These are serious charges, Mr. Moore."

"Yes, your honor. We don't argue the point that he'd been drinking, but let's remember that my client was enticed."

The judge looked over the paperwork. "I don't have any evidence to that, or the drinking."

"They probably didn't do a breath test, your honor."

"So your argument was that he was drunk, and therefore not responsible for his actions?"

"No, your honor. Our argument is that my client had been drinking and was presented with an offer by Ms. Reynolds, and he took her up on it." He shrugged his shoulders. "It was a lapse in good judgment."

The judge looked over the notes and the additional paperwork that Tim had given her.

"The charges are assault, attempted rape, and battery. That sounds like a lot more than a lapse in good judgment, Mr. Moore."

"As you can see from the photos, your honor—" He went forward and laid some pictures on the bench. "—my client was severely mistreated. If anyone should file assault charges, it's Mr. Buchard."

"And will you be doing so?"

"Oh, no, your honor. Mr. Buchard wants to put this behind him and return home to his expectant wife and business as a respected member of the community."

The disgust Jasmine felt moments before compounded. Not only was he refuting the charges, he was laying the blame for the incident at her feet.

"Let me understand what you are saying, Mr. Moore. Your client was solicited by Ms. Reynolds and accepted her solicitation because he'd been drinking. Then, at some point, Ms. Reynolds attacked Mr. Buchard?"

"Yes, your honor." The slender, well-dressed man seemed to grow horns and a tail under Jasmine's very eyes. How could anyone lie like he did?

"Did your client suggest a motive for Ms. Reynolds's behavior?"

"Ms. Reynolds had feelings for my client many years ago."

Jasmine shot forward in her seat, seething. Brandi put an arm out and gently pulled her back into her seat. She shook her head the tiniest bit and patted Jasmine's arm.

"We also believe Ms. Reynolds has emotional problems, judge." The defense lawyer gave her a sympathetic look that made her want to spit.

The judge picked up a stack of papers and read them again. "Do you know what I see, Mr. Moore?"

"No, ma'am."

"I see a stack of professional and personal character references for Ms. Reynolds—each one reports she is a woman above reproach. I also see a stack of auxiliary complaints against your client." She lifted the stack that was three times as high as Jasmine's stack. "Am I to believe that all these women solicited Mr. Buchard as well?"

At that point, Mr. Moore tugged at his collar. "No, ma'am. I'm not familiar with those complaints."

"Well, perhaps you should be. Your client has been a busy man. Not just here in Bright River, but in at least two other towns as well. I'm assuming there are more where this came from, Mr. Able?"

"Pouring in as we speak, your honor." Tim's tone was solemn.

"I see. In light of this new evidence, would your client like to change his plea?"

Moore leaned down to the now sweating, red-faced Dave, who'd already begun sputtering.

Dave leaned away from council. "No. I will not. I don't care what any of them say. I'm a pillar of the community!" Dave bellowed into the face of his lawyer. "She's a temptress!" He pointed a shaky finger in Jasmine's direction. She turned away, not facing him, and kept her eyes on Tim, whose eyes showed practiced, complacent indifference at Dave's words. He turned toward the judge.

"As you can see, judge, Mr. Buchard is a danger to the public. It's our request that he not be released on bail."

"Mr. Buchard, please rise."

Mr. Moore pulled Dave to a standing position.

"The request for bail is denied. Mr. Buchard will be held without bail until the date of his trial."

The gavel pounded down, and wailing filled the courtroom. Jasmine saw Marcy leaning into Lily, sobbing uncontrollably.

But the women who had been giving Jasmine accusing looks earlier were now looking in disgust at Dave. They filed out, murmuring their disbelief.

Lily helped Marcy stand and led her from the room; she never looked at Jasmine, not even once.

The officers hauled Dave from the room kicking and screaming. Jasmine kept her eyes averted. When the courtroom quieted down, she took a deep, stress-relieving breath. Tim collected his papers and headed toward them.

Bill stuck his hand out and shook Tim's hand. "Thanks."

"Sure thing. I knew a little push would be all he needed to hang himself." He glanced at Jasmine. "You'll have to come back to town for the trial. I'll give you a call and let you know more about that as the date draws nearer."

"When will that be?" The idea of coming back any time soon filled her with anxiety.

"Things are a bit backed up here in town. It might not be until early next year."

"I can't thank you enough, Tim. I don't know what I would have done without you." She put her hand out to him, and he took it, squeezing it gently. The warmth and safety that filled her at his touch surprised her. Their eyes locked a moment, before letting her go—and that lost empty feeling she'd experienced in Portland swirled around her once again.

"Will you join us for a celebratory lunch?" Bill invited.

Tim glanced at Jasmine. "No, I can't. I'll be in touch." He nodded toward her and made a hasty exit. Things would never be the same between them again.

Bill put his arm around her. "Don't look so hurt. He's honoring your wishes."

"I wish he'd be satisfied with just being friends."

Bill pressed his lips together but said nothing. They exited the building into the now-glaring light. Steam was rising from the dampened cars and streets.

"What happened to the cool fall weather?" Brandi fanned her face.

"Oh, it'll be back before we want it to be. When do you ladies leave?"

"I'd like to go see Misty and Dee before we head out of town."

Jasmine didn't know where all the talk of leaving had come from. Now that the trial was over, she felt like she was being dismissed. Her shoulders slumped at the thought. She'd never wanted to come here in the first place, she should be happy to go home. That's what she'd wanted all along.

After lunch, Jasmine and Brandi headed off to see Mrs. Craig. As they pulled up, Jasmine saw a newly made sign over the door. Bright River House of Hope on a carved wooden background edged in evergreen trees and a curling river.

"I love the name." Brandi smiled as she scanned the house. "It's big, how many rooms?"

"I think she said four. To be honest, I can't remember."

"Well, if I like Mrs. Craig as much as I like everyone else out here, I think we'll have a good solution for some troubling cases."

As they headed up the front steps, Mrs. Craig whipped open the door and gasped. "I thought you were the EMTs." A woman cried out from inside, and Mrs. Craig raced back through the door.

Jasmine followed her, passing the disarray in the living room. Cushions were off the couch and magazines strewn over the carpet.

"What's wrong?" Jasmine heard a scream from the dining room. She and Brandi rushed toward the sound and found Misty laying on the floor, towels under her bottom, a couch cushion behind her back, and Dee holding her hand.

"Breathe, Misty. Pant like they taught us in class," Dee coached her.

Jasmine shot a look at Mrs. Craig. "Isn't she early?"

"The doctor said she had five weeks to go yet."

"It hurts!" Misty's eyes rolled from side to side in panic.

"Breathe, pant, pant," Dee reminded her.

"You breathe!" Misty screamed at her.

The front door slammed open, and two EMTs raced into the room. Dee, Brandi, and Jasmine all stepped back, letting them get to work. They loaded her on a gurney and had her in the ambulance before Jasmine realized what was happening.

Mrs. Craig, Dee, Brandi, and Jasmine followed in her car.

"Will the baby be okay?" Dee's eyes locked on her own bulging stomach.

"We need to pray for both of them." Mrs. Craig still carried the sweet, grandmotherly tone, but Jasmine could see worry lining her face.

Jasmine wove her way through town as fast as she could, pulling in behind the ambulance and parking in the lot. They jumped from the car and raced into the ER. One of the EMTs stood at the nurse's station, filling out paperwork. He looked up and walked over to them. How could he be so calm when the adrenaline rush was still pumping through her ears?

"They've got her admitted. The baby was crowning as we moved her into the ER."

"She wasn't due yet." Jasmine couldn't quite believe this was happening. She thought Misty had more time to make a decision. Had Tim found another adoptive parent? Had Misty changed her mind about keeping the baby?

"I've seen my share of premature labors. I can't make any promises, but most turn out okay in the long run." He headed back to the station and left them sitting in the waiting room. About an hour later, a doctor came out of the ER.

"Mrs. Craig?"

Mrs. Craig motioned to him and he came over to them. "Hi.

I'm Dr. Shea."

She stood to face Dr. Shea. "How's she doing?"

"She's in recovery. The baby is in NICU. Her lungs are in fair shape considering her age. We'll need to monitor her closely for the next two weeks or so."

"It's a girl?" Jasmine found herself smiling, despite the situation.

"You can all go up and see her through the window. I'm afraid we can't let you in to hold her until she's more developed. As soon as we get a good set of vitals and warm her up, we'll bring Misty in for her first feeding."

"Where's Misty?"

The doctor checked her chart. "Room one-fifteen. Down the hall, take the next left."

As they walked up the hallway, Jasmine couldn't help but sense Dee's worry and anxiety. If she could say anything to comfort her, she would. This wasn't Jasmine's area of expertise. In fact, Jasmine had never felt more out of her element.

Inside the room, the nurse finished taking her vitals and offered Misty a glass of ice chips and apple juice. The other bed in the room was empty for now. Jasmine could see out through the window into a grassy garden area. Peaceful.

"We'll have dinner in a couple hours. If you need anything, push the call button." The nurse gave Misty a pat and smiled at them all as she left.

Jasmine approached her first. "How're you doing?"

Misty took a sip of juice. "Okay, I guess. It hurt a lot more than they told me it would." Dee inhaled sharply and Misty gave her an empathetic look. "Sorry, Dee. Have you seen her yet?"

"No, we'll see her next."

"She's so beautiful, Jazz." Her eyes grew teary. "I wish she wasn't early, though."

"You have some tough decisions to make. But don't think about that now. You need to do what's best for both of you, and that's rest."

"And feed the baby. They said that my nursing her would help us both recover faster."

"Good." Jasmine felt relief wash over her. Misty had finally let go of the idea of her adopting the baby.

"The doctor said her lungs and intestines have to mature, still." She glanced over at Dee and to Mrs. Craig. "Thanks for being there. I was so scared."

Dee didn't look comforted, but she smiled. She still had that deer-in-the-headlights look about her. Jasmine could hardly blame her.

"We're so glad you and the baby are safe." Mrs. Craig squeezed Misty's hand. "I have to be honest, though, you gave me quite a scare." She turned to Dee. "Don't you go getting in a rush now."

It wasn't clear if Dee understood Mrs. Craig's sense of humor or not. All she said was, "No, ma'am."

Misty leaned back into the pillows, releasing an exhausted sigh.

"We'll leave you to rest." Jasmine started to lead their crew out of the room.

"Thanks, Jazz. Would you let Tim know I'd like to talk to him?"

"Sure. Do you want him to come by tomorrow?"

"Yes, that'd be fine. Thanks."

The optimism Jasmine felt was palatable. She'd no longer have to consider her parenting skills, or lack there of—Misty would be keeping her baby.

Thirty-Two

"So we'll head back in the morning?" Brandi's question hung in the air between them as they sat on the back porch at Bill's house sharing takeout dinner from the sandwich shop downtown.

The last time Jasmine was in Bright River, she couldn't wait to leave. With the attack and public pressure, she should want to leave all the faster.

"I guess so." Jasmine chewed on the straw from her soda, looking out over the yard. The day had been unusually warm for that time of year. Summer didn't want to let go.

"Did you want to stay on for a few days? It's understandable."

"No. I've got a lot to do when I get back. And there's Oscar." Jasmine sat up in a panic. "Who's feeding Oscar?"

"Don't you worry about him. Officer Banner offered to pitch in. I told him to keep his fingers curled and not move suddenly." Brandi laughed.

Jasmine felt odd having Banner in her apartment when she wasn't home. But it was an emergency. Instead of reprimanding Brandi, she changed the subject. "So Mrs. Craig said they had four rooms in that house, and they were trying to buy the neighboring house, too. It would have six bedrooms."

"An excellent place to send some of our gals who need a place to hide and recuperate."

"Some of them anyway. They'll be focusing on giving shelter to homeless pregnant women."

"How will Mrs. Craig cover both houses?" Concern and curiosity filled Brandi's eyes.

"She has a good friend from her college years that wants to

move here and retire like Mrs. Craig."

"Probably the kind of retirement I'll have someday. Helping these young women is more than a job for me—it's who I am." Jasmine could imagine Brandi rustling around Bright River House of Hope, making cookies and delivering advice.

"I'm glad she'll have help. These women need another matronly woman like Mrs. Craig to befriend them."

"To love them." Brandi found loving easy.

Memories of Jasmine's mother flitted through her mind. She'd loved her the best she could. A sense of warmth and care filled her as she remembered Fiona. "Yes, to love them. Even if it's for a short time, it can make all the difference in the world." She thought for a moment. "Do you have anyone you could recommend as a counselor here?"

"I've got someone in mind, but we'll have to see." Brandi gave her a pointed look.

"You're kidding, right?"

"Why not? It'd get you out of the city, and you'd be able to work more personally with the girls."

"What's the old saying? You can't go home again."

"Maybe." Brandi sipped her soda and continued to give Jasmine the once over. She squirmed under Brandi's gaze.

"Besides, you'd be lost without me." More like she'd be lost without Brandi.

"You can work remotely."

Jasmine ignored her. "I'll put the word out with some of the local colleges. These women deserve to have someone really walk alongside them and get to know them. We can't do that from Portland." Her mind compiled a list of possibilities.

"You're right." Brandi stretched in her chair, but Jasmine knew she hadn't let go of the idea. "I really like your family. You are one blessed lady."

The words sank into Jasmine, and for the first time, she really thought about the blessing they were to her. She had Bill, Elsie, and the kids for keeps.

"Well, it's been a day, and we have an early morning ahead of us. I'm going to head back to the B and B." She picked up the garbage from her dinner and stuffed it in the takeout sack. "Thanks again for coming."

"I wouldn't be anywhere else." Brandi gave Jasmine's

shoulder a squeeze as she passed by and headed into the house. Jasmine could hear her saying good-bye to Bill and Elsie. A few minutes later, Bill joined her on the porch.

"So you're leaving in the morning?"

Jasmine tilted her head toward him. "It's time. But I know the way back."

A soft smile passed his lips. They sat in companionable silence for several minutes, watching the honeybees take advantage of what might be the last choice day of the season. Jasmine concentrated, mesmerized as one after another visited the flowers on the rail before flying toward the garden.

Bill's voice broke the stillness. "Are you doing okay?"

Glancing at him, she nodded. "I really am. It's been quite a few months, hasn't it?"

"It sure has."

"I don't know if I ever thanked you, Bill."

"For what?"

"Getting there in time." She reached a hand toward him. He grasped it in a warm embrace, and they watched the bees together.

"Bill, there's something I'd like to do before I go."

"Name it."

"I'd like to see Mom's gravesite."

Nodding his head, he gave her a knowing look. They climbed to their feet. Bill stepped inside to let Elsie know they were leaving and grabbed a couple coats before leading her to his truck.

Jasmine slid into the truck, pulling the heavy metal door closed, and waited for Bill. The older model truck was built like a tank and smelled like his aftershave. Bill climbed in, and they started the drive to the cemetery.

"Mom's headstone came in a few weeks after you were here. It's nice looking."

"Good." She crossed her arms over her chest. "I remember the last time I was out this way." Familiar road marks flitted by.

"When was that?" Bill kept his eyes on the road.

"Labor day, the weekend before I ran away. I went to visit Grandma's grave and cleared the weeds." It might have seemed odd to some that she'd visit the grave of someone she'd never met—but the grandmother she imagined in her mind was very real and had been her confidant on rough days.

"I'm sorry you never got to meet her. She was a great lady."

"How old were you when Grandma died, Bill?"

"About seven, I guess. I still remember images and feelings of her. She was the only one to ever hug me." Emotion choked his words. "Why did you go visit her?"

"It's silly, I guess."

"Tell me."

Jasmine took a deep breath. "Well, I really liked her photos. You know, the ones of you, Lily, and Grandma. You all looked so happy and safe. I imagined I knew her. She sort of became my invisible friend."

"The one you called Gee?"

"The letter G, for Grandma." Jasmine picked at the lint on her pants. "Did she know about Dad and his drinking?"

"I think so. She'd come to visit for a week here and there, baking up a storm. She'd take Lily and me to the park and out to eat. She'd spoil us like crazy, and for that week, he wouldn't beat us."

She reached her hand out for his and gave it a squeeze.

"So you went to say good-bye."

Jasmine nodded. "I felt like I had to leave everything behind, even G." Cutting ties to her whole life seemed like the best plan. Now, with gaps in her memory, doubts swirled around the truth of that.

Bill slowed the truck by a small flower stand on the corner run by an independent grower. The stand was unmanned, the honor can sitting on the back table. He put some bills inside the coffee can and picked up two bundles of flowers. He handed them to her as he climbed back into the truck. The aroma of fall flowers filled the cab with a musty sweetness.

They pulled into the country cemetery, and Bill drove his truck up a gravel road, stopping near a knoll. As they climbed from the truck, Bill handed her one of the woolen plaid coats he'd grabbed. She pulled it on, her small frame getting lost inside, grateful to have it. They headed up the knoll and stood in front of their family plot. She smiled softly at her grandmother's grave and moved over by Bill who stood at a spot to the left, marked off with bricks.

250

"That's new, what is it?"

"Mom bought spaces for us."

"Oh." She stared at the spots, imagining her brother and his family interred there. And Lily. Maybe she'd buy a spot out here, too. For some reason it bothered her to be buried away from everyone else.

"She bought spaces for you and the family you might have, too. Right there." Her section of plots was nearest her mother, furthest from her father. Even in death, she did her best to keep her safe.

"Oh, Mama." She sank down to her knees on the new growth of grassy covering. She ran her hand over the headstone, tracing her name.

"I think she did her best. It wasn't good enough, but it's all she had." Bill's voice shook. "I used to be so angry at her for staying, but I don't think she knew to do anything else. He beat all the fight and will right out of her."

"I know." Tears ran down her cheeks. She laid her bundle of flowers on her mother's grave. "I wish things could have been different, Mama." Bill sank down next to her and put his arm around her.

"They will be, now." He hugged her sideways as they cried together.

The next morning, Jasmine tiptoed downstairs with her bags, attempting to leave without waking anyone. The sight of the whole family on the couch brought her up short.

"I didn't expect you guys to be up." She hated good-byes.

"This is what family does." Bill gave her an encouraging smile.

"Thanks." She put out her arms to her sleepy niece and nephew. In a daze, they walked over and wrapped their arms around her waist. "I'll see you two soon."

Rose yawned. "When?"

Jasmine shot a look at Bill and shrugged.

"We'll plan a day to head into Portland. Remember Aunt Jasmine said she'd take us all to the zoo?"

"That's right. Your dad is going to call me, and we'll set up a zoo date." She hugged them and turned to Elsie.

"Thanks for everything."

"Come here." Elsie gave her a tearful hug and stepped back,

making way for Bill.

Bill embraced her in a long, comforting hug. When she pulled away, her eyes were full of tears. She heard Brandi's car drive up to the house.

"Brandi's here." She wiped the tears from her eyes and gave them all her bravest smile. An idea flitted through her mind, and she pulled out her phone.

"Smile."

"Oh no. I'm a mess." Elsie pushed at her hair, glancing down at all of their pajamas.

"Please?" Jasmine didn't have any photos of them, and she wanted to remember this moment, this family moment, for a long time to come.

They scrunched together in front of the couch and gave her their best, although sleepy, smiles. She took several and tucked her phone away.

Tears welled in her eyes once again. She grabbed her bag and rushed out to her car. Brandi called to her through the open window of her own car.

"Ready?"

All she could do was nod. Stashing her things in the backseat of her car, she began to follow behind Brandi. Before they could pull out, Tim pulled into the driveway, blocking them. Jasmine pressed her head against the steering wheel. The last thing she needed was a drawn-out good-bye with Tim. She heard tapping on her window and rolled it down to speak to him.

"I'm glad I caught you." He took a gasping breath. "Misty's gone."

Thirty-Three

As she climbed the steps of Bill's house and went back inside, she wondered what kind of Twilight Zone she'd entered. She'd nearly made it out of town this time, too.

Elsie came from the kitchen and distributed coffee to everyone, leaving a tray of bagels on the coffee table.

"How can she walk away like that? It doesn't make any sense. She knows how important it is for her to stay. She'd decided to keep the baby. What could have changed her mind?" Jasmine sipped the sustaining drink and waited for an answer from Tim. He wasn't making eye contact. That couldn't be good.

"She left a note." He pulled out an envelope.

As she reached for it, Jasmine saw her name written across the front. She slipped a finger under the flap and unfolded the letter.

> *Dear Jazz,*
>
> *If you're getting this letter, I've finally gotten the courage to do what's right. You're probably thinking I'm foolish and immature—you're right. But this decision isn't.*
>
> *I knew the minute I heard my little girl's heartbeat that I shouldn't be the one to raise her. She's got to stay safe, needs to be loved and protected. I can only promise to do one of those things—and I do love her, so much. So much so, I've prayed for the courage to leave.*
>
> *I thought I could stick around until she was out of the NICU—but every time I go to nurse*

*her, every time I see her so vulnerable, I ache
inside. The truth settles into me more and more.
I know I can never be what she needs. If she
were to go with me, one day social services
would take her away, and she'd be lost forever.*

*We both know having a child doesn't make
someone a good parent. So I'm doing the next
best thing. I'm choosing one for her.*

*I've not named her, I'm leaving that for
you, her new mommy, to do. Tell her I loved
her more than myself. Please tell her every day
God has a plan for her, and loves her, too. I am
certain in my heart He does.*

*Mr. Able has all the paperwork. I've signed
her over to you. You can do this. You inspire
me. Thank you from the depths of my heart.*

Misty

Jasmine read the letter again. As the weight of what
happened settled on her, she felt lightheaded. She blinked,
trying to regain her focus, and saw her family, Tim, and Brandi
staring at her. Her eyes darted to Tim's.

"She's really gone?"

"Yes."

"I didn't know she'd take off." Blood rushed and pounded
in her ears as panic built. Another idea settled and anger grew.
"She said you have the paperwork. You knew her plans."

"She kept saying it would all work out, I didn't know she'd
do something like this." He shook his head.

"But you didn't stop her. You didn't tell me!" She wanted
to hit him.

"Lawyer client confidentiality."

"I was your client first. This directly affects my life. And
I'm supposed to be your friend." Her voice shuddered with
rage and disbelief. "You forced this on me. After I told you
how I felt. I don't want to be a parent, I can't." Jasmine's eyes
blazed at him. "You've betrayed me and our friendship."

"Jasmine, I didn't know she'd run away."

"It doesn't matter. You should have talked her out of it. At
the very least, you should have found a prospective parent."

"I couldn't."

"Why in the world not?"

He sighed. "Because I agree with her choice."

The room went still. All she could hear was the sound of her breathing, the blood pounding in her head.

"Get out."

"Jasmine, please," Tim started, but she put a hand up, stopping him from continuing.

"I said get out." The sound of controlled vehemence laced her voice. "We are done."

Jasmine walked through the living room into the kitchen, keeping her eyes locked on the back door. The impulse to give chase after Misty, maybe even join her, buzzed through her thoughts. As she put her hand on the doorknob, she sensed a presence next to her. Brandi.

"Has he left?"

Brandi nodded.

So many different emotions flooded through her, she couldn't pick one to focus on—but one surfaced over all the others—fear.

"Let's you and me go for a walk."

Jasmine nodded and let Brandi lead her out the back door, down the side path, and out of the yard toward town. The crisp fall air bit into her cheeks, and she pulled her coat closer around her.

"Can you hear me?" Brandi knew her tendency to tune out better than anyone else in her life.

"Yes."

"I'm sorry this has happened."

Again, all she could manage to do was nod in response. The wounds she carried from Tim's betrayal grew deeper by the second. He'd tried to force her into what he believed to be the perfect life. She wouldn't be manipulated by anyone, especially not a man.

"I think he planned it all. I think he's known for months that Misty wouldn't change her mind. In fact, he probably encouraged her to do it. He can be very persuasive. You know—lawyer."

Brandi shook her head. "I wouldn't go there."

"Why not?" The curtness of her reply surprised them both.

"Tim should have told you Misty wasn't letting this go. He was wrong. But both you and I know she's had her sights set on you from the beginning."

"What kind of cosmic joke is it that I should be a mother? Look at me. I tune out when I'm overwhelmed. Don't you think taking care of a baby will overwhelm me? What do I know about being a mother? My own mother—" She broke off, putting a hand to her mouth to stifle a sob. "My own mother couldn't keep me safe. She hid in her backyard, dirt up to her elbows, and let my father hurt me." Tears flowed freely down her cheeks.

Brandi drew her by the arm into the park and led her to a bench, far back from the early morning foot traffic. Somehow they'd arrived at the town center.

"Can you see yourself doing that?"

"What?" Her eyes focused on Brandi for the first time.

"Letting your child be abused."

"How do I know?"

"You wouldn't."

Jasmine leaned down, cradling her face in her hands. "I sold drugs; I stayed with my rapist and convinced myself he loved me." She gagged on her words and took a steady breath. "I killed my baby." The last sentence of admission tore through her body. She rocked back and forth.

"Would you do it now?"

"What?" Brandi's question brought her up short.

"The abortion. Would you have one now?"

"No, I know the truth now."

"So the world lied, and you were desperate and believed it."

"Because I'm a stupid fool."

"And thus, you don't deserve to ever be happy?"

Jasmine couldn't say it, so instead she nodded.

"Oh, baby." Brandi put her arm around her. "Don't you think you've punished yourself enough?"

Again, to answer seemed too hard. She rocked back and forth on the bench, arms hugged across her chest.

"I'll tell you why Misty left her baby to you. She saw someone who had learned from her mistakes. She saw someone who took responsibility for her life and who loved others even when they made those same mistakes. She saw a survivor full of compassion."

Jasmine shook her head, unwilling to hear it.

"Have you asked God to forgive you?"

She nodded.

"Accept His forgiveness."

"What do you mean?"

"You're still punishing yourself. He's granted you forgiveness, child, and you are throwing it back in His face."

Blinking to clear her eyes, Jasmine's ears honed in on Brandi's words and her mind grappled to keep hold.

"Your heavenly Father forgives you—take it, or you'll end up hurting the both of you."

Truth washed through her, filled her extremities, and cradled her heart.

"Praise Him for His generous gift, and pray He'll show you what to do next." Brandi gave her a squeeze. "You've got to stop limiting yourself and embrace God's limits, instead." She handed her a tissue, and Jasmine cleaned up her face.

If Brandi was right, and she usually was, Jasmine hadn't been giving God much credit. It was hard to go from thinking of Him as a distant God to a loving Father. She needed practice.

They sat together, not speaking, for over an hour. Every now and then, Brandi handed her another tissue. After awhile, Jasmine's tears dried up, and life became a bit clearer.

"How come each time I think I'm all healed and ready to move ahead, I get tripped up again?"

"Sometimes God's got to heal us in stages because we won't let Him get close enough right away. He can take care of one spot, and that reveals another spot needing work."

"I sure wish He'd do it all at once."

"God's ways aren't our ways."

They watched the people walking by, a mother pushing a stroller; a father playing chase with his son.

"Do you think I should adopt Misty's baby?"

Brandi went still. "I think what you need to do is ask God what He wants for you. Is this part of His plan? I don't know—but it's a good question to ask."

Jasmine didn't know about much at that point. Except one thing—she'd packed her things, ready to leave, and once again, she wasn't going anywhere.

Thirty-Four

As Jasmine pulled into the parking lot of the hospital, a sense of foreboding filled her. After spending the better part of the day praying, or rather, talking things over with God, she'd ended up here. There wasn't an answer clear enough. She needed a memo signed in triplicate to feel secure in any decision at that moment.

She looked up at the ceiling of her car. "You know, this isn't fair. I don't want this. You need to make Misty come home." She released a defeated sigh when she heard the tone in her voice. She was dictating what she wanted rather than asking God what He thought was best.

Maybe she was afraid of the answer.

It'd been years since she'd felt this trapped, this hedged in by someone else's decision in her life. She stared out the car window at the one level, brick building. Inside people were healing, being born, and dying. Inside was a baby girl whose mother had abandoned her.

One thought comforted her. At least this baby was alive.

Jasmine had to give it to Misty—she'd carried this baby and allowed her a chance at life. Brandi told Jasmine it was the example she set. She didn't know if it was or not.

Climbing from the car, she headed inside the building to the NICU. As she peered through the single window, she could see that Misty's baby was the only patient. A nurse, covered in pink scrubs, turned and waved at her, opening the door. She spoke through her protective mask.

"Can I help you?"

Jasmine hadn't thought this through. "My name is Jasmine

Reynolds. I'm here to see..." She paused, not sure what to say. The foreign feeling of the whole situation threw her off-kilter.

"Oh, you're here to see your baby! I'm so glad to meet you. Misty told me all about you. I'm June." June knew, Tim knew—she seemed like the only one left out of the decision.

Before Jasmine knew it, June ushered her down the hall and covered her shoes, hair, and clothing in disposable green paper wrappers.

"Your daughter is doing fine. But we need to cover you up as a precaution. Her fragile system can't handle germs very well yet."

"Listen, I'm not—"

"Ready?" June's eyes scanned Jasmine's. "Don't worry; we never feel all the way ready to become a parent. I've got four, and each time I felt overwhelmed by the responsibility. You'll do fine." She led Jasmine back to the NICU and inside the room. After puttering around, she came back with a warm bottle.

"Misty pumped quite a bit and made sure we had a small supply before she left. Why don't you feed her?"

"No. Not this time. I came by to make sure she was doing okay." Jasmine backed away from the bottle-wielding nurse, hands up for protection.

"Don't be silly. Bonding happens during feeding. Sit down." She motioned to the gliding rocker chair near the baby's bed.

Something compelled Jasmine to comply. As she got comfortable in the chair, June handed her the smallest baby she'd ever seen.

"Wow. How much does she weigh?"

"Five and a half pounds. Putting on weight every day."

Amazed that something so small and helpless could survive, Jasmine continued to stare down at the infant. "That's amazing." The baby nursed the bottle until it was empty. June showed her how to burp her.

"And don't forget to talk to her." The nurse's eyes crinkled at the sides, and Jasmine could only speculate that there was an accompanying smile under her mask.

"Hey, baby. How was that bottle?" Jasmine rolled her eyes at her own inadequate small talk.

"It'll come to you as you practice." Again the crinkles

showed above June's mask. "So what are you going to name her?"

Jasmine's head shot up. "What?"

"We've been calling her Baby Reynolds. But she really needs a name."

The trap Misty had built became clearer and clearer. First, she showed up in town, looking all helpless. She wheedled her life into the community's compassion. Somehow she won Tim to her side. Leaving the baby, like a cute puppy in the pet store, unnamed and ready, felt like a box lid slamming against the top of Jasmine's head.

Jasmine glanced down at the baby, whose eyes were now staring up at her, seeming to peer into her very soul.

"I hadn't thought about it." At all.

"Well, it's a big decision." The nurse's voice sounded strained. "I would have thought since you were adopting her, you'd have a name all set."

That was the problem.

"Make sure it's something you can yell across a park or store quickly, in case you ever need to get her attention. Those really long names don't cut it."

Those seemed odd guidelines for naming a child. Her mother had named all her children after her favorite flowers. She probably even helped naming Rose. Somehow Jason had escaped. If it really was up to Jasmine, she'd have to give it some serious thought.

Jasmine stayed at the hospital for another hour, watching the baby sleep. She drove back through town, to the cemetery. Climbing the knoll, she sat by her grandmother's grave.

"I wish we could have met, G. I'd sure like some of your guidance today. What a mess I've stepped into." She picked the dead flowers from the old bunch she'd laid there the day before. "Most of my life, men have been making decisions for me, or about me. It's like I'm always along for the ride. First Dad. Then Rob. Now Tim. Tim's a huge improvement, mind you, over the rest of them."

Jasmine fiddled with the flower petals, plucking them one at a time, remembering the old rhyme from her childhood. She'd never played the fortune-telling game. Jasmine didn't want to know who loved her or not. She'd never wanted a boyfriend or husband. She never played house, let alone imagining herself as a mother. As a girl, she'd thought all the other girls were silly—even weak.

As the sun set, she thought about her baby, and what she might have named it. Different names flitted through her mind. She'd never known if it had been a boy or a girl. Even after talking to the woman at the shelter, she'd never allowed herself to think about meeting her child in heaven someday. What could she say? Sorry I ended your life.

A shiver coursed through her.

Jasmine stared up at the sky, hoping for a divine sign, but all she saw was a flock of geese heading south. Their arrow shape shifted here and there, breaking off and reforming to fit the new currents of air.

Slipping her purse off her shoulder, she pulled out the envelope of adoption papers Tim had left for her that morning. A tiny bunch of dried pink flowers clung to the corner, sprinkling out on the grass. The scent of jasmine lifted around her, filling the air with a musty sweetness, transporting her to another time. Jasmine opened it and read the forms. Her name appeared in several places near the word mother.

"Are you trying to give me a second chance here, God? The thing is, Elsie would make a much better mother than me. About anyone would."

Jasmine could picture it now. She, Oscar, and the baby sharing her one-room apartment. She and the baby going on emergency calls late at night. The two of them hanging out at the shelter together. The picture sure didn't fit.

"If I do this, I'll need to change everything about my life." She stared intently at her grandmother's gravestone, wondering what she'd do. Her cell phone rang, making her jump. Tim's face, this time holding a silly grin, flashed over the screen. Seriously? Again? She needed to keep a better watch on her phone. She should make him leave a message.

Better yet, she'd give him a talking to.

"Yes?"

"It's Tim."

"So I see."

"Oh. Yeah. That was for a joke. Before."

Before you started trying to control my life. "So a lawyer

and a pick-pocket. I think they could use you on the streets."

"You left it out one day, so I did it really fast." She could hear the embarrassment in his voice.

"What do you want?"

"Are you talking to me again?"

"Apparently." She hated how he did that.

"That's fair. I wanted you to know it looks like your house will sell. The realtor called. Jenny figured I'd like to give you the good news."

"Because we're such good friends, right?" The sarcasm-laced tone slipped out.

"Jasmine."

"Friends don't corner each other and keep things like babies and runaway mothers from one another. They don't try and force them to change."

"Can we talk in person?"

"No way." She picked up a small stone from the ground and tossed it toward the woods.

"Jasmine, please, for a few minutes. We can clear the air."

"Now you want to talk. Not before Misty hit the road. Not when you were writing my name all over those adoption papers."

"I was acting in everyone's best interest."

"You were playing God."

That got him. He didn't speak for several seconds.

"You're right."

Her eyebrows scrunched together. "I'm right?"

"Yeah. I had no business plotting a sneak attack like that. No matter that Misty had made up her mind, no matter that she was going to leave the baby, one way or the other. I should have come to you and told you. I'm sorry."

"Sometimes sorry doesn't cut it." She didn't know what she expected him to do at this point. She could hire a private detective to find Misty—but dragging Misty back wouldn't change anything, she'd run away again.

"I guess not." Again, he went quiet.

She checked her phone to make sure he hadn't hung up.

"If I don't do this, take the baby, what will happen to her?"

She heard him exhale. "At first she'll go into the system and be assigned to foster care. They'll try to find adoptive parents."

An image of the baby rushed through her mind, and she tried to imagine the family willing to take on her hospital bills and any residual health issues. She couldn't.

"How likely is it they'll find someone who wants to take on an abandoned premature baby?"

"I don't know."

Jasmine pictured the baby growing up alone and unwanted, handed off to one group of strangers after another, never belonging to anyone.

"Jasmine?"

His voice startled her, and she pulled back from the awful scenarios playing through her mind. She knew very well what happened to unwanted girls.

"Yes?"

"Congratulations on selling your house."

"Thanks." She'd forgotten all about the house for the moment. "Out of curiosity, do you know who bought it?"

An hour later, Jasmine paced back and forth in Bill's living room for what felt like an eternity before she paused to question Bill.

"What in the world is she doing?"

"I guess she wanted the house." Bill shrugged.

Jasmine shot a look to Elsie, who sat on the couch.

"It does seem odd, though." Elsie's brows crinkled in consternation.

"According to Tim, the realtor didn't even know we were related. She never even mentioned it."

"I guess there's no way to know what's going on in her head." Bill leaned back against the couch, putting his arm around Elsie's shoulder.

"Oh yes there is." Jasmine grabbed her car keys and stormed from the house before they could stop her. Had Lily gone insane? How was she paying for the house? Maybe she'd sold the other property to do it.

Jasmine parked her car and approached Lily's house. Before she reached the porch, Lily stepped outside, arms folded.

"That's far enough." Lily stared down at her from the top step.

"I came to find out why you're buying the house."

"Because I want it. It should stay in the family." The stress she put on the word family made Jasmine uneasy.

"But why buy it? I told you in the beginning I didn't want it. I would have given it to you."

"I wouldn't take anything from you." The sadness in Lily's tone took Jasmine aback.

"But how can you afford it?"

"I'm going to rent it."

Her mind rushed with questions, and Jasmine got the distinct feeling she was the last one at the party to get the joke.

"To who?"

"Marcy."

The coldness of Lily's tone hit Jasmine in the chest. Her mind went blank. Lily's hateful words came rushing back. She really had chosen Marcy over her. Jasmine couldn't help staring at her sister, a virtual stranger who carried a vendetta against her. There didn't seem to be anything else she could say. She turned in stunned silence to leave.

As she took a step toward her car, emotion stirred inside and spurred her to speak.

"You know what happened—the truth is rattling around somewhere in your warped memory. I pray someday you can accept it and ask God to heal you."

"Pray? God?" The hollowness of Lily's laugh made Jasmine's skin prickle.

Taking several steps backward, she reached the safety of her car. She climbed inside and rolled down the window. "You said you wished Dad had paid attention to you, Lily. Right now, I'm thanking the Lord he didn't. I don't think you would have survived."

Lily's jaw dropped a moment, before she ground her mouth into a hard down-turned grimace. "Get off my property."

At that moment, Jasmine wanted to do nothing more. She'd never convince her sister that the images she held in her mind were false. Lily would have to find the truth out on her own.

Thirty-Five

The hospital seemed to be the most peaceful place in town. Jasmine rocked the baby back and forth while she watched hersleep. She might be ready to leave the hospital in a week. Her time of decision was at hand.

If Jasmine adopted the baby, she couldn't stay in her old apartment. She would need the support of family. Her eyes lifted, looking at the wall, imagining the town outside. Could she live in a place where bitter childhood memories hid? Not only that, but Lily and her lancing comments would be another thing to contend with. Not to mention Marcy.

As she pondered these things, she heard a rap on the glass window. Tim waved at her, and his hopeful eyes brought another question to mind. He motioned for her to come out into the hallway with him.

Jasmine handed the baby to the nurse and left the room, removing the scrubs as she did.

"You look like a natural in there."

"Did you need something?" Try as she might, her guard was dropping again.

"To take you to lunch." He gave her a huge grin, one she could never have said no to as a kid. She apparently wasn't so great at it now, either.

"Where are we going?"

"You could sound happier."

"No, really, I couldn't. Where are we going?" Disappointment at herself grew by the moment.

"It's a surprise."

Tim escorted her out to his car. As she climbed in, he closed the door, and the noise reverberated like the clanging of a cage door. She pushed away the idea, breathing deep to relieve her stress. This was Tim. She trusted Tim. Well, mostly.

"How's the baby doing?" He started the car and they drove out of the lot.

"Much better. They're thinking of releasing her in a week, maybe sooner if she puts on more weight."

"Good. Great." The small talk died and left them both tongue-tied.

They drove through town. The question she knew he wanted answered hung in the silence between them. For once, he didn't press.

They rounded a corner, and she knew where he was taking her.

"I imagined a picnic, but with winter on the way, it's too cold out for that." Tim pulled up in front of his house. "So, I thought we could do a floor picnic."

Tim escorted her up the front steps of his house. As he opened the door, she saw he'd pushed all the furniture back, laid a plaid blanket down, and had place settings waiting for them. In the center sat a cooler. Tim helped her off with her coat and hung it on the tree near the front door. He knelt down by the hearth, stirred the fire, and got a warm blaze going in the fireplace.

"Have a seat."

As she did, a memory popped into her head—one that made her smile.

"We used to do this."

"Yes, we did. My dad would let us set up in the living room when the weather was bad."

"It was always so fun at your house. So safe." She brushed her hand over the blanket and saw a familiar purple spot. "This is the same blanket."

"How did you know?"

"This stain. You told a joke, and I laughed so hard I spit my grape juice out." She laughed reflexively at the memory and looked up into Tim's eyes, to find them shining down at her.

"We always had good times." He handed her a plate of fried chicken and potato salad.

Defenses gone.

266

The warmth of the fire seeped into her, and she relaxed for the first time in weeks. As they ate, Tim shared anecdotes from different trials he'd taken part in recently. Her smile was on autopilot, reacting at the right moments—but her mind wandered far away.

Tim. He'd always been there for her. Even now, when she was at her lowest, he'd been there. When she first hit town, he'd welcomed her home. Clearing out the house, finding the key, dealing with the camper and repairing her diary—he was there through all of it. When Dave attacked her, he'd come to her rescue. He'd protected her in court. He'd taken her tears and her anger and given her comfort. Really the thing he'd done wrong was help Misty give up her baby.

Granted, that was a big one.

Her mind came back into focus as he finished up another story, but she hadn't heard a word of it.

"You're like God." Had she said that out loud?

"Wait, what? I mean, I'm a pretty awesome lawyer, but…" He laughed, waiting for the punch line.

Jasmine's hand went up to her shirt collar and pulled it closed over the redness she knew had to be spreading up over her throat. "That's not what I meant."

"It's okay." He pulled her hand away from her neck and held it in his grasp. "Explain it to me."

After taking a steadying breath, her head cleared and everything came into focus. "All those times I felt most lost as a kid, I had you. You made me feel safe and normal when nothing was. And when I ran away, I had Fiona. Later, when I gave up and went with Rob, there were still people here and there giving me a chance and encouraging me. I didn't take it until I met Brandi. She was there, taking care of me—loving me when I didn't feel worthy of it. Even when I pushed her away over and over, she stuck by me.

"All those times I thought God didn't care, that I felt alone—I wasn't. God brought you, Fiona, Brandi, Bill and Elsie to me. He was waiting for me to come to Him and sent others to love me, even when I didn't feel like I deserved it."

Tears flowed freely down her face. "He never left me." The truth of it sank down on her, covering her like a mantle of protection. Tim's arms came around her, holding her and letting her cry.

As she pulled back from Tim, she sensed his reluctance to her go. She'd kept Tim at arm's length her whole life, like she'd done to Brandi. Like she'd done to God. She tried to protect herself—but by keeping everyone out, she'd hurt herself more. For the first time, she knew she could let him in. "I'm sorry for giving you such a hard time." She wiped at her eyes with her sleeve. "I've been keeping my guard up for so long, I'm just now learning how to let it down."

Tim reached for a napkin and dabbed the tears from her cheeks, the warmth in his eyes pouring into her. "I can be a little pushy sometimes."

She laughed. "You think so, do you?" Jasmine gave him a shove on the chest, and he caught her hand, holding it there.

"I know taking on this baby seems overwhelming. But you're not alone."

It had been ages since she'd allowed herself to get this close to anyone, but for the first time she could remember she wasn't afraid to let it happen. Jasmine let her hand rest against his chest and took comfort from his strength, from the beating of his heart under her palm. The plans that had taken shape in her mind over the past two days flowed freely.

"I think I'll move back here. I can get an apartment. Brandi would refer girls to Mrs. Craig's who needed distance and safety away from the city. I'd be the on-site counselor. Elsie and Bill would be here for us." She took a deep breath. "And you."

Tim's eyes sparkled at her. "I think that's an excellent plan." He reached up and brushed back her hair from her face with his free hand, letting it linger there, caressing her cheek. Heat raced through her, and Jasmine felt her heart race in expectation of his kiss. Even a week ago, the very idea would have sent waves of fear over her. But not now.

Leaning in, Tim brushed her lips with a delicate kiss, all the while keeping eye contact. She smiled against his lips. He closed his eyes and kissed her a second time. The sweet gentleness of it all brought tears to her eyes. He pulled her into an embrace.

"Have dinner with me," he whispered into her ear, sending shivers down her side.

"We haven't finished lunch yet."

He pulled back, locking eyes with her. "I meant forever."

Shock waves pulsed through her as she took in his meaning, and she leaned back in astonishment.

He cleared his voice. "I know. Pushy, right?"

At that point, Jasmine didn't know which worried her the most—that he'd proposed off-handedly, or that everything in her urged her to accept. A clear thought broke through her shock with a shudder.

"Listen, Bud, one change at a time here, okay? I'm about to become a mother."

"And usually that means you need a father." His voice lilted in suggestion.

"You mean an instant family?"

"Makes sense."

"You're incorrigible."

"Don't forget pushy." He rubbed his fingers over hers. "Well?"

Jasmine's emotions had ebbed and flowed so many times that week, she wasn't sure if she could trust herself to say what was in her heart.

"I'll tell you what. When I'm proposed to properly, after a decent period of dating and deepening friendship, I'll let you know."

"So that's a maybe."

"Did I say that?"

"I'm a lawyer—I'm very good at reading between the lines." He leaned in and was about to kiss her again when there was a knock on his front door.

"Don't move," he whispered against her lips before moving away.

"Do you always get what you want?"

"No, but I act like I do. All part of the image, remember." He winked at her and reached for the handle.

Jasmine's laughter stopped as he opened the door. There on his stoop stood a young woman, disheveled and cold, arms wrapped tightly to her chest.

"Misty?"

Thirty-Six

Jasmine leapt to her feet and pulled Misty into her arms, and led her inside to sit by the fire. "Where have you been?"

"I hitched up the road a ways, into Idaho. I tried to get a job but couldn't. I ended up in a shelter again."

Tim wrapped a blue wool blanket around her shoulders, and handed her a cup of tea. Jasmine fixed her a plate of food and brought it over to her.

"I saw her. The baby." A tear escaped down Misty's cheek. "I went to the hospital and watched her through the glass. She's doing good."

"She's doing fine." Jasmine's emotions raced. Just as she'd decided on a plan, here was Misty, back again. Without a doubt in her mind, though, she knew what should happen.

"Listen, Misty," Jasmine began, but Misty cut her off.

"Megan."

"What?"

"My real name is Megan." She sniffled. "That's why I came back. I told my story to this gal at the shelter. I told her I'd never given you my real name. She said the adoption wouldn't be legal if I didn't use my given name. And I realized I'd known that all the time." Sobs wracked her body. "I think all along I didn't really want to do it. I needed an out, you know? So one day when I'd gotten my act together I could come and say how it was never legal and take her back from you."

Misty wiped at her nose with her napkin. "But I know that's not right. I couldn't take her when you loved her all that time. And besides, I don't think I'm ever going to be okay. Look at me. Homeless, jobless, back in a shelter." She pressed her fingers to her eyes and rocked back and forth like a child.

"You can't do it on your own. No one can." Jasmine rubbed Misty's back until she calmed down.

"You could, Jazz. You've got it all together."

Jasmine shook her head, sure she'd misheard her.

"Hardly. The only way I could raise your baby was if I had the support of my brother and his family. And Tim. There's no way I could do it alone. And you don't have to, either."

Misty's eyes shot up in shock. "You haven't filed for adoption yet?"

"No."

"I kept thinking of her. I couldn't stop. My head told me that it was the right choice, but my heart kept telling me to come back."

Jasmine caught Tim's eye. His face didn't show any emotion at all, but she had an idea how he felt. She felt the pain, too. For a short time, she'd believed she would raise that baby. But now, she knew she wasn't supposed to.

"You're coming back to Mrs. Craig's. Once you've rested and settled in, you're going to take custody of your daughter."

"Won't they arrest me for abandoning her?"

Tim took that moment to interrupt them. "You didn't. You put her up for adoption and changed your mind. That's all."

Jasmine sent a grateful look in his direction and gave him a thankful smile, but he didn't respond in kind. The openness he'd shown her only minutes before was all but erased. Jasmine chalked it up to the loss of the baby.

"Tim, will you drive us to Mrs. Craig's?"

"Absolutely. Let's go." Grabbing his coat, he headed out the door and started warming up his truck.

Moments later, Misty ducked through the door of Bright River's House of Hope as if she wanted to remain unseen. Inside, Mrs. Craig and Dee sat talking about a job interview. When she spied Misty, she let out a yelp and leapt up to gather her into her arms.

"Oh, you dear girl. I'm so glad you're back."

Jasmine smiled at Tim, but once again, he didn't return it. Ever since Misty showed up, he'd been quiet and distant. Jasmine wished she could read his expression. Her eyebrows rose in his direction, waiting for a response—but he gave none.

A worried chill settled in the pit of her stomach.

"You're here to stay, aren't you?" Mrs. Craig held Misty at arm's length, searching her face.

"She's home to stay, Mrs. Craig. I'm going to the hospital to make sure they're aware of her return. Tim will take care of any legalities, I'm sure." She gave him a hopeful look, to which he nodded his agreement.

Well, at least he gave her that much.

"I'm so excited to have our first baby in the house!" Mrs. Craig pulled Misty into her arms again. "We have so many plans to make."

Misty spoke past the embrace. "You're not angry with me?"

"Child, I kept praying you'd change your mind. Now, let's get you upstairs, back into your old room."

Dee trailed behind them both as they climbed the stairs, a bright smile on her face.

Tim headed outside, Jasmine following, back to his car.

"Could you take me by the hospital to speak to the staff?"

"Sure." He opened his car door for her, climbed in the other side, and drove in silence.

There were more emotions than she knew what to do with racing through her. It wasn't quite like mourning the loss of a child, but the possibility of a child. She hadn't expected this ache now filling her.

Wrapping her arms around her chest, she tried to insulate herself from the pain. Life had turned into quite a roller coaster ride over the past few weeks. She'd gone from not feeling deserving of a child, or wanting a man in her life, to having both. She glanced sideways at Tim's stoic face. But now, did she have either? Maybe he only wanted the package deal.

As they pulled into the parking lot, the silence in the car felt deafening.

"I guess we might as well get this over with." Jasmine climbed from the car, assuming Tim would follow. Once inside they explained to the staff that Misty had changed her mind and would be back. The nurses patted her on the shoulder, giving her comfort and encouragement. By the time they left, exhaustion had set in. Despite it all, though, her stomach growled, reminding her she hadn't eaten all day. She grimaced in embarrassment and pressed her hand to her middle, trying to make light of the moment.

"Sorry about that. We didn't exactly get to eat any lunch, and I missed breakfast." She glanced out into the darkening neighborhood as they drove through town. "And it's past dinner time now."

"I'll drop you at Bill's."

The coldness in his tone surprised her. "I kind of hoped you'd take me back to our floor picnic."

Tim didn't say anything but kept his eyes intent on the road.

"Hey, is everything okay?" Jasmine reached out and brushed his arm, but he didn't respond to her touch.

"I've got a lot of my mind." He shot her a look. "I'm surprised you're taking all this in stride."

"Honestly, I'm not. I've got a lot of mixed feelings. When I look at the big picture, though, I'm glad Misty made the decision to come back. There will always be a part of me that wants that second chance to be a mother, but I know in my heart that her baby belongs with her. She just needs some help to get there."

As she finished talking, he pulled up in front of his house, staring at its darkened doorway. "I couldn't help imagining her little feet running up and down my stairs." His voice cracked.

"They still might someday. You don't know how long Misty will live here. You were there for her when she really needed someone. She won't forget that."

Again, tension filled the quiet space between them. Something was bothering him, something larger than Misty and the baby. This time, it was his stomach that growled.

Jasmine giggled. "We should go eat." Tim got out and opened the truck door for her. As they walked up the steps together, she tripped and he caught her.

"Sorry, I should have left the light on."

She'd expected to linger in his grasp, but he let her go right away. She shivered.

Once inside, she stirred the fire, using the dying embers to rekindle the flame. By the time he came out with their reheated food, she had a nice blaze going. As she turned to face him, she caught his pained expression before he could hide it from her.

"I've seen that look before. I was in the kitchen, washing dishes the first time you showed me your house." He looked away from her. "And again at the fair." She took a step forward, dying to know what was wrong, wanting to comfort him, but he stayed back.

Continuing to ignore what she'd said, he put the food on the floor. "It's nothing."

"You can't lie to me, Timmy—I know you too well."

He pressed his lips together at the use of her childhood name for him. "It's foolishness, that's all."

"Please, tell me." She pulled him down by the arm to sit by her on the floor.

"Sometimes I see you in a place I've imagined you to be many times, and then I'm reminded that it can't be." He shrugged, looking away from her

"You've imagined me washing dishes?" She tried to joke him out of it, but it didn't work. She took his hand, her voice barely a whisper. "Really, dishes? And here, in front of the fireplace?"

"Never mind." He offered her the dish of potato salad.

Jasmine knew he wanted her to drop it, and she knew it'd be easier that way. But she didn't want easy this time.

"Why can't it be?" She'd never imagined talking to so openly to anyone, but with Tim, she didn't worry, didn't feel on edge. This was Tim—and she was safe.

"Because in a couple days you'll head back to Portland, and I'll still be here." The quiet resigned tone to his voice told her what she needed to know. It all clicked as she connected the dots from the day.

He thought she was leaving.

"I told you, I'm moving here to help Mrs. Craig."

As Tim's eyes locked on hers, she saw a glimmer of hope.

"Misty needs me now, more than ever. Once Brandi starts referring girls this way, there'll be more. I want to be here, helping them avoid the same mistakes I've made."

"But I thought that since the adoption was off, you'd leave town. You don't need to be here."

"Did you arrange everything with Misty and the baby to keep me in town and get me to marry you?"

"Of course not. Sure, it was a catalyst, but not the reason. I've always—" He broke off and swallowed. "Of course not."

"So you were asking me to marry you?"

Although Tim kept a good poker face, Jasmine knew his tell. His ears were going three shades of red, although his face betrayed none of his emotions. She laughed.

"What?" He frowned at her.

"You'd better keep those ears covered in court; they've always been a dead giveaway." She snickered, picturing him in his suit in front of a judge. "A knit cap would do the trick."

Tim rubbed at his left ear, scowling at her. "Pass the chicken."

"Uh huh." She handed him the dish. Tim didn't like being out of control any more than she did.

"When do you think you'll move here?"

"First I've got to find a place that takes grumpy cats. I've got to take care of things with Brandi and network a bit at the shelter. Then pack." She listed the items off on her fingers and sighed. "There's a lot to do."

"As far as a place to live, we could just call—"

Jasmine stopped him with her finger on his lips. "Not Jenny." Ever.

"Right. What I mean to say is that I'll help."

"I was hoping you'd say that." She took a bite of salad, and the sweet sauce mixed with the perfect softness of the potatoes filled her mouth. "This is great, where'd you get it?"

He shrugged. "I made it."

"That's right. He cooks too." She gave him a huge grin.

The tension in the room disappeared, and Tim sat a bit taller. Cockier.

"My offer is sounding better all the time, isn't it? Solid home, good job, excellent standing in the community, and—" He paused for emphasis. "—great cook."

"Mmm. I'd be nuts not to consider it." Tim's eyes lit up at her as he leaned in to kiss her, but she put a hand on his chest, holding him back. "That is, when you've made me a firm offer."

"What's that supposed to mean?"

"Having 'dinner with you forever'—doesn't sound quite like a firm deal. Sounds more like a casual offer."

"Now you want formal?" He caught on to her teasing tone and raised his eyebrows in mock surprise.

Jasmine grinned at the game—she loved seeing him off

balance and insecure.

"I want the whole package. I want to be courted."

"Do people still use that word? It's like wooed. Who uses that?"

"You asked—I said." She shrugged and looked away, pretending to lose interest.

He teased her off and on through dinner. Before long, the clock on the mantle struck eight.

"I had no idea it had gotten so late." Jasmine glanced up at the clock, shocked at how fast time flew. They'd had such a nice night, it had kept her mind off the ache created by the lost chance to adopt the baby.

"I'd better get you home." He stood and held out a hand to help her up from the floor. She took it, and their eyes locked a moment. Their friendship had shifted to something else, something deeper, and they both seemed to sense it. "I can clean this up later." He motioned to the floor.

"Don't you want me to do the dishes?" She winked at him, and he groaned in response as she cleaned up the plates.

"Not going to let that one go, are you?"

"Hardly, lawyer man."

Once their picnic was cleaned up, Tim drove her home. As they pulled up in front of Bill's house, she saw the lights were still on inside.

"Do they know your plans?" Tim motioned toward the house.

"I thought I'd tell them tonight. It's not quite what I thought I'd be telling them, though."

"Will they be disappointed too?"

"I think so. Elsie loves children and was pretty happy at the thought of my providing a niece for her to dote on." She gave him a forced smile. It would take awhile before she could smile easily about it.

Well, she always had Oscar. She tried to picture dressing up Oscar as some women did their miniature dogs and winced at the image of her scratched and scarred arms.

"Maybe you'll give her a niece or nephew later." Again the suggestive tone—but this time, she didn't laugh.

"I can't." She didn't know it'd hurt so much to admit this to him. The brokenness inside amplified. Would he want her still?

"Can't what?"

"Have children." The pain from admitting it aloud flooded her core, and the car filled with a deafening silence.

A disappointed look crossed Tim's face, but it was gone in an instant. "Well, we already know I don't have anything against adoption." He kissed her cheek and nuzzled the side of her face with his nose. When he spoke, it sounded more like a promise than a simple statement. "There are a ton of kids out there who need to be loved. I think you're the mom for the job."

His ability to take things in stride never ceased to amaze her.

"That's it?" Her heart swelled with hope.

Tim tipped her chin up and looked deeply into her eyes. "I love you, Jasmine. And any child we bring into our relationship will be ours, even if it doesn't come from us."

Tears formed in her eyes, but she blinked them away. He loved her.

"You want me to walk you inside and help explain?"

"No, I'll be okay." She started to climb from the car, but he held her back with his hand, got out, and came around to open the passenger side door for her.

"I'm also a gentleman," he said, reminding her of yet another one of his attributes.

"That's true." She laughed. As they stopped at the gate, she reached up and kissed his cheek. "Thanks for being there."

"My pleasure." He watched her walk up the path to the front door before he drove away.

Inside, Bill sat near the wood stove, reading the paper. "Hey sis, have a big day?" He patted the chair next to him, inviting her to sit down. The kitchen was dark, and Jasmine could hear the kids laughing upstairs as Elsie corralled them into bed.

"As a matter of fact, I did." She filled Bill in on Misty's return.

"You doing okay?"

"Believe it or not, I am. It opened old wounds, but they don't ache the way they used to." She leaned her head on his shoulder. Brandi was right, God took healing in stages sometimes.

"When are you heading back to Portland?" She noticed he didn't use the word home. He kept referring to his house as her home. She smiled.

"In a couple days. I've got to find a place to live here first, and get all those loose ends tied up and pack."

Bill leaned away from her. "You're moving home?"

The sound of thumping feet on the stairs startled them both. Elsie stood at the bottom step, panting, eyes brimming with hope. "You're moving home?"

"You have excellent hearing." Jasmine laughed at the joy she saw in their eyes. "Yes, I'm moving home. But not here, I need my own place."

"Well, you can stay here until you find one." Elsie leaned down and hugged her. She knew if it were up to Elise, she'd never let her leave.

Jasmine's mind ran with plans and changes she needed to make. She'd always looked forward to work, to helping—but this new direction stirred a fire in her spirit that she'd never had before. There was so much to do, so many decisions to make.

Wonderful decisions.

"I'll need to stay a couple more days, to talk to Mrs. Craig and start looking for an office here in town. And an apartment." She chuckled, looking back and forth between her brother and his dear wife. "I never would have guessed I'd come home. Not ever."

"You never know what God has planned for your life, do you?"

"You've got that right."

Before they could discuss her plans further, the doorbell rang.

Elsie got up to answer the door, an expression of worry on her face. "Wonder who that could be at this time of night? It's nearly nine-thirty."

On the other side of the screen, Tim stood, dressed in slacks, and brown leather jacket, holding a bouquet of flowers.

"Sorry to call at such a late hour. If it's not too much trouble, may I speak to Mr. Reynolds?"

Jasmine put her hand to her mouth to stifle a laugh, feeling very much like a nervous schoolgirl.

"Uh, Bill, it's for you." Elsie stood back, a sparkle in her eyes.

Bill, eyebrows creased together, went to the door. "Tim?"

"Good evening, sir. I've come to ask permission to court your sister, Jasmine. As you know, I have very good prospects, and I'm an active community member."

"Court her?" Bill shot a worried glance at Elsie. Jasmine could almost read his mind. Tim had cracked.

"Yes. My intentions are honorable, sir. Do I have your permission?" Tim cleared his throat, and Jasmine could tell from the red hue of his ears that he was much more nervous than he was letting on.

"My heavens." Elsie sank down on the couch, overcome by the scene.

"I'm not sure?" Bill glanced at Jasmine, who nodded emphatically. "I guess you do."

It was Jasmine's turn to clear her throat, and she gave a look to Bill.

"I mean, yes, you have my permission to court my sister."

"Thank you, sir. Might she be at home?"

As Bill made to open the door and let Tim inside, Jasmine raced up the stairs. She stood at the top, listening, her hand over her mouth to quiet her breathing.

"I think so. I mean, she was here a minute ago." She heard Bill push open the screen. "Why don't you come inside and wait?"

"Nice home you have here, sir."

Bill, starting to catch on, entered the game. "Thanks, Son."

"I'll go and let her know you're here." Elsie headed up the stairs, nearly toppling Jasmine over as she hid at the top in the dark. They laughed together and headed into her room, giggling like teens getting ready for their first date.

Jasmine opened her closet and stood back, her face falling in dejection. "I don't have anything to wear."

"I'll be right back." Elsie left the room and came back in holding a long-sleeved sapphire blue dress.

"Oh, Elsie, that's beautiful. I couldn't."

"Yes, you can. Someone gave it to me years ago, and it's much too long for me—not to mention it's not my color at all, but it's definitely yours."

Jasmine took the dress and tried it on. It was like it was made for her, hugging her in all the right places, revealing a figure she'd forgotten she had. She grabbed a pair of black heels from her suitcase and slipped them on.

"You look amazing." Elsie's warmth and encouragement flowed through Jasmine.

"Thanks." She gave Elsie a hug, hoping she knew she meant it for much more than the dress. After brushing out her hair and putting on a quick bit of makeup, she was ready. Taking a deep breath, she headed down the stairs. Elsie followed her.

Bill and Tim, who had been making ridiculous small talk, stopped speaking as soon as she lit on the bottom step. Tim gasped when he saw her but made a quick recovery, holding out the flowers.

"These are for you." She could see his hand shaking, and knew he was taking this more seriously than he let on.

"Thank you." She took them and handed them off to Elsie. "Could you put these in some water for me?"

Elsie nodded and took them from her with a huge grin on her face.

"How nice to see you, Tim. What brings you by?" Jasmine fought the urge to cross her arms. She was used to pockets and didn't quite know what to do with her hands. Instead, she clasped them together and gave him her best innocent expression, eyebrows up in expectation.

"You're brother has given me permission to court you."

"Me?" Her voice lilted.

He gave her a pointed look and leaned closer. "Someone once told me to find the woman I wanted to spend the rest of my life with and pursue her. So that's what I'm doing."

It was Jasmine's turn to go red; she could feel the splotches growing down her neck. She remembered all too well the conversation he referred to. Tim reached out and held her hand down from covering her throat. He rubbed his thumb gently across the back of her hand, calming them both.

"Would you care to go to a movie?"

"Um…" She bit her bottom lip and glanced down at her formal dress.

"Oh. Right. How about dancing?"

"Excellent." She reached for her coat, and he helped her

into it, and put his arm out for her to take it.

Tim glanced over his shoulder at Bill. "I promise I'll have her back at a decent hour, sir."

"I should hope so. I think eleven would be a good hour."

"I was thinking more about midnight?"

"Well, I don't know." Bill gasped when Elsie gave him a quick jab to the ribs with her elbow. "Okay, midnight. Don't you two need a chaperone?" He stepped toward the coat rack, reaching for his jacket.

"No, that's okay, Bill. I trust him." Jasmine locked eyes with Tim, hoping to convey what she felt, what she'd known, for so long. The warmth in his eyes told her he did.

"That's good enough for me." Bill escorted them to the door.

Once outside, Tim leaned over and whispered into her ear, leaving a trail of shivers down her side. "Well, how am I doing so far?"

"It's a start." She put her hand out to him, and they walked down the sidewalk together, ready to see where these new paths would take them.

Acknowledgments

This is the part of the book where I get to write sentimental things to the people who have supported me during this time. I'm ever so glad to do it. As a writer and a person who suffers daily from chronic illness, I know full well I can't do a single thing alone.

First and foremost I want to thank my Lord and Savior, Jesus of Nazareth, without whom I would not be here. He encourages me to get out of bed each day and helps me put one foot in front of the other. He lifts my spirits and loves my soul—I am completely unworthy and eternally grateful.

To my love, Ken, and little loves, Madeline and Seth, you are my bright lights on dim days. You give me daily boosts of joy and support. My life would be so empty without you in it. I'll never be able to convey what huge blessings you are to me.

To the best four parents a girl could have: Richard and Andrea Johnson, and Allan and Carol Solstad. You have always encouraged me in whatever I tried to do—that's rare in this world. Thank you so much for raising me in faith and for believing in me.

To WhiteFire Publishing and my incredible editor, Roseanna White, thanks so much for giving me this opportunity. I don't have a clue how you accomplish all you do, Roseanna—you're an inspiration to me.

If you're a writer, you need to belong to an organization that provides continuing education, networking, support and encouragement like Oregon Christian Writers. They are an amazing organization.

To Regina Williams, editor, mentor and friend. Thanks for walking me through my first novel, holding my hand and pointing the way. You're a gifted teacher and talented author. I'm so glad I took your class and our paths met.

To my critique partner, anxiety counselor, and sister-scribe, Melody Roberts, thank you doesn't quite say it. Every writer needs a "you" in their corner. I'm so glad the Lord brought us together for this writing journey. And to the rest of my Encourager's Writing Group: Nancy Meacham-Cole, Danika Cooley, Louise Dunlap, Jac Nelson, and Mary Wilson. No writer improves their craft alone, thank you for sharpening my skills and giving me direction. You ladies are shining gifts.

To Anne Beals, Christine Collier, Janet Hewitt, Susan Moons, Billie Jo Robbins, Tammy Schwartz, Lynn Trachte, Laurene Wells, and Beth Zulaski: when we were transplanted in another state without family or support, you all stepped into the gap. I can never thank you enough for standing by us during times of celebration, illness, and trial; for your prayers, for transporting our kids and enriching their lives on days when I couldn't take another step, and for standing with us in this life. You are the epitome of what friendship means.

To Lee Ann Macklin: I'm so thankful for your years (and years) of constant friendship and support. Everyone needs a friend who thinks she can do anything she puts her mind to. Even writing a novel.

To Kristina Walker who never let me consider giving up and has been a constant captain in the cheering section—I'll never forget your words to me when I considered this writing thing: April, you have to do it! To LeAnna Murray and Susie Cartwright, who've known me since forever—thanks for your enthusiastic listening while I regaled you with wild (and mostly true) tales as a kid. You were my first wide-eyed audience. The seeds planted back then finally grew!

To everyone who encouraged, prayed, and counseled me on this journey—I couldn't have done this without you. And finally to Valerie Becker and Debbie Carpenter, inspiring women of faith: I want to be just like you when I grow up.

Author's Note

There are many reasons young people live on the streets—and none of them have to do with fun. Most of them are escaping from something (verbal/physical/sexual abuse/neglect) and running to a place that ends up putting them in even more danger (drugs, sex trafficking, crime, imprisonment, perpetual homelessness, disease). Here are some facts gathered from The National Clearinghouse on Families and Youth:

Every day, approximately 1.3 million runaway, thrown away, and homeless youth live on the streets of America. Children, both boys and girls, are solicited for sex, on average, within seventy-two hours of being on the street. Approximately fifty-five percent of street girls engage in formal prostitution; seventy-five percent of those work for a pimp. About one in five of these children becomes entangled in nationally organized crime networks and is forced to travel far from home and isolated from friends and family. A girl will first become a victim of prostitution between the ages of twelve and fourteen, on average.

If you're like me, all those statistics feel overwhelming. What can *you* do? First, if you know a young person in trouble, get involved. Encourage them to reach out to professionals that can help them. Secondly, support organizations out there doing the work to get them back off the street and making safe havens. Please donate to the Portland Rescue Mission's Shepherd's Door at: http://www.portlandrescuemission.org/lp/2013lp/jasmine/ (designate women and children's recovery) and at Door To Grace http://www.doortograce.org/. Both of these incredible ministries aid in rescuing, healing and restoring.

Other Titles

If you enjoyed *Jasmine*, you may also like these other titles from WhiteFire Publishing:

Paint Chips
by Susie Finkbeiner

What lies beneath the layers of hurt?

The Good Girl
by Christy Barritt

She survived her past...but can she face it?

Sailing out of Darkness
by Normandie Fischer

Love conquers all?
Maybe for some people.

CPSIA information can be obtained at www.ICGtesting.com
Printed in the USA
LVOW13s1028290713

345121LV00002B/58/P